Thomas Wright

Autobiography of Thomas Wright, of Birkenshaw, in the County of York, 1736-1797

Thomas Wright

Autobiography of Thomas Wright, of Birkenshaw, in the County of York, 1736-1797

ISBN/EAN: 9783337013189

Printed in Europe, USA, Canada, Australia, Japan

Cover: Foto ©Raphael Reischuk / pixelio.de

More available books at **www.hansebooks.com**

LOWER BLACUP, *as it appeared in November, 1863; the Residence of Thomas Wright, during his first marriage and widowhood.*

From a Photograph by Joseph Beldon, of Bradford.

AUTOBIOGRAPHY OF THOMAS WRIGHT,

OF BIRKENSHAW,

IN THE COUNTY OF YORK.

1736—1797.

EDITED BY HIS GRANDSON,

THOMAS WRIGHT, M.A, F.S.A., Etc.

CORRESPONDING MEMBER OF THE IMPERIAL

INSTITUTE OF FRANCE.

LONDON:

JOHN RUSSELL SMITH,

SOHO SQUARE.

1864.

PREFACE.

THE writer of the following Autobiography ſtates that it was deſigned for the inſtruction and amuſement of his children and deſcendants; but it has been thought by ſeveral friends who have read it, and whoſe judgment I reſpect, that it contains much that might be inſtructive and amuſing to other people's children alſo, and I have, therefore, ventured to give it to the public. Too long a ſpace of time has elapſed to leave any perſonal feelings or intereſts to be affected by it, and I myſelf in printing it look upon it only as a remarkable hiſtorical record, which gives us a curious and ſtriking picture—I may, perhaps, add almoſt unique—of domeſtic life among a very important claſs of Engliſh ſociety during the latter half of the laſt century, in what has ſince become one of the greateſt and moſt active manufacturing diſtricts in our iſland. Moreover, it preſents a very remarkable view of the effects, even on the relations of the domeſtic homeſtead, of thoſe violent religious party-feelings and contentions which raged more in this part of England than anywhere, during the laft century, and which, though they gave perhaps not an unhealthy activity to men's minds, were certainly far from improving their tempers, or encouraging among them fentiments of mutual charity.

Thomas Wright, of Birkenfhaw, was, as will be feen by his own writings, no ordinary man. Endowed with very confiderable talents, and with an earneft defire for knowledge and a love of literature, which might have raifed him to a diftinguifhed pofition in fame, he evidently, from his own account, often regretted that he had no guardians of his youth who could appreciate the real bent of his mind, and give him the education which his fortune, though not great, as well as his inclinations claimed. But left an orphan in his earlieft infancy, with none but diftant relatives, who thought only of fecuring a fhare of his property—at firft a fpoiled child, and fubfequently a neglected boy, nothing could fwerve his mind from its natural bent, and fome of his manufcripts in my poffeffion, as well as the reports of thofe who knew him, prove that he poffeffed an extraordinary extent of reading, a large amount of mifcellaneous knowledge, with power and judgment in the application of it, which muft have made him an object of refpect among the fociety of what was then rather a wild part of Yorkfhire. At an early age he went through the ufual courfe of Latin in the old and juftly celebrated free Grammar School at Bradford, which was the whole amount of what may be called his liberal education; and the writer of his brief " Life," prefixed to the fecond edition of his " Familiar Religious Converfation," printed in 1812, ftates that, " He was accounted very clever while at fchool ; and when he went home, it was with the reputation of being a youth of facetious difpofition, and of the moft ready wit and invention."

This part of Yorkfhire had always been a ftronghold of the Nonconformifts, and the Eftablifhed Church was comparatively weak in face of the violent diffenting Calvinifm which reigned there ; but at this time the far more liberal Arminianifm of Wefley and his party was labouring to eftablifh itfelf, and, as might be expected, met with the moft unfcrupulous perfecution. Thomas Wright, of Birkenfhaw, had a large fhare of the chivalrous in his character, and he took up the caufe of the new fect quite as much becaufe it was that of the weak oppreffed by the ftrong, as for the conformity of their opinions with his own liberal views. He tells us in the following pages the rather curious way in which he became firft acquainted with the Methodifts, as the followers of Wefley were already named ; his feelings in their favour, already well known, were no doubt ftrengthened by his marriage into a family who belonged to the leading and moft violent Calvinifts of this diftrict, and whofe hoftility difturbed the peace of his own family and the profpects of at leaft one of his children; yet he poffeffed no fectarian fpirit, and in fpite of the ftatement in the "Life" juft alluded to, appended to his "Modern Religious Converfation," I do not believe that my grandfather was ever what they call a profeffing Methodift—that is, a member of the Society, unlefs it were juft at the clofe of his life. He has defcribed his religious feelings very candidly in the following lines of this poem, where he, in his affumed character of "Richard," is accufed of being an Arminian, or Wefleyan (I quote from the firft edition) :—

> "I own ingenuoufly to you,
>   I think their doctrines nearly true;
>   I am not, Jemmy, of their fect,
>   Yet I the people much refpect,
>   Wifh well to what they chiefly teach,
>   And often go to hear them preach.
>   But bigot am I not fo hearty
>   To people, principles, or party,
>   But that if any one can fhew
>   My tenets are not juft and true,
>   I will renounce them gladly then,
>   And learn to think with wifer men."

Neverthelefs, "Tommy Wright," as he was popularly called in the phrafeology of the north country, was the champion of the Wefleyans in this diftrict, contributed largely to their triumph over perfecution, and obtained the acquaintance and efteem of the great leaders of the Arminian party, including fuch men as John Wefley himfelf and Fletcher of Madeley. An interefting account of his vifit to the latter in Shropfhire, in the year 1773, in the courfe of an excurfion for the purpofe of obtaining fubfcriptions towards the expenfe of building a Wefleyan Chapel at Height, within half a mile of his own houfe, is given in the following pages. The building of this chapel appears to have given great offence to the Birkheads of Brookhoufes, and explains the violent quarrel with his wife defcribed in the following narrative (page 104). He appears to have made the acquaintance of John Wefley during fome of the excurfions of the latter to preach his doctrines and principles in this part of the country, perhaps nearly about the fame date. From this time he entered warmly into the difputes between the Calvinifts and Wefleyans, and his alliance was the more valuable as he could handle with confiderable power the rather formidable weapons of fatire and ridicule; and, as his mind had a ftrong poetical turn, he ufually compofed his controverfial writings in verfe. Among the moft violent, and it may be added, the moft abufive of the writers of that time againft the Arminians, and efpecially againft Fletcher of Madeley, was Richard Hill, Efq., of Hawkeftone in Shropfhire, anceftor of the prefent Lord Hill, who fucceeded his father as Sir Richard Hill, Bart., in 1783, and was one of the reprefentatives of Shropfhire in Parliament during a great part of his life. In his " Modern Familiar Religious Converfation," the author characterizes this champion of the

Calvinifts, who was in the habit of prefuming
rather too much on his ariftocratic pofition, in
the following lines :—

> "Though high-born, felf-important Hill,
> In height of Calviniftic zeal,
> For want of better weapons, fight
> With fcorn, contempt, reproach, and fpite;
> And compafs you on every fide
> With laughter or difdainful pride;
> With this and that poor ftormy rail,
> Of bathing-tub, or comet-tail."

In 1775, Richard Hill, in a pamphlet entitled
"Logica Wefleienfis," publifhed one of the moft
fcurrilous perfonal attacks on Wefley he had yet
written, under the bantering title of a "Heroic
Poem" in his praife, in reply to which Thomas
Wright wrote a very clever parody, under the
title of "A Heroic Poem in praife of Richard Hill,
Efq." which is printed in the Appendix to the
prefent volume. It appears that he was prevented
from publifhing this poem by the opinion of "one
of no mean name," that fuch an anfwer to the
Calviniftic affailant was only returning "railing
for railing"—the perfon here referred to being,
I fufpeft, John Wefley himfelf; but he fent a
written copy of it to the Calviniftic champion
at Hawkeftone. Three years after this he publifhed a more general defence of the Arminian
party, alfo compofed in verfe, and entitled (a
parody on the title of Hogarth's celebrated picture) "A Modern Familiar Religious Converfation." The origin of this book is explained in

the author's addrefs to the reader. "The occafion of the following piece was rather accidental than defigned. Having had frequent occafion to take notice of the great variety of differing opinions amongft the profeffors of Chriftianity, and to remark their fpirit, practice, and manner of teaching each other, which I had done with fome degree of accuracy, and having been one day engaged with an acquaintance in a religious difpute, it afterwards proved an occafion of exciting in my mind the following thoughts:—I imagined to myfelf a perfon in great fufpenfe with refpect to his religious opinion, yet extremely defirous to learn, and fincerely willing to embrace the truth. I next imagined this perfon, in his fearch after truth, applying himfelf to the different fects of Chriftian profeffors one after another, for inftruction and direction: he would find every fucceffive party he applied to would, in its turn, affure him, in the moft pofitive manner, that theirs was the *only* true fyftem of religion, the *only* fyftem that was agreeable to the Word of God throughout; he would find them very ready alfo to cenfure and condemn (with no fmall degree of acrimony in general) every other party as (more or lefs) blind, ignorant, out of the way of truth, and involved in error. He would further find that every party would readily allow that the Word of God was uniformly and invariably true; and at the fame time he would find every one of them profeffing to ground their various, and even directly oppofite, opinions upon the *fame* Bible, and attempting to prove the truth of their *incompatible* fentiments from the *fame* book of God!　Under thefe circumftances, I beheld my imaginary inquirer in the utmoft perplexity and confufion; he had penetration enough to difcover, and generofity enough to difapprove, all the unfair, unkind, and unchrif- tian practices more or lefs made ufe of by moft parties, in order to blacken and difcredit thofe who differed from them in their religious fenti- ments; yet, at the fame time, he had fenfe enough to perceive, and candour enough to own, that, amongft all or moft of the profeffing parties, many perfons might be found of great natural abilities, various and deep learning, ftrict morals, and unblemifhed characters, both as men and Chriftians, in every practical refpect.　Yet all this did but ferve to heighten his dilemma and increafe his uncertainty: and being refolved to deal fairly and ingenuoufly with his own foul, and not to efpoufe any fentiment merely becaufe fuch a great man, or fuch a fafhionable or creditable party, had efpoufed it, I faw him fairly forced at laft to have recourfe to prayer and the Word of God, that by comparing what each party in its turn advanced for truth with that unerring ftandard, fairly taken together, he might be able to judge for himfelf.　Being in this train of thought, and having fomething of a poetical turn, I put down (dialogue-wife) fome of the firft para-

graphs of the following eſſay, without any farther
deſign, at that time, than to write a ſhort copy
of verſes for my own amuſement; but the ſub-
ject growing upon me as I proceeded, the conſequence was, I have drawn it out to the preſent
length." The further hiſtory of this book is
told as follows by the Weſleyan writer of the
"Life" of the author given with the ſecond
and poſthumous edition, who informs us that,
" poſſeſſing an excellent memory, he often entertained his friends by repeating to them a great
part of this poem. They generally expreſſed
themſelves highly delighted with it. The high
ſeaſoning of Hudibraſtic compoſition which the
author had imparted to it, excited their riſible
muſcles to a high degree; and they frequently
declared it to be a performance which contained
much matter in a ſmall compaſs. After mature
conſideration, he reſolved on publiſhing it. The
demand for it was much beyond his expectations.
In a very ſhort time there was not a copy of it
to be procured. It operated like an electric
ſhock on the Calviniſtic poetaſters and pam-
phleteers of that day. Not one of them found
it convenient to give a reply to what they termed
' a worthleſs production.' It ſealed up their
mouths in ſilence, and by the neighbouring ruſ-
tics it was thought to be unanſwerable."

As we may ſuppoſe from these latter remarks,
the author of this poem did not ſtrictly carry out
the deſign declared in his preface—it is a warm

and a fenfible defence of Arminianifm againft
Calvinifm. In the principal interlocutor Richard,
the defender of Arminianifm, the author has reprefented himfelf; and the narrative contains
feveral allufions to his own difputes with the
Calviniftic party. We learn from one part of it
that, fometime previoufly, on the occafion of one
of John Wefley's vifits to the north, a rather
zealous young Calvinift minifter of Stockport
in Chefhire, whom he defignates as the Rev.
T——s B——ke, after vifiting the meeting at
which he preached, and liftening to his fermon,
wrote to Wefley a very infulting letter, which
the great leader of Wefleyanifm did not think
worthy of a reply; but this letter having fallen
into the hands of "Tommy Wright," he favoured the writer with an anfwer, which appears
to have effectually filenced him. The poem of
which I have been fpeaking was printed at
Leeds, by J. Bowling, in the year 1778, under
the title of "A Modern Familiar Religious
Converfation, among People of Differing Senti-
ments: a Poetical Effay." It is a book of merit,
and from a perufal of it we can well underftand
how it muft have excited the hoftility of the
author's relatives at Brookhoufes. The firft edition, publifhed anonymoufly, is now a book of
extreme rarity; in fact, the only copy I ever
heard of, is the one I poffefs myfelf, and which
has defcended to me from the author. But in
1812, a fecond and pofthumous edition was

printed, intended, I believe, for the Wefleyans, under the modified title of "A Familiar Religious Converfation in Verfe, by Thomas Wright." The editor profeffes, and no doubt truly, that he printed it from "a copy which was corrected and amended by the author," but unfortunately adds that he had made alterations of his own, and he has given us no clue to enable us to diftinguifh his own alterations from thofe of the author. I have heard my father, who probably fupplied the copy with the author's alterations, complain rather bitterly of the unwarrantable liberties taken by the editor.

It is but juft to remark, that the brief "Life" prefixed to this edition of his book gives a qualified meed of praife to the perfonal character of its author, which was hardly fair to the memory of the man who had rendered fuch fignal fervices to the religious party for whom efpecially this Life was written. We are told that "he was not a man deftitute of religion," but "was favoured in his youth with the drawings of the Spirit of God;" that "when he arrived at riper age he felt the fame ftrivings within him," and that, when later in life he became more clofely connected with the Wefleyans, he was "not without having grievoufly to lament his frequent wanderings from God," becaufe "his popularity and his great vivacity were fources of great temptation and danger to him." In truth, "Tommy Wright," of Birkenfhaw, poffeffed

none of that fort of afcetic fpirit which the zea-
lots of either party were too apt to confider
as the chief proofs of true piety. He poffeffed,
from his fchoolboy days, a genial difpofition and
a readinefs of wit, combined with many focial
qualities, which, afide from the religious ani-
mofities, endeared him to all his acquaintances;
and I have heard, years ago, aged people who
had known him in the latter part of his life,
fpeaking of him with a feeling of affection which
can hardly be defcribed. They fpoke of him
as being well known as the friend of every one
who wanted honeft advice and affiftance; and I
have heard one of them defcribe how, when any
individual under fuch circumftances applied to
him, he took him into his kitchen, feated him by
the kitchen fire—which was in thofe days the
ufual place of intimate converfation—gave him
a pipe (for he appears to have been given to
fmoking), and then inquired into his wants, with
a friendlinefs which nobody could miftake. In
his earlier youth—although even then he was a
great reader—we find him, in his own narrative,
affociating largely with the people around him,
and he feems to have at times regretted the lofs
of time which, in an intellectual point of view,
might have been more profitably employed. He
was a good fhot, and loved the pleafures of the
chafe. He appears even to have mixed not un
willingly in the ruftic amufements of the people.
Under the character of Richard, in his " Modern

Familiar Religious Converfation," he intimates that one of the charges brought by his over-pious enemies againft him was that he had joined in the dance on the village green. When in Richard's abfence one of his religious opponents attempts to plead a little in his favour, another, more fevere, replies,—

> " 'Tis all hypocrify and pride
> (Mary with zealous warmth replied);
> I've known e'er now when he's been found
> Dancing upon the devil's ground,
> At wakes, and feafts, and fairs, among
> The thickeft of the carnal throng."

On which his feeble apologift remarks—

> " That may be too (fays Will), but what
> Would you, my friend, infer from that?
> A man may rife and fall, 'tis plain,
> And rife, and fall, and rife again.
> Judge as feverely as you can,
> 'Tis fettled habit fhows the man.
> Has Dick walk'd always thus contrary?
> Is it his conftant practice, Mary?
> Perhaps, when all the truth appears,
> It has been once in twice feven years.
> O Mary! were *you* fearch'd to th' quick,
> As narrowly as you fearch'd Dick,
> 'Tis like you never would be known
> To caft at Dick another ftone." *

Only a few years ago, many ftories were current in the locality where he lived, of the ready

---

* In the fecond edition, thefe lines are altered as follows :—

Mary. Yes, that may be; yet he's been found
       Dancing upon the devil's ground,
       At fairs and wakes, nor thought it wrong
       To be the foremoft in the throng:

wit, the *fang-froid*, and the ingenuity of "Tommy
Wright," of Birkenfhaw, which proved his great
popularity; and fome of them are ftill remembered among old people. I have heard one of
thefe old people tell how, in one of the lanes
through which he had to pafs on his way home at
night, he was attacked by a highwayman on
foot, or (in more technical language) a foot-pad,
who, with terrible threats, demanded his money.
My grandfather carried with him, concealed,
what was then either new, or newly improved,
and was almoft unknown in that part of the
country, a bull's-eye lantern, which, with a
threatening roar, he thruft out at arms' length
towards the face of his affailant. The latter,
who could not in the dark very well diftinguifh
the form of the man he had to deal with, was
taken entirely by furprife, and, believing that he
had met with fome fupernatural monfter, fell on
his knees in abfolute terror, and begged to be

This was when he had firft begun
After the Methodifts to run.

Will. What follows then? 'tis very plain
A man may rife and fall again.
Judge as feverely as you can,
Confirmed habits fhew the man.
Has this Dick's practice always been,
To dance upon the village green?
Perhaps, when all the truth appears,
'Twas only once in fourteen years.
Were you but fearched to the quick,
As narrowly as you fearch Dick,
You never would again be known
To caft at him another ftone.

forgiven for what he faid was his firft offence of the kind, which he promifed never to repeat if he might be allowed to go away unfcathed. On another occafion he played a practical joke upon a tailor. It was the cuftom, when any perfon wanted new clothes, to furnifh his own cloth, and to fend for the tailor to his houfe, who was ufually inftalled upon the kitchen table as his board, and who received fo much a day, and remained there till his work was finifhed. The tailor employed on this occafion, who was probably the only one near at hand, was rather noted for his idlenefs, and he was efpecially in the habit of falling afleep in the middle of his work. His employer determined to cure him of this, and he contrived that fome heavy weight fhould be fufpended above him in a manner the details of which I have forgotten, but it dropped on the table in the middle of the tailor's fleep with fuch a frightful noife, that he awoke in fo great an alarm, that he leaped from the table, ran away, and could never be perfuaded to return to the fame place again. Whether it cured him of his idle habits or no, I am not informed. Among many other ftories of this kind, of which I have but an imperfect recollection, I remember one, which, when but a mere boy myfelf, I have heard told by my father, and which always feemed to me an amufing example of cruelly tormenting.

As will be feen in the following narrative, "Tommy Wright" fet ftore on his orchards at Lower Blacup, and he was very much annoyed when, for feveral confecutive nights, he found them plundered by depredators. One day the elder "Tommy" told young "Tommy" to prepare his gun (both were good fhots, though the latter was but a boy), and to be ready to ftay up with him all night. He loaded both guns with fmall grains of hard rock-falt intead of fhot, and, taking his fon with him, placed himfelf in a place of concealment in one of the orchards, and waited the events. In the middle of the night feveral perfons came into the orchard furnifhed with large facks, which they began to fill with fruit, but the two watchers ftole from their hiding-place, gained a pofition at a diftance from which the fhot would penetrate only through the fkin, and then, giving the alarm, took aim at the lower and more tender parts of their bodies as they had turned their backs in flight, and fairly falted them alive. The known refult was, that the orchards at Lower Blacup were, for a long time afterwards, free from fimilar intruders.

Another anecdote of the ready wit of the writer of the following Autobiography enjoyed a greater local reputation than all the reft. At the time of his fecond marriage he had become bald, and was in the habit of wearing a wig. He employed a barber in Bradford, the neareft place it is to be prefumed where a barber capable of fuch a work could then be found, to make him a new wig, and this barber was named Jofhua Craven. He

appears to have been a very dilatory workman,
and the delivery of the new wig was delayed until
the patience of him for whom it was defigned
became exhaufted.　One day he called into his
house a neighbour who was paffing on his way to
attend Bradford market, and afked him to wait
while he wrote a line to his barber ; and in a
few minutes he gave him the promifed letter,
which he duly delivered as directed, and was furprifed at the broad laugh which burft from the
receiver when he had opened and read it : in fact
it contained the following extempore lines :—

" Mr. Jofhua Craven, I wifh your pate fhaven,
　　And over your fhoulders a twig ;
　I muft have this ado, to fend to and fro,
　　And yet you won't make me my wig.

" How long, with a vengeance ! muft I dance attendance
　　On you, you dilatory prig,
　And run in the cold, with my head bare and bald ?
　　And yet you won't make me my wig.

" Would you fend me my bob, to cover my nob,
　　Why then I might ftrut and look big ;
　Now I'm forced to be fquat, and keep on my hat,
　　And all for the want of my wig.

" Don't you know, blefs your life, I've got a young wife ?
　　And did you but hear her fweet voice !
　When fhe fees I am bald, fhe thinks I'm grown old,
　　And is fit to repent of her choice.

" I vow and proteft, if you don't do your beft,
　　And fend it by Saturday night,
　I'll furely refent it, and make you repent it,
　　As fure as my name's THOMAS WRIGHT."

It is to be fuppofed that fuch an appeal could not fail to have the defired effect.*

The author was celebrated for an extraordinary memory, of which I have heard feveral anecdotes. It is ftill remembered in one of the manufactories in which, when the increafe of his family called for all his refources, he took employment, that "Tommy Wright" could repeat the whole of Milton's "Paradife Loft" whenever called upon, befides the works of other poets ; and yet that he could not remember accurately for a few hours a common bufinefs commiffion. This is, perhaps, fomewhat exaggerated on the fide of the forgetfulnefs, although he had evidently no tafte for bufinefs ; but only a few years ago I heard directly the following anecdote from an old man, who may be ftill alive, and who was when young his intimate neighbour. This perfon, who was an intelligent man, and in eafy circumftances, ftated that, on the day when the "Leeds Mercury," then a young newfpaper, arrived, "Tommy Wright" ufually brought it with him to his houfe,

---

* Thefe verfes were inferted in the local newfpapers at the time of the author's death, and it is from a cutting from one of thefe in my own poffeffion that I give them here complete. Within the laft few weeks I have received from two different quarters in that neighbourhood the ftory, with imperfect copies of the verfes taken down from oral recitation, a proof of the popularity of the writer, and at the fame time a curious example of the length of time through which in fome parts of the country fuch traditions are preferved.

took his ufual feat by his kitchen fire, and, after both had lit their pipes, proceeded to read it through. The "Mercury" was then, of courfe, comparatively a fmall paper; but when he had once read it, if called upon immediately afterwards to repeat either the whole or any part of it, even an advertifement, he could do it without hefitation, and fo accurately that it was quite unneceffary to refer to the paper itfelf.

Birkenfhaw, with the name of which that of Thomas Wright is more efpecially connected, is even now a rather wild and ftraggling village, fpread over the top and fides of bleak elevated land; but in the laft century it muft have been a very dreary place. A houfe, or rather a cottage, the end one of a row, is ftill pointed out and known to fome of the inhabitants as the one in which he lived, after his removal from Lower Blacup. This latter houfe remains much in the condition which it prefented in his time. The front and larger part of it appears, indeed, from the ftone mullions and antiquated glazing of its windows, to be a building of fome antiquity, perhaps as old as the earlier half of the feventeenth century. He fpeaks of having let off part of it as a feparate tenement, which expofed him, through the difhonefty of his tenant, to a ferious robbery; and it ftill remains divided into two houfes. It is prettily fituated on the fide of the hills which form the fouth-weftern fide of a rich and picturefque valley, with a ftream immediately below, and a wood, once spreading eaftwardly over the fteeper fide of the hill above, and muft have been, in the laft century, before fo many factory chimneys had been raifed in its immediate neighbourhood, a fingularly rural and retired place. As this houfe was the fcene of a rather important and active period of his life, that of his firft marriage and widowhood, it has been thought that a view of it would form an appropriate frontifpiece to his Autobiography; and it has, therefore, been engraved from a very admirable photograph, made for me by Mr. J. Beldon, of Bradford, a young photographer of great talent, and who promifes to attain a high pofition in his art. Lower Blacup is rather more than three miles nearly fouth of Birkenfhaw, and about half a mile from Cleckheaton, which, though now a confiderable place, was then only a good-fized village. Bradford itfelf, four miles northward from Birkenfhaw, was then a fmall town in comparifon with its prefent extent.

Brookhoufes, which holds fo important a place in the following narrative, ftands alfo on the flope of the fame fweep of hills, but on the oppofite fide of Cleckheaton, beautifully fituated, with the little river Spen winding round the foot of the bank on which it ftands; and overlooking Cleckheaton, which occupies the rifing ground at a very fhort diftance on the other fide of the river. Through Cleckheaton, it would be lefs than a mile diftant from Lower Blacup, and the diftance

is not much more than a mile by the more pleafant road along the foot of the hills. The principal part of the houfe at Brookhoufes built by
the Birkheads ftill remains, but part of it has
been pulled down, and fome rather handfome
additions raifed on the fite. At a very fhort diftance behind the houfe, the old Balm Mill ftill
remains, the place where my grandfather ufed to
meet Mifs Birkhead during his courtfhip. Between it and the houfe runs the lane which leads
to great Gomerfall, and thence to Birkenfhaw
and to Birftall. The chapel at Cleckheaton,
that of the Independents, which the Birkheads
frequented, has been rebuilt fince that time; but
the tomb of Lydia Wright, with the infcription
raifed over her by her hufband, as defcribed in
the following pages, ftill ftands in the burial-
ground, and the tablet to her memory infide the
chapel; and near that of my grandmother ftands
the tomb of her brother and parents, which bears
the following infcription:—" May this marble
perpetuate the memory of William, Son of Mr.
William Birkhead, of Brookhoufes, who departed
this life the 25th of April, 1780, aged 21 years.
—Mary Birkhead, Mother of the above, died
April 29th, 1796, in the 80th year of her age.—
William Birkhead, Father of the above William
Birkhead, and Hufband of Mary, died March
3rd, 1797, in the 100ᵉᵈ year of his age."
    It muft not be fuppofed that in this country
Thomas Wright was buried among a population

of mere ignorant ruftics. A confiderable portion of the people around him were occupied in the cloth manufacture, and were fteadily laying the foundation of the prefent manufacturing wealth of the diftrict, and fome of them had already enriched themfelves by their induftry and intelligence. The very agitation of religious controverfy, whatever elfe it might do, tended to give activity to people's minds. There were, moreover, in the country around, a few men who had raifed themfelves to intellectual diftinction. At Bierley Hall, about two miles to the north-weft of Birkenfhaw, lived Dr. Richardfon, F.R.S., the eminent naturalift, with whom Thomas Wright was intimate in his youth. Field-head, in the parifh of Birftall, was the refidence of the Prieftleys, where they eftablifhed a celebrated boarding-fchool for ladies, to which he fent one of his daughters. As the celebrated Dr. Jofeph Prieftley, who was born at Field-head, was refident at Leeds during feveral years fubfequent to 1767, he muft have frequently vifited his near relatives at the place of his birth, and it is at leaft probable that my grandfather was perfonally acquainted with him. He vifited Mifs Bofanquet, fubfequently the wife of Fletcher of Madeley, at Crofs Hall, in the parifh of Batley, about three miles to the eaft of Birkenfhaw, and it was there that he heard the remarkable ghoft-ftory related in the following pages (p. 132). He defcribes as his friend, John Taylor, of Great

Gomerſall, little more than a mile to the ſouth of
Birkenſhaw, the enterpriſing and intelligent merchant and manufacturer, whoſe character is drawn
ſo admirably by Charlotte Brontë under the name
of Mr. Yorke, in the novel of " Shirley."

The manuſcript of the following Autobiography, in the hand-writing of the author, is in my
poſſeſſion, having deſcended to me as a ſort of
heir-loom. He appears to have commenced it
in the year 1795, when he was ſixty-one years
old, and to have intended to bring it down only
to that year, which he mentions more than once
in the text as the year in which he was writing;
but he ſubſequently continued it to 1797. In
the manuſcript he has further added notes of
events in the three following years, but as they
merely relate to private tranſactions and diſputes,
among ſome of the younger branches of the
family, and have no intereſt for the general reader,
I have judged it adviſable to cloſe it with the
year 1797, according to the original deſign. The
title in the manuſcript is, " Memoirs of Thomas
Wright and his Family, interſperſed with Remarks and Moral Reflections on Occurring Circumſtances, &c., written by Himſelf for the Information, Inſtruction, and Amuſement of his
Children, 1797." Autobiography ſeemed to me
a better title for it, when printed, than Memoirs.

As I learn from an entry in the manuſcript (in
the handwriting of my father), Thomas Wright,
of Birkenſhaw, died of an attack of typhus fever,

on Friday, January 30, 1801, at about feven
o'clock in the evening, eight days fhort of fixty-
five years of age.   He was buried at the White
Chapel, in the north of the parifh of Birftall, at
the lower end of the chapel, by the fide of his
daughter Hannah, his fourth child by his fecond
marriage, who had died only eleven days before
him, at the age of ten years and a half.   He retained his office of infpector of woollens (or,
cloth-fearcher) to the end of his life.

Thomas Wright appears to have been much
attached to his children, and he defcribes the
death of a favourite fon, named John, in a detailed account which is extremely pathetic. The
lofs of this child feems to have weighed heavily
on his mind for feveral years, in which he devoted
the anniverfary of the forrowful event to the
compofition of a fhort poem to his memory.
Thefe he has carefully copied, along with one or
two controverfial pieces in verfe, in a volume of
MS. accompanying the Autobiography, evidently
intending them as an appendix to it, and as fuch
I have printed them at the end of the prefent
volume.   The laft of thefe relates to fome local
controverfy, and would require an explanation
which I am not able to give, for local tracts of
this kind are very rare.   Mr. Thomas Taylor
was a well-known and diftinguifhed Wefleyan
itinerant preacher, who travelled in the Birftall
circuit in 1771 and 1772, and was appointed to
the Bradford circuit two years later ; he had been

a blackfmith.   Mr. John Knight, an early Wefleyan convert, who had been a poor collier, and
had afterwards turned Calvinift, attacked him in
a pamphlet, in which he fought to throw ridicule on his former occupation under the name of
Polyphemus the Cyclops.   "Tommy Wright"
came to the refcue of Taylor in a poem which
is full of humour, and contains fome powerful
writing.   I have not thought it neceffary to print
the rather long criticifm in profe on the controverfial notes to Knight's poem, which follows
in the manufcript.

I have only to add, that it was thought a few
explanatory notes, efpecially on the localities
mentioned in the Autobiography, would render
it much more interefting to the general reader,
and that I owe nearly all thefe illuftrations to a
very refpected friend in Bradford, Mr. Abraham
Holroyd, who is remarkably well acquainted with
the whole country around that town, and with
its hiftory and traditions.

THOMAS WRIGHT.

Sydney Street, Brompton, London.
December, 1863.

AUTOBIOGRAPHY OF THOMAS WRIGHT.

HOW exceedingly limited is human knowledge in this tranſitory and imperfect ſtate of things! Even men of the fineſt geniuſes and deepeſt reſearches, men of the greateſt parts, learning, and diligence, do but make low attainments in knowledge, comparatively ſpeaking, either with reſpect to the things of the natural or ſpiritual world ; but with reſpect to the bulk of mankind, comprehending the middle and lower ranks of people, they appear, with ſome exceptions, to be ſunk in ſtupid ignorance, and to know very little even of the world they dwell in, or the inhabitants thereof, much leſs of things of a more abſtruſe nature, but to content themſelves in general with a knowledge of thoſe mechanic arts, or manual employments, that are neceſſary to obtain riches or a greater or leſs plentiful ſubſiſtence in the preſent ſtate. Nay, how little is known by the generality of the people even of their own families, very few being able to trace back their defcent beyond their grandfathers ; and, indeed, there appears little defire in general to know either from whom or from whence it is we fpring ; notwithftanding the defire of remembering thofe, and being remembered by thofe, we moft efteem on earth, feems congenial to the human heart :—

> " For who, to dumb forgetfulnefs a prey
> This pleafing anxious being e'er refign'd?
> Left the warm precincts of the cheerful day,
> Nor caft one longing, lingering look behind?
>
> " On fome fond breaft the parting foul relies,
> Some pious drops the clofing eye requires ;
> E'en from the tomb the voice of nature cries,
> E'en in our afhes live their wonted fires."

If every father of a family who can read and write would take the pains to record the births, baptifms, marriages, deaths, and moft remarkable providential occurrences towards himfelf and the different branches of his family, while under his obfervation, it would be a circumftance that might prove in many refpects both ufeful and entertaining to his fucceffors.

I could wifh to give a more particular account of my anceftors than I am able, they all having died while I was very young ; and I, like moft of my neighbours, having received nothing but verbal accounts concerning them. However, I will put down all that has come to my knowledge concerning them, and be more particular when I come to myfelf and the affairs of my own more immediate family. It may fome time, perhaps, prove a leifure hour's ufeful amufement to fome branch of my family into whofe hands it may fall after I am gone.

Thomas Wright, my paternal grandfather, (after whom, I fuppofe, I was named,) fome time kept the Bowling Green Inn, in Bradford, York-fhire ;* where, after he married my grandmother,

---

* The Bowling Green Inn, Bradford, ftill remains, and is one of the beft in the town. It is a long old building, fronting on the level open fpace called from the earlieft times the Bowling Green, and is at the weft end of Bridge Street on the road from Wakefield. Outfide there are the marks of many alterations, fuch as windows walled up in fome places, and broken out in others ; doorways walled up, and frefh ones broken out in other parts. In the infide the rooms are fmall and low, and large fquare beams are thrown acrofs the whole to fupport the flooring of the upper rooms. This maffivenefs and ftrength was formerly no doubt meant to fupport properly the heavy ftone flags with which all rooms in this part were flagged. Wooden flooring, which is both warmer and lighter, has now become common in all new erections. Such is the account given me by Mr. Abraham Holroyd of Bradford, who adds, " My earlieft recollections of the inn reach to a time when one Joe Ward was landlord; and there ufed formerly to be held here meetings on particular fubjects, and the fpeakers addreffed the crowds affembled in the open fpace in front from an old balcony which yet runs the whole length of the hotel. It ufed formerly to be the beft hoftelry in Bradford, as the ftables in the rear yet teftify; and the mail coaches ufed to ftart from and arrive in here with tremendous ado. But this has all paffed away, and the inn is now the haunt only of the neighbouring tradefmen and of the country farmers, who put up here on the market-days; and it is a rendezvous alfo of that flitting race the commercial travellers. The other oldeft hoftelries in Brad-ford are the *Woolpacks, Pack Horfe, King's Arms,* and the *Bull's Head* in Weftgate, at which laft the farmers and others ufed to keep a market on both fides of the ftreet. At the Bull's Head in Weftgate our earlieft merchants and manufac-

he lived and died with credit and efteem amongft
his neighbours. I underftand by his will (which
I have by me) that he was by trade a cloth-
dreffer; and I have heard that the family came
originally from Keighley,* or its neighbourhood,
and fettled about Wibfey;† and fome of the de-

---

turers ufed to occupy the beft front room upftairs to hold a
kind of Chamber of Commerce. During the wars of England with the elder Napoleon the news from our armies
was retailed and difcuffed by thefe gentlemen when they
met on the market-day at the Bull's Head. If the news
was againft us, they broke up *early*, and all went to their
homes in the country in a ferious and defponding manner;
but if victory had been with our army, they feafted, ftayed
late, and got jolly well drunk on Mr. Illingworth's ftrong
home-brewed ale, like good fellows and lovers of their
country."

* Keighley, then a not very confiderable town, about
twelve miles to the north of Halifax, was celebrated for its
manufactures in cotton, linen, and efpecially worfted, which
were fold chiefly at Halifax and Bradford.

† Wibfey is now a very large village, and is in the
townfhip of North Bierley. It is nearly two miles fouth of
Bradford, and has in and near it three churches, and feveral
diffenting chapels. The great iron works of Low Moor are
near Wibfey. There is almoft everywhere a village which
is made the butt of thofe near it; and the Wibfey people
are fuppofed not to be fo fharp as their neighbours, and
hence are called by others, " Wibfey Geefe," " Hullatt
Wallers," and " Moon-rakers." It is reported of them, but
whether the ftory be true or not may perhaps be doubted, that
once upon a time, one of the Wibfey villagers faw fomething in a pond on the " Slack," which he fuppofed to be
a cheefe—this was at night, fo off he fet and collected
feveral of his companions, and they, with a few hay-rakes,
ftarted off to the place to recover the cheefe, if fo it might
be. After feveral fruitlefs efforts to obtain the cheefe by
raking for it in the pond, one of the party, poffeffed of a
little more fenfe than the reft, fuggefted that it might

scendants remain still in the adjacent country. This is all I know of my grandfather Wright prior to his marriage with my grandmother. If any of my family should be desirous to know more, they may probably find an account of their marriage and deaths in the parish register at Bradford. Martha Wright, my paternal grandmother, (whose maiden name, I have heard, was Hopkinson,) and who came from Batley, had been married before her connection with my grandfather to a Richard Horton, by whom she had issue, a son and daughter, whom I personally knew; namely, Abraham Horton, my half-uncle, a shoemaker in Bradford, who has left several sons that survive; and Martha Horton, my half-aunt, who first married a — Haworth, and was mistress of the old Cock Inn in Halifax,* with

---

be the shadow of the moon they saw in the water, as that luminary was shining brightly. Hence the name of " Moon-rakers," a term still applied to them. This, a little varied, is, it need hardly be stated, one of the well-known stories of the wife men of Gotham. But the Wibsey people are charged with something worse than this; it is said that they are, and have long been, great eaters of " howpeys " (horses). Forty years ago there was nothing in this part of the country to compare with the Wibsey people for all kinds of wickedness and low brutishness. Gambling and thimble-rigging were common, and rapes and murders were frequent. But cheap periodicals and the labours of the teacher are entirely changing the habits of these miners and iron-workers; and ere many years are past they will be changed entirely.

* The old Cock Inn, Halifax, is still in existence, and stands near the " Corn Market." I am told that it has

great credit and reputation, above thirty years;
but after the death of her firſt huſband ſhe married a Nathaniel Longbottom, who proved but a
very indifferent huſband, deſerted her, and went
to London, married a ſecond wife during her
lifetime, uſed to ſend threatening letters to extort
money from her, &c. She told me ſhe ſaw his
apparition the night of his death, as ſhe lay awake
in bed with a Mrs. Newton, with whom ſhe
lived at that time, and who was faſt aſleep by
her ſide—that ſhe looked earneſtly at the ghoſt
for ſome time, and it looked as earneſtly at her;
but at laſt ſhe covered herſelf with the bedclothes
and ſaw him no more. She told her bed-fellow
in the morning that Natty was dead; ſhe had
ſeen him in the night, and expected a letter with
an account of his death by the next poſt, which
happened according to her expectation. She told
me another inſtance of the kind, which is as
follows :—A Mr. Chriſtopher Laverack, a reputable tradeſman (a maltſter) at Spen, in the pariſh
of Birſtall,* who uſed to inn there, lying ſick at

---

undergone little alteration, and that it is ſtill a flouriſhing
hoſtelry.

  * Spen, or Spen Bank, lies between Cleckheaton and
Birſtall. There is a corn mill here, which was rebuilt ſome
few years ſince. Formerly the mill was managed by a
family named Mann. There are about a dozen cottages
near the mill; and at a ſhort diſtance on the hill there is a
houſe, rebuilt alſo a few years ago, called Spen Houſe.
The place is leſs than a mile from Cleckheaton as you paſs
towards Gomerſall and Birſtall.

home upon his death-bed: she was doing something in the bar one evening about ten o'clock, and happening to lift up her eyes she saw his ghost looking earnestly at her through the railing. She afterwards heard that he died exactly at that time. She always behaved very respectfully to me. She once visited and stayed with us a week at Lower Blacup,* and I usually called to see her when I went to town. She died in Halifax. I and my wife were invited to and attended her funeral. She was buried in Halifax Church, just within the large front door, on the left hand entering in. I do not know whether any of her issue survive.

Thomas Cordingley, my maternal grandfather, lived for many years in the later part of his life at the Mulcture Hall in Halifax, Yorkshire,† which, together with the mills, (namely, the Four Mills, Little Mill, Farrah Mill, and a frizing mill, with the grounds belonging to them,) he farmed

---

* Lower and Upper Blacup are two farms lying to the south-east of Cleckheaton, and are but a short distance from the latter place, perhaps half a mile. A friend tells me that the farm house at Lower Blacup is still a one-storey building all covered with thatch in its primitive condition. It is on the side of a footpath which leads to Hightown, or *Heetaan*, and to *Hatchett* or Hartshead Moor. The italics denote the way in which the people of the neighbourhood pronounce these names. Blacup is *Bleckup*.

† Mulcture Hall is also still in existence; but about twenty years ago it was altered, and converted into model lodging-houses. Before the date of these alterations it was occupied by an old gentleman by the name of Stott, a noted antiquary in his day. It stands by the side of the street called Cripplegate.

of Lord Irwin of Temple Newfome,* and which he occupied till he died. He had been married before his connection with my grandmother, and had iffue, two fons and a daughter, viz. Thomas, who lived and died near Farrah Mill,† without iffue. I have fince found he had another fon, my half-uncle Jofhua, who was poifoned in eating a falad, and lies buried by the fide of my mother, with this infcription upon his graveftone:—"Here lieth interred the body of Jofhua Cordingley, milner, who died 19th July, aged 23 years. 1730;" and Martha, who married firft an — Aked, by whom fhe had feveral children; and afterwards a Benj. Sutcliffe, a butcher, by whom fhe left no iffue. Not any of them now furvive. My grandfather, in his laft will, left me a fmall eftate called Oaks Fold, in Bowling,‡ from

---

* Temple Newfome, about four miles from Leeds, came early in the feventeenth century into the poffeffion of the Ingrams, who were fubfequently created vifcounts Irvine. The laft Vifcount Irvine died here in 1807. The eftate fubfequently paffed to the Marquis of Hertford.

† Farrah Mills, I am told, are in the valley between Halifax and Salterhabble.

‡ Oaks Fold is in Birch Lane, in Bowling Lane, Bradford (borough), and is about one mile from the centre of Bradford. The land around Oaks Fold is now divided between three owners; viz., Mr. Ripley, the dyer; the heirs of Mr. Wroe; and the Bowling Iron Works Company. The *Fold* has in it now three farm-houfes and four cottages. The largeft of the farms is occupied by a family named Benfon, and the houfe they refide in was built in 1617; and, as Mr. Benfon termed it, "had the top taan off abaat forty year fin'." The next farm, which is but fmall, and keeps only two cows, is occupied by Mr. Jofeph

whence, I fuppofe, the family originally came. He lies interred in the family burying-place in Halifax churchyard. Martha Cordingley, my maternal grandmother, was daughter of Matthias Whitehead of Streetfide, between Dudley Hill and Weftgate Hill, in the lordfhip of Tong. They were a pretty numerous family. I remember the names of four brothers and two fifters—Samuel, whofe only fon and child, Matthias Whitehead, inherits the family fettlement at Streetfide at this time (1793), and has iffue at prefent two fons and three daughters; Benjamin, who left feveral children of both fexes; Abraham; and Jonathan, of whofe family I have no knowledge; Lydia, who married Timothy Ellifon of Birkenfhaw (of whom more hereafter); Mary, who married a Mr. Richmond, diffenting minifter at Cleckheaton, by whom fhe had a fon Robert, who was afterwards drowned; and Han-

---

Wright. His father was a Thomas Wright, and he was in the fervice of the Low Moor Company. The father of this Mr. Thomas Wright was a George Wright, a farmer in Bowling, but which farm he held I have not been able to afcertain. The prefent Jofeph Wright has a family of five; and as the farm will not fupport them, he takes employment from Mr. Ripley, at his dye-works near by. The railway from Leeds to Halifax paffes only a few hundred yards from Oaks Fold, after you have paffed the Bowling ftation going towards Halifax. It is a nice fpot yet, and muft have been a lovely place before the towering mill chimneys began to pour or belch forth their volumes of black foot and fmoke; but if there ever were any oaks here there are none now.

nah, who died young, and who was remarkable, while yet a child, for being able to repeat feveral parts of the Bible by memory. This is moftly what I know of the progenitors or collateral branches of my mother's family. I have fince found a fon of my uncle Abraham Whitehead's, a Chriftopher Whitehead, a faddler, in North-gate, Wakefield.

John Wright, my father, was born at the Bowling Green Inn in Bradford; I have heard of a brother and feveral fifters, but know nothing of any certainty of any of them, except one. Upon inquiry I have found that my father had two other fifters :—Mary, who married a — Harper at Halifax; and Judith. My aunt Betty lived and died at Bradford. She married firft a W. North-rop, and afterwards a Thomas Craven, and left iffue by both hufbands; but I know little of any of them. She died in ftraitened circumftances, but was liberally behaved to while fhe lived by Mr. Jofeph Hollings of Cottingley, a diftant and fubftantial relation of the family. At a proper age my father was put apprentice to a Jer. Jagger, a cabinet-maker of Halifax, where he became acquainted with and married my mother, Elizabeth Cordingley, daughter and only child of my grandfather with my grandmother Cording-ley. After their marriage they dwelt as long as they lived at Mulcture Hall, with my grand-father and grandmother; and as my grandfather was old, and my father young and active, he took the care of the mills upon himself, which he superintended till his death. My mother bore him four children, namely—Mary, Martha, Thomas (myself), and Elizabeth, of whom she died in childbed. Elizabeth Wright, my mother, was born at the Mulcture Hall in Halifax, the latter end of November, 1711, and died at the same place when she had just entered her twenty-seventh year; and was interred in the family burying-place, a little above the lowest gate near the south front wall in Halifax churchyard, where a stone lies over her grave with the following inscription :—

" HERE lieth the body of Martha, the daughter of John Wright of Halifax, miller, who departed this life the 18th day of August, 1736, aged 2 years, 7 months, and 4 days.

" Also here lieth the body of Elizabeth, daughter of the above John Wright, aged six hours.

" And also Elizabeth, the wife of the above John Wright, who died February the 19th, 1738, aged 26 years and three months."

I know not where my eldest sister Mary was buried, but I suppose in the same place. My father died about two years afterwards, turned (I suppose) of thirty years of age, and lies interred by the side of my mother. I can just remember my father twice. Once I asked him for a halfpenny as he sat by the fireside in the hall ; he gave me one, which I well remember was a little thick one of George the Firft, rimmed round the impreffions, which drawing my notice, feems to be the circumftance that fixed the occurrence in my memory.   Another time, which was on a Sunday, my father went out of the great parlour, as we called it, down the orchard below the hall, my grandmother, or fome one elfe, fent me out after him to call him back.   I remember I faw him go down the orchard and climb over the wall at the bottom, as if going to the Mills.   I was juft then put into breeches.   I remember that I had on a white dimity waiftcoat, with a double row of buttons down the breaft; that I was in my fhirt fleeves, not having put on my little coat; that I fometimes called daddy and fometimes father.   I had been ufed to call him daddy, but hearing fome of the neighbouring boys call their father, I thought I would call mine fo too, which fomewhat embarraffing me in my mind at the time, feems to have been the circumftance which fixed the occurrence in my memory.   This is all I remember of my father. I cannot remember anything at all of my mother. After the death of my father and mother I was left to the care of my grandfather and my grandmother Cordingley.   My grandfather died not long after my father, and lies interred in the fame grave.   By the death of my father and grandfather, my grandmother was left very forlorn and expofed.   She was left with a pretty large ftock in her hands, in cafh and furniture,

and the articles of their bufinefs. The bufinefs
of the mills was extenfive and complicated, and
required far more management and attention than
fhe was capable of beftowing upon it; hence,
fhe was obliged to rely on the faithfulnefs of different perfons to tranfact her bufinefs for her,
which fhe did till nearly ftript of all her property. Her lofs on this occafion, I have reafon
to think, did not fall much fhort of a thoufand
pounds. I remember a circumftance (child as I
was) which, among others, fufficiently indicated
her critical fituation with regard to the rapid decreafe of her property, over which I remember
her forrowing very much. We had a woman
in the houfe fhe hired as a maid, and chiefly to
attend me as a nurfe; and as my grandmother
was very fond of me, fhe ufed to indulge me with
any thing to play with I took a fancy to. Among
other things fhe ufed to let me have twenty-feven
and thirty-fix fhilling pieces of gold coin,* and
when I was weary of them locked them up again
in her defk. My grandmother ufed to attend the
diffenting meeting-houfe on Sundays, and frequently left me and the maid at home by ourfelves on thofe days. I can remember the woman
having fweethearts attending her in my grand-

* The twenty-feven fhilling piece was the moidore;
the thirty-fix fhillings, the double piftole. Thefe coins
were properly Portuguefe and Spanifh, but they were introduced rather extenfively into our currency in the reigns
of the firft Georges.

mother's abfence. And when I was troublefome for playthings, and in particular for the gold pieces, to get rid of my importunity fhe produced a key which opened my grandmother's defk, and gave me the pieces to play with, with a ftrict charge not to tell my grandmother; and fhe took care to lock them up again before her return. It was therefore no wonder that her property wafted fo faft. Finding things go fo much the wrong way, my grandmother at laft gave up the mills to one Richard Aked, and removed to one of our own houfes at the bottom of the town, taking me and the maid along with her. The houfe is that which the widow of James Carleton occupies at prefent (1793). Here my grandmother foon fickened and died; leaving me and my concerns to the care of her fifter, my great aunt, Lydia Ellifon, of the parifh of Birftall—living at that time at the village of Birkenfhaw. My grandmother Cordingley was buried in the family burying-place before mentioned. I made a fhort ftay with my aunt Lydia at her youngeft fon's, John Ellifon's, at Birkenfhaw; and then, for the convenience of going to Bradford Free School, removed with her to her youngeft daughter Hannah's, who had married a Samuel Wood, a mixed clothmaker, refiding at a country place called Leifter Dyke,* about a

---

* Laifter Dyke is on the eaft edge of the borough of Bradford, and is now a very populous place. There are

mile from Bradford. At this place I refided for fome years, and went from hence to Bradford School, where I went through all the Latin forms under the ufher Mr. Thomas Northrop. The upper mafter at that time, who taught Greek and Hebrew, was the Reverend Mr. Butler. At this fchool they taught every day in the week, begun every morning at feven o'clock, and loofed every evening at five o'clock, except Wednefdays and Saturdays, the afternoons of which days were devoted to writing, and we lay by at three o'clock. This was the practice fummer and winter, fo that, living a mile off, I had to go and return morning and evening during every winter feafon in the dark. When I gave over learning at the Free School I went to learn writing and accounts with a Mrs. Betty Ward, who taught fometimes at her own houfe on the Broad Stones, and fome-times at the vicarage houfe oppofite the church, the houfe being at that time empty. I may ob-ferve here, that I learned to write a plain legible hand, fufficient for any purpofe of common life or common bufinefs; but believe I was in-capable of ever learning to be what is called a

---

large mills, and rows of houfes and ftreets there, filled with bufy workpeople. The Great Northern Railway to Brad-ford has a ftation here. The place is near both the old village of Tong and Birkenfhaw. It was perhaps called Laifter Dyke from the fmall " beck," or " dyke," which runs through it, but which is indeed at prefent very incon-fiderable.

fine, or becoming a very quick or ready writer. With refpect to accounts, I learned a good way, but never having occafion to make ufe of the more uncommon rules in the fubfequent fcenes of my life, I have now in a great meafure forgot them; though I fuppofe if neceflity required, the circumftance of having learned them once would make them more eafily attainable a fecond time. The common rules I retain ready enough. With regard to the other branch, or book learning, the bent of my genius lying ftrongly that way, I made a rapid proficiency above moft of my fellows; and here I muft regret, if at leaft we ought to regret any circumftance in life which appears to be more peculiarly permitted or brought about by the order of a wife and good fuperintending Providence, and in which our *own will* appears to have been little or not at all concerned, I fay, I muft regret the want of fome perfon or perfons attentive enough to my intereft to have noticed the bent of my difpofition and genius, and find out means (if means might have been found) to have put me out to fome of the learned profeffions. In this cafe I might perhaps have made a confiderable figure in the world, and thofe talents which fome have thought me poffeffed of might have enabled me to have fupported myfelf and a family genteelly through life, which now ftand me in little more ftead than to make me perhaps a more pleafing and entertaining companion among my acquaintance.

However, as I obferved above, as it appears to be the difpenfing of a wife and kind Providence, which appears in feveral inftances to have defignedly prevented me from appearing or acting in the more public fcenes of life, it becomes me to fubmit and be refigned, which I find myfelf the more readily difpofed to do, as I am fully perfuaded of the wifdom and goodnefs of Providence in its difpenfations towards every individual, and firmly believe that God is—

> " Good when He gives, fupremely good,
>   Nor lefs when He denies;
>   E'en croffes from His gracious hand
>   Are bleffings in difguife."

I here take notice of the comparatively fuperior happinefs of childhood and youth. Pleafed, if in health, with the prefent, unanxious for the future; roving at their leifure hours through the fields and groves in fearch of the little birds' nefts, or engaged in innocent plays or amufements with their fchool-fellows; when fometimes, perhaps, the fudden little unmalicious quarrel may excite " The tear forgot as foon as fhed," which, however, is foon over, and they are bufy at their little amufements again. What a contraft this to the fcenes that await them.

> " *Retired* we tread a fmooth and open way;
>   Through briars and brambles in the *World* we ftray.
>   *Stiff* oppofition, and *perplex'd* debate,
>   And *thorny* care, and *rank* and *ftinging* hate,
>   Which choke our paffage, our career control,
>   And wound the firmeft temper of the foul."
>   DR. YOUNG.

I never view thofe fcenes of my youthful amufements without feeling a deep regret for the lofs
of thofe happy hours, and exclaiming with the
poet,—

> " Ah happy hills, ah pleafing fhade,
>   Ah fields beloved in vain !
> Where once my carelefs childhood ftray'd,
>   A ftranger yet to pain !
> I feel the gales that from you blow
> A momentary blifs beftow ;
>   As waving frefh their gladfome wing,
> My weary foul they feem to footh,
> And, redolent of joy and youth,
>   To breathe a fecond Spring."
>   GRAY.

The uncommon word *redolent*, made ufe of
here by Mr. Gray, means fmelling fweet giving
a ftrong flavour, or reviving a lively, pleafing fenfation or idea of joy and youth. I never fee children or youth at their playful diverfions, but I
partake in a degree of their joy ; only regretting
for them the fhort continuance of their felicity.

> " Gay hope is theirs, by fancy fed,
>   Lefs pleafing when poffeft ;
> The tear forgot as foon as fhed,
>   The funfhine of the breaft.
> Theirs buxom health of rofy hue,
> Wild wit, invention ever new,
>   And lively cheer of vigour born ;
> The thoughtlefs day, the eafy night,
> The fpirits pure, the flumbers light,
>   That fly the approach of morn.

> " Alas, regardlefs of their doom,
>   The little victims play !

No fenfe have they of ills to come,
  Nor care beyond to-day.
Yet fee how all around them wait,
The minifters of human fate;
  And black Misfortune's baleful train !
Ah, fhow them where in ambufh ftand
To feize their prey the murd'rous band !
  Ah, tell them they are men !

" Thefe fhall the fury Paffions tear,
  The vultures of the mind ;
Difdainful Anger, pallid Fear,
  And Shame that fkulks behind ;
Or pining Love fhall wafte their youth,
Or Jealoufy with rankling tooth,
  That inly gnaws the fecret heart,
And Envy wan, and faded Care,
Grim-vifag'd, comfortlefs Defpair,
  And Sorrow's piercing dart.

" Ambition this fhall tempt to rife,
  Then whirl the wretch from high,
To bitter Scorn a facrifice,
  And grinning Infamy.
The ftings of Falfehood thofe fhall try,
And hard Unkindnefs' altered eye,
  That mocks the tear it forced to flow ;
And keen Remorfe, with blood defiled,
And moody Madnefs, laughing wild
  Amid fevereft woe.

" Lo, in the vale of years beneath,
  A grifly troop are feen,
The painful family of Death,
  More hideous than their queen ;
This racks the joints, this fires the veins,
That every labouring finew ftrains,
  Thofe in the deeper vitals rage :
Lo, Poverty to fill the band,
That numbs the foul with icy hand
  And flow-confuming Age.

" To each his fufferings : all are men,
  Condemn'd alike to groan ;

> The tender for another's pain,
>   The unfeeling for his own.
> Yet ah, why fhould they know their fate?
> Since forrow never comes too late,
>   And happinefs too fwiftly flies.
> Thought would deftroy their paradife.
> No more; where ignorance is blifs,
>   'Tis folly to be wife."

Yes, ye little fportive innocents, enjoy your happy ignorance, enjoy your childifh amufements, your youthful pleafures, while you may; the cares and anxieties of life are haftening on, and will put a fpeedy end to your felicity.

As I have been led infenfibly into fome account of myfelf, without beginning at my birth, I will now return and endeavour to give a regular and connected account of myfelf from that period.

I, Thomas Wright, of Birkenfhaw, in the parifh of Birftall, late of Lower Blacup, near Hightown, in the fame parifh, but originally of Halifax, was born at the Mulcture Hall, in Halifax, on Monday, the 27th day of January, 1736, about ten o'clock in the forenoon. (Feb. 7th, N.S. is now my birthday.) I was baptized at the parifh church of St. John's, in Halifax, on Monday, February the 24th, 1736. I lived with my father and mother, and grandmother and grandfather Cordingley, at the faid Mulcture Hall, where they all lived together, till they all died. My mother died in child-bed of my fifter Elizabeth, when I was fomewhat turned of two years old. My father died a year or two afterwards, leaving me and my concerns to the care of my grandfather and grandmother. My eldeſt ſiſter Martha, a beautiful little girl, having died ſometime before of the ſmall-pox, my grandmother, who was extremely fond of me, as the only remains of her only offspring, and conſequently very anxious to preſerve my life, was perſuaded by a Doctor Nettleton, who was intimate with the family, to inoculate me, as the ſafeſt method with that dreadful malady. I well remember the operation, it was on a Saturday; the doctor ſeated me in a chair in the left wing of the Hall, bared my arms, made an inciſion with his lance in both my arms above the bend of my elbows, introduced the matter, and then bound up the parts. A young man, an apprentice, I ſuppoſe, ſtood by all the time to obſerve the operation. The doctor gave me a penny, ſaying I was a fine boy, and obſerving that I was the firſt upon whom he had performed the operation who had not wept. The fever came on the Saturday following. The doctor, his wife, and apprentice, were affiduous in attending me, and very anxious for the conſequence, as the practice was new in the neighbourhood, and depended for its credit upon the ſucceſs of this and a few other inſtances. I well remember them bringing me ſyrups and ſweetmeats almoſt every day. However, by an improper treatment, that of keeping me too hot both without and within, which aftertimes and more improved knowledge have rectified, the eruption was great, and I was much hazarded. Several of thofe inoculated in the neighbourhood at the fame time, died, which brought the practice into difrepute at that time.

However, by the bleffing of God, I furvived, but was pitted a good deal, and a flight injury remained on my right eye, which now, in my more advanced years, I find the effect of, it being much weaker than the other. My grandmother kept a maid-fervant, who had been long in the family, her name Mary Moore, a daughter of Anthony Moore, a blackfmith at Smithy-ftake.* She kept this woman chiefly for the fake of nurfing and waiting on me. She afterwards married a John Wright, who came from Belly-bridge,† but followed his trade of joiner in the town. She was ftill retained in the family after her marriage till my grandmother's death, and my removal. They afterwards lived in one of my cottages in the Lower Church Steps till fhe died. She lies buried, at her own defire, in our family burying-ground. She left four children, John, Thomas, Elizabeth, and Maria. John en-lifted and went to America, where he died; Tho-

---

* Smithy Stake is the name of a diftrict in Halifax near Mulcture Hall.

† Bailiffe Bridge is in the parifh of Dewfbury, and is about fix miles from Halifax. As you pafs on the railway from Leeds to Halifax, it lies at lefs than a mile diftance on the left hand, from the Lightcliffe ftation. It is here fpelt " Belly Bridge," but is never named fo now. There are two mills in the place, and it is now a confiderable place. The road from Wibfey Low Moor to Huddersfield paffes through it.

mas (my namefake) died a boy, foon after he had been over at Lower Blacup to fee me ; both the daughters furvive, have both been married, and refide at prefent at the bottom of Halifax. The father in his old age was taken to the workhoufe, and died there. I have taken this notice of the family out of refpect to my old nurfe, who though I believe her to have been blameable with refpect to her freedoms with my grandmother's property, yet as I have reafon to believe fhe repented of this, and always manifefted a parental love and regard for me to the day of her death, common gratitude requires from me this little tribute to her memory. May fhe reft in peace ! After I recovered from the fmall-pox, I was fent to fchool ; firft to a petty fchool, taught by a Natty Binns, a lame man, in one of my own cottages at the bottom of the churchyard ; afterwards to a kind of free fchool, a little higher in the ftreet than our Hall, on the fame fide, taught at that time by a Mr. Thomas Simpfon. Here I learned till I attained a little writing, and Lilly's grammar in reading. In this interval my grandfather died, leaving my grandmother quite deftitute of all affiftance, an unhappy circumftance, as I have before obferved, both for my grandmother and me, whofe property from this time wafted faft. I ftop here to notice a few little circumftances. As foon as I became ac- quainted with letters, that inclination for reading and the acquifition of knowledge, which is one of the ftrongeft propenfities of my nature, difcovered itfelf. I was never weary of my book, and by the time I was feven or eight years old, I had read through the Old and New Teftaments, and was well acquainted with every remarkable ftory to be found there, and in the Apocrypha. I well remember our maid, with whom I flept in a clofe or ceiled bed, when engaged with her fweetheart, ufed to bring me a candle to bed, and fet it on a fhelf in the bedfide, and a quarto bible I ftill have in the family. On this I ufed to read till twelve, one, or two o'clock in the morning, till I fell afleep, a dangerous practice, though my nurfe came frequently to fee me. I notice alfo that my grandfather and grandmother dreffed me very well ; I remember wearing a filver-laced hat, a filver-laced waiftcoat, and my fhirt ruffled at the neck, breaft, and hands ; at the fame time I had pence for afking for to buy any kind of fpice or fweetmeats I pleafed, and the old people, though naturally careful, thought nothing too much they could do for me. I mention thefe things not out of vanity, but as indicative of the plentiful circumftances of my grandparents at that time ; a circumftance I have found corroborated fince by feveral elderly people, their contemporaries, I have occafionally met with, particularly the late Doctor Alexander, who was a neighbour to and familiar with the family. He told me that they were always confidered as a very creditable and fubftantial family. I notice the following inftance of my childifh ideas. A high hill, or mountain, called the Haynes, rifes very abruptly from the bottom of Halifax, to a confiderable height. Our Hall ftood not far from the foot of this mountain, which I ufed to contemplate very much from the top of our orchard. I verily thought the fky refted on the top of the hill, and was very curious to go up and examine how it was, and touch the fky. At length the time arrived to fatisfy my curiofity; my nurfe perfuaded my grandmother to let her go upon a vifit for three or four days to her hufband's father's, who lived at Belly-bridge, and to take me along with her. We fet off, accordingly, and I remember my nurfe, when we were afcending the old bank (which was the only road at that time), bid me obferve my affectionate grandmother, who was anxioufly watching us up the hill from the top of the orchard, hardly knowing how to venture me out of her fight for the time. Well, we arrived at Whifk'em Dandies, a cottage fo called, fituated where the road croffes a lower part of the top of the hill; but alas! the fky, which I thought to have touched, was retired far away. However, this being my firft excurfion from home, every view and every object was new to me, and I was fufficiently pleafed and gratified with my journey. We lodged and chiefly boarded at the public-houfe at Belly-bridge; we ftayed three or four days, and then returned. I notice the following inftance of ill-nature. When my grandmother gave up the mills, fhe retained the Hall and gardens till a time fixed for her departure. In this interval I had one day climbed a plum-tree in the fide of our orchard next the lane leading to the mills ; Richard Aked, who had taken the mills, was going down to them, and feeing me in the tree, threw a fharp-edged ftone violently at me, which cut a deep wound in my eye-brow, and fo frighted me that I leaped from the tree into the orchard, a confiderable height, but providentially efcaped breaking my bones and having my eye knocked out. My grandmother was very angry, and threatened to profecute the man. I notice another circumftance. My grandmother was weak enough to admit the company of feveral defigning and interefted men, who pretended love to her. Some of thefe, I have heard, tricked her out of feveral large fums of money a little before her death. I remember the names of two of them ; George Savage, and Abraham Baraclough. This latter was a cuftomer fhe traded with, and I remember took me with him to his houfe, fomewhere in Shelf, where I ftayed a week or more. I know he ufed to let me ride on a pretty little white galloway he had, and tell me it fhould be my own. I take notice of two or three of my childifh play-fellows who ftill furvive in or about Halifax. Richard Naylor, who lived in a cottage in our back-fold, and whofe mother was very fond of me, and ufed to entertain me with ftories, fome of which I ftill remember ; he enlifted into the army, where he remained many years; he was by trade a mafon, and is at prefent a penfioner. George Wallace, a breeches-maker; and Bobby Alexander, fon of a phyfician of that name in Halifax, where Bobby now refides, and follows the profeffion of his father; and Billy Wood, fon of a huckfter oppofite our houfe, and who follows at prefent the bufinefs of his father. After our removal to our own houfe at the bottom of the town, my dear grandmother foon fickened and died, leaving me and my concerns to the care of her fifter, my great-aunt Lydia Ellifon, of Birkenfhaw, whom fhe made the fole executrix of her will. I remember my nurfe took me to the bedfide to take my laft leave of my expiring grandmother. She turned her head on the pillow and looked at me with a look of inexpreffible love, affection, and concern, and had juft ftrength to exclaim, " Poor bairn !" deeply pierced, no doubt, with the forrowful reflection of the forlorn, comfortlefs, and deferted ftate fhe was leaving the little darling of her heart expofed to. She then ftretched herfelf out in the bed and expired. Thus did I lofe the neareft, deareft, and only difinterefted friend I had left in the world. Farewell, my honoured, beloved, and affectionate grandmother; great was your maternal care, love, and fondnefs for me. I was too young at the time to be duly fenfible of, or make a proper acknowledgement for your love and kindnefs, but I have felt deeply grateful for it fince, and as I hope and truft to meet you in another and better ſtate, I will thank you for it in heaven.

Divine Providence, ever wiſe and good, however myſterious in its operation, having thus deprived me of all my neareſt and deareſt friends, and caſt me a forlorn orphan upon the care of a diſtant relative, my great-aunt Lydia Elliſon, who had come over on the occaſion, after the funeral and family concerns were ſettled, I began my wandering pilgrimage by making my firſt remove with her, from Halifax, my native place, to Birkenſhaw. My old aunt had procured a large baſket, or wiſket * (as ſhe called it), which ſhe filled with delf and china ware, and carried on her arm, with no ſmall fatigue, to Birkenſhaw. We ſet off together on foot on the afternoon of

* A *Wiſket*, Mr. Holroyd tells me, " was a ſmall ſhallow baſket about ten inches in width, made ſometimes of wire and ſometimes of wicker-work : they were uſed in the ſpinning-mills to carry yarn. When hand-loom weaving was common in this part of the north, the worſted weavers had to ſteep the weft in water before they uſed it, after it had been wound on the bobbins. To get the water out again, theſe wiſkets or ſpool baſkets were ſlung in ſtrings, with a ring at the end to hold by, and were then ſwung ſwiftly round until the water had left the weft nearly dry again. There was a game when I was a boy common among children, which muſt have been ſuggeſted from the uſe of the wiſket as ſtated. The children formed a circle by taking hold of hands, and running around one way, and then the other, they repeated—

    ' A wiſket, a waſket,
     To buy a penny baſket :
     You a penny, I a penny,
     Turn round cheeſes.' "

a winter's day, and by the time we reached Oakenſhaw* it was dark. Being weary, I remember I thought the Cliff Hollings Lane a very long one; at laſt, however, we reached our journey's end, the houſe of my aunt's younger ſon, John Elliſon, at Birkenſhaw. Having been a much indulged child, and coming all at once to a ſtrange place, and among ſtrange perſons, I began to be very heavy-hearted. I ſlept with my aunt, and

---

* Oakenſhaw is a good-ſized village, about four miles ſouth of Bradford, not far from Cleckheaton, near the line of railway from Bradford to the latter place. It is built at a place where four roads meet; viz., thoſe from Bradford, Leeds, Cleckheaton, and Halifax. There is now neither church nor chapel in it, and the neareſt will be thoſe at Low Moor, and the White Chapel at Cleckheaton. This latter was erected by the Richardſons of Bierley Hall, and a public houſe near by is now called the " Richardſon's Arms." There uſed to be a public houſe here, bearing the ſign of the White Bear, and it was kept by a family of the name of Bateman for more than a hundred years. Some years ago, however, a perſon went and offered more rent than the Batemans paid, to the owner of the houſe and land. The greedy landlord, after taking off a piece of land, let the new tenant have the place, but the buſineſs ceaſed to pay from that time, and had to be given up, and the whole building turned into cottages. In the centre of the village there ſtand the remains of an old butter croſs, on which there uſed to flouriſh a weather-cock; but in a ſevere ſtorm about ſeven years ago, it was blown down. The inhabitants are principally colliers, and the reſt are farmers, and thoſe who work at the great Low Moor Iron Works. It was, even fifty years ago, a very ruſtic village. The inhabitants were almoſt wholly engaged in agriculture, and ſo rude were their manners that they became a bye-word. It was ſaid of them that their hair was unkempt from Sunday to Sunday, and that an iron comb was chained to the tree which ſtood in the middle of the village, for the uſe of all the inhabitants.

refrained myfelf while I thought her awake ; but as foon as I perceived her to be afleep, I burft out into a violent flood of tears, till I wept myfelf afleep. This I did many fucceeding nights, till my aunt difcovered me. She faid what fhe could to comfort me ; but I longed to return to Halifax, but knew not the way. However, there was a man in the village named Jofeph Tempeft, who walked regularly to Halifax market every Saturday ; him I refolved to follow at a diftance, that he might not obferve me, but to keep within fight, for fear I fhould lofe my way. However, he difcovered me ; but on my promifing to return with him, he fuffered me to go. I ftayed perhaps a week, and then John Wright, my nurfe's hufband, brought me back again on horfeback. John Ellifon was fond of fhooting ; I ufed to attend him in his excurfions, till I grew very fond of the diverfion myfelf. As there was no proper fchool at Birkenfhaw, my aunt removed with me to her fon-in-law's, Samuel Wood, at Leifter Dike, for the convenience of attending Bradford Free School. As I have taken notice of what happened to me in this fituation before, I will only notice a few additional circumftances. As I was returning home one winter's night in the dufk of the evening, in company with a fchoolfellow who was a neighbour, whofe name was Jofeph Bower, as we were entering into a field of about four or five acres, fituate on a declivity or hill-fide, the foot-path lying along the bottom, called the Gravemaker's

Clofe, becaufe at that time the grave-maker of Bradford Church farmed it, we obferved a woman, as we thought, dreffed all in white from head to foot, coming over the oppofite ftile into the fame field to meet us. The fingularity of her drefs attracted our notice. But fuddenly we had loft her; but looking about we difcovered her about the middle of the field, apparently aiming at the upper crofs-corner. The unaccountable quicknefs of this remove rather alarmed me, and I could not help turning my head to obferve her procedure; when fuddenly we had loft her again, but on looking about us, found fhe had got to the ftile behind us, which we had juft come over, with equally unaccountable fpeed as before, and as if fhe had taken that circuit to avoid meeting us. We both began now to be pretty much ftartled, and when we had reached the ftile, turning about to look after her, we faw her coming back after us, in the fame field. We were both now fufficiently frightened, took to our heels, and faw her no more. I could never be fatisfied what this appearance was, and muft therefore leave it undetermined. While I learned writing and accounts with Mrs. Betty Ward, there was a young, beautiful girl learned with her at the fame time, called Nancy Denifon. With the beauty of this girl I was greatly ftruck, but was too young and bafhful to fay anything to her in the way of courtfhip on my own behalf. However, as is ufual in fuch cafes, I was perpetually talking of her, till the people where I lived fufpected the caufe, and rallied me fufficiently on the occafion.   As the girl boarded with a Mr. Hardcaftle, the then minifter of the old Diffenting chapel at Bradford, where they attended divine worfhip, they thought fit to inform the minifter of the circumftance ; and the parfon fent me a jocofe invitation to his houfe, with an affurance of a cordial welcome, and free admiffion to the company of his amiable boarder ; but I was too bafhful to accept the invitation, and removing foon after, the impreffion wore off, and the affair dropped.   This was my firft love impreffion ; a difpofition, I may here obferve, to which, with refpect to the young and handfome part of the fair fex, I was very prone.   Being very fond of fhooting, and catching game, I ufed to go often out with a John Jobfon, a John Lumby, a Squire Booth, and a James Speight, neighbours, who were fond of the diverfion, till I became a tolerable proficient at fhooting flying. Befides thefe perfons I ufed to fhoot with, I will juft name the perfons who compofed the family I lived in at the time, fome of the neighbours I was moft intimate with, and fome of my fchoolfellows. S. Wood, his wife, and children. Jonas Bateman, John Webfter, and Humphrey Moore, fervants.   John Moore, John Webfter, and Grace Wilfon, apprentices.   Jofeph Gauk, Timothy Fawbert, Jofeph Shaw, John Speight, John Roberts, Richard Broadbent, neighbours.

Schoolfellows on my own form, William Northrop, Richard Shepherd, Thomas Hodgfon, Thomas Mafon, Jofeph Pollard, William Lifter; a William and Thomas Seargeantfon, and Samuel Difney of Wakefield; William Ambler from Norfolk, William Nichols from Wales, and Mr. Elmfall of Thornhill, afterwards fteward to Sir George Saville. Moft of thofe I have here named are at this time (1795) dead, fo fleeting is human life!

While I lived here I had a remarkable dream two or three times repeated; it was of the laft day and its procefs. It ftruck me very much, and made the firft confiderable religious impreffion upon my mind. But as I mean to include all my remarks on my religious principles and impreffions in one point of view, after I have run through my hiftorical fketch, I forbear faying anything further at prefent, and haften to take leave of this fcene of part of my youth. In this interval, my coufin John Ellifon died of a high fever. Mrs. Wood, his fifter, was fuppofed to have caught the infection at his funeral, as fhe immediately after fickened and died of the fame diforder. This event caufed my aunt and me to remove to North Bierley,* to her daughter Mary's,

---

* North Bierley is a very populous diftrict, a townfhip, and lies about two miles to the fouth of Bradford. It is celebrated for its extenfive coal and iron works, and comprifes Bierley Lane, Butterfhaw, Carr Lane, Hill Top, Hodgfon Moor, Woodhoufe Hill, Revoe Hill, Folly Hall,

who had married William Brogden, my aunt bringing Sufannah, S. Wood's youngeſt child, with her, purpoſing to bring her up. If my aunt at this time had put me out a regular apprentice to ſome ſuitable calling, as ſhe ought to have done, I might poſſibly have acquired ſome habit for trade, which might have been of uſe to me afterwards ; but this was entirely neglected, and I was ſuffered to paſs ſeveral years at this place doing nothing but ſeeking birds' neſts in the ſummer, and going a-ſhooting in the winter ſeaſon. This was a loſs of a very pre-

---

Wibſey Slack, Low Moor, and Wibſey. The Low Moor iron-works are very extenſive ; and Dr. Whittaker gives it as his opinion, that the manufacture of iron was carried on at North Bierley by the Romans. At theſe extenſive works, cannon balls for the uſe of hoſtile nations throughout the world are manufactured, or rather fabricated, as well as ſteam engines. Theſe works preſent a very ſtriking view to the ſtranger ; during the darkneſs of the night hundreds of flames ſeem to ſhoot up into the ſky, and throw a liquid light far and wide ; and during the day, the ſable appear-ance of the workmen, the hiſſing of furnaces, the heavy fall of hammers, the rumbling ſounds vibrating in every quarter, and the various ſhapes the red iron aſſumes, combine to produce upon his mind ſenſations of terror and bewilder-ment.

Bierley Hall, which was formerly the reſidence of Dr. Richardſon, is a very handſome edifice. Bierley Chapel ſtands near the Hall, and was founded by Dr. Richardſon, and licenſed as a place of worſhip ſo early as 1716, yet it was only conſecrated in 1824. It was enlarged in 1831, at the expenſe of Miſs Currer, of Eſhton Hall. Trinity Church, Low Moor, was erected in 1604. St. Paul's Church, Butterſhaw, was built at the ſole expenſe of John Hardy, Eſq., formerly member of parliament for Bradford. The Weſleyans have a chapel at Low Moor, and another at Wibſey. The Independents have alſo a fine chapel at Wibſey.

cious and critical portion of my time, and had a
confiderable influence for the worfe on the
events of my future life, and was in a great
meafure occafioned by neglect and inattention in
thofe who had the ordering of me and my concerns. I mention this circumftance, that if any
of my family fhould happen hereafter to be in a
fimilar fituation, they may profit by my misfortune. The perfons I have mentioned before, that
I ufed to go a-fhooting with at Sammy Wood's,
ufed to come conftantly to North Bierley two or
three times a week during the winter, to kill
game for Doctor Richardfon. I conftantly accompanied them, and after rambling through the
fields, woods, and groves all the day, we ufed to
retire to the Doctor's at night, where a fupper was
provided for us, and as much ale as we choofe to
drink, paying us for the game after the rate of
fixpence for a woodcock, fourpence for a par-
tridge, threepence for a fnipe, and twopence for
a judcock.* By this means I became a pretty
good proficient in the art of fhooting flying, an
amufement I practifed with fome avidity for
fome years afterwards.

I notice a fecond love affair that happened
while I remained here, with Nancy Hopkinfon, only daughter of John Hopkinfon, a tanner
of this place. A pretty lafs, but like myfelf, very young, about my own age, but a
tall girl of her years. On this occafion, though

---

* A judcock was a fmall fort of fnipe.

ſtill very baſhful, I went a ſtep farther than in my firſt amour, frequently preſuming to give her a kiſs; and one night, encouraged by a neighbouring man, a John Halmſhaw, who had acquaintance with the maid, I ventured to pay her a viſit after the family were gone to bed, and paſſed part of the night with her, while John wooed the maid. I remember I was terribly embarraſſed to keep up the converſation, ſhe not being a very talkative girl, and was ſo diſheartened with the circumſtance—with which, by the by, I ſhould not be puzzled now—that for fear of making myſelf appear ridiculous in that reſpect, I never durſt repeat my viſit afterwards, although the girl was coming enough. Soon after this, a young man from a neighbouring village formed a connection with her, got her with child, was hardly perſuaded to marry her; behaved unkindly. She was unhappy, bore a child, and died. I ſaw her interred in the White-chapel, near the pulpit. Farewell, poor Nancy Hopkinſon!

I obſerve that in both theſe love affairs the paſſion only played as a gentle lambent flame about my head, without ſo much affecting my heart as to give me any material uneaſineſs of mind. The next was more fatal to my peace of mind, as I ſhall note by and by. I obſerve that here alſo there is hardly a perſon in the village, except old Madam Richardſon, who were then in a ſtate of maturity, who now ſurvive; ſo tranſitory is human life!

At length I removed with my aunt and her little grand-daughter from this place to Birken-fhaw once again. It was now ordered that I fhould learn the white-cloth-making trade with Richard Ellifon, my aunt's eldeft fon. I accordingly attended and worked there at the trade, but continued to board with my aunt, and lodged with her and at Richard's alternately. I learned to weave with John Bentley and John Sykes. I ftayed here till Richard's death, which happened in the fpring of 1754, when I was about eighteen years old. I continued with his widow till fhe married again, when I purchafed the implements of the trade of her, in order to trade a little for myfelf. About this time I came of age, and of courfe had my concerns to fettle with my aunt as my executor. During my minority my half-uncle, Thomas Cordingley of Farrah Mill,* died : by his death, his fifter, my half-aunt, Martha Sutcliffe, became entitled to a legacy of one hundred pounds by my grandfather's will, which I had to pay her out of my Little Bowling †

---

* The Farrah Mill here meant is an old corn-mill which yet remains, and is fituated in a valley between Halifax and a place called Salterhebble, not far from Skircoat Moor. Formerly almoft every valley in the Weft Riding of York-fhire had its corn-mill, or mills (if there was a ftream in it, and a water-courfe or "goit" could be formed) for the ufe of the farmers in the neighbourhood. The millers were wont to mulct a certain quantity of the grain brought, as payment for grinding, and it is highly probable that *Mulĉture* Hall got its name from this ancient cuftom, as it is built near fome yet very large corn-mills.

† Little Bowling is up Manchefter Road, one mile from

eftate. She demanded the legacy at my uncle's death, but my executor finding that fhe could not pay it fafe till I came of age, it was deferred till that time : I then paid them the legacy, with about twelve pounds for intereft, upon a promife from them, that if (after having taken a lawyer's opinion on the fubject, which we agreed to do) it fhould appear that they had no right to the intereft, they fhould refund it without trouble ; which happening to be the cafe, I recovered, after much ado, about nine guineas from my interefted relations, and the attorney agreed to take what he could get of the remainder for his trouble. They manifefted a good deal of mean-nefs, and ill-will at this time ; and a William Aked, a fon of my aunt's by her firft hufband, was brutifhly abufive on my dear deceafed grand-mother on this occafion, as he fuppofed fhe had perfuaded my grandfather to leave me the eftate,

---

Bradford. There were two Bowlings, Great and Little, but the latter name has fallen into difufe. The old road from Bradford to Low Moor ran paft Little Bowling, which was a clufter of houfes at " Red Gin "—a public-houfe. The " *Gin* " was a machine for raifing coals out of the pit, and was worked by a horfe. The " Red Gin " is not many hundred yards from Oak Fold to the weft of the latter place. The Bowling Old Lane and Oak Folds dis-trict ufed to be called Far Bowling. As to the coal in Bowling, that in the vicinity of Birks Hall was got out without finking, but the whole of the coal in the townfhip of Bowling is all taken out now. The coal near Birks Hall was taken out by Mr. Charles North, and the iron-ftone by the Bowling Company, who have fome very ex-tenfive works clofe by.

which they wanted themſelves. The apoſtle ſays, " The love of money is the root of all evil." It often creates evil tempers, evil diſpoſitions, and evil diſſenſions among neareſt relations and deareſt friends : it is a pity ! I will beg of God it may never be the caſe among any of my deſcendants, if they ſhould have any property to quarrel about. I return to my executor.

All the time I had been under the guardianſhip of my aunt, I had fared very meanly, and been as plainly clothed. A meſs of boiled milk, and a little bread and milk, cold, to breakfaſt; about a print* of butter between two pieces of oat-bread, or ſometimes cheeſe, with a pint bottle of milk, or ſometimes beer, for my dinner and drinking ; and the ſame to ſupper as

---

* A *print* of butter meant generally a certain quantity, as a pound or a half-pound, which was ſtamped out, but here it is applied more particularly to a *ſmall* quantity, an ounce *or leſs* in weight, and about the ſize of a half-crown piece. In the country farm-houſes they are made for the children, and are intended as allowances by careful mothers, aunts, &c. They are ſometimes brought out at country inns, where the inn happens to be a farmhouſe alſo, when there are only one or two perſons to breakfaſt or tea. " I remember," a correſpondent writes, " being ſerved ſome years ago with two of theſe ſmall prints at Stanbury, which lies on the edge of the moors above Haworth, the lady of the houſe telling me that ſhe was churning, and ſuppoſed, as I was a *town's man*, I might like it freſh in that way. Theſe prints are generally ſtamped the ſame as the pounds are, but ſometimes the ſtamping is done with the end of the thumb."

breakfaft, with a little pudding and frefh or falt meat on Sundays, was my general bill of fare for moft of the time. Sammy Wood broke me off from fchool frequently to go with cloth to mill for him to the mills on the river Air, beyond Bradford, befides other errands for the family to Bierley, Birkenfhaw, &c., which took me much from the fchool, and all went for nothing to me. However, they took care to charge fufficiently for everything they did for me, and made more than a double charge for my board to what I had coft them; befides, my perfonal property— that is, the houfehold furniture and wearing apparel that came from Halifax—was feverely plundered amongft them under various pretences, fo that I came off a confiderable lofer from what I ought to have done. I perceived their aim was to make end and even, as we fay, or to make their charge equal to my income, that fo they might have nothing to pay me. By this means I was left deftitute of any ftock to trade with, or towards paying off the legacy I was charged with. I note that, with regard to the unfair dealing I met with on this occafion, in my opinion the chief blame attached to Sammy Wood, who was a narrow-minded, interefted man. My poor old aunt evidently irked with the bufinefs, but fhe had given up the manage- ment of all her concerns to him, in whom fhe placed an implicit confidence. His children by his firft wife were likely to obtain a good fhare of what the old woman might leave; he therefore became interefted to procure her all he could. I reafoned the cafe with him, and propofed to refer it to two indifferent perfons, but to no purpofe: I therefore took my leave of him with a recital of that paffage (which feemed to ftrike him), Exod. xxii. 22, 23, 24, " Ye fhall not afflict any widow or fatherlefs child; if thou afflict them in any wife, and they cry at all unto me, I will furely hear their cry, and my wrath fhall wax hot, and I will kill you with the fword; and your wives fhall be widows, and your children fatherlefs." I told him I had rather be the fufferer than the oppreffor, for fear of the confequences. I never hardly faw him afterwards, but he mentioned it and endeavoured to palliate his conduct, and to be greatly defirous that I fhould think more favourably of it; a circumftance which appeared to me as a ftriking proof of confcious guilt. He was at this time as careful, fober, and managing a man as any in the neighbourhood; but after the death of his firft wife he became an extravagant, quarrelfome, drunken fot, and fo, for aught I know, he lived, and fo he died.

Being thus left with little ready cafh, in order to pay off the legacy before mentioned, I fold Mr. A—— B—— of Bradford all the coals he could get in the land without putting down a pit within the ftakes of any of the outfences, for one hundred pounds, with which I paid the legacy, as I have noticed before. I notice the following circumſtance on this occaſion. When I met Mr. B—— and the attorney (Mr. Jno. Eagle of Bradford, who had made the writing) at the Talbot Inn in Halifax, in order to receive the money and execute the deed, Mr. Eagle gave it me to look over before I ſigned it; and I found it left Mr. B—— at liberty to come within and break up my land, only paying me for the damages. I told Mr. Eagle this was contrary to bargain, to which Mr. B—— with much confuſion was obliged to aſſent. Mr. Eagle was very angry, and ſpoke ſome very ſharp words to Mr. B—— on the occaſion, and immediately eraſed the objectionable paſſage, and interlined words punctually expreſſive of the bargain; but I was ſo ſtruck with the meanneſs and apparent diſhoneſty of the trick deſigned to have been put upon me, that I could hardly perſuade myſelf to ſign the writing till I had got it examined; but Mr. Eagle aſſuring me upon his honour it was right, I ſigned it, but immediately ſhowed it to another attorney when I got home, who aſſuring me it was ſafe, I was eaſy. Mr. B—— had told me that he was very intimate with, and had a great reſpect for, my father, and on this account profeſſed a great friendſhip and reſpect for me; hence, being young and unexperienced in men and manners, I was led to expect a very friendly and generous behaviour from him, when, alas!

the very firſt opportunity that occurred, he was aiming to trick me out of my property e'er I had well got poſſeſſed of it, and that to a conſiderable amount too, as it would have proved; while I was unexperienced with men, and a novice in the world; a moſt ungenerous attempt.

So deceitful is the human heart, and ſo little dependence is to be placed in general on profeſſions of human friendſhip! While a perſon can ſerve a turn by you, or make you or yours in any reſpect ſubſervient to his intereſts, you may expect plenty of theſe profeſſions; the moment you do *not* need their aſſiſtance they are ready to do you any kindneſs; nay, they will even obtrude their friendly favours, as they call, and you may think, them, upon you, becauſe they run no riſk, and ſee a probability, if nothing more, of your returning their friendſhip in kind, or by ſome ſimilar or greater favour; but the moment you *do* ſtand in need of their aſſiſtance, and are, perhaps, reduced to a condition not to be able to make any great, if any return at all for their kindneſs but gratitude, you will ſoon ſee their friendſhip aſſume a different aſpect, and find them very ready to abandon an unprofitable connection. Do you think—taking the world before you—you would be able to find above one perſon in a million capable of performing an action of *purely diſintereſted* friendſhip of any conſiderable conſequence, to ſave you or your family from a prifon or the workhoufe? Nay, in general—

> " The kindeft but your prefent wants allay,
>   To leave you wretched the fucceeding day."

If they have paffed for your friends in a ftate of profperity, on a change of circumftances with you for the worfe, common decency indeed may induce them to fhow you fome fmall kindnefs, in order to juftify in fome meafure the character they have borne to the world; as to afford you an occafional treat, or perhaps to fpare or beftow a few fhillings, or at moft a few pounds, for your affiftance or in your favour. This, in general, is the moft you may expect or will experience. In the mean time you may expect a rapid decreafe in their outward civility and refpect; nay, if occafion offers, they may probably proceed to oppofition, detraction, and abufe, if they do not go farther ftill, and add injury to outrage, *becaufe* you are *unable*, or at leaft, *lefs able* now than you was once either to return a favour or retaliate an infult. Such behaviour indeed indicates a mean, ungenerous heart, and demonftrates the falfity of their pretended friendfhip. This, however, is what we have to expect from moft profeffors of friendfhip in the world, although, perhaps, in our better days, we may have laid them or theirs under preceding obligations. Good, therefore, is the advice of the prophet, "Ceafe ye from man, whofe breath is in his noftrils, for wherein is he to be accounted of?" Well does old Homer, the poet, advife—

> " That fince of fallen mankind fo few are juft,
> Think all are falfe, nor even the faithful truft."

Needful, abfolutely needful, is an attention, an invariably clofe attention, to the advice contained in Tim a' Lee's old cautionary proverb, *Truft no mortal!* No, let my children, or any perfon who may read this manufcript, be advifed by me—Whatever profeffion of friendfhip any perfon may make, however highly you may think of their friendly difpofition at prefent, leave yourfelves, I advife you, as little at their mercy as you poffibly can. If you do not, it is five thoufand to one you are deceived, and will find reafon to repent feverely, when it is too late, of your imprudence. This was one of the firft inftances I met with of the deceitfulnefs of pretended friendfhip, but I have known many of them fince, and perhaps not many perfons have been more a dupe to them than myfelf; hence I advife caution in reliances of this nature. He is well helped who, when he can, helps himfelf. I know there is fomething extremely difagreeable to an open, generous mind to treat every perfon we may have to do with as if they were not to be trufted : 'tis true we may and ought indeed to do this as decently as we can, but ftill, in my opinion, it is for the moft part abfolutely needful.

When, therefore, you have affairs of any confequence to tranfact, fecure your own interefts yourfelf as far as you decently can, and *truft no mortal!*

I proceed to take notice of the following circumftance, which happened about this time. My aunt Betty, who lived at Bradford, made an attempt when my father died, to wreft me and my property from the care of my grandfather and grandmother Cordingley, but as they knew fhe did this from interefted motives, to get me and what I had into her power, they withftood and caft her; the law, however, was expenfive, but as fhe was caft in cofts, fhe was liable to pay, or go to prifon; but as fhe was poor, and a near relation, they chofe rather to pay the cofts themfelves and let her alone. When I fold the coal, as noted before, fhe thruft herfelf officioufly into the bufinefs, and went, or pretended to go, feveral times betwixt me and Mr. B—— on the occafion, without being either ordered or defired by me. After this fhe made a charge of what fhe had done in the above affair twenty years before, and what fhe had done now, till fhe had got it above ten pounds. To this pretended debt fhe fwore, and arrefted me; I gave bail to the writ, determined in my firft chagrin to ftand her out and punifh her, as I underftood I might certainly have done; but upon fecond thoughts, confidering fhe had a numerous family, and was very poor and diftreffed, the certain expenfe that would attend the conteſt, and that putting her or her huſband in priſon would do me no good, I was perſuaded by Mr. Joſeph Hollings of Cotting-ley* to drop the conteſt : I therefore paid her the money and quit my hands of her. She after-wards ſent for me on her death-bed in great diſtreſs. I ſent her three ſhillings, and went afterwards to ſee her : I forgave her, and took a friendly leave of her, but from that time have had no connection with the family. This affair, firſt and laſt (for all the expenſe fell ultimately on me), was, I ſuppoſe, not leſs than fifty pounds out of my pocket.

I began now to acquire a pretty large acquaint-ance among the fair ſex, and to form ſome par-ticular connections ; but as I had made but little ſhow in trade, having, indeed, but little ſpare money, I found myſelf much objected to on this

---

* Cottingley is a ſmall village four miles to the north-weſt of Bradford. It lies on the north ſide of what uſed to be Cottingley Moor, but during the laſt few years the whole of this waſte land has been encloſed and let out in ſmall lots for almoſt nothing, by the owner Busfield Fer-rand, Eſq. M.P. for Devonport. The high road from Bradford to Bingley paſſes near it, and it is about two miles from the latter place. There are two or three old houſes in it, and the ſcenery in its vicinity is of the moſt beautiful kind. During the latter part of laſt century a Mr. Wickham, a juſtice of the peace, reſided in an old hall which ſtands by the ſouth-eaſt end of Cottingley Bridge, and he was the only juſtice then near Bradford. Hence the ſaying among people generally, "O'll carry tha ovver Cottingley Moor if tha dus'nt mind." That is, to the juſtice.

account, and having by this time entered into a particular attachment to a neighbouring girl, of whom I became extremely enamoured, in order to remove this odium, and show myself to the best advantage, I borrowed 200*l.* on my little estate. Confidering that I had always a natural averfion to trade, and had but been very imperfectly initiated in the bufinefs I propofed to follow with this money, this, at the time, was a very imprudent action, and the firft ftep that tended to break into and leffen my little property. Had I done a little with what I could have fpared out of my annual income, till I had become gradually more perfectly acquainted with the bufinefs, and increafed my ftock when I had known better how to have ufed it, I had acted far more wifely than I did; but as I hinted before, my eagernefs to remove the odium of following little or no trade out of the way of my being accepted as a hufband, was my chief motive of action on this occafion. Well, having been chiefly while with Richard Ellifon confined to the working part of the bufinefs, and feldom or ever been taken to the markets, I was of courfe unacquainted in a great meafure with buying and felling, and being diffident of my own abilities, I entered into a kind of partnerfhip with a neighbour. This alfo was a weak imprudent meafure, by which I fuffered lofs, and for which I blame myfelf. We continued to make and fell cloth for fome time, till finding

my partner in an unfair practice, and that my
stock diminished very fast, I gradually withdrew
from the connection.

I proceed now to give some account of the
attachment I mentioned before, with the circumstances attending it. The girl was very young,
and a very pretty girl; we lived near together,
and had very frequent opportunities of enjoying
each other's company. My fondness for her
kept increasing, till I became very unhappy in
her absence. The idea of any other man forming a connection with her gave me exquisite pain
of mind; and, in short, I was deeply in love with
this girl, and experienced, as occasion offered, all
the varieties of that baneful passion. She was
sent one summer to a boarding-school at Bolton
in Lancashire, where I visited her twice during
her stay. These journeys were very expensive,
and I was profusely lavish of my money over
this girl, buying her anything she desired, or
whatever I thought would please her, whatever
it cost me. I was likewise very liberal to her
mother, and father-in-law, and their family,
partly for her sake, and partly from the respect I
had entertained for them from being familiar
with them from my infancy; and they were at
this time in straitened circumstances.

I notice here the extreme folly and imprudence
of this conduct in young fellows. The girls
love them never a whit the better, but often the
worse for such profusion. They consider it as a

bait thrown out for their affections, and contemn,
defpife, and ridicule the man who aims at obtaining them by fuch paltry methods.

" Can gold gain friendfhip (or love) ? Impudence of hope !
  As well mere man an angel might beget.
  Love, and love only, is the loan for love."

I therefore advife any young man who may
happen to be entangled, more or lefs, in this
foolifh paffion, to keep his money in his pocket ;
or if he does anything in this way, not to go
beyond trifles. If he cannot obtain and fecure
his fweetheart's affections by other means, money,
or anything which money can do, either for him
or her, will never be able to effect it ; he may
take my word for it if he pleafes. And in cafe
he fhould drop the connection, or be fupplanted
by another man, he will fubject himfelf to the
difagreeable alternative of either making himfelf
appear mean, interefted, and ungenerous, by re-
tracting or endeavouring to retract his favours,
rather than another man fhould enjoy them ; or
of being heartily laughed at for his weaknefs
and folly by his more fuccefsful rival. I never
reflect upon my own actions in this cafe without
being deeply ftruck with a painful fenfation of
fhame and regret for the weaknefs and folly of
my own conduct.

I return to my ftory. After keeping up our
acquaintance for feveral years, fhe went to
refide for fome time with an aunt fhe had (her
mother's fifter), at two or three miles' diftance.

The uncle followed a large bufinefs, and had a great many men and boys about him; his niece was a fond* girl, and remarkably weak in her conduct in this refpect. This, therefore, was a dangerous fituation for her. I apprifed her mother of the circumftance, and advifed her to order her home; fhe laughed at me, and obferved that I only wanted her home that I might have more of her company myfelf. This was partly true. However, it foon appeared that to have followed my advice was extremely neceffary; reports of a flanderous nature were prefently propagated concerning her, with refpect to feveral men, both at home and in the neighbourhood. I queftioned her very clofely on the fubject, but fhe conftantly denied that there was any foundation for fuch reports. I told her my defigns were honourable, and my love difinterefted, but that if fhe preferred any other perfon before me, if fhe would let me know it I would give her no further trouble, whatever uneafinefs of mind it might fubject me to. She denied any other attachment, and feemed very unwilling to drop the connection. As the reports ftill continued—particularly with regard to one of her uncle's apprentices—I was refolved, if poffible, to find her out, and underftanding that they ufually met in the dyehoufe, after the

---

* *Fond* in the dialect of this diftrict means *filly, in dotage, an idiot.* It is fometimes ufed as a term of endearment, thus: "He's varry fond on her," that is, he doats or thinks much of her.

fervants had laid by their work, I went down one winter's evening and placed myfelf in a corner of the dyehoufe where I could fee what paffed without being obferved. Some of the boys after fupper came into the dyehoufe, and placed themfelves round the low lead fires,* and he came amongft the reft. The fires were low, and caft little or no light upwards; the place was therefore very gloomy. She prefently came in, and he immediately joined her, the other boys taking little or no notice of them. He brought her upon a heap of cloth very near me: I foon obferved improprieties pafs between them, which fatisfied me of the truth of the reports that paffed. In the midft of their play I ftepped fuddenly up to them; they were both afhamed and confounded, and feparated immediately. She went into the houfe, and I followed her, acquainted her aunt with the circumftance, told her I fhould trouble her no more, and wifhed them a good night. I afterwards fent her my farewell advice in the following ftanzas:—

---

* Formerly the vats in all the dye-houfes were made of lead, and as the tops of the vats muft of courfe be on a level with the floor of the workroom, the place for the fires, to be below the vats, muft alfo be below the level of the ground. The way to the firing-up place was down fome fteps, and led between the vats. Thefe lower regions were always termed "below the leads," or "below the lead fires," and were the favourite reforts of youngfters (where it was permitted) during the long evenings of winter, for the fires were feldom allowed to go out entirely.

TO EMMA.

I.

Dear Emma, will you deign to hear,
  And heedfully attend,
The counfel which thefe verfes bear,
  The counfel of a friend.

II.

Who with the warmeft wifhes fraught
  Your happinefs to fee,
Feels all at leaft that friendfhip ought
  For your felicity.

III.

A friend whofe bofom once you knew
  With generous ardour burn,
Although that ardour met from you
  A moft unkind return.

IV.

'Twas faithful love which you fuppreffed,
  'Twas true, and free from art,
As e'er poffeffed a human breaft,
  Or warmed a human heart.

V.

Difinterefted, genuine, free,
  It knew no felfifh aim ;
But you unkindly damped its fires,
  And quenched the rifing flame.

VI.

But may the wrongs I fuffered be
  Eternally forgot,
Nor of them rife the leaft idea
  To form one future thought.

VII.

Though difappointment ftung me fore,
  Though grieved and pained I was,
Refentment now exifts no more,
  But pity takes its place.

VIII.

How oft I've thought, when I've beheld
  Th' imprudence of your ways,

Along the fatal paths impelled
  That led to dire difgrace,

IX.

Thoughtlefs, and wild, and void of care,
  To your own errors blind.
What pity that a form fo fair
  Should want an equal mind.

X.

But won't experience now at laft
  Unfeal your clofed eyes?
Will Emma never fee her faults?
  Will Emma ne'er be wife?

XI.

On every coxcomb will fhe choofe
  Her favours to beftow?
Emma, affume a confcious pride,
  And fcorn to ftoop fo low.

XII.

Oh, could I learn what counfel giv'n
  Might to your good redound,
'T fhould flow as free as dew from heaven
  Upon the thirfty ground.

XIII.

For now the cankered, pois'nous tongue
  Of calumny and fpite,
In blafting of your character
  Enjoys a fell delight.

XIV.

Exulting malice fhrugs the head,
  And deeply wounds your fame,
And envy and ill-nature join
  To vilify your name.

XV.

But if you're free, may you perfift
  To keep your virtue ftill,
And difappoint th' ill-natured hope
  Of fuch as wifh you ill.

XVI.

Your nature, over-fond, reftrain ;
    Learn th' happy mean to fteer,
Betwixt a conduct light and vain
    And one that's too fevere.

XVII.

Our fex, remember, little prize
    What little trouble gains ;
An eafy conqueft they defpife,
    And love what cofts them pains.

XVIII.

Let prudence, then, direct your ways,
    And reafon fway your will ;
And wifely fhun the devious paths
    That lead to certain ill.

XIX.

Accept this counfel fairly meant,
    And honeftly defign'd,
And may it leave a good imprefs
    Upon your thoughtful mind.

XX.

Think not I've any felfifh view,
    Or finifter defign ;
I know I never can be yours,
    You never can be mine.

XXI.

'Tis real friendfhip prompts my pen
    This plain advice to give,
And if your intereft it promote,
    Then I my wifh receive.

XXII.

May Emma's fame, though now obfcured,
    Shine out more fair and bright,
With friendly warmth and beft good-will
    So wifhes Thomas Wright.

Here ended my connection with this girl, and though it gave me some uneasiness of mind, which gradually wore off with time, considering the nature of her future conduct, it was well for me that it did ; I should have been one of the most unhappy mortals under the sun, had I been brought into the situation her future husband happened to be. I had reason therefore to be very thankful to a kind Providence, which would not suffer me to enjoy my eager and baneful desire.

> " Heaven's choice is safer than our own ;
>   Of ages past inquire.
>   What the most formidable fate ?
>   To have our *own desire*.
>
> " If in your wrath the worst of foes
>   You wish extremely ill,
>   Expose him to the thunder's stroke,
>   Or that of his *own will*.
>
> " What numbers rushing down the steep
>   Of inclination strong,
>   Have perished in their *ardent wish ?*
>   Wish ardent, ever wrong."
>   DR. YOUNG's *Resignation*.

As she has now (1795) been dead many years, I will just give some of the outlines of her history from the ceasing of our connection to her death. She soon after proved with child by the aforesaid apprentice ; her relations would not suffer her to marry him. She bore the child, and it died. After some time an acquaintance of mine married her ; she bore him a son in twenty weeks after their marriage. They lived together to have fix children, who all died : fhe afterwards proved unfaithful to his bed; they quarrelled ; he left her and went to London, where report faid he married another wife, and had two children by her before his firft wife died. She at laft fell into a confumptive diforder, and, reflecting on her former life, appeared to be very penitent. I called to fee her, and fhe defired me to write her a penitent letter to her hufband, a copy of which I here fubjoin.

Dear B——,

I know not whether you have heard that your wife is in a very bad ftate of health or no, but fhe appears to be in a deep confumption, and near approaching the borders of the grave. I have feen her now and then lately, and have been glad to obferve a ferious and fettled concern upon her mind for her future welfare ; fhe appears to be truly penitent for her paft fin and folly, and as a proof of this fhe has defired me to write you this for her, wherein fhe requefted me to let you know that fhe is very deeply fenfible of the offences fhe has formerly committed againft you, defires to confefs them before God and you, and take all deferved fhame to herfelf upon the account, and earneftly begs your pardon. She fays it has been for fome time one of the greateft burdens upon her mind, and that after having made this free confeffion and requeft, fhe can be fo far eafy. That fhe could be glad to fee you, to acknowledge her faults, and be reconciled to you in perfon before fhe dies ; but if you cannot fhow her that favour, fhe hopes you will write immediately and let her know if you are enabled to forgive her; and in the meantime fhe bids you farewell, and recommends you to the protection and favour of God, of whom fhe trufts to have her fins (though great) forgiven, and with whom fhe trufts to be reconciled and accepted through the mediation of an infinitely gracious Saviour.   And if fhe muft fee you here no more—of which fhe confeffes herfelf unworthy—fhe hopes to meet you, fhe fays, where all weaknefs, fin, and forrow will be done away, in a better and happier world.   Your wife appears to be very fincere in her defire of reconciliation with you, very fenfible of and repentant for her crimes ; and earneftly defirous of being reconciled to God ; and I think will not be long before fhe dies.   If it fuits your convenience and inclination, I could wifh you to fee her once again to exchange forgivenefs and part in peace; if not, I defire you would not fail to write to her immediately, as it may be a fatisfaction to the repentant fpirit of one that has been dear to you and that ftands in a near connection to you ftill. I hope this will find you in health, as I and my children are at prefent.   I fhall always be glad to hear of your welfare, and remain, dear B———, yours with great fincerity of affection,

T. Wright.

He came not down, but wrote a letter, in which he forgave her. Soon after this I called to fee her, juft as fhe was expiring, and ftood by her till fhe died, June 25th, 1779. She was buried near the low gates in Birftall church-yard. Farewell, Emma!

During my love affair with this girl two young women and a widow thought fit to think favourably of *me*, and took care to let me know it. The widow, who was a good deal elder than me, was very importunate, and deeper in the paffion, if poffible, than myfelf; but as my affections were pre-engaged, all their attempts to engage my attention were vain.

I ftop here to make fome reflections on this ftrange paffion, fo common, in a greater or lefs degree, among the youth of both fexes, and fometimes attended with very ferious confequences.

" What art thou *Love!* thou ftrange myfterious ill ? "

It has been obferved that perfons of the moft generous, open, and good-natured difpofitions are of all others the moft fubject to this paffion ; that perfons of a four, ill-natured turn of mind are feldom or ever engaged in it ; and that in Africa, where the heat of the climate is fuppofed to render the inhabitants more favage, the paffion is unknown.

" Love dwells not there,
The foft regards, the tendernefs of life,
The heart-fhed tear, th' ineffable delight

> Of sweet humanity: thefe court the beam
> Of milder climes; in felfifh, fierce defire,
> And the wild fury of voluptuous fenfe,
> There loft."
>
> THOMSON's *Summer.*

Whether thefe authors have fufficient grounds for what they affert of thefe Africans, I know not. The former part of the obfervation I believe is a fact : it therefore behoves young perfons of this defcription, of both fexes, to be doubly careful how they fuffer their affections to be engaged upon improper objects, or to an improper degree, if they mean to avoid the follies, inconveniences, and vexations of this befooling paffion.

Dr. Young, in his " Eftimate of Human Life," Third Edition, p. 30, has, I think, given the beft account of it I have met with. He obferves, that love " implies difcontent, that is *pain;* for he that defires is diffatisfied with his prefent condition, be it what it will ; and the pain is in proportion to the defire. To fay the leaft to the difadvantage of this paffion, it is putting your peace in the power of *another,* which is rarely fafe even in your *own.*" He obferves further, that " Love is *all* the paffions in *one :* it is *anger* that it *cannot, fhame* that it *does not, fear* that it *fhall not* enjoy its object. It is *envy* of and *hatred* to thofe that poffibly may ; for *envy, hatred,* and *fufpicion* form love's conftant companion, *jealoufy;* which therefore ftings deeper than *either* of them, becaufe it is *all.* Now, as many paffions as love has, fo many pains. Be it therefore a maxim, he that was never *pained* never *loved*. But though this paffion has pains, leads it not to *pleafures?* It *may* fail of them, and then it is *defpair*, which is moft terrible; if it attains them they may not be lafting, for moft pleafures, like flowers, when gathered, die. Love has under its banner *watching, ficknefs, abafement, adulation, perjury, jealoufy,* and fometimes it lifts anger's moft dreadful followers; the only difference is, *there* they are ftanding troops, *here* cafual recruits; there they are *volunteers,* here they are *preffed* occafionally into the fervice; for they do not *naturally* belong to love." I will conclude thefe fhort reflections on this fubject with a tranfcription of Mr. Thomfon's beautiful and ftriking defcription of and diffuafive from the wild and irregular paffion of love, oppofed to that of a pure and happy kind.

> " And let the afpiring youth beware of love,
> Of the fmooth glance beware; for 'tis too late,
> When on his heart the torrent foftnefs pours.
> Then wifdom proftrate lies, and fading fame
> Diffolves in air away; while the fond foul,
> Wrapt in gay vifions of unreal blifs,
> Still paints th' illufive form, the kindling grace,
> Th' enticing fmile, the modeft-feeming eye,
> Beneath whofe beauteous beams, belying Heaven,
> Lurk fearchlefs cunning, cruelty, and death:
> And ftill, falfe-warbling in his cheated ear,
> Her firen voice, enchanting, draws him on
> To guileful fhores and meads of fatal joy.
> E'en prefent, in the very lap of love
> Inglorious laid—while mufic flows around,
> Perfumes, and oils, and wine, and wanton hours—

Amid the rofes, fierce repentance rears
Her fnaky creft: a quick-returning pang
Shoots through the confcious heart; where honour ftill
And great defign, againft th' oppreffive load
Of luxury, by fits, impatient heave.
　　But abfent, what fantaftic woes, aroufed,
Rage in each thought, by reftlefs mufing fed,
Chill the warm cheek, and blaft the bloom of life!
Neglected fortune flies; and, fliding fwift,
Prone into ruin fall his fcorn'd affairs.
'Tis nought but gloom around; the darken'd fun
Lofes his light. The rofy-bofom'd Spring
To weeping fancy pines; and yon bright arch,
Contracted, bends into a dufky vault.
All nature fades extinct; and fhe alone
Heard, felt, and feen, poffeffes every thought,
Fills every fenfe, and pants in every vein.
Books are but formal dullnefs, tedious friends;
And fad amid the focial band he fits,
Lonely and unattentive. From his tongue
Th' unfinifh'd period falls: while, borne away
On fwelling thought, his wafted fpirit flies
To the vain bofom of his diftant fair;
And leaves the femblance of a lover, fix'd
In melancholy fite, with head declined,
And love-dejected eyes. Sudden he ftarts,
Shook from his tender trance, and, reftlefs, runs
To glimmering fhades and fympathetic glooms;
Where the dun umbrage o'er the falling ftream
Romantic hangs; there, through the penfive dufk
Strays, in heart-thrilling meditation loft,
Indulging all to love; or on the bank
Thrown, amid drooping lilies, fwells the breeze
With fighs unceafing, and the brook with tears.
Thus in foft anguifh he confumes the day,
Nor quits his deep retirement, till the moon
Peeps through the chambers of the fleecy eaft,
Enlighten'd by degrees, and in her train
Leads on the gentle hours; then forth he walks,
Beneath the trembling languifh of her beam,
With foften'd foul, and woos the bird of eve
To mingle woes with his; or, while the world
And all the fons of care lie hufhed in fleep,

Affociates with the midnight fhadows drear;
And, fighing to the lonely taper, pours
His idly-tortured heart into the page
Meant for the moving meffenger of love;
Where rapture burns on rapture, every line
With rifing frenzy fired. But if on bed
Delirious flung, fleep from his pillow flies;
All night he toffes, nor the balmy power
In any pofture finds; till the grey morn
Lifts her pale luftre on the paler wretch,
Exanimate by love: and then perhaps
Exhaufted nature finks a while to reft,
Still interrupted by diftracted dreams,
That o'er the fick imagination rife,
And in black colours paint the mimic fcene.
Oft with the enchantrefs of his foul he talks;
Sometimes in crowds diftrefs'd; or, if retired
To fecret-winding flower-enwoven bowers,
Far from the dull impertinence of man,
Juft as he, credulous, his endlefs cares
Begins to lofe in blind oblivious love,
Snatch'd from her yielded hand, he knows not how,
Through forefts huge, and long untravell'd heaths
With defolation brown, he wanders wafte,
In night and tempeft wrapt'; or fhrinks aghaft,
Back from the bending precipice; or wades
The turbid ftream below, and ftrives to reach
The farther fhore; where, fuccourlefs and fad,
She with extended arms his aid implores,
But ftrives in vain: borne by th' outrageous flood
To diftance down, he rides the ridgy wave,
Or, whelm'd beneath the boiling eddy, finks.
   Thefe are the charming agonies of love,
Whofe mifery delights. But through the heart
Should jealoufy its venom once diffufe,
'Tis then delightful mifery no more,
But agony-unmix'd, inceffant gall,
Corroding every thought, and blafting all
Love's paradife. Ye fairy profpects, then,
Ye beds of rofes, and ye bowers of joy,
Farewell! ye gleamings of departed peace,
Shine out your laft! the yellow-tinging plague
Internal vifion taints, and in a night

Of livid gloom imagination wraps.
Ah ! then, inſtead of love-enliven'd cheeks,
Of ſunny features, and of ardent eyes
With flowing rapture bright, dark looks ſucceed,
Suffuſed and glaring with untender fire ;
A clouded aſpect, and a burning cheek,
Where the whole poiſon'd ſoul, malignant, ſits,
And frightens love away.   Ten thouſand fears
Invented wild, ten thouſand frantic views
Of horrid rivals, hanging on the charms
For which he melts in fondneſs, eat him up
With fervent anguiſh and conſuming rage.
In vain reproaches lend their idle aid,
Deceitful pride, and reſolution frail,
Giving falſe peace a moment.   Fancy pours
Afreſh her beauties on his buſy thought ;
Her firſt endearments twining round the ſoul
With all the witchcraft of enſnaring love.
Straight the fierce ſtorm involves his mind anew,
Flames through the nerves, and boils along the veins;
While anxious doubt diſtracts the tortured heart:
For e'en the ſad aſſurance of his fears
Were eaſe to what he feels. Thus the warm youth,
Whom love deludes into his thorny wilds,
Through flowery-tempting paths, or leads a life
Of fevered rapture, or of cruel care;
His brighteſt aims extinguiſh'd all, and all
His lively moments running down to waſte.
   But happy they ! the happieſt of their kind !
Whom gentler ſtars unite, and in one fate
Their hearts, their fortunes, and their beings blend.
'Tis not the coarſer tie of human laws,
Unnatural oft, and foreign to the mind,
That binds their peace, but harmony itſelf,
Attuning all their paſſions into love ;
Where friendſhip full exerts her ſofteſt power,
Perfect eſteem enliven'd by deſire
Ineffable, and ſympathy of ſoul ;
Thought meeting thought, and will preventing will,
With boundleſs confidence : for nought but love
Can anſwer love, and render bliſs ſecure.
Let him, ungenerous, who, alone intent
To bleſs himſelf, from ſordid parents buys

The loathing virgin, in eternal care,
Well merited, confume his nights and days;
Let barbarous nations, whofe inhuman love
Is wild defire, fierce as the funs they feel:
Let eaftern tyrants from the light of heaven
Seclude their bofom-flaves, meanly poffefs'd
Of a mere lifelefs, violated form;
While thofe whom love cements in holy faith
And equal tranfport, free as Nature live,
Difdaining fear.   What is the world to them,
Its pomp, its pleafure, and its nonfenfe all!
Who in each other clafp whatever fair
High fancy forms, and lavifh hearts can wifh;
Something than beauty dearer, fhould they look
Or on the mind, or mind-illumined face—
Truth, goodnefs, honour, harmony, and love,
The richeft bounty of indulgent Heaven.
Meantime a fmiling offspring rifes round,
And mingles both their graces.   By degrees,
The human bloffom blows; and every day,
Soft as it rolls along, fhows fome new charm—
The father's luftre, and the mother's bloom.
Then infant reafon grows apace, and calls
For the kind hand of an affiduous care.
Delightful tafk! to rear the tender thought,
To teach the young idea how to fhoot,
To pour the frefh inftruction o'er the mind,
To breathe the enlivening fpirit, and to fix
The generous purpofe in the glowing breaft.
Oh, fpeak the joy! ye, whom the fudden tear
Surprifes often, while you look around,
And nothing ftrikes your eye but fights of blifs:
All various Nature preffing on the heart—
An elegant fufficiency, content,
Retirement, rural quiet, friendfhip, books,
Eafe and alternate labour, ufeful life,
Progreffive virtue, and approving Heaven!
Thefe are the matchlefs joys of virtuous love;
And thus their moments fly.   The feafons thus,
As ceafelefs round a jarring world they roll,
Still find them happy; and confenting Spring
Sheds her own rofy garland on their heads:
Till evening comes at laft, ferene and mild;

When after the long vernal day of life,
Enamour'd more, as more remembrance fwells
With many a proof of recollected love,
Together down they fink in focial fleep ;
Together freed, their gentle fpirits fly
To fcenes where love and bliss immortal reign."

I take notice here of a circumftance which fhould have been mentioned when I related the behaviour of my aunt. As fhe would have heired part of my little property if I had died inteftate, and as I thought fhe had rendered herfelf peculiarly unworthy of anything that was mine, in order to prevent this in cafe of anything fudden happening to me, I made a will, which coft me about half-a-guinea, wherein I left John Ellifon junior (fon of the before mentioned John) all I had, I having the greateft refpect for him and the family of any relation or friendly acquaintance I then had. I note alfo that during this interval I bought many books, and read much—divinity, philofophy, history, poetry, voyages, travels, &c., &c. ; and having a good memory, by this means I acquired a good deal of various knowledge, which, qualifying me for converfation, I contracted a very large acquaintance with fome of the moft fenfible men and beft families in the country round about. I alfo learned to play a little upon the violin and German flute. During this period alfo I made feveral excurfions into the furrounding country. I went with Mr. R—— B——, of Cleckheaton, and his fifter to Hull: we croffed the Humber to Barton in Lincolnshire, where we purchased some wool, and returned. We stayed about a week with an aunt of Mr. B——'s, at Hull, and returned home by the way of York. I went also to the Spa at Scarborough several seasons, and I took a journey to London with Mr. Martin Charlesworth, of Little Gomersal.* We resided at the Talbot Inn, in the Borough, Southwark: we went down to Greenwich and Woolwich to see the men-of-war, &c. I was on board the Sterling Castle, of 74 guns. We went to St. James's Chapel, saw the old king, George II., the present king, George III., then Prince of Wales, and most of the Royal Family. I saw also during my stay some of the principal public places and curiosities of the city and its neighbourhood. We stayed about ten days, and then returned. I went also with an acquaintance to Harrogate, and forward to Ripon; and this, I think, is nearly the extent of my travels to this period.

---

* Little Gomersall is a part of Great Gomersall, and is in the same township. It is in the parish of Birstall, but by a singular arrangement, Birstall is in the township of Gomersall. There is a chapel of ease in it, and a new church was erected about twelve years ago. The Wesleyans have a chapel here, and there is a Moravian chapel which is of a very old date. The trade of the place is the woollen manufacture, particularly that of blanketing. It is about five miles south-east of Bradford. At this place lived the prototype of Mr. Yorke, a character in the late Miss Brontë's novel of "Shirley;" the real name was Taylor.

After my affair with the laft-mentioned girl, an old Methodift in the town, called Benjamin Boys, obferving me look more folid and thoughtful than ufual, concluded that I was under fome religious impreffion, and invited me to go with him to hear the Methodifts preach: I complied with his requeft, and hence began my acquaintance and connection with the Methodifts, of which more hereafter. I was fo deeply difgufted with the vexation and difappointment I had met with in my late love affair, that I was almoft ready to forfwear all future connections with the fex, and was for fome time without any intercourfe of the kind; but by and by a circumftance happened which yoked me again. J—— B——, my late fweetheart's father-in-law, became fo ftraitened in his circumftances, that he was obliged to retire to London to avoid the perfecution of his creditors and recover himfelf; his wife and children locked up the houfe for fear the creditors fhould break it up, and I took them to me into my houfe, and accommodated them the beft I could till he returned and paid his creditors, which after fome time he honeftly did. During their ftay with me, Mrs. Birkhead of Brook-houfes,* near Cleckheaton (a near relation

---

* Brook-houfes. This beautiful place is rather lefs than half-a-mile up the ftream from Spen Bridge, and is but a fhort diftance to the north of Cleckheaton. One of the houfes—the Hall—is built of ftone, and was erected about thirty years ago when the old one was pulled down.

of Mrs. B——'s), attended by her eldeſt daughter Lydia, paid her a viſit. I was much taken with Miſs Birkhead, who was a very beautiful girl, and when they returned home in the evening, bore them company moſt of the way. As ſhe was at this time but very young—about eleven or twelve years old—I came to a reſolution in my own mind to wait about three years, and then, if we both lived, try if I could not obtain her for a wife, and I punɗually kept my reſolution.

At the end of three years Miſs Birkhead and her ſiſter Betty happened to be learning writing and accounts with a Mr. John Whitford, at that time miniſter of the Red Chapel* at Cleckheaton, who taught a ſchool on the week days,

---

The other part conſiſts of two cottages built of brick, which ſtand with the end towards the back of the hall. The buildings are beautifully environed in trees, and the whole neighbourhood as far as Spen Bridge looks like an ancient park. A clear ſtream runs juſt below, and all down the valley towards the eaſt there are ſome ſplendid bits of woodland and park-like grounds. An old foot-road leads down to Spen Bridge, paſt a mill-dam, and the walks are very carefully kept. Such is the Brook-houſes at the preſent day.

* Red Chapel, Cleckheaton. The old Independent chapel in Cleckheaton was built of brick, as are many of the houſes in that place. I ſuppoſe it was called the *Red Chapel* from that circumſtance, or it might be to diſtinguiſh it from the *White Chapel*, which ſtood at a ſhort diſtance from it. The Red Chapel has been replaced ſome years ſince by a very handſome new one of ſtone, and it is, perhaps, the beſt building in Cleckheaton at preſent. The White Chapel is built of ſtone.

and taught his fcholars at this time in the chapel. As I was well acquainted and very familiar with this gentleman, I called in one day to fee him while teaching his fcholars in the chapel, and the Mifs Birkheads being there, I went into the feat to them and helped them to finifh their fums. After they had fhown them to the mafter and returned, I took Lydia behind the pulpit, where I paid my firft addrefs to her in the way of courtfhip. The minifter obferving this haftened to loofe his fcholars, and left us the chapel to ourfelves.

I continued to cultivate my acquaintance with this girl for feveral years, till we had formed a pretty clofe connection. I obferved that fhe was remarkably backward in admitting my vifits at her father's houfe, though extremely willing to oblige me with every other opportunity: I found this arofe from a fear of her parents becoming acquainted with our connection, which fhe endeavoured to conceal from them as much as fhe could. I afterwards underftood that they not only difapproved of me for a hufband to their daughter, but were bitterly prejudiced againft me on other occafions. I was fo difgufted with the mean pride, contempt, and ill-nature I heard they expreffed on this occafion, that it caufed me to drop our correfpondence for fome time. In this interval I accidentally became acquainted with a Mifs C—— H——, a very handfome, genteel, young lady, near Mirfield,* whofe father could give her fome fortune, had given her a good education, and who was likely to make a very agreeable, managing wife. I kept company with this girl during the whole interruption of my correfpondence with Mifs Birkhead, and for aught I know, had I been fo determined, might have had her for a wife ; but meeting again with Mifs B—— at a friend's houfe, we made up the breach, and I was of courfe obliged to drop my correfpondence with Mifs H——. This young lady afterwards married a Mr. M. F——n of Raftrick, went with him to America, bore him two children there (daughters), and died. He himfelf foon after perifhed in a voyage upon bufinefs to the Dutch ifland of St. Euftatius. The veffel, it was fuppofed, foundered at fea, and all on board perifhed, as fhe was never heard of after her departure from the American port. One of the girls furvives, and has fince come over to fettle with her relations in this country. I heard the following ftory concerning her (Mifs H——) related as a fact:—That while her hufband and fhe were at fea, on their paffage to

---

* Mirfield, or Mirefield, is a prettily fituated village about three miles and a half to the fouth-weft of Dewfbury. It is rather celebrated in the legendary hiftory of this part of the county, and near the church there is a large conical mound, and the remains of an ancient manor-houfe. In modern times it has been beft known as one of the chief feats of the woollen manufacture.

America, her mother faw her apparition one evening pafs out of one room into another, with a candle in her hand, looking more than ordinarily thoughtful. If fo, I think it feemed to betoken that fhe was never to fee her again in this world.

I return to my own ftory. My fweetheart and me began now to think of marriage, in fpite of the old folk's oppofition, and in one of my vifits I propofed it to her. She was willing, but did not know how we fhould accomplifh it, fhe being under age, and her father refufing to give his confent. I told her there was one way ftill; fhe faid, what was that? I told her to take a trip to Scotland, and afked her if fhe would go? She declared fhe would whenever I pleafed. We then proceeded to fix a day for our adventure; it was Thurfday evening, fhe obferved, that her father and mother would have to attend what they call a church-meeting at Heckmondwike,* that day three weeks; that they would fet off by one o'clock paft noon, and be detained till the evening; that if I would, in their abfence, come down the private lane at the back of her father's houfe with my mare and a pillion, fhe would ride off with me to Leeds, where we could take the chaife for Scotland. On this footing we parted

---

* Heckmondwike. A confiderable place, eight miles fouth of Bradford. Here are extenfive blanket and carpet manufactories. It is but a fhort diftance from Liverfedge and Cleckheaton, on the Lancafhire and Yorkfhire Railway from Bradford to Mirfield and Huddersfield.

at this time. I had propofed the meafure without much thought or confideration, and when I came to confider it with attention, it gave me no little uneafinefs; not but that I loved the girl well enough, but I was afraid of the old people's after behaviour; and indeed, I had much more reafon to dread this—as I found to my coft afterwards—than I was at prefent aware of. However, as I confidered myfelf as equal to them, at leaft, in family, fortune, education, or moral character, and that if I behaved refpectfully they could not retain their refentment long, I determined to make the venture. The Sunday following I rode to Cleckheaton Chapel, and put up my mare at the public-houfe at Heaton Gate. My fweetheart, amongft other children, was faying her catechifm that day to the parfon. At noon a friendly acquaintance of mine (Mr. John Broadley, of Rawfolds *) invited me to dine with him, as he ufually did. I accordingly went and dined with him, and in returning to chapel after

---

* Rawfolds is near Liverfedge, and has become a famous place fince the novel of " Shirley," by Mifs Brontë, of Haworth, was publifhed. The mill, or manufactory, here is celebrated for its fuccefsful and fanguinary refiftance to the Luddite rioters on the 11th of April, 1812, under its proprietor, Mr. Cartwright. It is about a mile from Roe Head, near Heckmondwike, where Mifs Charlotte Brontë (Currer Bell) went to fchool, and fhe has introduced it prominently in the ftory of "Shirley." An interefting account of it will be found in the life of Charlotte Brontë, by Mrs. Gafkell. At prefent there are cloth-works and dye-works carried on in the mills at Rawfolds, or " Rawfuds."

dinner, I obferved Ifaac Taylor coming to meet me in a field called Rawfolds Pafture. I immediately fufpected that he came with fome meffage from Mifs Birkhead, which proved to be the cafe. This man lived in a little ftraw-thatched cottage at a place called Goofe Hill,* juft at the back of Mr. Birkhead's houfe, in the croft where the Balm-Mill ftands. We ufually called it the Ivy Hall, from its being much overgrown with ivy at the weft-end of it ; at this place Mifs Birkhead and me ufually met during the greateft part of our courtfhip, hence the family became a kind of confidents in our amour, and did all they could to promote our defign. He told me that Mifs Birkhead had been over at his houfe fince I faw her, and that fhe had laid a new and a fpeedier plan for our being married, which was as follows :—She and her fifter Betty were to go over in the morning (Monday) upon a vifit for fome time to her coufin, Sammy Webfter's, at Morley ; that I fhould go over with my mare and pillion, her riding drefs, &c., in the evening, put up my mare at the public-houfe, vifit her at her coufin Sammy's as a fuitor ; that fhe would ftay with me till they were fettled in bed ; that then I

---

* Goofe Hill. This name is no longer ufed, but the hamlet now paffes as Balm Mill, or in the dialect of the diftrict, *Bome Miln* ; it ftands about one hundred yards to the weft of Brook-houfes, and is only divided from the latter place by a narrow green lane, a beautiful clear ftream of water, and a croft.

fhould fetch the mare from the public-houfe, and fhe would ride off with me to Leeds, where we might take the chaife for Scotland. I fhould have noticed firft, that he told me fhe had got her riding drefs out to his houfe, that I was to ftay at the public-houfe till dark ; that then he would meet me at Spen Bridge* with her clothes, which I fhould take home with me, in order to carry them to Morley, to put on for her journey. All this was fudden ; entirely of her own contriving, and bound me to put or put up, and from the fhortnefs of the time, ftunned me a little. However, as I was fond of the girl, and hoped (as obferved before) that the circumftance the moft frightful to me, the old people's prejudice, might probably be furmounted, I fent her word that I would comply with her plan, and that fhe might expect me the next evening at Morley, according to appointment. I accordingly ftayed at Abraham Smith's, the public-houfe at Heaton Gate, till dark ; met Ifaac, and took her clothes with me to Birkenfhaw. I muft here notice another circumftance. Mr. Timothy Crowther, a friendly acquaintance of mine in the fame village, had been married fome time before to a Mifs Nancy Brooke, eldeft daughter of Mr. Jofeph Brooke,

---

* Spen Bridge is a fine ftone bridge near Spen Mill. On the eaft fide of the bridge there are large factories which have been built by Mr. Atkinfon. The owner of Spen Mill is a Mr. Mann, and the leffees of the mill are Meffrs. Firth and Blackburn.

of Hall Mill, at the bottom of Mirfield Moor. The girl was of age, and therefore at her own difposal, but her mother was fo averfe to parting with her, that we had her to get away as we could. I went early one fummer's morning with a horfe and a pillion, and fhe met me at the bottom of the common; fhe leaped on behind me, and a fervant met us up the fields with her clothes; we rode to a neighbouring ale-houfe, where we met her intended fpoufe and one or two companions; here fhe dreffed, and we walked to the church and had them married. On this occafion Mr. Crowther declared that if ever I ftood in need of fimilar affiftance, he would go with me wherever I went. He and his father and brother traded into Scotland; I therefore the rather claimed his promife at this time, as I had been little ufed to travelling, and he knew the roads and the country, having been there before. After fome little hefitation on the fhortnefs of the time, he declared he would bear us company; he therefore fpoke to his father and his brother, and they arranged their mercantile concerns for the journey as fpeedily as they could. I had never afked her father's leave to wait on her, but I determined to do it that day— though I knew I fhould be denied—that he might not have it to fay I had never afked him. I accordingly afked, and was refufed, but with more civility than I expected.

I made what fpeed I could in getting ready

for my journey, as to money, linen, &c., and in the evening rode over to Morley according to my promife, accompanied by Timmy Crowther, Benny Beaumont, and John Barrans. We put up our horfes at Morley Hole, where I left them and my companions, and attended my fweetheart. S. Webfter was acquainted with her parents' prejudice againft me, but, however, behaved very civilly, and invited me to fup with them. We were obliged to acquaint the maid with the affair, whom we obliged to fecrefy : fhe was very willing to oblige us, and obferved that fhe herfelf had a fweetheart that night, and that when they heard them ruftle and whifper, they would imagine it to be us, and they would carry on the deception as long as they could. When it approached eleven o'clock my fweetheart was impatient to be gone. I had ordered one of my companions to attend at the back-door when it grew late, and I would ftep out and let him know when we were ready, to fetch the mare; I therefore ftepped to the back door and told him, and he ran over for my mare and the reft of the company. She got on behind me from the wall near the windmill, and we proceeded to Mr. George Efh's, the Golden Lion Inn, at the bottom of Briggate, Leeds, the place I ufually inn'd at when about my bufinefs. She here changed her drefs (fhe was in mourning at tnis time for her uncle Tommy), the chaife was got ready with fpeed, we put a bottle of wine and fome cake in the box, and mounted. As the dread of her parents' malevolence ftill hung upon my mind, I looked folid and thoughtful; Mifs Birkhead obferved this and faid jocofely that if anybody faid a few words, I fhould run back of my bargain. At this my companion (a funny fellow) laughed heartily, and bantered me freely on the occafion. Our two companions returned, taking the horfes, &c. back with them, and we ftarted on our journey.

We were juft paffing through Shipfcar turnpike as it was chiming twelve o'clock at night at Leeds old church, and we reached Knaresborough early in the morning. Here we changed our carriage and horfes and proceeded to Boroughbridge, ftill in the dark; here we called them out of bed, changed our carriage and horfes again, and proceeded to Northallerton. Here we got our breakfaft, and then rode on to Darlington; here we dined, and then proceeded to Durham; here we drunk tea, and then proceeded through Chefter-le-ftreet to Newcaftle-upon-Tyne, which we reached about fix or feven o'clock in the evening of Tuefday, Nov. 18th, 1766. The driver took us to the Queen's Head, Pilgrim Street; here we fupped and refted awhile. Mr. Crowther was weary and fleepy, and propofed going to bed, but Mifs Birkhead and I were afraid if anyone happened to purfue us it might prove difagreeable, and therefore urged our proceeding with all fpeed, although fhe declared if anyone fhould overtake us, fhe would not return with them, at which Mr. Crowther laughed heartily again, and declared, No, we would fight blood to the knees before! I called the driver and gave him a fhilling extra; he told me he would put two as good horfes in the carriage as there was in Newcaftle, and drive us merrily; he was as good as his word. We went on the canter almoft all the way to Morpeth, where we called them out of bed, changed our chaife, and proceeded to Alnwick. Here we called them out of bed again, got a bottle of wine and fome little refrefhment, and rode on to a village they call Belford;* here fome of the tackle of the chaife had broken, and the driver had to call up a blackfmith to repair them; we fat in the chaife the while, and then proceeded to Berwick-upon-Tweed, which we reached foon after daybreak. Here we ftaid breakfaft and dinner, as Mr. Crowther had fome cuftomers to tranfact bufinefs with at this place. We then proceeded over the Scotch moors to a large, lone inn's-houfe called Old Camus. The roads were bad, fo that we had to alight feveral times and walk, the horfes having enough to do to draw the empty carriage. The face of the country fuddenly changed from a country en-clofed and adorned with trees and hedges, to a

---

* Belford is not a village, but a fmall market-town, about fourteen miles from Berwick-upon-Tweed.

black, barren, dreary wafte, where no fence, and
hardly a tree or a bufh were to be feen for long
together ; the cattle alfo had a very different
appearance ; the fmall, black, Scotch heifers and
the diminutive fheep on the wafte grounds of
Scotland, formed a very ftriking contraft to the
large cattle we had juft left behind in fome of
the northern counties of England. We reached
Old Camus at laft, changed our chaife, and proceeded to a village they call Broxburn.* The inn
where we alighted was no other than a ftraw-
thatched cottage with an earthen floor ; the
waiter, a ftrong-limbed, brown, Scotch girl, bare-
legged and bare-footed, and fpeaking the broad
Scotch dialect. Mifs Birkhead was ftartled with
the oddnefs of the fcene. After getting fome
refrefhment at this place, we proceeded to Had-
dingtoun, the capital, I fuppofe, of Eaft Lothian,
in North Britain ; we arrived at this place about
fix o'clock in the evening of Wednefday, Nov.
19th, 1766. We alighted at the chief, or one of
the chief inns in the town (I forget the fign),
and immediately fent for a minifter ; they prefently brought one ; he required a large fee at
firft, but I told him as we were but common
people, and not marrying from interefted motives,
he muft be content with lefs ; we agreed for two

---

* Broxburn is the name of a river which runs through
Haddingtonfhire to the fea, which it enters at Broxmouth.
The village of Broxburn ftands on the banks of this river.

guineas the minifter, and five fhillings the clerk, which I gave them, and he married us in a chamber of the inn about feven o'clock in the evening. My wife went to bed immediately, and after chatting awhile with my companion and the parfon, I followed her. The parfon told us the following ftory, which he had juft been concerned in a little before he married us.

A gentleman of London, of good fortune and character, wooed a lady of the fame place of a good fortune likewife. The gentleman was an unexceptionable match, but the lady's father was a fingular conceited fellow, and, as his daughter was under age, utterly refufed to give his confent to the marriage; the young couple, however, were determined on the meafure, and laid their plan accordingly. The gentleman hired a chaife and four in the neighbourhood to be ready at a certain hour, and as he knew that the lady's father was a fharp, active man, that their elopement could not be long concealed from him, and that he would follow them with all fpeed, he took the precaution to fend off a fervant, poft, with orders to keep a ftage before them all the way, and to fee a chaife and four ready harneffed at each ftage, and a fupply of wine and victuals in the box for them to fubfift on by the way, that they might ftep out of one carriage into another, and proceed with the utmoft fpeed without a moment's delay. By this means they prefently reached Haddington, and alighted at the fame inn which we did, but as they knew the activity of the old gentleman, they were afraid they would not have time to complete the ceremony before he was at their heels ; they therefore requefted the miftrefs of the houfe to fhow them a bed-room, and they would undrefs and get into bed, and if the old gentleman came, to tell him they were married and a-bed. She promifed to follow their directions, and by the time fhe had well left them the old gentleman was rattling in a chaife and four at the door ; he immediately inquired for the young couple ; fhe told him they were a-bed. "A-bed!" he exclaimed with aftonifhment ; " what, were they married already?" fhe told him, yes. After furioufly walking backwards and forwards for fome time, he defired to be fhown to their bed-room ; fhe accordingly introduced him into the room ; the young folks apologifed and begged his pardon : after fwearing and raving furioufly for fome time his paffion at length remitted, and he invited them to rife that they might drink together before he returned. He retired, and they arofe, dreffed themfelves, and joined the old gentleman, where they became tolerable friends over a bottle. The lady's father then got into the chaife, and returned home again. They then fent for the parfon (the fame who married us and told us the ftory), got married, went to bed, and the next morning followed the old gentleman to London.

The minifter wrote me the following certificate or teftimonial of our marriage :—

" Thomas Wright, of the parifh of Birftall, in the county of York, clothier, and Lydia Birkhead, of the fame parifh, fpinfter, were married at Haddington, in Eaft Lothian, N. Britain, according to the form of matrimony prefcribed and ufed by the Church of England, on this nineteenth day of November, 1766, by

J. Buchanan, Minifter,

In the prefence of { Timothy Crowther.
{ Bartholomew Bower."

In the morning, while breakfaft was preparing, I overheard the miftrefs of the houfe remarking to fome of the family, that the young lady (my wife) was a very pretty young lady as moft fhe had feen, and looked well ; but that the gentleman (myfelf) looked but poorly, and fhe thought the young lady would foon have a new hufband to feek. I thought, " I hope not, miftrefs, I do not think of dying fo foon as you feem to imagine." My wife had never had the fmall-pox, was in the bloom of youth and beauty, and at this time looked very well. I myfelf always looked pale, was at this time much fatigued both in body and mind, and had got little or no reft or fleep for three or four fucceffive days and nights, fo that at this time I looked poorlier than ordinary. Mr. Crowther and Mifs Birkhead flept foundly in the chaife, but I could not. But alas ! how

was our landlady miftaken ! The young blooming beauty, my wife, who was at this time like
the picture of health, and whofe look feemed to
promife many long years of life, health, and
vivacity, has now (at the time I am writing this
—September, 1795—after living with me in
wedlock near eleven years, and bearing me feven
children), been dead near eighteen years ; and
the poorly-looking gentleman who, in the judge-
ment of the landlady, feemed to be *then* near the
borders of the grave, after living with his then
wife near eleven years, and having feven children
by her, as mentioned above ; after living above
four years in a ftate of widowhood, and after
being married a fecond time to a younger wife
than his firft, with whom he has lived near fourteen years, and had five children by her, which
makes up his whole number twelve, is at prefent
in a comfortable ftate of health and ftrength for
his time of life. So uncertain is human fore-
fight, and fo liable is human judgment to be impofed upon by deceitful appearances.

We now concluded to bear Mr. Crowther
company the reft of his journey amongft his
cuftomers, and return home again together.
After breakfaft, therefore, we took the chaife
and proceeded to Edinburgh. This is the capital
city of Scotland, and here we ftayed feveral days.
We took a walk to Leith, the fea-port for Edinburgh, and about a mile diftant, and took a view
of the harbour, the fhipping, &c. We alfo took

a walk to Holyrood Houfe, where the Scottifh
kings ufed formerly to be crowned. The houfes
in this city (efpecially High Street) are remarkably high, from four to twelve or fixteen ftories,
fo that a perfon walking beneath feems buried
between the houfes, which appear the height of
fteeples on each fide, and gives a perfon a remarkable idea of his own littlenefs. The different
ftories of thefe lofty buildings are afcended by
flights of fteps, which they here call winds, and
at each ftory—for the moft part—a different
family dwells, with an infcription over the door
containing the perfon's name and occupation.
My wife and I afcended, I think, feventy-one
fteps to our bed-room. The inhabitants of this
city are not accommodated with neceffary houfes;
each family, therefore, provide themfelves with
clofe-ftools; at ten in the evening a perfon goes
about the city with a drum, to give notice to the
people in the ftreets to get out of the way;
every family then empty their clofe-ftool-pots
out of the windows into the ftreets, and early in
the morning perfons appointed for the purpofe
clean the ftreets and take as much of it away
as poffible, leaving the reft in vacant places,
covered with afhes, to take away afterwards.
This practice caufes a nafty fmell in the ftreets,
which is very difagreeable, efpecially to ftrangers;
I hardly durft venture out in a morning before I
had got my breakfaft. I obferved that they were
almoft univerfally fnuff-takers in this place, and

fomebody told me that they had adopted this cuftom as an antidote againft the bad fmells arifing in the ftreets, occafioned by the aforefaid dirty practice. We refided in one of the principal inns and one of the principal ftreets in the city, but I forget both the fign of the houfe and the name of the ftreet. One day while we remained here two of the maid fervants quarrelled about their work; they fcolded loud and feverely in the broad Scotch dialect; they appeared very droll to us, as we hardly knew a word they fpoke, although we could fee they were very angry.

Mr. Crowther having finifhed his bufinefs at this place, we took the coach one morning and proceeded to the city of Glafgow, which we reached in the evening. We refided during our ftay here at the firft inn on the right hand entering the city. The name of the perfon who kept the inn was, I think, at that time Tenant. The landlady of this inn was the biggeft, moft corpulent, and heavieft woman that ever I faw in my life; fhe told us her weight, but I have forgot it. She had a little wide carriage, like a cart, in which fhe rode out to take the air, for fhe was too heavy and overgrown to walk five yards: fhe faid when fhe was young fhe was as fmall as my wife; however, fhe would have made half-a-dozen of her now. This city, for its bignefs, is one of the prettieft cities I ever faw; it appears to have been laid out on a regular plan, all the ftreets croffing each other at right angles. The buildings are lofty, grand, and regular, and the principal ſtreets accommodated with piazzas, which are very agreeable to foot-paſſengers on a hot or rainy day. I called in one day at one of the bookſellers and purchaſed Gay's "Beggars' Opera," to read for amuſement during our ſtay: the bookſeller underſtanding I came from Yorkſhire, aſked me if I knew Mr. Edwards, of Halifax? I told him, "Yes, very well;" he ſaid, "If you ſpear him, he will ken me; my name is Robinſon." In returning down the ſtreet a poor boy aſked me for twa bawbees; I told him he was too greedy, and gave him one (a halfpenny). On Sunday we attended two of their kirks to hear divine ſervice; one of them, a new-erected building and highly finiſhed, where the quality reſorted. I obſerved ſeveral women in the ſtreets whoſe petticoats reached very little below the knees, and one old woman whoſe petticoat did not reach the knees: this appeared very odd, becauſe, perhaps, unuſual, to me. We drunk tea with ſeveral of Mr. Crowther's cuſtomers, and after ſtaying moſt of a week in this city, we took the coach and returned to Edinburgh. We had a kind of a ſhip-captain, a paſſenger with us in the coach part of the way. The man was drunk, and therefore diſagreeable company; he chewed tobacco, and ſitting next my companion, ſlavered and ſpat upon his coat. At this Mr. Crowther was offended, and ſpoke rather ſharply to the man;

the fellow immediately challenged him out of the coach to fight, but Mr. Crowther treating him with the contempt he deferved, the man foon after fell afleep, and the affair dropped.

One of the fervant-girls—a ftrong-made, hardy-looking, Scotch lafs—would gladly have come with us as a fervant, from the inn we refided at in Edinburgh; fhe faid if we would accept her fervice, fhe could run on foot after the chaife all the way; and obferved, that fhe could milk the cows, tend and clean them or other cattle, look after the dairy, and upon occafion, do any genteeler work; and I do believe if we had ventured to bring her, fhe would have made an excellent fervant. We returned from Edinburgh by a different road from that which we came, till we got to Newcaftle. We flept the firft night at a place they call Gingle-kirk; in the morning Mr. Crowther had his eyes almoft fwelled up from being bit by the bugs, but though I thought I felt them run over me in the night, neither I or my wife were bitten by them the whole journey. We proceeded from hence through Wooller to Newcaftle, from whence we returned by the route we came, through Chefter-le-ftreet, Durham, Darlington, Northallerton, Boroughbridge, and Knarefborough, to Leeds, where we arrived on Tuefday, December 2nd, it being juft a fortnight the night before fince we left the place. It being marketday, my friendly acquaintance foon flocked round me and acquainted me with the terrible hubbub our adventure had raifed, and the rage and malevolence of my wife's parents. Mr. John Broadley, of Rawfolds, near Littletown* (a gene- rous little fellow), infifted that I and my wife fhould go home with him, where we fhould be as welcome as day, till we could accommodate ourfelves with a proper fettlement—for at this time I was no houfekeeper, but boarded out. He faid farther, that if I could purchafe a foil anywhere nigh, and make it convenient to build, he would give me the ftones out of his own quarry to build the houfe, if I built one as large as Bilton's Hall,† and help me lead the materials into the bargain. Mr. Richard Brooke, of Cleckheaton, declared he would help me alfo to lead the materials. I fhould certainly have accepted Mr. Broadley's propofal, but Nathaniel Brooke, of Cleckheaton, my wife's uncle (her mother's youngeft brother), obferved that it would be more prudent for us to go home with him, as we fhould be nearer the old folk ; that they would be better pleafed with our being there, he being fo near a relation, and that he would have a better opportunity of promoting a reconciliation. On thefe confiderations we agreed to his propofal, and accompanied him

---

* Littletown is a part of the townfhip of Liverfedge.

† I am told that there was formerly a popular saying in this part of Yorkfhire, in the form, " I'll build a houfe as big as Built-ons Hall," or " Bilton's Hall ; " but it appears to be now obfolete.

home that evening, where we had an upper and lower room appropriated partly to our use, and in which we resided till we removed the May-day following to a farm I had taken in the meantime.

The terrible task was now to be undertaken of attempting to propitiate the dreadful wrath of those high and mighty, sorely-offended, deeply-injured, self-important, and eminently religious people; and as much fear and cringing, adulation, self-abasement, and submission was thought requisite on this occasion as if we were approaching the grand Turk, or some equally dreaded, powerful, and offended tyrant! Nathaniel Brooke, my wife's uncle—a sneering, scornful fellow, a characteristic of the family—was our professed mediator on this occasion, and proposed to introduce us to their offended majesties. He represented the absolute necessity of great submission in order to avert their anger, and obtain their favour; and said so much, that, as I was greatly desirous of peace and quietness, he persuaded me to comply with the abject circumstance of asking their pardon, together with my wife, upon my knees, for having married their daughter without their consent, who was no better than myself, and sprung from a family no better, if as good, as my own, a circumstance for which he himself afterwards laughed me to scorn, in consonance, indeed, to his family disposition. To a worthy, generous-minded person I might have happened to affront or disoblige, I should have esteemed it no difhonour to have made the humbleft reafon-able acknowledgment and fubmiffion; but to ftoop fo low to ftupid, fordid, unfeeling people, who never manifefted one generous principle that ever I could perceive during my whole acquaintance and connexion with them, was too unworthy and difgufting an abafement for an open, ingenuous mind ever to reflect upon with patience; and I never recall the circumftance to my memory without feeling a painful fenfation of fhame and indignation. They received our humble addrefs and requeft with the ftupid, un-feeling indifference and difregard peculiar to their character and difpofition, and we returned on pretty much the fame terms we came, except-ing a baneful admiffion, obtained by my wife, to vifit them occafionally, to hear them contemn, abufe, and vilify her hufband, and afford them an opportunity to fay and do all that lay in their power to alienate her efteem and affection from her partner, and ruin the peace and comfort of our family. This purpofe, wicked as it was, through the weaknefs and indifcretion of my wife, they at laft completely effected. I had fondly imagined that thefe venerable people, who were grown gray in the profeffion of religion, and had paid a ftrict conformity for many years to the *formalities* of their party, and paffed among their neighbours for mighty pious folks, who could fay with the Pharifee (Luke xviii. 11,) "God, we thank thee, that we are not as other men are, extortioners, unjuft, adulterers, or even as our comparatively more profane and lefs formal neighbours: we pray twice in our family every day (it feems *fafting* was not in their formulary), in contributing to the fupport of the church (as they call it) and its minifters, entertaining the faints, &c. &c : we pay tithes of all that we poffefs, we pay a facred regard to the *fabbath* by attending conftantly at the chapel that day ; we give a ftrict attendance on the ordinance (as they emphatically call it), and receive the Sacrament of thy Body and Blood every month, &c. &c. : we muft furely, therefore, be far more eminent Chriftians than thofe of our neighbours who pay little or no regard to thefe, or many of thefe formalities."

I fee nothing amifs in all this for thofe who choofe to follow it, but I conceive this is not Chriftianity. I had fondly hoped, as I faid before, amidft all this eclat and parade of *profeffion* and *formality*, to find fome *reality*; to find them in poffeffion of fome tolerable meafure of the genuine *fpirit* and *practice* of Chriftianity ; to find them paying fome deference, regard, and attention to fome of the moft important commands and precepts given by that divine perfon to his followers, whom they affected to call Mafter ; precepts, the obfervation whereof was of the laft confequence to the peace and comfort both of fociety at large, to every family, and to every individual ; I mean thofe of mutual love

and forgivenefs, to which he required an un-
qualified obedience. But, alas! I was miferably
difappointed in my expectation; they appeared
to be utterly unacquainted with the divine commands and injunctions, or, what was worfe, to
pay an utter difregard to them; their whole
fpirit and *conduct* towards me on this occafion,
for near *thirty* years together, being—if I have
a fingle grain of true judgment in the cafe—
diametrically oppofite both to the *fpirit* and
practice of Chriftianity. The gofpel commands
every man not to think of himfelf more highly
than he ought to think, but to think foberly;
but thefe people thought highly of themfelves,
not only on account of the little wealth they
had acquired more than the generality of their
neighbours, but alfo on account of their ftrict,
religious formalities, from whence they concluded
themfelves righteous; and, with the ancient
Pharisees, thofe religious devils incarnate, def-
pifed others—efpecially myfelf—whom they affected to treat with the moft fovereign contempt,
and vilified me in the moft vulgar, infulting, and
abufive language, as if I had been the vileft
character in the country. Jefus Chrift fays,
" If thy brother fin againft thee feven times in a
day, and feven times in a day turn again unto
thee, faying, I repent, forgive him." His beloved apoftle, John, declares, " If any man fay
he loves God, and hateth his brother, he is a
liar, and the truth is not in him." And left any

narrow-minded sectary should attempt to restrain the meaning of the word *brother* to those of their own party (as the self-opinionated Jews were strongly inclined to do), Jesus Christ teaches them better in the amiable and affecting parable of the Good Samaritan, wherein he gives his narrow-souled querist in a very forcible manner to understand, that it was his duty to confider any individual of the human race, even though an enemy, that might happen to stand in need of his kindnefs or assistance, as his neighbour or his brother.   But William Birkhead wished his knife in my heart, and declared to a friend of mine (Mr. John Broadley) that he would never forgive me! My friend observing, that then he must never say his prayers, he declared he did not care if he never did; and whatever he may have done since as to saying his prayers, which I think means very little, he seems firmly to have kept his purpose of bearing me a deadly hatred to this day.

I mean by and by to give a few short notices of both these people's families as far as I have been able to trace them out; in the meantime I return to the thread of my story. My wife continued to repeat her visits, while I was kept at a distance, as a dishonour to the family. These visits soon operated for the worse on my wife's mind and behaviour, and I presently found, to my extreme regret, that by attaching myself to this family, I had attached myself to family difquiet and unhappinefs; to grief, vexation, mifery, poverty, and ruin.

We were now to make our appearance and receive the vifits of our friendly acquaintance according to cuftom; but my wife's two beft gowns—one green, and the other blue filk—were at Brook-houfes, and her parents refufed to let her have them. I told her not to mind this, that I had feven filk gowns which had been preferved from the wreck of my mother's wardrobe, and fome of them better than hers, that as fhe feemed to be about my mother's fize, fhe fhould have one of the beft of them altered into the prefent fafhion for her to appear in on the prefent occafion. For this purpofe we immediately fent for the mantua-maker, but her mother hearing of the circumftance, her pride, fuch as it was, induced her to fend over the two gowns immediately. We accordingly made our appearance and received our vifitors, and had a good number of our common friendly acquaintance to fee us. At May-day, or thereabouts, 1767, we removed to Lower Blacup, in the townfhip of Liverfedge, on the north fide of the hill facing the turnpike-road leading from Cleckheaton to Hartfhead Moor.* The farm I had taken of Mr.

---

* Hartfhead Moor is a place near the village of Hartfhead, and is about two miles to the fouth-eaft of Cleckheaton, the village of Hightown lying between them. The Moor is now all enclofed, and covered with thriving farms. There is an ancient crofs where this moor was, in

Richard Brooke, of Hoyland,* for fifteen pounds per annum. It was but mean land, and had a very difficult and inconvenient road to it, but was very quiet and retired—a circumſtance which ſuited my fancy very much—had a number of good fruit trees—plumbs, apples, and cherries in the two gardens or orchards planted by the laſt tenant, William Cordingley. We had one quiet neighbour under the roof with us, Tere Lee, with whom, upon the whole, we lived very peaceably during our ſtay together, which was fourteen years. Tere Lee had dwelt long at

---

a lane near the church. Parts of the church are very ancient, and there is an arch in it which bears a great reſemblance to the beautiful arch now to be ſeen in Addle, or Adel Church. "I have viſited Hartſhead Church," Mr. Holroyd writes, "and am of opinion that it was built in the earlier part of the twelfth century. Its ſituation is ſplendid, and embraces a view of the whole of the vale of the Calder, except that part above Halifax. Kirklees, and the wood where bold Robin Hood is ſaid to lie buried, lie below, a few miles to the ſouth ; and the ſcene is indeed charming. In the early part of the preſent century the Rev. Patrick Brontë was the incumbent of Hartſhead, and it was to this place he brought his young Corniſh wife, the ſame lady who afterwards became the mother of Charlotte, Emily Jane, and Anne Brontë, of Thornton and Haworth, to which places their father afterwards removed."

* Hoyland. There are four places bearing this name in the Weſt Riding of Yorkſhire, viz. High Hoyland, a pariſh ſix miles north of Peniſtone ; Swaine Hoyland, two miles north-eaſt of Peniſtone ; and Upper and Nether Hoyland, five and a half miles ſouth-ſouth-eaſt of Barnſley. Very likely the latter is the Hoyland referred to in the text, having over two thouſand inhabitants.

the place, I fuppofe near forty years. Some houfehold furniture I had, which had been faved from the wreck of my family's furniture, which did fomething towards furnifhing the houfe; I had alfo purchafed fome other pieces of furniture when I occupied a room or two at Birkenfhaw; thefe made out a little further, and after fome time we had the following articles from Brookhoufes. A new oak defk and drawers—this they had back again when my wife died; a new fmall mahogany tea-table, price one pound; one old-fafhioned oak bedftead, and part of the old bedding, of fmall value; one little ftand table to fet a candle upon : thefe I ftill retain. An old cradle—this they had back again alfo; a fmall, old-fafhioned filver table-fpoon; this, with many other things belonging to me, they afterwards fhamefully, unjuftly, and wickedly perfuaded my children to purloin from their father's houfe, and being but children, and not knowing confequences, they were eafily impofed upon by the fpecious pretences that a fecond wife would fhut them, but that they would take care of them for *their* ufe; but alas! they took care that they were never a farthing better for any or moft of them afterwards, fo that they were entirely loft both to them and their father; a piece of bafe injuftice, and little, if anything better than if my houfe had been rifled by a common houfebreaker. But I return to my ftory. I was obliged to purchafe what further neceffary things I wanted for the houfe and the farm. I bought a cloth-tenter as it ftood in the tenter-croft, and a little old cart and its furniture, and other old goods and implements for the houfe and barn, of William Cordingley, the late tenant, for which I paid him twenty pounds; but I afterwards thought this a dear bargain. Our marriage adventure had coft me a good fum of money; we were more than a fortnight abfent, and had travelled 500 miles, more or lefs, in carriages; it will be eafily imagined, therefore, that it muft have been very expenfive : this, with following expenfes, by the time we had got fettled on the farm, had nearly drained my pocket of ready money. However, they ventured fo far at Brook-houfes as to fend us a pack of wool to begin cloth-making with; we accordingly begun and did a little, as our fmall ftock would allow.

I proceed to relate another circumftance. I had a fmall eftate at Halifax, in cottages, at the bottom of the churchyard; two or three of thefe, which fronted into the churchyard, were mean and made little rent, and I was advifed by fome of my acquaintance to pull them down, and build new ones on the foundation. I complied with their advice, and for this purpofe borrowed two hundred pounds of Mr. Samuel Webfter, of Morley,* and gave him fecurity of the place.

---

* Morley is in the parifh of Batley, eight miles fouth-eaft of Bradford, and four miles fouth-weft of Leeds.   It

This money, together with moſt of fifty pounds I had at Brook-houſes, was expended on this occaſion, and when the affair was completed, the rent which they let for paid about five per cent. for the money, ſo that I had better have let it alone. I was ſoft and unacquainted with affairs and bargains of this nature, and the artful work-men impoſed upon me much, ſo that the build-ings coſt me much more than they might or ought to have done. I remained at Lower Blacup in the whole fourteen years. Soon after we came to this place, my wife's father *lent* me fifty pounds, for which I gave him a note, but not to pay intereſt. Moſt of this, as I obſerved before, I laid out at Halifax. About the year 1773, there being a briſk trade, and having but little ſtock, my wife's father lent her another fifty pounds, and I made cloth for ſome time. My family increaſed apace, and about this time my wife lay badly a long time, in lying in of her fourth child (Sally), which proved a very expenſive ſeaſon, and I found, upon calculation, my family expenſes greatly exceeded my income. I acknow-ledge I was no great adept in trade, however, as I never did but little in this way ; if I got nothing I could not be ſuppoſed to make myſelf much worſe. Our fifty pounds dwindled very faſt,

---

is a very populous village, and the inhabitants live by the manufacture of clothing. Batley, near by, is the centre of the " ſhoddy " trade.

owing chiefly to the extraordinary expenfes of my family. I afterwards endeavoured to adjuft my family expenfes to my annual income, that I might be enabled to keep even in the world as long as I could. I did my beft to live on friendly terms with my wife's parents, and fometimes we feemed pretty agreeable, but this never lafted long, and as I could not put up with foul looks and difrefpectful behaviour, I was finally forced to withdraw myfelf as much as poffible from all intercourfe with them. My wife, however, continued, and would continue, her vifits in fpite of all I could fay to perfuade her to the contrary; and they continued to blackguard, villify, and abufe me in her prefence with all the virulence and malignity that the blackeft and moft diabolical pride and malice could infpire. This foon had its effect on my wife's mind and temper, and entirely ruined the peace and happinefs of our family. Notwithftanding I did all that lay in my power to oblige her, and put up with the infults of her parents with a degree of patience which, confidering the natural warmth of my temper, I have often fince been aftonifhed at, yet fhe feldom came from thence but in a bad humour, and would have abufed me in the moft provoking language for hours together, when I have hardly uttered a word in reply; indeed, I am forry to fay it, but it is a fact, and I record it, not to expofe *her* (for I write this only for my family's perufal), but as a *warning* to the different branches of my family to avoid the same shameful and fatal evil; I say she seldom came sober from Brook-houses, and in such cases always in a bad, abusive humour. I seldom contested with her on such occasions, as I deemed it absurd, but got her to sleep as soon as I could. This practice, I am certain, very much injured her health, and shortened her life : it also affected the life of one, and injured the health of several others of her later children. When the notoriety of her conduct had unavoidably exposed her to the observation of all the neighbourhood, and her parents could no longer deny the fact (though it terribly mortified their religious vanity), they endeavoured to throw the odium upon me by saying, that it was grief and vexation of mind because I did not follow a trade, &c. that induced her to adopt the fatal practice; but this assertion was false as hell—the propensity was natural, strengthened and increased, very probably, by habit, for the old people always kept a dram by them, and any of the children that happened to be so disposed, could easily find access to the bottle.

I did not fail to admonish her when she was properly herself of the pernicious consequences likely to attend so imprudent a conduct, in the most loving, affectionate, and respectful manner I possibly could, but it had no effect; and, indeed, the continual, reiterated contempt and abuse she heard uttered by her parents against me, in her frequent vifits to fee them, appeared to have entirely divefted her of all proper regard and affection for her hufband; and her behaviour in general was what I might have expected from fuch an unhappy difpofition of mind. In vain did I beg of her with the utmoft earneftnefs and good-nature to forbear her vifits, as the effects of them were fo unfavourable to the peace of our family; in vain did I tell her fhe fhould be welcome to fhare the laft penny I had or could honeftly procure, and that I would never upbraid her with her want of fortune, if fhe would ftay by me and not join my enemies, but let us do the beft we could for ourfelves and our family. She told me to my face fhe would not, but that fhe would go and fee them whenever fhe pleafed, whether I would or no, whatever was the confequence; and that fhe did not care if I was utterly ruined the next day! I told her I hoped her laft words were a flip of the tongue, and that upon fecond thoughts fhe would recall them. She protefted fhe would not, and vehemently affirmed that it was the fettled difpofition of her mind! I told her I was forry for it, and that it was fo much the more pity; and Mary Gomerfall, a neighbour-woman (a Quaker) who fetched milk, and happened to be then in the houfe, cried out, " Nay, miftrefs, for fhame; thou muft not fay fo!" I own this repeated declaration (which fhe never afterwards retracted) entirely overturned my efteem for her, and it was never in my power afterwards, to the day of her death, to regard her with that degree of love and affection I always had done before; and the recollection of it to my mind, even at this diftance of time, is highly difgufting ftill. Hence I advife all my children of both fexes that may happen to enter into the matrimonial connection, to be doubly careful how they make ufe of fuch imprudent and difrefpectful expreffions to their partners; for though they may be uttered in paffion, and perhaps afterwards retracted, yet are they apt to make fuch unfavourable impreffions, and create fuch averfions in delicate minds, as perhaps they may never afterwards be able to furmount as long as they live—a moft unhappy circumftance between a married couple. However, I was enabled to behave refpectfully and even tenderly to my partner to her laft hour, notwithftanding the ungenerous return I continually met with.

In the fpring of the year 1774, my wife one morning propofed to go over to her father's and fpend the day with them, as fhe very frequently did; to oblige her, I accompanied her within a field of the houfe, and carried the child for her, and then returned home again to look after our family affairs. I had told her I would meet her in the evening, and help her to bring the child home again. We had ploughers in the field, and they had promifed to plough me a headland to plant potatoes upon. Towards evening I locked the door, and went to see what they were doing. I found they had left the field without performing their promise; I followed them to a blacksmith's at the top of the hill, where I heard they were, and engaged them to come again and plough it for me, and then returned home immediately. When I got within view of our house I saw my wife at the door, and hasted down to open it. Her brother Willy had brought her and the child behind him on her father's gray mare. When I reached the house I found my wife in a furious passion on the supposition that I had been attending the masons who were at that time erecting the Methodist preaching-house on the top of the hill; in this she was mistaken; however, she proceeded to abuse me at a great rate. I said little, but told her that if she could not see her parents and come home peaceably and in good humour, I wished she would stay with them, while she was there. She immediately put on her cloak and marched off, leaving the little child in the cradle. Her younger sister afterwards fetched the child while I was out of the house, and I followed them to Brook-houses, where I received plenty of abuse, and many warm words passed between us. I left her, and she stayed with them about three weeks, when, understanding that she wished to be at home, I went over and fetched her and the child back again. On this occasion more warm words passed between us, and her mother told me, with a spirit of the moft perverfe malignity, that fhe had rather fhe had married a chimney-fweeper; nay, that fhe had rather follow her to her grave, than fee her return peaceably home with her hufband! This was an old woman making mighty pretences to religion, but where, I wonder, on this occafion was her Chriftianity? No wonder, that being conftantly under fuch baneful influence, my wife—a weak, unreflecting girl—fhould behave with impropriety towards her hufband. I told her, as we returned home, that I was no longer difpofed to put up with fimilar infults to thofe I had received formerly, and that I infifted upon better behaviour for the future; otherwife, fhe might depend upon it, I would take more fevere methods with her. This feemed (partly, at leaft) to have its effect, as fhe behaved afterwards, though not very refpectfully, yet in a lefs offenfive manner towards me to the day of her death.

I have noticed before that my wife lay a long time ill when fhe bore her fourth child, and I think it may not be amifs to give a more particular account of that circumftance in this place. I fhall be excufed for the plainnefs of my narration, as, firft, the fact itfelf was made as notorious as it could be to all the neighbourhood by her own conduct; and fecondly, I write this only for the perufal of my family, to whom it may prove a fuitable admonition; and thirdly, I have forgiven my wife for her mifconduct towards me, and, though I know nothing of her prefent fituation, yet, as fhe is in the hands of a God of infinite goodnefs, wifdom, and power, I am fatisfied that all will be done for her that is neceffary, *when* it is neceffary and *as* it is necef-fary, to reftore her again to holinefs and happi-nefs, to the full perfection of her nature; in which ftate, through divine goodnefs, I doubt not, one day, of meeting with her again. I proceed. By the imprudent ufe of fpirits fhe had much injured her health and conftitution, as well as the health and conftitution of the child fhe was pregnant with, and it was with difficulty it was reared afterwards. The child was to bring up by the fpoon, and fhe herfelf, after the birth, lay confined to her bed for the moft part for three months, caufed, I am fatisfied, principally, if not folely, by a *continuance* of the fame baneful practice. I obferved this with extreme forrow and regret, but knew not how I could peaceably prevent it. If I had complained or withheld it from her, her parents would have abufed me beyond meafure, as being unwilling to allow her what fhe ftood in need of. I hoped her fifter or mother, who frequently attended her, would have noticed the circumftance, and have had good fenfe and refpect enough for her, to have interpofed; but I expected this in vain.

Mr. James Scott, the minifter of the Calvin-iftic Chapel at Heckmondwike, of which her parents were members, paid her a vifit, to pray with her and adminifter ghoftly comfort and confolation. I *knew* her to be very unfteady in her head at the time, yet fhe quoted the common-place fcriptures fhe had been wont to read, talked to the parfon in the cant ftrain of the party, and profeffed great fpiritual comfort and confolation. Difgufting circumftances thefe to a fober, obfervant byftander. The minifter was impofed upon, and departed without ever difcovering (that ever I could perceive) anything at all of her real fituation. The doctor, however, took notice of this, and afked me how much rum we ufed in a week? I told him we had ufed more than a gallon for many weeks together. He held up his hands, and declared we fhould kill her. I told him I was aware of it, and informed him of my critical fituation He pitied me very much, but declared that if we continued the practice we fhould infallibly and fpeedily deftroy her. In a day or two after this, old Dame G——d, a difcreet, difcerning old woman, a diftant relation of the family, paid her a vifit. She had fagacity enough to difcern her *real* fituation, and after afking fome queftions of me as to what we gave her to drink, &c., feemed to be fully aware of the danger of it. She faid nothing to me of her intention when fhe left us, but I was pretty certain from what fhe faid, and what followed, that fhe immediately acquainted her mother with the circumftance, and the impropriety and danger of the practice; for the next forenoon fhe came up in a great chafe, and almoft out of breath, and the firft word fhe faid after fhe came into the houfe was, " Take away that bottle, fhe fhall not have another drop!" I thought, that is well, then my wife will get upon her legs again. The bottle was taken away, fhe had no more rum, and fhe *immediately* recovered. It had been well if fhe had never tafted it more; it might have been fome addition to her days; but alas! the propenfity was too deeply rooted, and fhe could not or would not deny herfelf of the baneful practice, as opportunity offered, till at length it deftroyed her health and life together.

In the autumn of the year 1773, I took an excurfion into the country, in company with Mr. Jofeph Jackfon, a currier of Hightown,* to folicit the affiftance of the Methodifts in different parts in defraying the expenfe of erecting the new Methodift Meeting-houfe at Height. We proceeded through Halifax, Rochdale, Manchefter, Bolton, and the intermediate towns, to

---

* Hightown, in the townfhip of Liverfedge, lies between Cleckheaton and Hartfhead, and is, as its name imports, fituated on elevated ground. The Wefleyan Methodift Meeting-houfe referred to as about to be built at " Height," probably refers to the " *theykd* chapel " at Hightown, which was erected on a piece of high land. This place of worfhip was pulled down a few years ago, and a more commodious one was erected on, or near, the fame fpot. Hightown was formerly noted for its blanket and card manufactories.

Liverpool; we then croſſed the river Merſey to
Eaſton Ferry; we paſſed thence to Cheſter, into
the edge of Wales, and places adjacent. We
then croſſed the country to Shrewſbury, the
capital of Shropſhire. Here we paſſed the night
at one of the principal inns in the town, and in
the evening the maſter of the inn informed us of
the ſituation of a young man in the town priſon
under condemnation to death for a highway
robbery, and who was to ſuffer the next day.
I expreſſed a deſire to ſee him, and the landlord
told us that he had been ſo uncommonly rude
and ſavage in his behaviour during his confine-
ment, as to intimidate moſt people from viſiting
him; but that if we durſt venture, he would
accompany us to the priſon to ſee him in the
morning. We agreed to his propoſal, and the
next morning, in company with our hoſt, paid a
viſit to the priſoner. We found him in a chamber of the priſon, ſitting beſide the fire, heavily
ironed; another priſoner ſat on the other ſide of
the fire, with heavy irons upon him likewiſe,
and the keeper of the priſon's daughter (as I
took her to be), decently dreſſed in black, ſat
ſewing in a window not far from the priſoner we
came to viſit. I aſked him if he was the perſon
who was to ſuffer to-day? He looked earneſtly
at me and replied, yes. I noticed the awfulneſs
of his caſe, and expreſſed my pity for his unhappy
ſituation. He was looking very earneſtly in the
meantime at Mr. Jackſon, who ſtood at my right

hand (I was betwixt them), and faid, " I took that perfon at firft for my profecutor, and was juft looking for the poker to dafh out his brains!" This declaration alarmed my partner not a little, who fhrunk back with fear, and was fo ftruck with the circumftance, that he did not choofe afterwards to vifit him a fecond time. I afked if he thought himfelf wrongfully profecuted ? he faid he was fure of it. I faid, be that as it might, it was wrong to bear malice even to an enemy, and peculiarly dangerous to a perfon in his awful fituation. He faid, " I know it," and earneftly added, " but what can a man do?" I told him it was true, that of *ourfelves* we could do nothing, but that through Chrift ftrengthening us, we could do all things ; and earneftly advifed him to pay a clofe and ferious attention to the concerns of a future world the little time he had to remain in this, and urged fome fcripture promifes for his encouragement. He told me he knew the fcriptures as well as me, and quoted (I think) that paffage in the prophet Jeremiah x. 23, " The way of man is not in himfelf, it is not in man that walketh to direct his fteps." He faid that he had been in battle, and that he had been fhot through his hat, his coat, &c. and yet had never received any harm ; that he believed everything was *fated* to come to pafs as it did come to pafs ; that every man was *fated* to die when he did die, and that therefore he might as well die like a man, as like a fool. I told him that his reasonings and conclusions were equally false; that I was sorry he had got involved in that common error, and advised him not by any means to rely upon his opinion for safety, or expect to get rid of his own evil conduct and its consequences, by vainly attempting to father it upon *fate* or the Divine decree. I assured him if he did he would find himself dreadfully mistaken. I told him we were strangers to each other, that I had no interest in his concerns but what arose from the common love I bore to my species, that misery always attracted my pity, and the greater the misery and the danger attending it, the greater my concern for the sufferer; that I should feel myself peculiarly happy to see him manifest a proper sense of his present condition, and genuine penitence for his sin and folly, that he might be able to entertain a well-grounded hope of better-ing his condition in that future world to which he was hastening, and begged him to cry earnestly for mercy. He heard me with attention, seemed much affected with what I said—his heart ap-peared to be full, and the tears stood in his eyes. I told him if he was truly penitent I was sure God would accept him through a Mediator, and encouraged him to hope for mercy. The time of his execution drew nigh, and we were obliged to leave him; I gave him my hand and bid him farewell. He held my hand hard for some time, and seemed to part with it with reluctance. As soon as he could—for, as I observed before, his

heart was full—he very kindly and very refpectfully bid me farewell, and we departed.

We were invited to dine at a houfe in the
town where they received the Methodift preachers. We repaired thither, and a gentlewoman
of the town named Lady Glynn, a lady of
fortune, and a favourer of the Methodifts, fent
us a number of difhes to dinner; but before we
had quite dined fhe fent up her maid in hafte, to
inform us that what I had faid to the prifoner
had affected him to fuch a degree, that after we
left him he burft into a flood of tears and begged
them to fend for a minifter to pray with him,
which fhe looked upon as fo extraordinary a
circumftance after his former defperate and
hardened behaviour, that fhe wifhed I would go
immediately to the prifon, and, if I could gain
admittance, to repeat my endeavours to engage
his ferious attention to his future welfare. To
oblige her ladyfhip, we left our dinner immediately and walked to the prifon, but were too late
to fpeak with the prifoner, as they were juft
bringing him out to execution. We attended
him to the gallows—nearly a mile out of the
town, amongft a prodigious concourfe of people.
A young man fat by him in the cart with a book
in his hand, who read and fpoke to him by turns,
but we could not hear what he faid. By his
demeanour in the cart, he feemed to be either
drunk or ftupified with the apprehenfion of his
near approaching fate. His behaviour at the

gallows while the minifter was praying with him, appeared to me in the fame light, and in his addrefs to the people, I was forry to hear him declare his belief in the fame erroneous fentiment of fate he had done to us before, a fentiment in which he feemed to take refuge to the laft moment of his life. The cart was then drawn from under him, and he was launched into the unfeen world.

This young man was only twenty-four years of age, was fprung from a reputable family, who had given him a liberal education; he turned out wild, enlifted into the horfe-guards, deferted from them, taking his horfe along with him, and committed the highway-robbery near Shrewfbury for which he fuffered.

I wifh here to take notice of the dangerous tendency of this erroneous doctrine of *Fate* or *Predeftination*; of which, the practical ufe which this unhappy young fellow made of it, is an undeniable inftance. The favourers of this opinion may perhaps fay, that people may abufe any opinion. It is true, moft opinions, however true or innocent, may be abufed by inattentive and difengenuous minds; but this is no abufe of this opinion, for, if it be true, the inference drawn from it by the highwayman is a fair, natural, and neceffary confequence of the principle.

In the morning (Sunday) we proceeded from hence to Madeley, to vifit the Rev. Mr. Fletcher.* In paffing through Coal-brook-dale we paffed over the broken ground caufed by the earth-quake which happened the preceding May,† and faw the new track which the river had wrought itfelf through an adjacent meadow, after being forced by the moving earth out of its ancient courfe. We attended the forenoon and after-noon fervice at Madeley Church, and were much edified with the company of this truly learned and pious man, who was at this time writing his " Equal Check," the manufcript of which he

---

* The life of this remarkable man has employed the pens of more than one writer, the beft being that by the Rev. J. Benfon. John William Fletcher, whofe real name was Jean Guillaume de la Flechere, was a Swifs by birth and family, who fettled in England, and became a clergy-man of the Englifh Church. His ftrong feelings againft the doftrines of Calvinifm had prevented his entering the church in his native land. He was prefented to the vicar-age of Madeley, in Shropfhire, in the year 1760; fo that at the date mentioned in the text, he had held the living thirteen years. He died at Madeley in 1785, and was buried in the churchyard of that parifh, where his tomb is yet fhown. Madeley is fifteen miles to the eaft of Shrewfbury.

† This refers to an extraordinary movement and break-ing up of the ground which occurred on the 27th of May, 1773, at a place called the Birches, about half-way between Buildwas and Iron-bridge, which lay on the way our travellers would take to proceed from Shrewfbury to Madeley. Buildwas is about eleven miles from Shrewfbury, on the river Severn. An account of the circumftances of this extraordinary occurrence is given in the " Gentleman's Magazine " for 1773, p. 281. A more detailed account was publifhed by Mr. Fletcher—who vifited the fpot imme-diately after it occurred—in a pamphlet entitled, " A Dreadful Phenomenon Defcribed and Improved," printed at Shrewfbury. Fletcher had preached a fermon on the

fhowed me.* We paffed the night with him, and in the morning we proceeded on our journey through Shiffnall, Congleton, Newcaftle-under-line, Boflam, and other places, to Macclesfield in Chefhire. We paffed from hence over the mountains, through Buxton, Tidfwell, &c. to Sheffield. We paffed the night at the Methodift preacher's, and after fupper, Mr. Jackfon being very weary and fleepy, was in hafte to get to bed. While he was undreffing—having heard much of the bugs at Sheffield—I took a candle and examined the bed-ftocks, in a knot-hole of which I difcovered a whole fwarm of bugs. My partner was furprifed, and afked me if they were bugs? I told him, yes. He was prefently dreffed again, and declared he would not fleep there for five guineas. "Come, Tommy," fays he, "we have often fpared a night's fleep with our fweethearts ; let us fit by the fire till morning rather than hazard the taking any of thefe vermin home with us." The people of the houfe would fain have perfuaded us to go to bed, telling us they

---

occafion, which was printed in this pamphlet. It was looked upon at the time as the effect of an earthquake, and it is ftated in the " Gentleman's Magazine," that the convulfion of the earth was felt at Wenlock, and at Bridge-north, a ftill greater diftance.

* This was Fletcher's well-known work entitled, " An Equal Check to Pharifaifm and Antinomianifm." The firft part was publifhed late in the fpring following this vifit defcribed in the text. The preface to this firft part is dated " Madeley, May 21, 1774."

did not bite all perfons, but no arguments could prevail on Mr. Jackfon to venture himfelf amongft fuch company. We accordingly fat or lay upon the chairs, by the fire, all night, and in the morning proceeded through Barnfley and Wakefield home again, where we arrived that afternoon, after having been about a fortnight abfent.

I underftood from my neighbours that my wife had been very imprudent in the indulgence of her peculiar weaknefs in my abfence; a circumftance which fhowed me the inexpediency of leaving home, and made me much regret my journey. As my family now increafed apace, and my income began to pinch us, I propofed to my wife to folicit for her fortune; not to trade with, for fear it fhould be leffened or fpent, but to put out on intereft to increafe our annual income; at the fame time I propofed to fecure it to her and her children by a jointure on my own eftate equal to the fum advanced. Had this plan been adopted, I might have been enabled, with good economy, to maintain my family comfortably at leaft, if not genteelly, without breaking any farther into my little patrimony. My wife, I fuppofe, never mentioned the matter, for what reafon I know not. The confequence was, I was obliged finally to fell my land—a moft unfortunate circumftance both for me and my family, as if I had had it to difpofe of at prefent, from a concurrence of circumftances fince that period, I fuppofe it might have fetched above

2000*l.*: this I owe to the carefulness, prudence, foresight, wisdom, and piety resident at Brookhouses. I wish here to remark, that as I did not make myself, my want of talents or propensity for trade, &c. is no *moral* defect; it is therefore no *crime*, brings no *guilt* upon my mind; nor can any person *justly* blame or despise me on that account. I notice here also that I never engaged in trade but I had a secret misgiving upon my mind that it would not do well. Had I despised the censures of the world, and paid more attention to this silent monitor, it might have been some hundreds better for me at present than it is. But so far for this.

I proceed to take notice, that during my residence at Lower Blacup my wife bore me the following children in the following order :—

ELIZABETH WRIGHT, my first child and first daughter, was born at Lower Blacup, near Hightown, on the north side of the hill facing the turnpike-road leading from Cleckheaton to Hartshead Moor, in the township of Liversedge, in the parish of Birstall, within six miles of Halifax, in the county of York, on Saturday, the 30th day of January, 1768, at half-an-hour after two o'clock in the afternoon, one year, ten weeks, and two days after our marriage. She was baptized by the Rev. Mr. James Scott, minister of the Independent Congregation at the Old Chapel in Heckmondwike, on Tuesday, the 22nd day of March, 1768.

MARY WRIGHT, my fecond child and fecond daughter, was born at Lower Blacup likewife, on Wednefday, the 22nd day of November, 1769, about feven o'clock in the evening, one year, ten months, two weeks, and two days after the birth of her fifter Elizabeth. She was baptized by the Rev. Mr. James Scott of Heckmondwike likewife, on Monday, the 5th day of February, 1770. Mary Wright, my fecond daughter and fecond child, died at Lower Blacup on Friday, the 25th day of May, 1770, between eleven and twelve o'clock in the forenoon, and was buried in the Old Red Chapel at Cleckheaton, at the bottom of the alley, at the foot of her great uncle Thomas Birkhead's gravestone, which now lies in the New Chapel yard, near the low wall, and is broken acrofs the middle, but has this year (1796) been taken up to receive the corpfe of her grandmother Birkhead. Between the foot of this ftone and the low wall, Mary, my fecond child, and James, as I call him for diftinction fake (though never-baptized), my ftill-born male child, lie fide by fide. She was interred on Monday, the 28th day of May, 1770, aged twenty-fix weeks, one day and a half. She was a remarkably beautiful and good-tempered child, and apparently likelier for life than any child we had; but by fome means or other (we never knew how) contracted a cough, which grew more and more violent, till it wafted her away, and defpatched her infant foul to Paradife.

THOMAS WRIGHT,* my third child and firſt ſon, was born at Lower Blacup alſo, on Friday, the 8th day of March, 1771, eleven minutes before five o'clock in the afternoon, one year, three months, three weeks, and one day after the birth of his ſiſter Mary. He was baptized by the Rev. Mr. James Dawſon, miniſter of the Independent Congregation, at the Old Red Chapel in Cleckheaton.

SARAH WRIGHT, my fourth child and third daughter, was born at Lower Blacup likewiſe, on Wedneſday, the 5th day of March, 1773, a few minutes after ſeven o'clock in the evening, one year, twelve months, three weeks, and three days after the birth of her brother Thomas. She was baptized by the Rev. Mr. James Daw- ſon of Cleckheaton likewiſe. Sally was a very weakly child when born ; ſhe had been much injured in her conſtitution by her mother's im- prudence, and it appeared very doubtful whether we could raiſe her or not. I had deſigned to name her Lydia, after her mother (whom ſhe very much reſembles both in perſon and diſpo- ſition), but as her mother and her friends thought it probable ſhe would die, they diſapproved of my deſign, and I therefore gave her the name of Sarah. Her mother lay badly long after her

---

* The father of the editor of the preſent volume. It may be remarked that this practice of marking the exact moment of births with ſo much care, aroſe out of the old belief in aſtrological influences.

birth; we had her therefore to bring up by the spoon, which proved a very troublesome business. However, she survived to attain maturity, and is at present (June 1796) married and has two children.

JAMES WRIGHT, my fifth child and second son, was born at Lower Blacup likewise, on Monday, the 7th day of February, 1774 (the birthday of his father since the alteration of the style), twelve four-week months and two days after the birth of his sister Sarah. I had designed if the child survived and proved a son, to have called his name John, but being born dead, for distinction sake I named him James. This child, who never saw the light of the sun, fell a victim to his mother's imprudence in the womb, and was buried at the bottom of the alley in the Old Red Chapel at Cleckheaton.

> " Happy the infant dead ; but happiest he
> Who ne'er must sail on life's tempestuous sea ;
> Who, with blest freedom, from the general doom
> Exempt, must never force the teeming womb,
> Nor see the sun, nor sink into the tomb ! "

JOHN WRIGHT, my sixth child and third son, was born at Lower Blacup likewise, on Thursday, the 2nd day of February, 1775, at eight minutes after nine o'clock in the evening, twelve months, three weeks, and two days after the birth of his brother James. He was baptized by the Rev. Mr. James Dawson, of Cleckheaton, on Monday the 27th day of February, 1775.

WILLIAM WRIGHT, my seventh child and fourth son, was born at Brook-houses, in the township of Gomersall, in the parish of Birstall, aforefaid, twelve weeks and two days before his mother's death, fhe having been gradually declining of a confumption during moft of the time of her pregnancy with him, on Monday, the 28th day of July, 1777, half-an-hour after eight o'clock in the evening, two years, fix months, one week, and one day after the birth of his brother John. He was baptized by the Rev. Mr. James Scott, of Heckmondwike, on Monday, Auguft the 18th, 1777. William Wright, my feventh child and fourth fon, died at Brook-houfes, of the fmall-pox, on Sunday the 10th day of March, 1782, about feven o'clock in the morning, and was buried on Tuefday, the 12th day of March, in the New Chapel yard, at Cleckheaton, clofe by the north fide of his mother's tomb, and rather under the edge of it, aged four years and feven months. This child alfo fuffered feverely in his conftitution from the fame unhappy caufe before mentioned. I put him out to nurfe, where he continued till he was almoft gone; his grandmother then propofed to take him to herfelf, to which I agreed, and with much care and attention fhe recovered him, and he was become a fine lovely boy, remarkably good-natured and intelligent, and that engaged the old people's affection very much, efpecially his grandfather's, who forrowed exceedingly for his death. He was a very weakly child when born, and long after being raifed with great difficulty, his mother having left him a ftrong taint of the confumptive diforder of which fhe died, and which he never got clear of, always breathing fhort whenever he was the leaft hurried, which plainly indicated a defect in the lungs. This was a very unfavourable circumftance for him under the diforder with which he was afflicted, and was probably the greateft natural impediment to his ftruggling through it with life, as his eldeft fifter did, who was afflicted with the fame malignant kind of pox. However, he was grown a beautiful lovely child, was frefh and fair-looking, and very forward and intelligent for his years as to his mental abilities, and of a moft fweet and engaging difpofition and temper, which had greatly endeared him to me and to his grandparents, with whom he had lived fince he came from the nurfe when part of a year old. They had been very tender over him, and taken great care and pains to rear him, but death fnatched him from all our hopes, and tranfported his infant foul to his brother and fifter in Paradife. I note, they had a carelefs girl for a maid, who fhould have watched with him that night, while the old people were at reft ; but fell afleep, and in the morning found the child fallen from a high bedfide, cold and dead, or nearly fo ; a deplorable circumftance and matter of pungent grief to furviving relatives.

EPITAPH.

I.

Infant.

To the dark and filent tomb
Soon I hafted from the womb ;

Scarce the dawn of life began
   E'er I meafur'd out my fpan.

II.

I no fmiling pleafures knew,
   I no gay delights could view;
Joylefs fojourner was I,
   Only born to weep and die.

III.

Anfwer.

Happy infant! early bleft!
   Reft, in peaceful flumber, reft;
Early refcu'd from the cares
   Which increafe with growing years.

IV.

No delights are worth thy ftay,
   Smiling as they feem and gay;
All our gaiety is vain,
   All our laughter is but pain.

V.

Infant.

Are then all your pleafures vain?
   Is there none exempt from pain?
Is there no delight or joy
   But your fondeft hopes will cloy?

VI.

Anfwer.

Short and fickly are they all,
   Hardly tafted e'er they pall;
Lafting only and divine
   Is an innocence like thine.

VII.

Infant.

Sickly pleafures all adieu!
   Pleafures which I never knew,
I'll enjoy my early reft,
   Of my innocence poffeffed:
Happy, happy, from the womb
   That I hafted to the tomb.

I take notice here of the following circumstances, which may ferve to difplay the nature of
their fpirit and conduct towards me at Brook-
houfes. The night before my child died, I went
over to fee him, and found him forely afflicted
indeed. While I was forrowing over him, he
put me from him, and faid (if I underftood him
right, for he could hardly fpeak plain), "I do
not like you." This cut me to the heart. I
knew from whence it came : my child was
guiltlefs, not being arrived at an age to diftinguifh between good and evil ; but thofe people
who, by abufe and mifreprefentation, had infufed
the averfion into my infant's mind againft his
own father, furely were highly culpable. Was
this the fpirit and conduct of Chriftians, to lead
my child—if he had lived—into the hazard of
bringing himfelf under the weight of that fentence,
(Deut. xxvii. 16,) "Curfed be he that fetteth light
by his father." It will be obferved that in order
to bring the account of this child altogether to
his death, I have anticipated the time ; his
mother being at this time dead, I having been
a widower above four years, and was at this
time married to my prefent wife. I note next,
that when my fon died, they never fent me any
notice of his death any more than if I had been
nothing related to him, nor did I hear anything
of it till fome neighbours brought me word
towards noon. Was this the behaviour of Chriftians ? or would it not have done difcredit to the

manners and feelings of a heathen? I note next, that when my child was buried they refused to admit my wife to the funeral. She was not fond of going, but the contrary, on their account; but I was grieved to fee them exert their malice, ill-nature, and ill-manners on fuch a forrowful and improper occafion, rendered more affecting by the lofs of a favourite child. One would have imagined that the folemnity and diftrefs of fuch a circumftance might have foftened their malice and ill-nature for the moment, and induced them to behave, if not with kindnefs, with common decency at leaft; but this, it feems, was not to be expected from fuch characters. We met accidentally at O. Brooke's, to buy funeral attire, where many warm words paffed between us, and I threatened to take the child home and bury him myfelf. On this occafion, Willy Birkhead, my late wife's brother, behaved very commendably, and it is with pleafure that I record his affability and good nature. He appeared to be much diftreffed with the behaviour of his parents, apologifed to me for their conduct, faid they were old and tefty, and begged I would excufe them, and contain my paffion, fo as not to utter any harfh expreffion. For his fake I bridled a good deal. He went to his parents, wept bitterly, and perfuaded them to agree for my wife to come to the funeral. He returned with his mother, and they told me if I pleafed I might bring my wife with me. I told my brother that

I was obliged to him for *his* good will and the propriety of *his* behaviour; but that my wife fhould not come amongft them, that neither would I nor the children, but that we would meet my child's corpfe by the way and accompany it to the grave. At this declaration he burft into a violent flood of tears, and earneftly begged that I would go, and take the children with me, at leaft; he faid, elfe it would look fo badly. I told him I was fenfible of that, but could not help it; it was their fault and not mine. Here his mother joined her entreaties, and defired me to go. I told her I did not choofe to go where I knew I was not welcome: fhe faid I was welcome. I looked her in the face, and afked her if fhe could fay from her heart, and without hypocrify, that I was welcome? She faid fhe could (how truly, God knows!). Upon this I promifed to go, and accordingly next day I and the children went over and accompanied my dear, and lately beautiful, lovely, and intelligent boy to the grave. There may he reft in peaceful flumber till the archangel's trumpet awake him into a renewed, immortal, more happy and more perfect ftate of exiftence.

I return to the thread of my ftory. In the clofe of the year 1776, and the beginning of 1777, I was attacked with a fevere fit of the rheumatifm, which confined me to my bed for feveral weeks. I recovered about February, when my wife began to feel ftrong fymptoms of a defect in the lungs, and an approaching decline. She was fresh and corpulent, and looked very well when she began, but the disease altered her very fast. As our house stood on the north side of a steep hill, the doctor advised her to reside some time at her father's house, for the benefit of a better air, as the weather was cold, and it enjoyed a warmer and more southerly exposure. With my consent, therefore, she went over to her father's house, where she resided afterwards for the most part till her death. We were at this time without a maid; I was left alone with the children. I hired a neighbour woman to do our occasional work, but as I was obliged to be often from home, and the children were little ones, I suffered much by her dishonesty. I paid my wife all the attention, and procured her all the assistance, in my power, but found myself in an unpleasing situation from the unkind and disrespectful behaviour of her parents. I therefore insisted on her returning home, and I would procure her all needful attendance and assistance. She wished to stay, observing that she could not be so well pleased with anybody to wait upon her as her sister, and she could not make it convenient to attend her at our house. This was her *declared* motive for desiring to stay, but I very well knew she had another and a stronger motive for wishing to remain at Brook-houses. I threatened to take her home by force as I could not visit her there with satisfaction, but as she begged with tears and a good deal of respectful submission when she saw me angry, that I would indulge her at least for a while, I consented, and she rode over home once or twice to see us. I was there every day, sometimes twice a day; but, from the influence of her parents, as I had reason to believe, she did not always behave very respect-fully. The day before her death—if I remember right—finding her very weak and not likely to live long, after returning home and looking after my family affairs, I went over again about eight o'clock in the evening, and took all the children with me, to take, as I thought, and as it proved, their last leave of each other. When I got there, I found Sufy Clough, the neighbouring miller's wife, come in to see her, and standing by the bedside. I told my wife, that finding her so weak, I had brought the children to see her. She replied very angrily, that she wondered I should hurry them over thither, that I was always there, and that it would seem me much better to stay at home and mind my busineſs. I told her that, judging her near her end, I thought she would be pleased to see the children, as it might probably be the last time they might see each other in this world ; that I was sorry to find her so unkind and ill-tempered at such a time and in such a situation, and wished her in a better state of mind. Sufy Clough held up both her hands in amazement, and I have heard her mention it with astonishment several times since.

We bade her a laſt farewell, and as I paſſed through the houſe I told her mother I could like to be with her when ſhe died: that I would have watched with her all night, but I had nobody to attend the children ; but if any change was likely to take place before morning, I would take it kindly if they would let James Walker, at the neighbouring cottage, know, and they would ſend ſome of the family to inform me, and I would pleaſe them for their trouble. She gave me no anſwer, nor ever ſent me any word. When they waked next morning, about ſix o'clock, they found my wife dead. They laid her out, but never ſent any notice of the event either to me or the children any more than if we had been nothing related to her. Was not this ſtrange behaviour in people making large preten-ſions to Chriſtianity? and as it evidently aroſe from a proud, contemptuous, reſentful, and malicious ſpirit, and was exerted at ſuch an improper time, and on ſuch a ſolemn and diſtreſſ-ing occaſion, how did it accord with the humble, loving ſpirit which Chriſtians ought to manifeſt on all occaſions ?

Lydia Wright, my firſt wife, died at Brook-houſes on Wedneſday, the 22nd day of October, 1777, about ſix o'clock in the morning, aged thirty years, nine weeks, and four days. She was nineteen years, thirteen weeks, and five days old when ſhe was married, and the time between her marriage and death was four weeks

fhort of eleven years. She was buried within
the Old Red Chapel at Cleckheaton, clofe by
the wall, under the lower back window; but
fince it was pulled down and the ground thrown
to the New Chapel-yard, I have placed a tomb
over her grave, with the following infcription :—
" Beneath this ftone lies interred the body of
Lydia, wife of Thomas Wright, late of Lower
Blacup, near this place, who died October 22nd,
1777, aged thirty years. Alfo, three of their
children lie adjacent, namely, Mary, who died
May 25th, 1770, aged fix months; William,
who died March 10th, 1782, aged four years
and feven months; and a male child, ftill-born."
There is alfo erected within the New Chapel a
fmall, neat, marble monument to the memory of
my wife's younger fifter Betty, upon which, after
her fifter's epitaph, one is infcribed for her as
follows :—" Likewife, Mrs. Lydia Wright, fifter
to the above, who died in the full triumph of
faith, October 22nd, 1777, aged thirty years.
' Behold, God is my falvation ; I will truft and
not be afraid, for the Lord Jehovah is my ftrength
and my fong ; he alfo is become my falvation.'
Alfo two of her children." Ifaiah xii. 2, the
verfe from which Mr. Scott preached her funeral
fermon at Heckmondwike Old Chapel.

In the autumn of the year 1780, I happened
upon occafion to be one afternoon at Crofs-hall,
near Brunt-cliffe,* the houfe of a Mifs Bofan-

---

* The village of Bruntcliffe, in the parifh of Batley,

quet,* a maiden lady of confiderable property. She was a very religious and charitable lady, and much attached to the Methodifts. She had afked me to drink tea with her, and juft as we rofe from the table a Mr. John Hampfon, fenior, a Methodift preacher, happened to drop in from Wales, and as I had contracted a little acquaintance with her, fhe afked me to ftay fupper, and bear the preacher company; which I accordingly did, and during fupper he acquainted us with a circumftance which had come to his knowledge

---

is built on the junction of four roads; thofe leading to Bradford, Wakefield, Leeds, and Birftall. It is only a fhort diftance from Adwalton, or Atherton, and Birkenfhaw; and is feven miles from Bradford. It is fometimes called Bruntcliff Thorn, and is not far from the Gilderfome ftation, on the Bradford and Wakefield branch of the Great Northern Railway. Crofs Hall is a little to the eaft of Bruntcliffe, built by Mifs Bofanquet.

* Mifs Bofanquet. This was the lady who afterwards became Mrs. Fletcher, of Madeley. Her memory feems to have lafted traditionally in this part of the country. Mr. Holroyd has obtained for me from a very old man from Morley, the following account of Mifs Bofanquet of Crofs Hall, which I give in the language of the relator, who has confounded a Swifs with a Swede.

"I knew Mifs Bofanquet varry weel when I were a lad. I've heerd mi father tell at fhoo com thro London, where fhoo hed a brother at wer a parliament man; an as luck wod hev it, fhoo wer convarted under owd Wefley, an then fhoo com doon thro London an belt Crofs Hall, an browt a weggan load o young wimmin, all orphans, an fhoo kept em wol they gate up ta be owd enef ta keep therfevs. Shoo led clafs-meetings, and preycht tu, an a rare gooid preycher fhoo wor. I remember fhoo gate wed tul a gentleman o't name o Fletcher, a Swede, an they went ta live at Gilderfome, where I think they both deed."

a little before he left Wales, and of which he gave us the following relation.*

It had been for fome time reported in the neighbourhood that a poor unmarried woman, who was a member of the Methodift Society, and had become ferious under their miniftry, had feen and converfed with the apparition of a gentleman, who had made a ftrange difcovery to her. Mr. Hampfon being defirous to afcertain if there was any truth in the ftory, fent for the woman, and defired her to give him an exact relation of the whole affair from her own mouth, and as near the truth as fhe poffibly could. She faid fhe was a poor woman who got her living by fpinning hemp and line ; that it was cuftomary for the farmers and gentlemen of that neighbour-hood to grow a little hemp or line in a corner of their fields, for their own home confumption, and as fhe had a good hand at fpinning the materials, fhe ufed to go from houfe to houfe to enquire for work ; that her method was, where they employed her, during her ftay to have meat, and drink, and lodging (if fhe had occafion to fleep with them), for her work, and what they pleafed to give her befides. That, among other places, fhe happened to call in one day at the Welfh Earl Powis's country feat, called Red-

---

* This curious relation is written at the end of the manufcript of the autobiography, but I have reftored it to its place in the narrative. Mr. Hampfon was one of the diftinguifhed preachers in the early days of Methodifm.

caftle,* to inquire for work, as fhe ufually had done before. The quality were at this time in London, and had left the fteward and his wife, with other fervants, as ufual, to take care of their country refidence in their abfence. The fteward's wife fet her to work, and in the evening told her that fhe muft ftay all night with them, as they had more work for her to do next day. When bedtime arrived, two or three of the fervants in company, with each a lighted candle in her hand, conducted her to her lodging. They led her to a ground room, with a boarded floor and two fafh windows. The room was grandly furnifhed and had a genteel bed in one corner of it. They had made her a good fire, and had placed her a chair and a table before it, and a large lighted candle upon the table. They told her that was her bedroom, and fhe might go to fleep when fhe pleafed : they then wifhed her a good night, and withdrew altogether, pulling the door quickly after them, fo as to hafp the fpring-fneck † in the brafs lock that was upon it. When they were gone, fhe gazed awhile at the

------

* Red Caftle. This—in Welfh, Caftel goch—was the old name of Powis Caftle, and is faid to have been given to it from the red colour of the ftone of which it was built. I have not been able to difcover if this very remarkable ghoft ftory is ftill remembered there, but I have heard that there is a room in the caftle ftill called the haunted chamber.

† Spring-fneck. *Sneck*, in the dialect of Yorkfhire, means a door-latch.

fine furniture, under no fmall aftonifhment that they fhould put fuch a poor perfon as her in fo grand a room and bed, with all the apparatus of fire, chair, table, and candle. She was alfo furprifed at the circumftance of the fervants coming fo many together, with each of them a candle; however, after gazing about her fome little time, fhe fat down and took a fmall Welfh Bible out of her pocket, which fhe always carried about with her, and in which fhe ufually read a chapter—chiefly in the New Teftament—before fhe faid her prayers and went to bed. While fhe was reading fhe heard the room door open, and, turning her head, faw a gentleman enter in a gold-laced hat and waiftcoat, and the reft of his drefs correfponding therewith. (I think fhe was very particular in defcribing the reft of his drefs to Mr. Hampfon, and he to me at the time, but I have now forgot the other particulars.) He walked down by the fafh-window to the corner of the room, and then returned. When he came at the firft window in his return (the bottom of which was nearly breaft-high) he refted his elbow on the bottom of the window, and the fide of his face upon the palm of his hand, and ftood in that leaning pofture for fome time, with his fide partly towards her. She looked at him earneftly to fee if fhe knew him, but though, from her frequent intercourfe with them, fhe had a perfonal knowledge of all the prefent family, he appeared a ftranger to her. She fuppofed afterwards, that he ftood in this manner to encourage her to fpeak; but as fhe did not, after fome little time he walked off, pulling the door after him as the fervants had done before. She began now to be much alarmed, concluding it to be an apparition, and that they had put her there on purpofe. This was really the cafe. The room, it feems, had been difturbed for a long time fo that nobody could fleep peaceably in it, and as fhe paffed for a very ferious woman, the fervants took it in their heads to put the Methodift and fpirit together, to fee what they would make of it. Startled at this thought, fhe rofe from her chair, and kneeled down by the bedfide to fay her prayers. While fhe was praying he came in again, walked round the room, and came clofe behind her. She had it on her mind to fpeak, but when fhe attempted it fhe was fo very much agitated, that fhe could not utter a word. He walked out of the room again, pulling the door after him as before. She begged that God would ftrengthen her, and not fuffer her to be tried beyond what fhe was able to bear; fhe recovered her fpirits, and thought fhe felt more confidence and refolution, and determined if he came in again fhe would fpeak to him if poffible. He prefently came in again, walked round, and came behind her as before; fhe turned her head and faid, " Pray fir, who are you, and what do you want?" He put up his finger, and faid, " Take up the candle and follow me, and I will tell you."

She got up, took up the candle, and followed him out of the room. He led her through a long boarded paffage, till they came to the door of another room, which he opened and went in; it was a fmall room, or what might be called a large clofet. "As the room was fmall, and I believed him to be a fpirit," faid fhe, "I ftopped at the door; he turned and faid, 'Walk in; I will not hurt you;' fo I walked in. He faid, 'Obferve what I do;' I faid, 'I will.' He ftooped, and tore up one of the boards of the floor, and there appeared under it a box with an iron handle in the lid. He faid, 'Do you fee that box?' I faid, 'Yes, I do.' He then ftepped to one fide of the room and fhowed me a crevice in the wall, where, he faid, a key was hid that would open it. He faid, 'This box and key muft be taken out, and fent to the earl in London'* (naming the earl and his place of refidence in the city). He faid, 'Will you fee it done?' I faid, 'I will do my beft to get it done;' he faid, 'Do, and I will trouble the houfe no more.' He then walked out of the room and left me. (He feems to have been a very civil fpirit, and to have been very careful to affright her as little as poffible.) I ftepped to the room-door, and

---

* The Earl in London. This was the laft of the earls of Powis, of the family of Herbert. He fucceeded his father to the title in 1749, and died in 1801, after which it was conferred upon Lord Clive, who had married the earl's fifter.

fet up a fhout. The fteward and his wife, with the other fervants, came to me immediately; all clung together, with a number of lights in their hands. It feems they had all been waiting to fee the iffue of the interview betwixt me and the apparition. They afked me what was the matter? I told them the foregoing circumftances, and fhowed them the box. The fteward durft not meddle with it, but his wife had more courage, and, with the help of the other fervants, tugged it out, and found the key. She faid by their lifting it appeared to be pretty heavy, but that fhe did not fee it opened, and therefore did not know what it contained;—perhaps money, or writings of confequence to the family, or both." They took it away with them, and fhe then went to bed and flept peaceably till the morning.

It appeared afterwards that they fent the box to the earl, in London, with an account of the manner of its difcovery, and by whom; as the earl fent down orders immediately to his fteward to inform the poor woman who had been the occafion of the difcovery, that if fhe would come and refide in his family, fhe fhould be comfortably provided for the remainder of her days; or, if fhe did not choofe to refide conftantly with them, if fhe would let them know when fhe wanted affiftance, fhe fhould be liberally fupplied at his lordfhip's expenfe, as long as fhe lived. And Mr. Hampfon faid it was a known fact in the neighbourhood, that fhe had been fo fupplied from his lordfhip's family from the time the affair was faid to have happened, and continued to be fo at the time fhe gave Mr. Hampfon this account. She told him that fhe was fo often folicited by curious people to relate the ftory, that fhe was weary of repeating it, but to oblige him had once more related the particulars, and wifhed now to have done with it. Mr. Hampfon faid fhe appeared to be a fenfible, intelligent perfon, and that he faw no reafon to doubt her veracity. I know many perfons in the prefent day laugh at fuch ftories, and affect very much to doubt their reality, while others totally deny the poffibility of their exiftence. However, fcripture, and many well-attefted relations, feem to favour the idea, and the prefent ftory appeared fo fingular and fo well attefted, and I had it fo near the fountain-head, that I thought it might perhaps be worth preferving, and I have therefore taken the pains to record it. Admitting it to be true, it fhould feem that the confequences to the family of what the hidden box contained, was the formal caufe of the fpirit's difquiet, and of its difturbing the houfe fo much and fo long, in order to bring about a difcovery; but why a departed fpirit fhould concern itfelf in the affairs of this world after it has left it, or why they fhould difquiet it fo as to caufe it to reappear and make difturbances, in order to difcover and have things righted, as in the preceding cafe, or why this fhould be done in fome cafes of apparently lefs moment, while in other cafes much greater family injuries feem to be fuffered, and no fpirit appears to intereft itfelf in the cafe, are circumftances for which we can by no means account. The cloud fits deep on futurity, and we are fo little acquainted with the laws of the fpiritual world, that we are, perhaps, incapable, in our prefent ftate, of comprehending its nature, or of giving any fatisfactory account of thefe matters.

I continued in a ftate of widowhood four years and two weeks, during which interval I fuffered much from the difhonefty of people I had occafionally about me. The firft fervant I had after my wife died was B—— B——, a daughter of one of my late wife's uncles ; but this was a very honeft girl for aught I ever faw by her, but during her ftay with me the following circumftance happened.

I had imprudently let the loom-fhop—as I did not ufe it—to a collier and his family. It adjoined upon the houfe, opened on the fame front, and was very near my own door, fo that it was very opportune for a perfon flipping out of one houfe into the other. The collier's wife was a woman of an exceeding bad character. I that year ferved the public office of collector of the land-tax and window money. I had collected, I think, about eighty pounds, which I had put in a fmall drawer in my defk, which ftood in the houfe, within about three yards of the houfe-door. By fome means or other I had fpoiled the lock of my defk-lid, that I could not lock it, and thought I would remove the money into a box in the chamber where I could lock it up in fafety ; but believing my maid honeft, and never fufpecting any other perfon would have the impudence to come into the houfe and go in to my defk in the day-time, I had neglected this for feveral days. At laft I went to remove it, and found a great part of it gone ; I think near thirty pounds. I had that fum to borrow of a neighbour to make it up. The maid protefted her innocence, and I was fatisfied of it ; fhe faid the collier's wife had obferved that I placed great confidence in her (the maid) to leave fo much money in the houfe with her, unlocked. This fhowed fhe had noticed the circumftance, and the maid faid, fhe believed fhe had watched her out of the houfe when fhe went to the brook to fetch water, and left the houfe door unlocked, and had gone in and ftole the money out of the defk in her abfence ; which I doubted not was the cafe. As they were bad neighbours, I had been endeavouring for fome time to get rid of them, but could not ; but as I had made a noife about this affair, and threatened, if I could find out the thief, to profecute feverely, the next morning I found they had removed their goods in the night, and were gone ! She afterwards bought a profufion of fine clothes at the rag-fhop and elfewhere, which fufficiently pointed out the thief; but as money could not be fworn to, and was an article fo eafily concealed, I had no chance to recover it, fo was obliged to fit down with the lofs, which tended much to my further embarrafsment.

They kept my daughter Sally and my youngeft fon Willy at Brook-houfes, but took no notice of me, but to hurry all they could from me, and I was weak and foft enough to fuffer myfelf to be terribly plundered by them. For this purpofe, foon after my wife's death, her youngeft fifter came and wheedled me out of every rag of her clothes, under pretence that fome of them would be fpoiled if they were not wafhed, &c., and that they would take care of them for the children, and I might have them again when I pleafed. However, I never received any of them again, and I underftood afterwards, that fhe appropriated moft of them to her own ufe, and that my children got little or nothing belonging to them afterwards. A piece of conduct this, which evinced fuch a degree of difhonefty and meannefs of fpirit, as no perfon poffeffed of a fingle grain of generofity would have been concerned in, as feveral of the articles were new or nearly fo, and lately purchafed with my own money. Being willing to give my eldeft daughter Betty the beft education I could—fhe being grown a fine girl, and taking learning very readily—I fent her to the boarding-school at Birstall-field-head, taught by Mrs. Priestley,* at an expense, indeed, beyond my abilities; she stayed here half-a-year, and I believe it was of considerable service to her. I notice here, that her grandmother took no notice of her all the time, never paid her a single visit, or offered me the least assistance, or gave her a single rag or a single shilling from first to last: nay, they had lent her an overworn bed-sheet, of very small value, to serve her for a change during her stay; and they made such a clamour for this being returned, for fear they should lose it—even before the child came home —as if it had been a thing of the greatest importance;—another instance of their inherent meanness of spirit.

About this time I had two successive servants, or housekeepers, who both turned out very bad. One was an incurable drunkard, and proved very expensive to me; the other, the greatest liar and the greatest thief that ever fell under my observation. She turned the house upside down, and plundered it through every time I turned my back, and carried out (when ever I was absent) to her father's and relations, meal, flour, butter, eggs, ribbons, small linen, beer, and

---

* The celebrated Dr Priestly was born at Birstall-field-head; so that the person here mentioned was, no doubt, a near relation of his, possibly his mother, but more probably a sister or sister-in-law. Formerly maiden ladies often took the title of Mrs.

bottles of rum ; in fhort, whatever was portable, and told fome of them that I had fent them for prefents. At the fame time, fhe had a brother, a boy as bad and thievifh as herfelf, who came miching* daily into our barn, and picked up all the eggs which nine or ten hens produced during the height of their laying, for weeks together. At the fame time I fummered her father a cow, and her mother and her met every morning and evening at the milking-place ; here they changed the ftrippings of our cows for the firftings of theirs, and by this means they got almoft all the butter, and we got next to none. At laft fhe proceeded to break open the locks on the drawers, and I turned her out of doors. I might have hanged her, but I did not choofe the trouble, though I knew nothing of the extent of my lofs by her at this time. This girl's name was R-ch-l R-b-rtfh-ed, the daughter of a near neighbour, whom I had laid under repeated pecuniary obligations, by lending him money when he was ftraitened. He was alfo an old profeffing Methodift, and muft have known fomething of his daughter's illicit practices, from the quantity of purloined ftuff fhe carried home, till it fell under the obfervation of the neighbours, and could not well be fuppofed, therefore, to efcape his obfervation. My drunken fervant was alfo a profeffing Methodift ; joined in clafs,

---

* *Miching.* Sneaking and prowling about, thieving.

and always very happy at the claſs-meetings. So difficult is it, very frequently, to reconcile people's profeſſions with their conduct. I had this girl eight weeks, and in that time ſuffered, I believe, as many pounds by her, at leaſt; but, indeed, I never did, and I believe never muſt, know my loſs by this girl and her family.

I now plainly perceived that I muſt have a wife, or be ruined; but who would be a ſuitable wife, or who I was to pleaſe—myſelf or other people—in the choice of one, was a queſtion. Some people adviſed me to marry an old woman that would have no more children, and talked in ſuch a manner as if they ſuppoſed that I might accommodate my fancy and affection to any old creature, with as much eaſe as I might chooſe a joint of meat to get my dinner upon. Theſe people ſeemed to think, that if a perſon has been married once, and got ſome children, he muſt have loſt all the finer feelings of the human heart; or, at leaſt, that he could be juſtified by no other motives to a future marriage, than thoſe mean and ſordid ones, intereſt and convenience. I cry thoſe prudent people's mercy. I am, and muſt be, of a different opinion; for though I readily allow that it is quite neceſſary on ſuch occaſions to make uſe of all the care and prudence that the circumſtances of the caſe will admit of, yet I think there are circumſtances of greater importance to be conſidered in this caſe than even thoſe of wealth and convenience; not but that I think, as I faid before, it is every one's duty and intereft to obtain as much wealth and convenience as he fairly and honeftly can ; yet I judge the matter of greateft moment is, if the parties love each other for their own fakes, with a love of difinterefted efteem and affection. This I look upon to be abfolutely neceffary, as the foundation of matrimonial happinefs, and which, I conceive, cannot poffibly fubfift without it. Here, perhaps, fome wifeacre may afk me, with a fneer, what I have got by indulging my head-ftrong will in this cafe ? I will tell him. I have got an agreeable partner, whom I love and efteem, and with whom, fo far, I am happy. I have got a houfe full of fine children, and ftraitened circumftances ; and I had a thoufand times rather choofe this fituation, than be bound for life to a perfon I could not love, though in the midft of affluence and worldly profperity ; for in this cafe, my mind is fo conftituted, I fhould be one of the moft unhappy creatures under heaven. However, I do not fuppofe that the increafe of my family (the confequence of my marrying a young woman) is a *principal*, or even any *confiderable*, caufe of the reduction of my property. No, this had other unhappy caufes, with which this had no connexion ; though it is certain, that my having a young and numerous family in my advanced years, under the prefent reduced ftate of my original property, and at a time when the price of all the neceffaries of life are fo unreafonably enhanced, tends greatly to increafe my prefent embarraffments ; but as this is the common lot of humanity, and we cannot help it, we muft endeavour to be as content as we poffibly can.

I return to my ftory. I found that fervants and houfekeepers were not to be trufted, I had no old grandmother, no mother, no fifter, as many others in my fituation have, upon whom I might rely, and who might, in a good meafure, fupply the place of a wife, in taking care of my children and looking after the concerns of my family. I had it not, therefore, in my choice, in a confiftency with my intereft, *to marry* or *not to marry.* No, imperious neceffity, arifing from the ftate of my family, required me to get a wife as fpeedily as poffible. During the ftate of my widowhood, for want of a wife in the houfe when I was abfent, I had already fuffered, to my own knowledge, to the amount of forty or fifty pounds at leaft, by downright thievery ; fo that continuing as I was, I had no profpect before me but ruin. I could not fancy an old woman. Does fome felf-important fellow with a fapient face afk me, why I could not ? I fhould deem the queftion abfurd, and afk him in my turn, why he chofe his wife (if he has got one) in preference to any other woman ? If he fays he cannot tell ; that it happened fo ; becaufe he liked her beft ; I return him the fame anfwer. I therefore chofe to take a young woman whom

I could love, and with whom I could be happy, though attended with almost a certainty of being encumbered with more children, rather than take an old woman, to avoid that inconvenience, whom I could not love, and with whom I could not be happy. This is the true state of the case, and I have been so particular upon the subject, that I might present a fair view of the case, that from a just representation of the subject, any impartial person may be able to draw a just conclusion; because I have been so severely censured for my conduct on this occasion by many persons who were "as wise in their own eyes as seven men that can render a reason;" but it is much easier for a half-thinking person to shake the head, and, with a solemn face and magisterial air, pronounce an ill-natured and ill-founded censure upon his neighbour's conduct, than it is to advance one solid reason in support of such a censure. Yet there seems to be as many persons in the present day among Christian professors as there was eighteen hundred years ago, who can see, or *think* they can see, a mote in the eye of their neighbour, while they quite overlook the huge beam that is in their own eye. Peace be to all such persons, and a better spirit.

About this time I saw a young woman I thought I could fancy. She was, indeed, very young, but had got a tolerable education, had very good hands, was very ingenious, solid, and senfible. I therefore formed a connection with her immediately. This foon reached the ears of my bitter enemies at Brook-houfes, and awakened all their malice, which flowed in a plentiful ftream of abufe and invective againft me from their envenomed lips. By fpecious mifreprefentations of the cafe, they endeavoured to deprive me of my children's affections, debauch them from their duty, and make them believe that I had acted unkindly, unjuftly, and wickedly with refpect to them in this cafe ; and fo far fucceeded, that my two eldeft children became very faucy and difrefpectful, which procured them both a more fevere beating than ever I had given them before. However, by appealing to their filial affection and good fenfe, by fhowing them the impropriety and bad confequences of their liftening to fuch people, and following their pernicious counfels, I brought them back to their duty, and we foon recovered and maintained the wonted peace and quietnefs of our family, notwithftanding all the infernal efforts of thofe fpiteful people to deftroy it.

I proceed to relate the following unfortunate circumftance, which happened at this time. A neighbouring man, who lived about a quarter of a mile from us, on the oppofite fide of the hill, over againft our little farm, feeing me mowing my own grafs in the fields, came frequently to me, and talked of trade and what profit he was certain might be obtained by dealing in fuch and fuch articles. He had a fmall eftate on which he lived, but it was very deeply encumbered, and I believe he was at this time in a very difficult fituation for want of money to enable him to carry on a trade to maintain his family. He knew I had it in my power to raife fome money, and therefore propofed that I fhould borrow fome more money on my land, throw up my farm, go live in a part of his houfe, and enter into partner-fhip with him, and he doubted not we fhould perform wonders. I was weak and unwary enough to liften to his propofals, and borrowed an additional two hundred pounds on my land, threw up my farm, went to live in a part of his houfe, and entered into partnerfhip with him; but as he had little or no money to advance, I was obliged to lend him fome of mine, for which he was to pay me common intereft; fo he joined with me at my own money. We went immediately into trade; bought and fold, and trucked a variety of articles, till at laft we got into the liquor bufinefs. We went to Man-chefter and Liverpool to buy goods, fought cuftom amongft the publicans, and foon had a great many bad debts on hand, which, whether they were ever all paid, or no, I know not to this day. We took out a retail licence, and my partner's wife was intrufted with this bufinefs, which required more honefty to do juftice to the partnerfhip than falls to everybody's fhare. The houfe, however, began to be very well accuſtomed, and preſented a very promiſing proſpect for trade ; but my money vaniſhed like a miſt, payments came on, more money was wanted, my partner could raiſe no money ; I ſold a pitſtead in my land for eighty pounds ; this went into the old ſwallow, and diſappeared in an inſtant as if it had been thrown into a coal-pit. Stupid, and dull, and fooliſhly confiding as I had been in this caſe, I now began to ſee I was in the wrong box ; indeed, my wife (for I was now married), who was a much cloſer obſerver than myſelf, had given me repeated hints of the circumſtance before. I was determined to be rid of this ruinous connexion as ſpeedily as poſſible, if I eſcaped with the ſkin of my teeth ; and my partner and his deep-contriving wife ſeemed very willing to diſpenſe with my company, and quite agreeable to appropriate all the proſpect of advantage, obtained at my coſt, entirely to themſelves. In balancing our accounts I was brought in debtor, though I had raiſed nearly all the money—and over and beſide, my partner was engaged in an expenſive chancery law-ſuit all the time—yet he came off creditor. All was imputed to my extravagance, and two of my old acquaintance, whom I had got to ſcrutinize the cunning of my opponents, entered into their idea, and ſuppoſed me inattentive and extravagant enough to run through all that money in two years' time, and ſo, inſtead of doing me any ſervice, they encouraged my opponent, and did me a great deal of hurt. Extravagant! when I was never drunk all the time, and my partner hardly ever came home fober; when he had a more numerous and expenfive family to keep, and had nothing to keep them on but what he got by the trade, and I had a lefs numerous and expenfive family, and an eftate of near thirty pounds a year befides the trade to keep them on. Add to this, my partner was engaged in an expenfive law-fuit, which coft him a good deal of money. Yet he came off on the faving fide, and I juft quitted the connection in time to efcape a gaol. I believe I fuffered by this connection, in the courfe of about two years, little lefs than three hundred pounds. This was a bad affair for me, and threw me into difficulties immediately, which I have laboured under ever fince. I thus became a ftepping-ftone for my partner, who trod me and my family into the duft to mount himfelf and his family into affluence and profperity.

I ftop to notice fome occurrences in my family during this period. We unfortunately left Lower Blacup, after refiding there fourteen years, and removed into Cleckheaton upper-lane, May the 12th, 1781. I was married a fecond time on Sunday, the 4th day of November, 1781, to Alicia Pinder, eldeft daughter of Thomas Pinder, farmer, of Upper Blacup, a few fields from my former abode, after remaining in a ftate of widowhood four years and two weeks. We were

married at the parish church of Birstall, by the
Rev. Mr. Reuben Ogden; present only besides
ourselves, the minister, Jo. Shaw, the clerk, and
my wife's father. Alicia Pinder was born on
Monday, the 19th day of May, 1766. She was
baptized at the White Chapel, in the North, by
the Rev. Mr. Jonas Eastwood, on Sunday, June
the 15th, 1766, and was fifteen years and a-half
old when she was married. Soon after we were
married my wife was attacked by a severe rheumatic fever, which reduced her very low. Before
she was quite recovered, in the end of the year
1781, and the beginning of the year 1782, my
children were attacked by that dreadful distemper
the small-pox, which at this time raged in the
neighbourhood, and was of a very fatal and
malignant kind. Betty was near fourteen years
of age, Tommy was near eleven, and John near
seven. They had often begged to be inoculated,
but as their grandparents were bitterly prejudiced
against the practice, to oblige them I had forbore
to do it. For this I afterwards blamed myself
much, as their prejudice was so inveterate against
me, that it appeared impossible for me to conciliate their favour by anything I could do; and
it exposed my children to more than double
hazard and suffering. Betty's was of a most
malignant kind, and she was rendered one of
the most deplorable objects I ever saw, and was
literally flayed from head to foot. However, it
pleased God to spare her life, contrary to the

expectations of all who faw her, and even of the phyfician who attended her. I regretted very much the ravage this naufeous diforder had made in her fine countenance, which was fo great, that if I had been abfent for the time, I fhould have been unable at firft to have recognized my own child. However, I was thankful that her life, her eyes, and limbs were fpared. Tommy was more favourably dealt with ; his pocks were of a better kind, his countenance little or none altered, and he got through them the eafieft of all the three. John was very full ; his lovely countenance much altered, yet he got through them with much lefs trouble and danger than his fifter did.

During this troublefome and diftreffing fituation of my family, my wife—though ftill very weak—affifted me in waiting upon the children with the greateft tendernefs and affiduity. I was myfelf fix or feven weeks and never had all my clothes off, was engaged day and night going up and down ftairs and from one chamber to another almoft without intermiffion, and my fleep departed from mine eyes ; yet a kind Providence fo ordered it, that I neither felt much over-fatigued, nor greatly to want my fleep during the whole time, though one might have imagined, from the conftant fatigue I underwent, and the depreffing forrow of mind I was under for my fuffering children — efpecially for my eldeft daughter, whofe death I apprehended every hour

—that it would have been impoffible I fhould have bore up under it. When my three children at home were recovering, my other two at Brook-houfes begun, though none of the family had ever come near our houfe while we had them. Sally got very favourably through them, but they proved fatal to my youngeft fon Willy, the circumftances of whofe death I have previoufly related.

I ftop to notice the following little circumftance. John, who was uncommonly fond *of*, and, of confequence, equally dear *to* me, the morning he found himfelf blind, when in the fmall-pox, I being in bed with him, faid haftily, " Daddy, I am dead ! " I faid, " No, my dear ;" but then he faid, " I am dying." I faid, " What for, my love ?" he faid, " Becaufe I cannot fee." I told him to be content, and not pull his eyes open, and he would fee again after a fhort time. He was fatisfied, and very patient, but added, " Daddy, I could not like to die." I afked him if he was afraid to die ; he faid, " No ; but I could not like to leave *you*," and earneftly added, " Blefs you! everybody fays you are a good daddy to your children, and fo you are." (The poor child had heard the family at Brook-houfes abufe me and fay I was a bad father to my children, and behaved ill to them ; he had heard all the neighbours fay the contrary, and from the tendernefs with which I treated him and all my children, was fatisfied of the contrary himfelf.

This was the caufe of my child's remarks on this occafion.) He then fondly embraced, kiffed, and bleffed me. Such was the endearing prattle and behaviour of my beloved child, whom death, to my heavy afflidion, has fince fuddenly fnatched from my embraces. I note here again the wicked perverfity of Mr. and Mrs. Birkhead's condudt on this occafion, in thus perpetually endeavouring to infpire my children with a bad idea of their father, and to rob me of their duty and affedion ; and I appeal to the judgment of every candid and unprejudiced perfon, if fuch a condudt was not abfolutely inconfiftent with their high profeffion of Chriftianity. I take notice here alfo, that a little before we left the Lower Blacup, my eldeft daughter Betty lay feveral weeks dangeroufly ill of a fcarlet fever, of which feveral had died round about us. My fon John was poorly alfo, and about this time they all three had the meafles, which were attended with much fever, and I was in fear I fhould have loft John, he was fo bad. We were without fervant ; I therefore waited on my fick children myfelf, and I dare appeal to my neigh-bours, that they were carefully and properly attended.

On Monday, the 12th day of May, 1783 (old May-day), I removed with my family to Birkenfhaw, the place where I had lived before I was married the firft time, into the loweft but one of John Ellifon's new-built houfes. I ftop here again, to notice the following circumstance, which I had overlooked in its place. Old Mrs. Birkhead, some time before my second marriage, having heard of my intention to marry, came wheedling over to my house, and said, "Tommy, you always said that Betty and Sally should have your mother's clothes between them." I said, "Yes; I mean so." She said, "Will you oblige me in letting me have them to our house to keep? I will take the best care I can of them for the children." I perceived she was afraid of a second wife getting them ; but as I always meant my girls to have them, and as the *hypocrite* appeared in high good humour—which it seems she could assume to serve a turn—and as I was greatly desirous of living on peaceable terms with them if possible, I told her, that the clothes had been kept with great care almost from my birth, but that if she thought them safer in her keeping than mine, if she would promise me to take good care of them, and let my daughters have them when they wanted them, I had no great objection to oblige her in this case, for the sake of peace, as neither I nor the person I was aiming to marry, had any desire to deprive my children of them. If, therefore, she would come over to my house some day when I was at leisure, I would look them over, and let her have such as I intended for them. With this promise she departed for the present, and sometime afterwards, instead of coming on a day when I *was* at home, she contrived—in concert with my daughter Betty, I make no doubt—to come on a day when I *was not* at home, on purpose to have the opportunity of plundering my house uncontrolled. This they did in a shameful manner; so that with what they took now, and what she and her agents had taken before, they almost entirely stripped my house both of bed-linen and wearing apparel, save that which the children and I had in common use, besides a variety of other articles; nay, she had even the meanness and impudence to take my own mother's wedding-ring, which, however I sent for back again, and was almost in mind to have entered a legal process against her for burglary. My daughter Betty, to be sure, was young, and deceived and misled by her grandmother's specious though false reprefentations; and these circumstances may, perhaps, form a tolerable excuse for my daughter's conduct on these occasions; yet she was certainly very blameable, as she was old enough (fourteen) to have known better than to have joined a mean, interested woman in plundering her father's property; but the old woman herself, or any other person of the family, who either took it themselves, or encouraged my children so to do, were no better than thieves and robbers. After they had thus stripped my house of all my wife's clothes and all my own mother's clothes, bed-linen, &c. &c., instead of keeping them sacred for the children, as they pretended, her aunt B——y carried off one part, and had the extreme meanneſs and impudence to wear ſome articles of my own mother's till they were good for nothing ; her grandmother ſeized and diſtributed another part ; and a diſhoneſt ſervant-girl they had, cut, and ſpoiled, and ſtole another part ; ſo that, ſave ſome of the larger articles of my mother's, as her gowns, &c. which they could not well take without being obſerved by every-body, the greateſt part of the property thus filched from my houſe was entirely loſt both to me and my children ; whereas, had they ſtill continued in my keeping, they might have enjoyed every individual article.

I will beſtow a few reflections on theſe people's conduct towards me on this occaſion.   I believe if they could have ſtripped me naked and turned me out upon a common, it would have pleaſed them to have done it.   Their oſtenſible reaſon for this manner of proceeding was, " A ſecond wife will get all that is left ; " and this plea they ſeemed to think ſufficient to juſtify *them* in doing all that lay in their power to accompliſh *my* ruin. What ſtrange reaſoning, and what abſurd and inconſiſtent conduct was this ! Mrs. Birkhead's own father married a *ſecond* time, after having married a *firſt* wife, with whom he had iſſue. Mrs. Birkhead herſelf was a fruit of that ſecond marriage.   Her father married a third wife, to whom, fame ſays, he and his family did not behave over-kindly. Now, if her father's child or children by his firſt wife, or their relations, had acted upon the ſame principles with reſpect to him and his future family which ſhe and her family acted upon with reſpect to me and mine ; if they had endeavoured to prejudice his child or children againſt him, to debauch them from their duty, and rob him of their affection ; if they had rifled, or encouraged his child or children to rifle his property, even to the hazard of his ruin, for fear his ſecond wife and ſecond children—of whom ſhe herſelf was one—ſhould have anything left to ſubſiſt upon afterwards ; what would Mrs. Birkhead have thought or ſaid of ſuch a proceeding ? What indeed ! doubtleſs, if it had been her *own* caſe, ſhe would have thought, and ſaid too, that they were a ſet of wicked, unjuſt, ungenerous, and unfeeling raſcals.

I return to my narration. When we came to Birkenſhaw, my wife was in a very weak ſtate of body ; ſhe was juſt recovering from a ſecond attack of her old diſorder, the rheumatic fever. She was obliged to wean the child (Patty) when about fifteen weeks old, who was poorly alſo ; but after this they both recovered pretty ſpeedily. About this time I was obliged to ſell my land—one of the moſt unfortunate actions for my worldly welfare that ever I did in my life, as I have hinted before. After paying off the mortgage, I put one hundred pounds of the ſpare money into the hands of ſome friendly acquaintance in the wool trade, on condition that I fhould have a proportional fhare of the profits arifing therefrom. However, I never received anything but fimple intereft for my money, and took fome of the ftock now and fome then, till I had taken it all. We tried to keep a fhop, but this would do nothing for us; we loft money by roguifh cuftomers. We next tried to teach a fchool, and could get the trouble and inconvenience of fcholars, but could get no pay for many of them; we therefore gave this up. I next got in to be book-keeper at the furnace for Meffrs. Emmets,* which place I held about a year, and had about two fhillings a day. This helped us for the time, and then we parted. My family was increafing all this time, and of courfe my difficulties. A friendly ac-quaintance of mine (Mr. John Taylor, merchant, of Great Gomerfall),† having, I fuppofe, intelli-gence of this, paid me a vifit, and kindly in-quired into my fituation. He had lately built a

---

* The father of the prefent Emmanuel Emmet, Efq. of Birkenfhaw, had a foundry and iron-works at Birkenfhaw during the laft century, and the earlier part of the prefent. Both the Coles and the Billingfleys, late of the Bowling Iron Works, were in the employ of the Emmets before they came to Bowling.

† This "Mr. John Taylor, merchant, of Great Gomer-fall," was the identical perfon who afterwards figured as Mr. Yorke in Mifs Brontë's novel of "Shirley." He was a man of great energy, was quite a charaćter, and became rich by trade. He built a chapel at Gomerfall at his own fole expenfe, and preached in it himfelf.

pretty large mill for carding machines, to which he had attached four ſtocks to mill woollen cloth in. He wanted a cloth ſearcher, and propoſed to me to endeavour to obtain the place, and he would aſſiſt me. He obſerved, it would be good for nothing the firſt year, being only four pounds for the year; but that the year following it would be advanced to ten pounds, he made no doubt, and eventually to fifteen or ſixteen pounds. That it would put me in the line of the buſineſs, and give me an opportunity of future advancement to better places. I thanked him, accepted the propoſal, and obtained the place. As he obſerved, I loſt by it the firſt year; the ſecond year it was raiſed to ten pounds a year, which was the ſalary affixed to it when I threw up the place; but it was afterwards raiſed to fifteen or ſixteen pounds a year, and, with other emoluments, is worth twenty, or near twenty pounds a year to the preſent officer. Mr. Taylor at the ſame time allowed me eight ſhillings a week for keeping the books and aſſiſting to overlook the ſervants and work of his carding machinery. Both the places together made me about twelve ſhillings a week, which, added to my own pittance, enabled me to ſubſiſt my family pretty comfortably. When I had been here better than two years, two perſons at Birkenſhaw—the village where I reſided—built a ſcribbling-mill;* another

---

* A *ſcribbling-mill* is a mill where wool is prepared for ſpinning, previous to being woven into cloth. The labour

had been built about the fame time about a mile from the village, and to both thefe mills two ftocks were attached for milling cloth ; thefe required a fearcher to attend them, and our fupervifor faid that I was like to take them, as they could not pretend to appoint an additional fearcher to thefe fmall places, while I was near them.   To this I agreed, rather than quit the connection, though I loft four fhillings a week by the circumftance, as I could not poffibly attend Mr. Taylor's bufinefs and thefe additional mills too ; but I knew Hunfworth * mill was likely foon to be advanced.   At this crifis the principal partner at Birkenfhaw mill afked me if I was difengaged from Mr. Taylor.   I told him yes, as I could not poffibly overlook *all* the mills and Mr. Taylor's work too.   He then propofed, that, if I would throw up Hunfworth mill, and retain only the two mills at Birkenfhaw (for which I had got ten pounds a year allowed), and come and keep their books, and affift in over-feeing their work as I had done for Mr. Taylor, they would give me the fame wage, namely,

---

of fcribbling is now done by machinery, worked by fteam ; but formerly this kind of work ufed to be done by hand-machines, or machines moved by the hand.

  * Hunfworth is a village near Oakenfhaw, in the parifh of Birftall, four and a half miles fouth of Bradford, and has a population at this time of twelve hundred.   The Old Mills ftill remain.   The corn mills are worked by Mr. Thomas Briggs, of Hunfworth ; and there are alfo extenfive woollen manufactories and dye works carried on by the Meffrs. Taylors, of Hunfworth.

eight shillings a week, which would put me precisely on the same footing I was at Hunsworth; and he observed, that it would save me much walking every morning and evening, that I should be at home, and that I might get warm meals, &c. I told him I was aware of these advantages, but asked him if I might depend upon the *continuance* of the place, because I was sure of the mill, and the salary was likely soon to be advanced to an amount which would be worth as much to me—or nearly so—as the wage of their place, besides the choice of another mill at Heaton if I thought I could serve them all; and these I was pretty sure of for life, except an opportunity offered of getting a better place; but if I threw it up, I lost it entirely, and if I lost their place too, I should be in a shabby situation indeed, with Birkenshaw mills only. He said I might *depend* upon it. I spoke to Mr. Taylor and Mr. Thompson. Mr. Taylor was for me keeping the mill and refusing the place; Mr. Thompson said, if I thought I could confide in my supposed friend, to be sure it would be much easier for me. I verily thought I could, and therefore threw up the mill and accepted the place.

This was another very imprudent action into which I was betrayed by a too great confidence in professed friendship. I put them in a commodious way of keeping the books, which I had practised at Hunsworth. When I had been with them about two years, one Saturday evening, without a moment's notice, or any other reason assigned, the other partner told me drily, that they thought they could keep the books themselves, and had no further occasion for my service. I was astonished at this, and looked upon it, as it certainly was, as a very mean, as well as a very unfriendly, unfair, and ungenerous action. I had not sought the place; indeed, I had no thoughts about it. I was solicited to come to this place, and to throw up my searching at Hunsworth for this purpose, though I knew it was likely soon to be worth as much, or more, to me as theirs, and which, in all probability, I might retain, if I pleased, for life. The only difference was, their work was near home. I was promised I might *depend* upon the place, and was then presently kicked out of it; so that it looked as if a scheme had been formed by my professing friends to deprive me of the comfortable situation and prospect I had obtained through Mr. Taylor's favour, and turn me adrift in search of new prospects.

> " What then is friendship ? 'tis a name,
>   A charm that lulls to sleep ;
> A shade that follows *wealth* and *fame*,
>   But leaves the wretch to weep."

This event confirmed my conviction of the great sanity of Tim a' Lee's proverb, and the general necessity of acting upon his maxim, Trust no mortal.

This event ftripped me of all my before-ac-
quired benefits and profpects, and left me only
the ten pounds a year for Birkenfhaw mills, at a
time when all the neceffaries of life were greatly
enhanced, and my family increafed with feveral
more children. We ftruggled with the difficulties
brought upon us by this event for more than two
years, and it was a lofs to us of near forty pounds,
which was wrung from the backs and bellies of
me and my family in a very difficult period.
Mr. Thompfon and feveral others of my friendly
acquaintance had promifed me to do their beft
the firft opportunity that occurred, to obtain me
a better fituation. In the mean time we troubled
nobody with our complaints; we fuffered in
filence, and endeavoured to make the beft of
our fituation. The infpectorfhip of Gomerfall
diftrict was divided into two rounds, with an
annual falary of twenty-feven pounds annexed to
each of them. Jofhua Dixon, of Birftal, furveyed the one, and Robert Goodalls, of Church
lane,* the other. During this period Jofhua
Dixon died, and the two rounds were thrown
into one. Robert Goodall had five pounds added
to his former falary, which made it thirty-two
pounds per annum, for which he furveyed both
the rounds. Robert Goodall died in the month

---

* Church Lane is probably what is now called Thirk
Lane. It is the road leading from Cleckheaton to Birftall
by way of Spen Bridge and Spen Houfe. This road leads
through the hamlet of Gomerfall Hill Top.

of January, 1796, and I obtained the place January the 27th, 1796, which I ftill retain at this time, April the 19th, 1797. As I obferved before, the falary was thirty-two pounds per annum, befides fome other fmall emoluments arifing from ftamping blanks for the merchants and clothiers, &c.

I defire here to take notice—to the praife of a kind Providence, which, I am firmly perfuaded, prefides, governs, and difpenfes with infinite wifdom and goodnefs, towards *every individual*, and towards his *whole* creation—the critical timing of my obtaining this place. It was when I could fubfift my family no longer without breaking into my little real or perfonal property, and thereby greatly injuring my annual income or prefent convenience, either of which we could ill forego. Bleffed be God for his goodnefs !

I return to take notice of the feveral events which happened in my family during this period ; that is, from my fecond marriage to the prefent time, April 20th, 1797. Mrs. Birkhead perfuaded my daughter Betty to refide with them, and I gave my confent. This was from no *liberal* motive, but fhe engaged Betty to do the fervant's work, and had only a little meat to find her, for I myfelf found her clothes, even to the value of a coarfe linen brat to wafh up the pots in. The family, therefore, which I brought to Birkenfhaw confifted of myfelf, my wife, my eldeft fon Tommy, my third fon John, and my little daughter Patty, about fifteen weeks old. I sent Tommy to school to my old acquaintance Benny Brooke, at Tong,* and John to Eaft Bierley school (it being much nearer) to Mr. William Kellet.

Nine weeks and five days after my coming to Birkenshaw, I was visited by one of the moft severe trials I had ever experienced hitherto, in the sudden death of my darling child, John Wright, my third son and sixth child, who died in my arms on Saturday, July the 19th, 1783, about three o'clock in the afternoon. He was buried on the Monday evening following, being the 21ft of the fame month, in the New Chapel-yard at Cleckheaton, clofe by the north fide of his brother William's grave and his mother's tomb. There his beloved remains reft in the peaceful grave, in a fure and certain hope of a joyful refurrection to eternal life when the Arch-angel's trumpet fhall give the final fummons, " for the trumpet fhall found and the dead fhall be raifed incorruptible." † This glorious hope

---

* Tong, in the parifh of Birftall, is a quiet rural village, four miles from Bradford, and the population of the town-fhip in 1861 was 3035. This is the Tunic of the Domef-day Book, and is generally called the Lordfhip of Tong. The heirs to thefe fertile lands from the times of the Saxons have been the families of the Tongs, the Mirfields, and the Tempefts; and Colonel Plumbe Tempeft is now lord of the manor, and refides in an old hall built of brick which overlooks a beautiful vale, on the other fide of which ftands the eftablifhment of Fulneck, the feat of the Mora-vians in Yorkfhire.

† 1 Cor. xv. 22.

we owe to Jefus' dying love, who will moft affuredly raife to a new, a happy, and an endlefs life, the diffolved bodies of all thofe who fleep in Him, as I doubt not *all* thofe who die in their infancy moft certainly do.   No ftone or tomb-ftone has yet been laid or erected to his memory, the ftraitnefs of my circumftances have hitherto prevented me from doing it; but if ever I am able I mean to do it with the firft opportunity that may offer; and if I never fhould be able, I will endeavour, if it be poffible, to engage fome branch of my family to do it for me fooner or later.   Meanwhile I have prepared the following epitaph, which may be fhortened, if need be, of the four laft lines in the poetry, or fome words, perhaps, in the preceding part.   For John Wright's tombftone :—

In Memory of

JOHN WRIGHT,

Third fon of Thomas Wright, of Birkenfhaw, whofe body refts in hope within this tomb, and who died fuddenly, in his afflicted father's arms, on Saturday, July the 19th, 1783.
Aged 8 years and 6 months.

Here all the flattering hopes of youthful bloom,
Untimely blafted, wither in the tomb :
Sudden death fnatch'd him from his guiltlefs play,
And clos'd his eyes, to wake in endlefs day.
Grac'd with each merit years like his could boaft,
So foon difcovered, and fo early loft ;
Studious by every pleafing art to prove
The endearing tendernefs of filial love,

Which, guided ftill by Nature's gentleft voice,
Prepar'd him for that Heaven he now enjoys.
O let not grief pronounce that doom unjuft,
Which lays a parent's faireft hopes in duft.
Lord, I fubmit to Thee, all good and wife,
And yield the infant victim to the fkies.

John Wright was near two years and three quarters old at the time of his mother's death. I always fufpected he was hurt by a fright his mamma gave him, by fuddenly fcolding and fhaking him when he cried and was troublefome one night in bed, when he was a little one, which at the time nearly threw him into fits, and I had much ado to recover him from the fright. He was ever after fubject to be frighty upon any fudden alarm, and would frequently get out of bed in dreams, and fometimes awoke out of his fleep under an unaccountable fright and tremor; which I always fufpected to be caufed, or at leaft increafed, by the above-mentioned fright, though I may be miftaken, and it might be purely natural : however, it is needful to be as careful as poffible not to give children any fudden fright. As he grew up he was very remarkable for the fondeft filial affection, and would frequently be telling me in his childifh way how dearly he loved me beyond everything elfe in the world. If I had at any time been out late, if he had been a-bed and awoke when I came in, he would have leaped out of bed, run to my embraces, and welcomed me home with the tendereft expreffions. He was remarkably folicitous about his prayers, and before he had learned the Lord's Prayer by heart, would have called on me, if I forgot, to teach him them before he would have gone to fleep. A few weeks before his death, being playing with his brother Tommy at Brook-houfes, he got fomething into his ear which frighted him; they put a drop of rum in his ear, which, they faid, brought out fome kind of a fmall black infect. One night foon after, I had been from home, and when I came in in the evening, he came weeping down ftairs, and faid fomething made a noife in his ears which frighted him, and thought it was fomething he had got in his ear at the time above mentioned. I took him on my knee and it ceafed, and I put him to bed, and he complained no more of it afterwards. Whether this circumftance might be any caufe of the ftrange diforder which afterwards cut him fo fuddenly off, I cannot tell; God knoweth.

On Thurfday, the 10th day of July, 1783, there came on, about ten o'clock in the evening, one of the moft dreadful ftorms of thunder and lightning I had ever beheld. It was extremely awful and alarming indeed. I got my family to bed, where, I think, they would have remained pretty compofed, but a neighbour woman coming in with her children, extremely frightened, alarmed my children too, fo that they and our maid (a Matty Webfter from Tong) ran from their own bed to my wife and the little one, where, with two of our neighbour's children, there were feven in one bed, at the head and feet. John was between two at the feet. I told him not to be afraid, but to commend himfelf to the divine protection, which I believe he did. He afterwards called me to him : when I came I found him bathed in fweat, occafioned by lying over-head in bed, to avoid feeing the lightning. He faid, " Daddy, I will fall afleep if I can, and then I fhall not fee the lightning. Will you pray for me ? you know, when I am afleep I cannot pray for myfelf." This requeft, uttered by my dear child with a fteady ferioufnefs, ftruck me greatly, and I immediately went to my knees to recommend him to the divine mercy and protection. A few days before he died, John Kitfon, fon of Jonathan Kitfon, near whom we had lived before we came to Birkenfhaw, came upon an errand to our next door neighbour, and had a little bay galloway with him ; at that time, Tommy and John, my two fons, were going to fee their grandfather at Brook-houfes, and John Kitfon told my younger boy, that if he would go the lane way with him, he fhould ride upon the galloway, of which he was fo fond ; and importuned me fo much to let him go, that I confented, upon John Kitfon's promifing to let him ride, and to proceed flowly and carefully ; but as foon as he was out of my fight he made my boy difmount, and then fet off on the full trot down the lane, and my boy ran after him moſt of the way to Gomerſall.   I was exceeding unhappy after I knew this, as the day was uncommonly hot and ſultry, and muſt almoſt ſuffocate the child to run after the horſe ſo far and ſo faſt under a burning ſun; and I have often been afraid the overheating himſelf ſo much on this occaſion, and bathing in cold water while he was yet hot (as I underſtood he afterwards did), might contribute to the bringing on that diſorder which ſoon after put a period to his life. Whether it was ſo or not, I cannot tell, but I have often reflected upon it with extreme regret, that ever I ſuffered him to go with that unlucky, miſchievous boy; and if I had known the trick he would have played him, he ſhould not have gone with him upon any conſideration.

On Friday, the 18th of July, 1783, he got a milk breakfaſt as uſual, and was impatient with the maid to get it ready, as he was afraid of his maſter being angry at his being late to ſchool. When he was going he looked fondly at me, and I aſked him if I muſt go part of the way with him—as I frequently did—and he ſaid, "Yes, if you pleaſe, daddy."   I accordingly went with him over the firſt field, and over the ſtile into the ſecond, where we ſtood to part. He turned about, and ſtroked his hands over his little thighs, and ſaid, "Daddy, I am ſomehow ſtiff over here, and it almoſt makes me lame." I told him he had, perhaps, been running or leaping, which had occasioned it, and I hoped it would be better soon. He said yes, he hoped it would. I suppose his running after the horse, above mentioned, so far and so fast, might be the occasion of this stiffness. He then came and kissed me, and blessed me, and bid me farewell, as he almost always did when he parted with me; but having gone a few steps he turned about and said, " Daddy, stay on that pit-hill * (a pit-hill that was just by) while I go up the Kirkgate, and I can turn about and look at you." I said, " Well, my dear," and he proceeded. As I looked after him I thought he looked a very poor look, as if he was not very well, as indeed, he had done for some days; and my heart ached in an uncommon manner at parting with him, as if foreboding the heavy affliction which awaited me. It was much I did not take him back with me, but as it was now about nine o'clock, and he would be down to his dinner, I thought it would not be long ere I saw my child again. I little thought this would be the last interview I should ever have with my dear little boy *out of doors;* yet so it proved, to my unspeak-

---

* This would very likely be an accumulation of rubbish thrown out of some coal-pit, on the side of the road from Birkenshaw to Bradford, as such heaps are yet very common. There is a lane still called Kirkgate, which leads up to an ancient cross, on the hill. The fact of this cross being on the hill, must have given rise to the name (Kirkgate), as there was not, until a few years ago, any church at Birkenshaw.

able affliction. I ftood near the place till he walked up the oppofite field, called the Kirkgate, where he turned about, as he had faid, to take *from thence* his laft look at his daddy. I waited till he was out of fight, and afterwards returned home. He ufed to come to his dinner towards one o'clock, but falling badly at fchool, his mafter fent him home fooner, and it was about twelve o'clock at noon when he came in at the back-door and up the entry, weeping, to me, as I was fet in the houfe rocking the little child in the cradle. I afked him what was the matter, and he faid, " Daddy, my head aches." I faid, " Does it, my love?" and he faid, " Yes, fadly, and I have thrown up my breakfaft at fchool." I told him not to cry, it would make his head worfe, and he immediately forbore. I took him upon my knee, and tied my pocket-handkerchief about his head, and being fet in a rocking-chair, he lay his head back in my arm, and I rocked him upon my knee. He prefently afked for fomething to drink ; the weather being very hot, our beer was turning hard, and I thought it would not be proper for him; I therefore afked him if he would choofe fome milk? He said, yes. I got him fome, of which he drank, then lay in my arm again, and feemed difpofed to fleep. I told him if he could fleep, I would carry him, if he would, into our bed, and he would lie eafier, and I hoped fleep would cure his head, to which he confented. As I was carrying him up-ftairs, he afked to drink again ; and after laying him in bed, and taking off all his clothes but his ftockings, I fetched him the milk again, of which he drank a fecond time, and compofed himfelf to fleep. I went down to the child in the cradle (my wife being out of the houfe), but he prefently called upon me again, and I ran up-ftairs. He was reaching to puke ; I held my hand on his forehead, and he threw up the milk he had drunk, which came curdled from his ftomach. I fuppofe clear water would have been beft to have given him, if I had known it, for he was much worfe than I imagined, as I took it to be nothing more than a common fit of the headache, occafioned, perhaps, by the un- common heat of the day, and from which fleep would effectually relieve him. I went to fee him often, and he feemed to fleep kindly, which abated my fears, and I concluded he was doing well. I ordered my wife to get fome tea and bread and butter ready againft he awoke, as I thought he muft be hungry then, as he had parted with his breakfaft before, and tea would be more fuitable for him than ftronger meat. She accordingly got it ready, and fet it by the fire to keep warm againft he awoke ; but alas ! my dear poorly child never eat more. In the forenoon Mr. William Johnftone, of Gomerfall- hill-top,* had called upon me as he went to

---

* Gomerfall Hill Top. A hamlet a little to the fouth- eaft of Gomerfall, and not far from Birftall. It lies exactly

Bradford, and engaged me to meet him at Mr. James Wilkinfon's, at five o'clock in the afternoon. I carefully attended, and very frequently went to look at my child, till betwixt five and fix o'clock in the evening, and though I thought he flept *long*, yet I thought he flept kindly, and ftill hoped he would be well when he awoke. I therefore ventured to fulfil my engagement, after leaving a ftrict charge with my family to obferve him with the utmoft care.

I obferve here, that fome unfriendly perfons, and particularly one perfon, who profeffed the greateft refpect and friendfhip for me, and even affected to confider me as one of her own family, and to whom, and to whofe family, I had behaved with the greateft generofity and good nature, laid hold of this circumftance to reprefent me as wanting in affection to my child ; as being *all* the afternoon from him, and taking little notice of him, which flander was as falfe as it was malicious in every circumftance. They alfo reported that the milk I gave him to drink was four ; but if it was (for I did not tafte it), it was more than I knew, and when I queftioned our maid about it fhe pofitively afferted the contrary. Nay, the perfon above referred to, went fo far as to infinuate (to Mrs. Birkhead, her near relation, and my greateft enemy), that we had poifoned

---

between Great and Little Gomerfall, and at about equal diftances from each of thefe places.

the child. I believe this lying flander was aimed chiefly againft my wife, though fhe told her alfo that I was a furious fellow, and curfed and fwore like a common collier, &c. &c. This, indeed, was a notorious falfehood; yet I believe what fhe faid againft me caufed Mrs. Birkhead to behave in a worfe manner than ufual to me about this time, and muft therefore attach no fmall guilt to the perfon's mind, as a common tale-bearer and mifchief-maker. What her motive could be for this proceeding, I know not, except it was to curry favour with her relation, with whom fhe had been but on fhy terms for fome time paft; yet I have heard Mrs. Birkhead repeatedly fpeak of her and her family with the utmoft difrefpect and contempt. This was an inftance of fhameful ingratitude, and an additional proof of the *general* invalidity and infincerity of common profeffed friendfhips. I certainly wanted not affection to induce me to do the beft I could for my own child, whofe life and welfare were, if poffible, dearer to me than my own.

I returned from Mr. Wilkinfon's a little after eight o'clock, fo that I had been fomewhat more than two hours away. When I came near home I obferved our maid running to meet me, and my fpirits immediately funk, for I feared my child was worfe. I afked her what was the matter? and fhe faid John had awoke, and was on a very ftrange fafhion. I ran immediately to him, and found him apparently in convulfions.

The neighbours flocked in, and as he lay upon one of their knees, I thought he was expiring. It is impoffible to exprefs the extreme agony of forrow with which this fudden, fevere, and un-expected ftroke overwhelmed me. It pierced like a fword through my foul, and almoft rendered me diftracted. Mifs Wilkinfon (Sally), who had come in amongft the reft, came to me and de-fired me to go down ftairs, " for," fhe faid, " you diftrefs the child; bad as he is, he follows you with his eye wherever you go, and anfwers you groan for groan." I went down into the kitchen, and as I thought him expiring, earneftly recom-mended his foul to God. Prefently one came, and faid, " Tommy, do not forrow fo exceed-ingly, your child is coming to himfelf again." I faid, " Is he alive?" They faid, " Yes, and feems coming out of a fit." I blefled God there was yet fome hope for his life, and immediately defpatched a perfon for the doctor with all fpeed. He fent him directly, and ftayed behind himfelf to bring the medicines he might order for the child when he returned. The doctor feemed at a lofs to know what the child ailed, but finding him very delirious, and to complain much of his breaft, exprefled a fufpicion that he had got fome-thing he could not digeft, and afked if I had got any fpirituous liquors? but this was not the cafe, nor had he taken anything which anyone knew of, which could poffibly do him the leaft harm. I have fince fufpected that as the fummer had been uncommonly hot, he might, when heated with play at fchool, have drank of the ftanding water in the ditches (as there was no good water near the fchool), and taken in the fpawn of fome animal, which might have bred in his ftomach, and killed him, but this is only conjecture. The doctor propofed to bleed him and give him a clyfter, which he did, and he faid—I heard—afterwards, that but for this he would not have furvived two hours. When he returned, he fent him a thin mixture, and a bottle of drops. We gave him fome little of the mixture two or three times, and one of the drops—in number twenty. I perceived the doctor thought he would die immediately, but in this he was miftaken. Old Matty Birkhead, and a young woman named Betty Fox, and myfelf, watched all night with him, and a fore, afflicted, agonizing night he paffed. I could have been extremely glad if my child had been able to have talked fenfibly with me, if it had but been a little ; but this could not be obtained ; only now and then when his eye catched me, he would call me his bonny daddy, and repeat other fond expreffions he had before been wont to make ufe of ; and once he faid, " Come daddy, lie down by me, and let us fall afleep together," and threw his arms eagerly about my neck, and was foon toffing and agonizing again.

I had fent early in the morning by Betty Fox for his fifters from Brook-houfes, and they got up fome time before he died. At intervals he knew his eldeft fifter, and called her once or twice by her name. As he continued fo long beyond the doctor's expectations, I began to entertain hopes that he might be fpared ; but I was miftaken. About three o'clock in the afternoon (Saturday, July the 19th), my family being at dinner, he feemed to recover his reflection, and be pretty compofed, and feeing me weeping over him, he fuddenly ftretched out his little arms, and with a look of inexpreffible love and pity, and the fondeft concern to comfort me, cried out, " Come daddy, come joy, come joy, come joy ! " I faid, " I will, my dear," and bent down my head to meet him. He threw his arms about my neck, preffed me to his bofom, and eagerly kiffed and bleffed me. He held me clofe fome time, but at length flacking his arms, I raifed my head ; he ftill followed me with his eyes, and appeared very much concerned to fee me in fo much forrow. I afked if he would kifs me again ; he quickly and eagerly replied, " Aye, bonny daddy, I will ! " and ftretched out his arms to embrace me again. He kiffed me with great fondnefs, and faid with much earneftnefs, " Blefs you, my daddy ! blefs you, my bonny daddy ! " This was the laft affectionate embrace which my beloved John gave his afflicted daddy, and thefe the laft loving words he uttered. Soon after he had fpoken them, he turned his head upon the pillow and feemed inclined to puke. His fifter

Betty, who was standing by me, said, "Daddy, if he could get something up, it would perhaps ease him." I thought it perhaps might, and therefore took him gently on my knee, lay my hand upon his forehead, and leaned him towards the floor. He threw up about two spoonfuls of the mixture he had taken, and immediately his hands hung down, and I perceived his head would fall too if I took away my hand. I told his sister Betty he was dying, she cried out and alarmed the family, and they alarmed the neighbours, who came running up to us. One of them would have taken him from me, saying I sorrowed so violently; but I said, "No, he shall die in his father's arms, where I am sure he would choose to die if he was capable of choosing." I accordingly kept him in my arms, and, while he was expiring, recommended his precious departing soul into the hands of his gracious Saviour.

Thus did I lose, as to *this* world, my darling child; thus was the desire of my eyes taken from me at a stroke; suddenly snatched from my paternal embraces, painfully torn from my bleeding heart! The killing image is still before me; my imagination recalls the distressing scene! I still hear thy last affectionate words calling upon me to come to thee, and pronouncing blessings upon me with thy expiring breath! I still see thee gasping in my arms, and resigning thy last breath in thy father's bosom! Farewell, my son, my son; my dearly beloved John! very pleasant haft thou been unto me; thy love to me was wonderful, furpaffing the common inftances of filial affection. I am diftreffed, I am exceedingly diftreffed for thee, my darling child! Thou fhalt no more play around thy daddy, and entertain him with thy engaging and affectionate prattle! Thou fhalt no more be at a lofs for comparifons and numbers to exprefs the greatnefs of thy love to me! I fhall no more hear thy fweet voice eagerly bleffing me, and when returning home, thou

> "No more fhalt run to lifp thy fires return,
> Or climb his knees the envied kifs to fhare."

I fhall no more behold thee on this fide the grave, but I fhall fee thee again at that day—the day of the glorious appearing of our Lord and Saviour the Lord Jefus Chrift, who fhall change our vile bodies, that they may be fafhioned like unto his glorious body, according to the mighty working whereby he is able to fubdue even all things unto himfelf. Till then, farewell, my beloved John! Thou art engraven on the palms of my hands; yea, upon the table of my heart! I fhall go mourning to the grave for thee, my fon! Farewell, my fweet babe, till we meet again in happier regions, beyond the reach of fin and forrow, pain and death; farewell, till we meet again to part no more,

> "High in falvation and the climes of blifs,"

and join together—with the reft of our family, I

truft, through the goodnefs of God in Jefus
Chrift—to blefs, and praife, and adore our gracious Redeemer for his unfpeakable goodnefs and
mercy for ever and ever.

The forrow of mind to which this event fubjected me, funk my fpirits fo very low, that the
doctor began to apprehend very much danger,
and I was obliged to exert my utmoft refolution
to furmount the afflictive impreffion ; yet I fuffered confiderably in my health on this occafion,
and feel, or imagine I feel, the effects of it to
this day. Some perfons cenfured me pretty freely,
as forrowing over much ; but it is an eafy thing
to find fault. Different perfons have different
feelings, and it had pleafed my Maker to endow
me with very acute ones, efpecially with refpect
to my children. I murmured not at the divine
difpenfation—I knew that God did all things well
—but I could not diveft myfelf of the nature
which he had given me ; and whether my cen-
furers know or know it not,

" Full well I know the twifted ftrings
Of ardent hearts combined,
When rent afunder, how they bleed,
How hard to be *refigned.*"

I may obferve here that I had wrote an elegy
on the death of my daughter Mary, confifting of
ninety-five verfes, with notes. Mr. John Wefley
publifhed about one half of thefe verfes in the
" Arminian Magazine," * for, I think, February

* My grandfather's memory has been a little at fault in

1778. I wrote alfo feveral copies of verfes at different times, and in different metres, on the death of my fon John. Thefe I mean to tranfcribe, and put all together, and the reader may probably find them attached to thefe papers.

In the end of the fummer of 1786 I was made a commiffioner in a chancery law affair, refpecting the eftate of my deceafed friend, Mr. John Broadley, of Rawfolds. I was called to a meeting on this account at Wakefield, where it was thought neceffary that I and the attorney who was employed in the affair—a Mr. L-m-top, Bradford—fhould proceed immediately to Sir George Robinfon's,* in Northamptonfhire, to obtain the fignature of a young woman who was concerned in the cafe, and who, at this time, refided in Sir George's family. This journey being unexpected by me, I had provided no money but what I happened to have in my pocket, which amounted to three or four pounds, and knowing that travelling in the chaife would be very expenfive, I afked my companion if he was provided with fufficient cafh for the journey? He affured me he was, which made me remain

---

this date. The " Arminian Magazine," edited at firft by John Wefley, commenced with the beginning of the year 1778. The poem here alluded to, which is printed complete at the end of the prefent volume, was inferted in the " Arminian Magazine " for February, 1779, vol. ii. p. 96.

* Sir George Robinfon, Bart. was elected member for Northampton in 1774. His feat was at Crauford, near Kettering, in Northamptonfhire.

eafy on that account. We accordingly hired a chaife, and proceeded on our journey, through Barnfley, Sheffield, Chefterfield, Mansfield, Nottingham, Loughborough, Leicefter, and foon to the feat of Sir George Robinfon in Northamptonfhire. We found the family gone from home on a party of pleafure, and the young woman we were in fearch of was gone along with them, and it appeared they were not expected home again for fome weeks or months to come. We of courfe did not obtain the defign of our journey, but were obliged to return home again without our errand.

As Sir George's feat was fituated about the midway between what is called the upper and lower roads to London, we concluded to crofs the country forwards to the lower road, and return home again that way. We therefore ordered the poftilion to drive forwards to the next market-town, which was called Oundle. In this paffage my companion told me that he had expended all his cafh, and had not as much left as would pay for our prefent paffage. I had fufpected fomething of this nature before, as he had fpunged all my cafh from me, except five fhillings I had referved which he did not know of. I think I never felt fo chagrined and embarraffed in my mind in all my life as I did upon this occafion. At a diftance of 140 or 150 miles from home, riding in a chaife and appearing and living like gentlemen, without money in our pockets, and unacquainted with a

fingle perfon in the country, was a moft morti-
fying circumftance indeed.   I fcolded my companion moft feverely for the abfurdity and imprudence of his conduct, efpecially as I had warned
him of the circumftance before we fet off from
Wakefield.   He kept his temper, however, and
affected to laugh at my chagrin; faid I was a
young traveller, that he had been in worfe fitua-
tions than this, and faid, "We will find fome
way to extricate ourfelves, I'll warrant you."
We arrived at Oundle, and my companion immediately walked off into the town, defiring me to
fit down in the inn till he returned.   I waited,
however, at the inn door all the time, under no
fmall anxiety of mind, for fear he fhould defert
me, and leave me in the lurch.   However, he
foon returned, and produced cafh to pay our fare
and expenfes at the inn.   We then hired the
chaife to Wansford, where he paid the fare, and
for a genteel dinner alfo.   It feems he had pawned
a pair of valuable knee-buckles for a prefent
fupply, and fupplied their place with a pair of
plain fteel ones; but his cafh again running low,
he hired a feat in a ftage-coach that was paffing
by, and I took one on the outfide, to Grantham,
where we arrived in the evening.   Here our
finances were quite run out, except the two
dormant half-crown pieces in my pocket, which
I kept as a laft referve.   I was therefore obliged,
though very unwillingly, to pawn my watch for
one guinea, which had coft me four guineas, and

was a very good one, and a favourite, under a promife, however, from the perfon who had it, that he would return it again when we fent back the guinea, and one fhilling for intereft; and my companion promifed pofitively that he both could and would obtain it for me again when we got home. However, I never faw it fince, although, I may note here, that I afterwards fent him a guinea and fhilling to fulfil his promife, and get my watch again. However, I never heard more of it, and I loft this money too, as he never re-paid it me again; but he lent me a pretty good watch of his own, which wanted fome little repairs, till he fhould obtain mine: this I never returned, and mean to retain it ftill, in lieu of my own.

We hired places on the outfide the York ftage-coach, to Doncafter the next day, and fet off early in the morning. Soon after we fet out, a dog brought a hare acrofs the road, and killed her juft by us. The coachman alighted, and fecured pufs in the coach-box, and then drove on again. As there happened to be no infide paffengers, he permitted us to fit within the coach; fo that this proved a cheap and an eafy ftage for us. We reached Doncafter in the afternoon, and inquired for fome of the diligences, to obtain a lift to Wakefield, but they were all gone. However, in returning over the bridge, we met with two chaife-boys returning with four empty chaife-horfes to Wakefield, two of which had faddles upon them. We bargained with them for half-a-crown for a ride to Wakefield, which we reached after dark in the evening. My horfe was a very uneafy one, and I was much fatigued when I got to Wakefield, but after getting fome refrefhment, I was determined to walk home on foot that night. My partner was tired, and wifhed to ftay till morning. I told him I thought *he* had better, but that I could walk home well enough. He fwore he could walk home better than me, for he was but half as old; and he was determined, if I walked home, he would too. I faid it was right, fo we fet off homewards late in the evening—perhaps nine or ten o'clock. By the time we were turned of Ardfley, he was taken ill of the belly-ache. He groaned and cried out bitterly, walked double-fold, and we could hardly get any forwards at all. It was near midnight, people all a-bed, and nobody ftirring, and I did not know what to do with him; but by-and-by a bailiff overtook us, upon a little galloway, with whom he was acquainted. He offered him to ride, and we helped him on; he rode about two or three hundred yards, and then could bear to ride no farther. We helped him to difmount, and the bailiff was obliged to leave him upon my hands. I had a bad job of it, and feared I fhould have to ftay all night in the lanes with him; however, I encouraged and haled him forwards as well as I could, till we reached the firſt public-houſe on this ſide Tingle-moor turnpike-bar. Here he was ſo ill, that he would have us try to gain admiſſion and relief; we therefore ſhouted the landlord out of bed, who came in his ſhirt and talked with us through the window. We told him our names and where we reſided; that the gentleman was taken ill on the road, which had thrown us late; that he wanted ſomething warm to relieve him, for which he would pay, and we would leave the houſe again immediately. But in ſpite of all we could ſay, the fearful landlord would not open the door nor afford us any relief. My companion was chagrined and highly affronted, and almoſt ready to weep, and threatened the man with proſecution for refuſing to relieve a gentleman taken badly on the road. But all would not do, and we were forced to proceed on our journey to Adwalton. We reached this place early in the morning, and by good fortune found the family up, they having been detained late with company the night before. We ſat down by a good fire, called for a bowl of rum and milk, which I helped my ſick companion to drink a part of, and then reſumed my walk for home, which I reached before break of day, with my two half-crowns in my pocket, after the moſt fatiguing journey, both of body and mind, that I ever experienced. Nine or ten years afterwards I received nine or ten pounds as a compenſation for the trouble and expenſe I was at on this occafion, which did little, if anything, more than barely reimburfe me for the expenfe I was at out of my own pocket.*

I have mentioned before that my daughter Betty went to refide at Brook-houfes fome time before we removed to Birkenfhaw. About this time the old woman at Brook-houfes behaved remarkably ill, and did all fhe could to prevent my children (for Sally was there alfo) from coming to fee me. I had wifhed to fee and fpeak with my daughter Betty, and had fent for her repeatedly in vain. I had to go to the balm-mill—which was juft by the houfe—from whence I fent a perfon to defire my daughter to ftep over to the mill and fpeak with me. She fent me word her grandmother would not fuffer her to come. Provoked at this, out of all patience, I went over myfelf in much warmth, determined to take her home with me, and in my way met with the old, religious, wicked woman. We fell out feverely, and I followed her to the door-ftones and ordered my daughter to gather up her clothes and come away immediately. She faid fhe would as fpeedily as poffible. While fhe was doing this, the old woman told her, that if fhe would forfake and difown her father, and never look the way he was, or call him father again, fhe was welcome to ftay there. To this wicked and

---

* This narrative alfo is inferted here from the end of the original manufcript of this autobiography.

fhameful propofal my girl anfwered, as it was her duty to do, that fhe would not. I told the old woman we had heard that fhe faid we had poifoned my lately deceafed child. She faid, " No, it was my *great friend* at Birkenfhaw that faid fo," meaning the perfon before alluded to. I took her (Betty) with me to the mill, and her fifter Sally followed us, and begged to go home with me too; elfe, fhe faid, they would never let her fee me. I therefore took them both home with me. All the clothes on Sally's back were, perhaps, not worth fifteen pence; I therefore had new clothes to buy her, and I fent her to fchool with her fifter Betty. After fome time, my girls had to go to the mantua-maker at Height with fome new coats to make, and they afked my leave to call at Brook-houfes as they paffed by, and afk the old people how they did. I gave them leave, and they called as they returned. The old woman detained Sally, although I had charged them not to ftay, but to return home ; and when Betty urged my order, and her fear of my being angry, fhe faid fhe might tell her father that fhe could not fpare Sally yet, and he muft let her ftay awhile there. I ordered Betty to tell her when fhe faw her again, that I had no objection to any of my children going to fee them, or ftaying with them awhile, lefs or more, provided they did not abufe me to my children, nor attempt to alienate their affection from me, nor hinder them from coming to fee

me when I or they defired. This laft article they
complied with pretty well afterwards, becaufe
they were otherwife afraid of a difagreeable vifit
from me again ; but they continued to abufe me
to my children behind my back, with as much
virulence as ever. They had not liberality enough
to fend Sally to any genteel place of education ;
fhe was only fent occafionally to the petty fchools
in the neighbourhood, and even there, for the
moft part, I had her fchool-wage to pay myfelf.
She was kept great part of her time immured in
a chamber, fpinning worfted, fecluded from all
company but that of a few neighbouring cottagers
and themfelves, from whom fhe could never learn
one liberal fentiment. Hence, the child was left
very deficient in her manners and education, from
the fordid avarice of her grandparents. However,
fhe refided with them from this time till her
marriage. Betty dwelt with me a confiderable
time after this, and I fent her to fchool to learn
writing and accounts. At length her grandmother
happened to be without a fervant again, and, wifhing to engage Betty to fupply the place of one,
at a cheap rate, as fhe had done before, fhe
therefore encouraged her to go live with them.
Betty was perfuaded, and obtaining my confent,
fhe went and refided with them from this time
till her marriage alfo. However, fhe found her
fituation very difagreeable ; fhe was obliged to do
all their drudgery work, and was fubjected to the
difagreeable neceffity of hearing her father abufed

in the moft illiberal manner eveiy time he was named ; and as fhe had a tender affection for her father, this circumftance hurt her filial feelings not a little. She was almoft reduced to a fkeleton, and I was much afraid fhe was haftening into a decline, and had thought of taking her home again immediately, when fhe was relieved from her painful fituation by marriage.

I fent Tommy to fchool all the time he was with me at Birkenfhaw. I put him apprentice to Meffrs. John and George Nicholfon (father and fon), bookfellers, ftationers, and printers, at Bradford, in March, 1787, for five years, ending March, 1792. I note, his grandfather advanced twenty pounds for him on this occafion, which was required as a premium by his mafters. I take notice next, that my fecond wife during this period bore me the following additional children, at the following places, and in the following order :—

MARTHA WRIGHT, my fourth daughter and eighth child (the firft by my fecond marriage), was born on Tuefday, the 28th day of January, 1783, a quarter paft two o'clock in the afternoon, one year, twelve weeks, and one day after our marriage, and five years and a half after the birth of my fon William, in Cleckheaton-upper-lane, under the roof with Jonathan Kitfon's. She was baptized by the Rev. John Croffe, the *prefent* (1797) vicar of Bradford Church, at the Old White Chapel, in the north, on the 4th day of

April, 1783.   Sponfors, its father, mother, and grandmother Pinder; alfo Mrs. Elizabeth Wilkinfon and the clerk were prefent.

ANN WRIGHT, my fifth daughter and ninth child (the fecond by my fecond marriage), was born at Birkenfhaw, on Monday, the 27th day of June, 1785, a quarter paft one o'clock in the morning, two years, twenty-one weeks, and three days after the birth of her fifter Martha.   She was baptized by the Rev. Mr. Reuben Ogden, at the parifh church of Birftall, on Saturday, July the 30th, 1785.   Sponfors, its father, mother, and Mary Davifon.   The clerk was Jo. Shaw.

BENJAMIN WRIGHT, my fifth fon and tenth child (the third by my fecond marriage), was born at Birkenfhaw alfo, on Thurfday, the 20th day of September, 1787, half-an-hour after one o'clock in the afternoon, two years, twelve weeks, and one day after the birth of his fifter Ann.   He was baptized by the Rev. Mr. Reuben Ogden, at the parifh church of Birftall, on Friday, the 23rd day of November, 1787.   Sponfors, its father, mother, and grandfather Thomas Pinder.   Jo. Shaw, clerk.

HANNAH WRIGHT, my fixth daughter and eleventh child (the fourth by my fecond marriage), was born at Birkenfhaw alfo, on Friday, the 25th day of June, 1790, twenty-five minutes after four o'clock in the morning, two years, thirty-nine weeks, and four days after the birth of her brother Benjamin.   She was baptized by the

Rev. Mr. Reuben Ogden, at the parish church of Birstall, on Thursday, the 22nd day of July, 1790. Sponsors, her mother, her aunt Hannah Pinder, and her uncle William Pinder. Jo. Shaw, clerk.

JOHN WRIGHT, my second son of that name, my sixth son and twelfth child (the fifth by my second marriage), was born at Birkenshaw also, on Saturday, the 21st day of September, 1793, half-an-hour after five o'clock in the morning, three years, three months, and three days after the birth of his sister Hannah. He was baptized by the Rev. Mr. Rueben Ogden (Jo. Shaw, clerk), at the parish church of Birstall, on Tuesday, the 22nd day of October, 1793. Sponsors, his uncles Thomas Brooke and John Pinder, and his aunt Hannah Pinder. N.B. Ann Pinder, my wife's sister, was married to Thomas Brooke, of Birstall, joiner, the same day.

JOSEPH WRIGHT, my seventh son and thirteenth child (the sixth by my second marriage), was born at Birkenshaw also, on Friday, the 10th day of June, 1796, at half-an-hour after three o'clock in the afternoon, two years, thirty-seven weeks, and four days after the birth of his brother John. He was baptized by the Rev. Mr. Rueben Ogden (Jo. Shaw, clerk), at the parish church of Birstall, on Tuesday, the 27th day of September, 1796. Sponsors, his father, mother, and John Walker of Toftshaw-moor-side.

It is somewhat singular, that the preceding six

children were born precifely in the fame order that my firft wife bore her firft fix children, viz., the two firft births girls ; the third, a boy ; the fourth, a girl ; the fifth and fixth, boys ; which is one boy fhort of my firft wife's number.

In my account of John I have mentioned a remarkable thunder-ftorm which happened on Leeds' fair-day, at night, July the 10th, 1783.* I will juft notice the circumftances that fell under my obfervation on that occafion. The fummer had been unufually hot and fultry, and the air appeared to be uncommonly charged with fulphureous vapours, and we had received repeated intelligence in the public papers of deftructive earthquakes having happened in Italy and the adjacent countries. The ftorm came on from the north-weft, about ten o'clock in the evening. A diftant rumbling of the thunder was heard for fome time before, but it approached us faft, and we were foon furrounded by the loudeft and moft tremendous peals and crafhes of thunder I ever heard, and involved in almoft perpetual flafhes of the moft vivid lightning I ever faw. The fcene

---

* The month of July in the year 1783 is memorable for the terrible ftorms which traverfed almoft every part of our ifland, doing incalculable mifchief. Many people were killed, and there was a great deftruction of cattle and of other kinds of property. Accounts of the effects of thefe ftorms in many parts of the country, are given in the " Gentleman's Magazine," for this month and the month following, vol. liii. pp. 621, 707. It was the year of the great earthquake in Calabria.

was truly awful and alarming indeed, and accordingly, moſt of the neighbours were terribly alarmed, eſpecially the women, ſome of whom were nearly frightened into fits. Indeed, none who were awake could avoid being awed, except a ſet of drunken fellows in the neighbouring ale-houſe, who ſeemed inſenſible of the tremendous ſcene, and who were, perhaps, incapable, in their preſent condition at leaſt, of being alarmed even with a view of hell itſelf. There was one perſon there, however (a T——s R——s, a butcher from Gomerſal) whom the ſtorm caught ſober, though in the habit of being frequently drunk, in which ſituation he was remarkable for an overbearing, rude, and profane behaviour. This perſon appeared the greatlieſt alarmed I ever ſaw. He came to me, as I ſtood before my own door obſerving the ſtorm, apparently under the greateſt agitation of mind, and aſked me, weeping and greatly trembling, "Tommy, do you think it is the laſt day?" I ſaid, "No, it is a dreadful ſtorm of thunder and lightning; are you affrighted?" He ſaid, "Yes; but I am not ſo much afraid of the thunder as I am afraid of being killed, becauſe I am not fit to die." I told him that was a very ſufficient cauſe for fear, and recommended to him to acknowledge his ſin to God, and beg his pardon. He ſtepped into the public-houſe, and kneeling down by a table —utterly regardleſs of the taunts of the drunken company—wept and prayed very heartily. Yet, (alas! for the weaknefs of human refolutions,) I foon after faw him in the fame houfe, drunken, and profanely fwearing at a great rate. I gently reminded him of his fright in the thunder-ftorm; he blufhed, was afhamed, and acknowledged the impropriety of his conduct. He is long fince gone into the unfeen world. I watched till about three o'clock in the morning, and obferved the progrefs of the ftorm as accurately as I could. None of the flafhes feemed to come very near us but one, when the flafh and report were exactly together. It burft from a low cloud, apparently forty or fifty yards from us, with a horrid crafh, and took a direction down the caufeway, about a yard and a half above it. It ran in a zigzag form, or that of acute angles, and appeared to me for the moment fomething like a ftream of the moft glowing melted metal, iffuing from the furnace. John Green, a neighbour, who ftood by me at the time, faid he faw it burft from the cloud, and that it appeared to him like a globe of glowing fire. He would have it that it hurt one of his eyes, of which he did not fee perfectly for fome time afterwards. If it was fo, it muft have proceeded from the ftrong glare of the lightning from being fo near us—perhaps ten or twelve yards diftant. The report of the thunder fhook the houfes to the very foundation. There were three principal ftorms at the fame time: one fouth-eaft, over the top of Birftall from us; another towards Cleckheaton, fouth-weft; and a third, north, towards Bradford and Bingley. Thefe played againft each other for feveral hours, flafh for flafh, and roar for roar, like batteries of cannon. The intermingled flafhes fucceeded each other fo rapidly, that it was impoffible to diftinguifh to which flafh each clap of thunder belonged. The whole hemifphere appeared like a glowing oven, except in the very fhort intervals of pitchy darknefs; and I could fee the diftant Derbyfhire hills through a blue fulphureous medium, conftituted by the almoft conftant glare of the ftreaming lightning. The ftorm abated as the morning approached, and by three o'clock it had nearly fubfided altogether.

Upon the whole;—the dreadful rattling of the rolling thunder, and the frightful flafhes of the darting lightning; the burning glare of the glowing hemifphere, contrafted with the fhort intervals of black, pitchy, midnight darknefs; the fhaking of the houfes and windows at every repeated clap of thunder; and the furious dafh-ing of the rufhing rain; the folemn hour of the night, and the general affright and confternation of the neighbours, contributed, all together, to render it one of the moft awful and alarming fcenes I had ever beheld.

I tranfcribe the following defcription of a thunder-ftorm from Mr. Thomfon's "Summer," v. 1128, &c.

" 'Tis liftening fear, and dumb amazement all,
When to the ftartled eye the fudden glance

> Appears far fouth, eruptive through the cloud ;
> And following flower, in explofion vaft,
> The thunder raifes his tremendous voice.
> At firft, heard folemn o'er the verge of heaven,
> The tempeft growls ; but as it nearer comes,
> And rolls its awful burden on the wind,
> The lightnings flafh a larger curve, and more
> The noife aftounds : till over head a fheet
> Of livid flame difclofes wide ; then fhuts
> And opens wider ; fhuts and opens ftill
> Expanfive, wrapping ether in a blaze.
> Follows the loofen'd aggravated roar,
> Enlarging, deepening, mingling ; peal on peal
> Crufh'd horrible, convulfing heaven and earth.
> Down comes a deluge of fonorous hail,
> Or prone-defcending rain. Wide rent, the clouds
> Pour a whole flood ; and yet, its flame unquench'd,
> Th' unconquerable lightning ftruggles through,
> Ragged and fierce, or in red whirling balls,
> And fires the mountains with redoubled rage.
> Black from the ftroke, above, the fmouldering pine
> Stands a fad fhatter'd trunk ; and ftretch'd below,
> A lifelefs group the blafted cattle lie.''

I will next relate another incident that fell under my obfervation during this period. The cafe was this. A William Secker, a poor man who lived in a cottage in a valley called Cotterf-dale,* about a mile below Drighlington,† and who had a wife and a number of fmall children, was found dead one winter's morning in the fields,

---

* Cotterfdale, now called Cockerfdale, is a valley which lies about a mile to the north of Driglington and Gilder-fome Chapelry, and is about five miles eaft of Bradford, in the direction of Tong.

† Driglington, a ftraggling village, in the parifh of Birftall, is five miles fouth-eaft of Bradford. It is chiefly famous as a mining and coal diftrict, and contains 4,274 inhabitants.

laid on his back upon the fnow, by the fide of a fmall brook, in a valley that lies between Tong and Drighlington, about fifteen or twenty yards from a footpath that paffes between the two villages. No outward wound was found upon him when he was difcovered, except that a moufe or fome other fmall vermin appeared to have been upon his face in the night, and to have gnawed the fkin of his forehead a little in two or three places. He was conveyed home, and I was called to be upon the jury at the coroner's inqueft. The preceding evening to his being found was a remarkably ftormy one; it had fnowed violently all the afternoon, and continued to do fo moft part of the night, attended with a very ftrong eafterly wind, and extremely cold, which rendered it very incommodious and uncomfortable to fuch as were expofed to the inclemency of the weather. It appeared that Secker had called, when it was far in the evening, at a Michael Jilfon's, a public-houfe in Adwalton,* where he got a pint of ale, over which he fat, to warm himfelf, during the ftorm, for fome time. That, being a clothier by

---

* Aldwalton is in a flourifhing diftrict, on the high-road from Bradford to Wakefield, and is about five miles fouth-eaft from Bradford. In 1643 a fanguinary battle was fought here between the royalift army, under the Duke of Newcaftle, and the parliamentary forces, under Sir Thomas Fairfax, in which the latter were defeated, in confequence of which Bradford was befieged and taken by the royalifts. The place is generally called Atherton in the neighbourhood.

trade, he had a very fmall fadge of wool with him, in a fheet or poke ; that he departed from thence at a late hour, to go directly home, during the fury of the ftorm, and faid to Mr. Jilfon, when he fet off, " I will now go home and give them a duft," meaning his wife and one Snowden, whom he expected to find together ; and that this was the laft place where any one would own he was feen alive, being found dead early the next morning. He was diftinctly traced through the fnow down the footpath to his own door, as near as the intermingled footfteps of the neigh-bours would admit. He, *or fome other perfon*, was then traced back again over the laft ftile he had come over in returning home ; the perfon then left the footpath on the left hand, and proceeded at random through the fields and hedges, where there was no path, till he arrived over againft a place called Sha-field,* perhaps a mile from Secker's houfe ; he then turned through a bufhy place to the right, down the hill-fide towards Tong, and had left the aforefaid fmall parcel of wool hung in one of the hedges. He then pro-ceeded to the place where poor Secker's body was found laid upon its back in the fnow, by the fide of the brook before mentioned. It appeared that the returning track was fprinkled with blood *all* the

---

* Shafield, now called Shawfield, is a fhort diftance from Tong, in the direction of Weftgate Hill, or Wifket Hill; and is not far from the Bradford and Wakefield highroad.

way from Secker's houfe to where his body was found. This circumftance we (the jury) attempted to account for from the bleeding of his legs, being found with the ftockings down, and the legs appearing much fcratched in paffing through the hedges. This being admitted, together with the circumftance of *only one* man's footfteps appearing in the track, led me and the reft of the jury, for want of better attention, into what I have always confidered fince as .a miftaken verdict, of accidental death; for afterwards, when I came to think more clofely on the circumftances, I was fully convinced that foul play had been fhown to the poor man. A neighbour who was on the jury alfo (Mr. James Wilkinfon), to whom I communicated my fufpicions, and my reafons for them, thought exactly the fame with me, and feemed once almoft determined to have the body taken out of the grave for re-examination, but this dropped. The following are my reafons for my faid fufpicions :—

There was a man who was a widower, named John Snowden, who dwelt in a cottage adjoining to Secker. The neighbours had long and very much fufpected that a criminal correfpondence was carried on between Secker's wife and this fellow; Secker himfelf was jealous, and it had already produced feveral quarrels between the parties. As Secker was unreturned at fo late an hour, his wife and her gallant might conclude he would not return that night, efpecially as the

night was fo very ftormy; coming therefore un-
expectedly, he might probably furprife them together. It is natural to imagine a furious quarrel
would enfue, and the adulterer, by a blow with
a ftick, a poker, or the like, might kill the
hufband (whether *defignedly*, or by a *cafual* blow
in his own defence, God knoweth). Secker
being dead, the guilty pair would next confult
how to difpofe of the body, in order to conceal
the real caufe of his death ; when Snowden, being
a ftrong-built, middle-fized man, might eafily
take the corpfe on his back, with the legs over
his fhoulders, and the head hanging down behind ;
the wife would faften the little fadge of wool
about his neck, and he would proceed on the
returning track (leaving the little fadge in one of
the hedges by the way, as though Secker had
dropped it himfelf), to the place where the body
was found, and after having dropped it, go the
few remaining yards down the fhallow brook,
without ftepping in the fnow till he reached the
footpath which led him back home, and where
his footfteps would be mingled with thofe of
other paffengers, and almoft obliterated before
morning by the falling fnow. By this difpofition
of the body and fadge, they might fuppofe that
people would be led to conclude that Secker
himfelf had wandered from his own houfe in the
ftorm, and perifhed in the fnow; and for want
of accurate attention in the jury, their expectations were but too well verified. I went with

my fellows of the jury to view the body; the
other jurors took a flight view of it as it lay
upon the floor, and then withdrew. I ftayed
behind and looked at it more carefully. I obferved that the hollow of the right ear ftood full
of blood, which drained from the cavity of the
ear, and had trickled plentifully down into his
hair, as the body lay upon its back upon the floor.
This circumftance evidently denoted violence,
and we ought, by all means, to have procured a
furgeon to have examined the head very accurately. Secker's fhoe ought alfo to have been
compared with the impreffion in the fnow; but
both thefe circumftances were overlooked. It
is well known that a fmart blow on the back of
the ear will break the jugular vein without breaking the fkin, which, by inundating the brain with
blood, is known to be inftant death. This was
probably the cafe with poor Secker, and accounts
for the blood in his ear at this time, as well as
for the blood that was fprinkled through the returning track to where his body was found; and
it was obferved that no blood was feen in Secker's
track from Adwalton to his own houfe. His
ftockings being down and his legs fcratched, is
eafily accounted for from the man's holding him
on his fhoulders by the legs, and paffing through
fo many hedges with him in that pofition; befides,
blood was found in the *firft* field, *before* any hedge
was paffed, and could not therefore proceed from
the fcratching of his legs; and it was utterly

improbable that, after he had gained the comfortable fhelter of his own houfe, on fuch a dreadful night, and at fo late an hour, he fhould come out again immediately, encumbered, too, with the fadge, without any reafon, to wander fome miles through the pathlefs fields and hedges during the fury of the ftorm, and at laft lie him down to die in the fnow. All thefe circumftances put together, ftrongly corroborate the fufpicion that Snowden had killed him, and difpofed of the body as aforefaid. We fent for the man to examine him at the public-houfe where the inqueft was held, and though he would confefs nothing to criminate himfelf, yet the ftrongeft marks of guilt and confufion appeared in his countenance. Soon after Secker's death he married the widow, in fpite of common decency and the confirming afpect it bore upon his fufpected guilt. They removed to Batley,* or its neighbourhood, where, frequently quarrelling, the wife was heard to threaten him with hanging (for fome fecret fault of his fhe was acquainted with), if he did not amend his behaviour ; a further proof of the reality of his guilt.

Poor Secker's cafe was truly pitiable. To come home to his reft from toiling abroad for the fupport of his family ; to be knocked on the

---

* Batley, nine miles to the fouth-eaft of Bradford, is a very ancient town. Of late years it has grown fafter than any other place in Yorkfhire, chiefly on account of its trade in fhoddy, and blanketings, and cloth.

head by an adulterous rafcal, in his own houfe, in the prefence, and perhaps with the affiftance, of his guilty wife, and amidft his innocent fleeping children, was very deplorable indeed. The man is fince gone—gone into the unfeen world; where (if he did not fincerely repent of his wickednefs in this), he will be certain to meet with his deferved punifhment.

I have related this affair fo circumftantially, to make fome amends for my *inattention* at the time, and as it may *poffibly* happen to prevent a like overfight on fome future fimilar occafion.

I return to my family. My eldeft daughter, Betty, was married to Jofeph Greenwood, tobacconift, in Lower-head-row, Leeds, fon of Thomas Greenwood, farmer, of Cleckheaton, at St. Peter's Church, in Leeds, by the Rev. Mr. Fawcett, on Sunday, the 25th day of December, 1789, in the twenty-fecond year of her age.

William Birkhead Greenwood, her firft furviving child and eldeft fon, was born on Wednefday, the 2nd day of September, 1791, four minutes paft nine o'clock at night. He was baptized on Tuefday, the 29th day of September, 1791. William Birkhead Greenwood died the 24th day of April, 1793, ten minutes paft twelve o'clock at noon, and was buried on the 27th, in St. John's Churchyard, Leeds, 1793, aged one year and a half, three weeks, and one day. His days were few, and full of forrow, he was greatly afflicted from his birth to his death, and gave occafion for his mamma to exhibit a very eminent degree of maternal tendernefs and affection towards him during his ftay. He now refts in peace, and will be found again by his feeling, affectionate parents in that day.

Thomas Greenwood, her fecond furviving child, and fecond fon, was born on Sunday, the 12th day of May, 1793, eleven minutes before five o'clock in the afternoon. He was baptized on Thurfday, the 30th day of the fame month.

Lydia Greenwood, her third furviving child and firft daughter, was born on Friday, the 9th day of October, 1795, at fix o'clock in the morning. She was baptized on Friday, the 30th day of the fame month.

Befides thefe, fhe has had three mifcarriages, and appears at prefent near the birth of her feventh child. Betty was always a feeling, affectionate child towards her father ; and, I doubt not, will make a feeling, affectionate wife to her hufband, and mother to her children. They are fettled in a pretty way of bufinefs, with (I hope) a promifing profpect before them. May every needful bleffing from their heavenly Father reft upon them and their offspring, to the lateft generation.

Sally, my third daughter, and fourth child, was married to Timothy Greenwood, furgeon and apothecary, of Cleckheaton, fon of Benjamin Greenwood, clothier, of the fame place, on Monday, the 17th day of June, 1793, by the Rev. Mr. Rueben Ogden, at the parifh church

Birftall, in the twenty-firft year of her age. Jo. Shaw, clerk.

John Brook Greenwood, her firft child and firft fon, was born at Cleckheaton, on Friday, March the 14th, 1794, about eleven o'clock in the forenoon. He was baptized by the Rev. Mr. James Dawfon.

Mary Ann Greenwood, her fecond child and firft daughter, was born at Brook-houfes, on Monday, the 9th day of May, 1796, about eight o'clock in the evening. She was baptized by the Rev. Mr. John Ralph, the minifter of the Independent Congregation at Cleckheaton, on Wednefday, the 9th day of June, 1796.

They fettled firft at Cleckheaton. They afterwards removed to Bradford, and then back again to Brook-houfes, where they remain at prefent. Sally behaves kindly and refpectfully to her father, and her hufband is poffeffed of a promifing bufinefs, and feems to be particularly efteemed in that branch of it which concerns the women. May every neceffary bleffing from their heavenly Father reft upon them and their offspring to the lateft pofterity!

Thomas, my third child and firft fon, was put apprentice to Meffrs. Nicholfons of Bradford (as has been obferved before), at the age of fixteen, with whom he remained till he attained the twenty-firft year of his age. With thefe people he acquired a pretty good knowledge of his bufinefs, but fome unfortunate circumftances attended him in this place, which proved an unhappy occasion of his being afterwards unfairly and cruelly deprived, by the machinations of inconsiderate, interested, malicious, and evil-dipofed perfons, of nearly the whole of his expected property at Brook-houfes. I will endeavour to give a fair and candid account of this matter, without *partiality* to my own child, on one fide, or *prejudice* againft thofe whom I confider as his and my enemies, on the other.

Mr. S. Nicholfon, my boy's mafter's youngeft fon, was poffeffed of a confiderable fhare of good fenfe, and had a good hand at his bufinefs; but affected to live and appear in a higher ftyle than his means would allow; and this, of courfe, led him into pecuniary embarraffments; and on this account he was on bad terms with his father, who greatly difapproved of his conduct in this refpect. He wifhed his father to take him in as a partner and allow him a fhare of the profits of his trade; this the old man utterly refufed, for the aforefaid reafon; he therefore left him in difguft, and fet up a fhop for himfelf in New Street, which he furnifhed with a very fcanty ftock, as his ftraitened circumftances would allow. Being defirous of availing himfelf of my fon's affiftance, and having gained an afcendancy over his mind, he encouraged a fhynefs between his old mafter and him; and by reprefenting to him that' he was much better able to finifh his inftructions in his bufinefs than his father was (which was partly true), he perfuaded him to leave his old mafter and dwell with him, which he accordingly did during a fmall part of the conclufion of his apprenticefhip. Mr. S. Nicholfon, however, finding that his fhop would not anfwer his purpofe, and (as it appeared afterwards) having a defign to marry and remove elfewhere, took the following meafures to fupply himfelf with money through the medium of my fon. Being acquainted with Tommy's expectations at Brook-houfes, he took occafion to commence an acquaintance with the family, by means of vifits made along with my fon, &c., and having a genteel appearance, and infinuating addrefs, he foon recommended himfelf to the notice and good opinion of old Mrs. Birkhead, the chief conductor of the family affairs. He then artfully propofed that Tommy, upon the conclufion of his apprenticefhip, fhould purchafe his ftock at a valuation, and he would give up his fhop and cuftom to him, which would afford him a fine opportunity of beginning bufinefs, with a good profpect of advantage. He had the addrefs to bring the old woman into his fcheme, and to engage her confent and promife to raife the *money* neceffary for this purpofe, and my boy entered eagerly into the project, with all the incautious truft and fanguine expectation incident to youth and inexperience. It is to be obferved, that fuch was the inveterate prejudice which Mrs. Birkhead had entertained againft me, that fhe ftrictly forbade the parties to inform *me* of.

or confult *me* at all upon, the occafion, as fhe wifhed *me* to know nothing of or have any hand in the matter; hence, whatever degree of praife or blame attaches to the tranfaction, they fhare it all among themfelves, as I had no hand in it. However, my fon had acquainted me with the affair, and from the firft I apprehended a good deal of danger in the cafe, and warned him repeatedly to take the utmoft care that he was not impofed upon, as I myfelf had been not long before, in a fomewhat fimilar cafe to this. However, Tommy's implicit confidence in Mr. Nicholfon's integrity,* and the fanguine expectations of youth, rendered my cautions void. The

---

* Samuel Nicholfon was the youngeft of John Nicholfon's three fons. The eldeft fon, George, was a very remarkable man, and may be confidered as having almoft worked a revolution in the publifhing trade. After remaining fome years at Manchefter, he went to Ludlow in Shropfhire, and eftablifhed himfelf at the beautiful hamlet of Poughnil in 1799, near that town, where he continued for fome years to publifh books, which were remarkable for their good tafte and good printing, and which had a large circulation. My father either accompanied or followed him into Shropfhire, which was the caufe of the editor of the prefent volume being a native of that county inftead of a Yorkfhireman. Mr. Nicholfon was his own compiler and editor, and his own traveller; and he performed the latter tafk almoft always on foot. His "Cambrian Traveller's Guide," firft publifhed in 1808, but much enlarged and improved in a fecond edition in 1813, is ftill the beft work we have on Wales. My father had the greateft perfonal efteem and refpect for George Nicholfon, and their friendfhip continued till the death of the latter in 1825. He had left Poughnil before the publication of the fecond edition of the "Cambrian Traveller's Guide," and eftablifhed himfelf at Stourport, on the river Severn, where he died.

bargain was made, the price of the ftock fettled (at much more than it was worth, as I believe my boy never made one half of the money of it which it coft), the fhop was given up, Tommy took poffeffion of the premifes, and the old woman paid a part of the purchafe-money. In the meantime S. Nicholfon got married and re-moved to Manchefter, where, being needy, he fent frequent and preffing letters for the payment of what remained. Mrs. Birkhead wifhing, I fuppofe, to raife the money without the know-ledge of the old man, found fome difficulty in doing this as fpeedily as S. Nicholfon's needs required; and as he had taken the precaution of taking fecurity for the money, he proceeded at laft to fend a threatening letter. This dunning fo irritated and difgufted her, that fhe began to view the whole affair in a different light, and, by the laft circumftance in particular, Mr. Nichol-fon entirely forfeited her good opinion. How-ever, the money was at laft paid, and that was all Mr. Nicholfon either wanted or cared for. My fon paid a very high rent for the premifes he occu-pied, and, as he had but a fcanty ftock, and of courfe fmall cuftom, it was eafy to forefee that, except he could increafe his ftock, it would do nothing for him.

I take notice here, that the money advanced by Mrs. Birkhead for Mr. Nicholfon on this occafion (which was 120*l.* or 140*l.*, I know not which), was not *given* to my fon, but *lent* in the firſt inſtance, to Joſeph Greenwood, of Leeds, who had married his ſiſter, who gave his note for it to William Birkhead, and my ſon gave Joſeph Greenwood his bond for it for his ſecurity, till the note was cancelled. I never approved of the ſcheme my ſon had adopted, but had much rather he had gone out as a journeyman for ſome time, gained a more perfect knowledge of his buſineſs, and waited the event of the old people's death ; a circumſtance which was not likely to be long ere it took place. In this ſtate of things old Mrs. Birkhead died ſuddenly in the month of April, 1796. This event rouſed every perſon who had expectations from the old people, and immediately introduced a lawſuit between the parties. I will endeavour to give as juſt, impartial, and diſpaſſionate an account of this diſagreeable, unjuſt, and unhappy affair, as I am able ; but before I proceed, I ſtop to notice, that the old woman died *ſuddenly*, as might have been expected from exiſting circumſtances ; that ſhe died in her ſeventy-ſixth year, and was buried in the ſame grave with her huſband's younger bro-ther Tommy, in Cleckheaton Chapel-yard, and had afterwards—as is uſual with the party—the parade of a funeral ſermon preached for her. It was curious to obſerve upon this occaſion, how a perſon who had ruined the peace of my family, alienated the affections of my wife from me, connived at her vicious weakneſſes, and induced her to behave with the utmoſt diſreſpect and im-

propriety towards her hufband to the last moment
of her life ; who had uniformly and invariably to
the laft, as occafions offered, faid and done all
that lay in her power, to inftill a bad opinion of
their father into the minds of my own children,
to deprive me of their filial affection, and detach
them from their duty; who had—for anything
that appeared to the contrary—carried her implacable malice and refentment againft me to the
grave ; and who had, with the help of her coun-
fellors and affiftants—except fhe herfelf was impofed upon by thefe, of which I have a ftrong
fufpicion, the affair is fo atrocious and unnatural
—difpofed of the old man's property contrary to
his mind, as evidently appeared from what he
himfelf repeatedly faid afterwards, and contrary
to her own folemn promife to me in her lifetime;
and who had, by this conduct, done the greateft
injury to fome of her own offspring, and given
occafion for the moft implacable animofity to
arife between the parties, who were near relations, immediately fprung from her own family,
and which malice and animofity will probably be
tranfmitted to future generations; when an equitable difpofal of the property, as juftice required,
might have preferved and induced a fpirit of
Chriftian love and unity amongft the different
branches of the family ;—I fay it was curious to
obferve (for me, at leaft) on this occafion how,
by the peculiar addrefs and dexterity of the
preacher, fuch a perfon as this could be meta-

morphofed into an eminent faint and a mother in Ifrael! The preacher did not deal fairly with his auditory on this occafion; he only gave them the bright parts of the picture, extremely heightened in the colouring. He ought to have given the fhades alfo, and fo prefented them with a perfect whole. If he was not prepared for this part of his fubject, there were perfons prefent who could eafily have fupplied him with *genuine* materials. His hearers then might have been able to have formed a juft and conclufive judgment upon the fubject.

Funeral fermons are, of late years, become fo common in this part of the country, amongft the Methodifts and fome of the different diffenting parties, that they feem to be confidered as a necef-fary appendage to the exit of every faint—fo called —in the neighbourhood; and one may as certainly expect one of thefe funeral harangues upon the death of every member of the different parties, as one may expect to hear *confeffions* cried about the ftreets upon the execution of every felon at Tyburn. Religious pride may, perhaps, be as predominant amongft profeffors, at prefent, as it was formerly amongft the ancient Pharifees. I remember, the perfon whofe funeral fermon has given occafion for these reflections, was fo terri-bly chagrined that her youngeft brother was con-figned to the grave without this badge of religious honour being attached to his memory, that fhe exclaimed in an agony of difappointed pride,

"Died my brother as a fool dieth!" It was evident from the import of her exclamation, that it was the want of the fuppofed *honour*, rather than the *ufefulnefs* of the circumftance, which her pride fo feelingly regretted. Indeed, thefe difcourfes, as they have been generally managed, have been ftuffed with fo much fulfome panegyric on the deceafed, as to render them extremely difgufting to every fenfible hearer; and were fome of thefe flattering funeral effufions to be printed, one might well addrefs the author in the language of the poet on a fimilar occafion—

> " Sir, in your funeral talk I'm griev'd,
>   So very much is faid;
> One half will never be believ'd,
>   The other never read."

Indeed, a preacher may be frequently led into a very unpleafant and difagreeable fituation in this refpect, if he be not *fully* acquainted with the *whole* character himfelf which he has to fpeak to. He generally receives a flattering and exaggerated account from fome party-man—friend or relative —of the virtues and piety of the deceafed, without one word being faid of their failings; hence he is led to give a very *partial*, if not a very *falfe*, reprefentation of the cafe, which may tend to hurt his own character as to his *veracity* or *prudence*, in the judgment of thofe who knew the perfon better, and may do material mifchief to fome of his fimpler hearers, who may well be suppofed to argue in this manner: "To be fure, if my neighbour can be efteemed fo great a faint by thefe eminent profeffors (who, to be fure, muft be capital judges of the nature of Chrift- ianity), notwithftanding *I know* he or fhe has in- dulged to the laft fome evil difpofitions and evil practices, very contrary to the *fpirit* and *duty* of a Chriftian, I need not, then, be over anxious to mortify fome of my own evil propenfities and practices, which ftick very clofe to me, but which, I am fure, are of a lefs blameable nature than thofe of my neighbour. It feems I may indulge them to the laft with the utmoft fafety, as well as he or fhe did, and remain a good Chriftian ftill, even in the judgment of thefe great and pious preachers, and go to heaven at laft for all that." So, poffibly, nay, very probably, may fome of his hearers argue, to the great hazard of unhappy confequences. A preacher ought, therefore, to be *fully* acquainted with the *whole* character and conduct of the perfon of whom he is fpeaking *himfelf;* or, otherwife, be fully and fairly informed of it by fome candid perfon able to give that information, before he ventures to give fo high and heavenly a character before a whole congregation of a finful mortal he knows little or nothing about. He ought alfo to be entirely uninfluenced by party-prejudice, or any other finifter motive in this cafe; but, indeed, the whole affair of funeral praife is of fo ticklifh and delicate a nature, that I think it is much better let alone altogether ; except, perhaps, in fome very exempt cafes. This is my private opinion ; however, I blame nobody for thinking otherwife. It is certain, thefe funeral adulations are nothing to the dead. No ;

> " Can ftoried urn or animated buft
> Back to its manfion call the fleeting breath ?
> Can *honour's* voice provoke the filent duft,
> Or *flattery* foothe the dull cold ear of death ?"

No, it may ferve to foothe the pride and vanity of fome furviving relative or party-profeffor, but can anfwer no valuable purpofe that I can conceive. The words with which (I am told) a late refpectable minifter in this neighbourhood ufed to addrefs his hearers on thefe occafions, are, I think, very fuitable and very fenfible : " Friends and brethren, whatever you have obferved in this perfon's conduct and converfation agreeable with the *fpirit* and *practice* of Chriftianity, be fure you carefully endeavour to *imitate ;* whatever you have feen of a contrary nature, be fure you carefully endeavour to *avoid*." This, I think, is enough in confcience to be faid for any man, and I am glad to hear that fome of the more judicious preachers in the neighbourhood are laying afide the aforefaid practice of funeral panegyric, and, as the relations of the deceafed will, for the moft part, infift on the ufual honour of a funeral fermon for their deceafed friend, they give them a good edifying difcourfe on the occafion, faying nothing, or as little as may be, concerning the dead. For my part, I fhould be utterly afhamed to have the *whole* of my conduct expofed before a crowded audience, and fo (I fuppofe) might the *beft* and *greateft* faint amongft any of the religious parties in the country ; and fhould any perfon pick out a few of mine or any other perfon's beft actions, or what may be efteemed fuch, and exhibit them as forming our character before a great congregation, I fhould think it a very partial, unfair, and unjuft mode of proceeding. I am concerned (though perhaps not fo much as I ought to be) to fecure the approbation of my Maker. I defire alfo to behave in fuch a manner that the good and worthy part of my neighbours and acquaintance may be able to think and fpeak of me and my conduct with complaifance and general approbation after I am gone. As for the ignorant, the uncandid, the malicious, and the cenforious, I am altogether unconcerned at anything they may think or fay concerning me. It is enough for me that my allwife, good, and gracious Maker is perfectly acquainted with me, my propenfities, my actions, and all my concerns ; that he knows how to rectify his own work, when it is got out of order ; that his goodnefs will certainly difpofe him to do this ; and his wifdom and power will enable him to accomplifh it in his own time and in his own manner, and I can, with the moft pleafing confidence, " caft my care upon Him, believing that he careth for me," and can fay to furvivors, in the language of the poet, with refpect to the foregoing fubject—

"No farther feek my *merits* to difclofe,
 Or draw my *frailties* from their dread abode,
 (There they alike in trembling hope repofe)
 The bofom of my Father and my God."

I return to the beginning of the family conteft before mentioned. Timothy Greenwood and his family, upon the death of the old woman, were left fettled at Brook-houfes, fo that the old man, with the houfe and farm, came more immediately under his care and management. The old woman had, before her death, dictated to one Thomas Exley, who had taken it down in writing, how fhe would have fuch and fuch parts of the houfe-hold furniture, bedding, filver-plate, linen, &c., difpofed of amongft the grandchildren immediately after her death, though fhe had no *right* to do this without her hufband's confent. With this divifion of perfonal property, Timothy Greenwood and his wife were not fatisfied, as believing fhe had not left them their fair fhare. It was known that the old man had made a will, or rather, that the old woman and her accomplices had made a will for him. It appeared from exifting circumftances, that Jofeph Greenwood and William Birkby knew in general—if they had not a hand in the will-making—that the will was very much in their favour; hence they became extremely interefted to fecure its validity, and exceffively jealous of Timothy Greenwood, for fear he fhould, as they faid, perfuade the old man to make a new will. However, as the old man was beft acquainted and fatisfied with my daughter Sally, as fhe had been brought up with them, Timothy Greenwood and his family were fettled at Brook-houfes, and it was agreed that he fhould have eighteen fhillings a week allowed for the care and maintenance of the old man, as long as he lived. I was pleafed with this circumftance, as hoping it would prevent litigation among the parties, at leaft, during the old man's life ; but I was miftaken. The mutual hatred and jealoufy of the parties foon found and gave occafion for frefh difturbances.

There was a field of grafs to be fold, belonging to the farm, and as Timothy Greenwood kept a cow and a galloway, he wifhed to purchafe the grafs himfelf, efpecially as it lay fo convenient for him. Jofeph Greenwood objected to this, except he bought it in bidding among others at a public auction. Whether Jofeph Greenwood was actuated on this occafion by a fear that if Timothy Greenwood bought it he either *could* not or *would* not pay for it—or by a fear that he fhould get it for *lefs* than it was worth—or by a principle of mere *ill-will* and *oppofition*, is beft known to himfelf. The two parties were *own* brother's children, had married two *own* fifters, and of courfe were nearly related in blood, and a fhare of the property of the grafs in queftion belonged to Timothy Greenwood as one of the perfons interefted in the eftate. To raife, therefore, a contention for a trifle of two or three guineas at moſt, which proved the *cauſe* of introducing contention and miſchief between the parties *much ſooner* perhaps than it would otherwiſe have taken place, was very *imprudent*, to ſay the leaſt of it. Well, a day was appointed, and the graſs put up to be ſold by auction; and on this occaſion Joſeph Greenwood himſelf became a bidder, and bid ſo high a price for it as Timothy Greenwood thought was much more than it was worth, and was much piqued at the conduct of his kinſman on this occaſion, as ſuppoſing it proceeded from mere oppoſition and ill-will to him. However, Joſeph was the buyer, but was tied to have it mowed by ſuch a day, or the bargain to be void. The weather proved unſettled, the day came, the graſs was uncut, and the bargain forfeited. Timothy Greenwood now got a neighbour to value the graſs, bargained for it with the old man, gave him half-a-guinea earneſt, and took poſſeſſion of it immediately. This proceeding irritated Joſeph Greenwood and his party, and they talked of applying to the chancellor immediately, to appoint a guardian for the old man, in order to get rid of Timothy Greenwood. The conteſt being thus commenced, I one day received the following letter:—

"Mr. Thomas Wright, Birkenſhaw.

"Sir,

"This is to deſire the favour that you will call upon your ſon-in-law, Mr. Timothy Greenwood, to-morrow forenoon, and come to my houfe, and, as it is on a particular occafion, I wifh for no other perfon with you.

I am, Sir, yours to command,
THOMAS EXLEY.

Spen, Thurfday noon."

I immediately conceived that he wanted me on fome occafion of the prefent difference, and as I wifhed to meddle as little between them as poffible, I called upon Thomas Exley the next morning, without taking Timothy Greenwood with me. I told him that I fhould be pleafed to *fay* or *do* anything that lay in my power to promote peace and quietnefs between the families, but that as I ftood *nearly* and *equally* related to both parties, I wifhed not to take, or feem to take, any decifive part with either againft the other (except I difcovered *unfair* and *unjuft* defigns in the conduct of either of the parties), that I might, if poff.ble, avoid giving any *juft* occafion of offence on either fide. That for this reafon I had not called upon or brought Timothy Greenwood with me, and wifhed to be excufed from taking any part in the affair. Thomas Exley, however, pleaded that his defign was to promote peace on this occafion, and preffed me pretty much to go over to Timothy Greenwood and bring him with me. Accordingly, in my return from my circuit in the evening, I called upon Timothy Greenwood, and he walked with me over to Thomas Exley's.

I note, that before we left Brook-houfes, old William Birkhead faid, "Doctor, how happens it that Thomas Exley does not come down? I want to fee my will, and to hear it read, that I may right what is wrong in it," or words to that purpofe. Timothy Greenwood replied, "I am juft going over to his houfe, and will tell him what you fay." The old man faid, "Do." In our way thither, Timothy Greenwood told me that, perceiving Jofeph Greenwood and his party were doing all they could to rid him from the place, he had, for his own fecurity, prevailed on the old man to make him a leafe of the place, together with a right to receive *all* the old man's rents and profits to maintain him on during his life, and the obligation to ceafe at the old man's death; and that he had alfo made him a deed of gift for, I think, part of the houfehold furniture. I told him, I hoped he had done nothing to injure any other perfon concerned in the affair. He affured me he had not. We proceeded to Thomas Exley's, whom he alfo acquainted with what he had done, at which he feemed pretty much alarmed, and told us in return, that he and his colleagues had determined to apply to the Lord Chancellor to appoint a guardian for the old man. Before we left the houfe, Timothy Greenwood delivered William Birkhead's meffage, to which Thomas Exley replied, "William Birkhead fhall neither *fee* nor *hear* his will read, nor fhall it go out of my houfe while William Birkhead liveth." They came to no agreement in their propofals, and we departed.

About this time, a friendly acquaintance of mine became acquainted (by information from Thomas Exley) with the principal difpofals contained in the paper which was called William Birkhead's will. Thefe circumftances he communicated to me, and they were faid to be as follows : " The Lower Brook-houfes to William Birkby's youngeft fon William and his heirs for ever, fubject to a legacy to be paid out of it to his elder brother, or fome of his fifters. A field in Cleckheaton-upper-lane, and fome cottages at Heaton-gate to William Birkby's eldeft fon John and his heirs for ever. A fmall eftate in land and houfes at Heckmondwike, of 15*l.* per annum, to my eldeft daughter Betty, wife of Jofeph Greenwood, and her heirs for ever. The *annuity* for life of another eftate in land, at the fame place, of 15*l.* per annum alfo, to my younger daughter Sally, wife of Timothy Greenwood, and at her death, to her children and their heirs for ever. An *annuity* for life of 13*l.* 10*s.* out of the Upper Brook-houfes eftate, to my eldeft fon Tommy, and the eftate itfelf was left, at my fon's death, to Jofeph Greenwood's children." The farm was let at this time for 21*l.* per annum. The truftees were empowered to borrow 150*l.* on a mortgage upon the farm, and the intereft to be paid out of the rents arifing from the place, and to accumulate for a portion for William Birkby's youngeft daughter; my fon only to receive the remainder of the rent for life, namely, 13*l.* 10*s.* It appeared afterwards, that the will-maker had taken peculiar care to exclude my fon from ever coming into *poffeffion* of the eftate, in order effectually to debar him from ever making any further advantage of his miferable donation, by felling the wood or coal, or advancing the rent upon the expiration of the leafe. But the truftees were to receive the rents, and pay him his pitiful pittance half-yearly, as a pauper receives his monthly allowance at the hands of a parifh-officer. As foon as I became acquainted with this difpofition of the old man's property, I faw at once into the *real* motives and defigns of the feveral parties concerned in the affair. I knew very well that Jofeph Greenwood had from the commencement of his connection with the family, been very affiduous in currying favour with old Miftrefs Birkhead and her chief confidant and counfellor Thomas Exley. Exley was poor, and full of religious pride and prejudice; Mrs. Birkhead alfo had her full quantum of thefe laft qualities, to which fhe added a moft difgufting degree of mean family pride and felf-importance, fordid avarice, and the moft perverfe and unremitting malice, that ever I experienced, or that ever fell under my obfervation. Jofeph Greenwood applied, with a good deal of addrefs, to their particular foibles, and by means of fuitable prefents and flatteries, well-timed and circumftanced, and profeffions and appearances at the time of great management and fuccefs in his bufinefs, fucceeded in obtaining their confidence and good opinion in a very high degree. I did not think amifs of this circumftance at the time, as I conceived it to be Jofeph Greenwood's defign to counterwork the *undue* influence of William Birkby's family, and prevent them getting *more* than their *fair* fhare (and one penny *lefs* I never wifhed them to have). In this light, therefore, I thought his policy commendable. But, alas! as it proved afterwards, I was quite miftaken in my furmifes. It was not, it feemed, to guard againft any unfair practices of William Birkby's family that the manœuvres of Jofeph Greenwood and his affiftants were directed : no, but againft my poor, foft, good-natured boy,—the eldeft male branch of the family, and the eldeft and only furviving brother whom Jofeph Greenwood's wife had left alive by the fame mother ; and who, notwithftanding fome blameable indifcretions which he was drawn into almoft in his childhood, and under very mitigating circumftances, which rendered him altogether as much an object of pity as blame ; and whofe after conduct to this day has abundantly proved that they were more the refult of thefe unhappy circumftances, than any natural propenfity to the crimes themfelves ; I fay, who, notwithftanding thefe accidental failings, had always been remarkable for the kindeft fraternal affection to his fifter, and the warmeft filial love to his father; whofe moral conduct was at this time unblameable, and who had, by mere dint of exertion, carefulnefs, and induftry, obtained a refpectable acquaintance, and eftablifhed himfelf in a promifing little bufinefs, with fairer profpects before him if he could have had that property which he had a right to expect, to affift him. I fay it was againft this brother their ungenerous attempts were directed, to undermine and fubvert him in the old people's affection and good opinion, to deprive him of his fair fhare in their property, to turn him and any family he might have out to poverty and ruin, and obtain what ought to have been his portion, for Jofeph Greenwood's and William Birkby's children.

But I return to take notice, that William Birkhead immediately after his wife's death, began to exprefs great uneafinefs of mind on account of the paper which was called his will, and which was in Thomas Exley's, the willmaker's, keeping, *becaufe*, he faid, *he had not done juftice* to Tommy Wright's children. He defired, therefore, earneftly to hear it read, that he might rectify what was amifs; but this reafonable requeft was utterly refufed him by Thomas Exley. The old man continued to be very uneafy for many days, and to exprefs an eager defire to alter the will, and do right to my children, till at length it engaged the attention of his attendants, relations, and neighbours, and a meeting was

called of feveral refpectable perfons in the neighbourhood, to queſtion the old man and judge of
his intellects. The perfons called in were Meſſrs.
Richard and Thomas Brooke, and the Rev.
Mr. John Ralph, of Cleckheaton, Mr. William
Williamfon, of Snelfons,* and Mr. — Sykes,
furgeon, of Gomerfall. It was agreed that Mr.
Sykes ſhould queſtion the old man, and he aſked
him, " Are you not fatisfied with your will?"
He anfwered, " No, I am not." He aſked
again, " How do you defire to alter it?" He
anfwered, " I would leave this lower Brook-
houfes to Tommy Wright (meaning my fon);
you know he is my eldeſt daughter's fon, and
has the greateſt right to it." It was obferved
that it was fenfibly anfwered, and a good reafon
given for it. He then aſked him, " How would
you leave the reſt of your eſtate?" He faid,
" There is a woman in the chamber (meaning
my daughter Betty), and Tommy Exley, who
know how I would leave the reſt." At this
juncture an impertinent fellow (Obadiah Brooke)
came into the room, and with matchlefs impudence, ſhouted out, " William, do not alter your
will; your will is right; it is agreeable both to
my fiſter's mind and yours, and you will make
it worfe if you alter it," &c. This ſtunned the
old man, and he walked out of the room and

---

* Snelfons is an eſtate near Cleckheaton, on the road
to Low Moor. The railway to Bradford paſſes near it.

could not be prevailed upon to come amongſt them again. Mr. Richard Brooke ſtepped up to Obadiah Brooke, and blamed him much for the rudeneſs and impropriety of his interpoſition. He told him they were not come there to exert any unfair influence upon the old man's mind, but to learn, if poſſible, what was his *real* mind and will, uninfluenced and unperſuaded by any perſon ; and that, therefore, he thought his ad-dreſs to William Birkhead very unfair, and very blameable. He churliſhly anſwered, that he would not be hindered from ſeeing his brother, and ſaying what he pleaſed to him. This broke up the meeting, and it was propoſed to meet again the following Monday, if required. How-ever, this was never put in execution.

Obadiah Brooke's conduct on this occaſion was certainly very wrong and very cenſurable. In the firſt place, it was very *impertinent*, as he was not called upon in the affair, neither had he any buſineſs or concern in the matter. In the next place, it appeared to be very *malicious* to ſome of my children, eſpecially to my ſon ; as it was plain, from what he ſaid, that he *knew* the contents of the will, elſe how ſhould he be able to *ſay* whether it was *right* or *wrong?* He *muſt*, therefore, be acquainted with the ſhameful in-juſtice done to my ſon in that paper ; and my boy may, therefore, juſtly conſider him as one of his greateſt enemies on this occaſion, as he ſaid and did all that lay in his power to eſtabliſh the authenticity of that villainous paper which deprived him of what ought to have been his property, and to prevent William Birkhead from rectifying what he had been perfuaded by malicious and interefted perfons to do amifs, which his *confcience* told him was wrong, and which he repeatedly *declared he had done wrong*, and which he manifefted, not only a *willingnefs*, but the *moft anxious defire* to rectify ; and which (there are people who believe) he *would* have rectified *at this time*, if it had not been for Obadiah Brooke's wicked interpofition. I wifh my children therefore to take notice that as Mrs. Birkhead *hated* me, with a *perfect hatred* to the day of her death, fo did fhe alfo diflike all my children, in fo far as they were related or fhe thought them to bear any fimilarity *to* their father. I wifh them to note alfo, that moft of her neareft relations, by her own family fide, are more or lefs inimical both to me and to every branch of my family, where fome particular intereft does not intervene, and to beware of them accordingly.

It now began to be rumoured that William Birkhead had made another will, under the influence of Timothy Greenwood. Timothy Greenwood's opponents had induftrioufly reported it through the country, that the deed of gift before mentioned, conveyed *all* the old man's property to him, and deprived all the reft of the grandchildren of their fair fhares. This report, though utterly falfe, was generally believed in the neighbourhood, and operated much to the prejudice of Timothy Greenwood's character ; and although the making of another will proved to a demonstration the falsity of this report (because, if he had made *all* he had away by a deed of gift *before*, he could not possibly devise it to any other person *afterwards* by a will), yet they encouraged a similar report on this occasion; namely, that Timothy Greenwood had persuaded the old man to leave *him all* or *most* of what he had, in this will, to the prejudice of the other parties. This report also was generally believed by his already-prejudiced neighbours, to the further detriment of his character, till the *real* contents of this will were afterwards brought to light. Joseph Greenwood and his associates acted with much what the same policy in this case, as Mr. Pope's "Wife of Bath," and might justly have adopted her language on this occasion—

> "I, like a dog, could *bite* as well as whine,
> And *first* complain'd whene'er the fault was mine."

When I heard of this report I asked Timothy Greenwood if it was true ? He said it was, but declared that the old man had done it of his own mind, and dictated the whole himself, without any unfair influence. Mr. Lambert, the attorney who wrote the will, declared the same. The other party asserted the contrary, and believed, or affected to believe, it to be Timothy Greenwood's will, and that it was framed by and under his influence. However, be this as it may, I believe it to be a real fact, that the old man was *as liable to be*, and *actually was*, as unfairly dealt with in framing the firft (efpecially the unjuft, mifchief-making codicil), as he poffibly could be in framing the fecond will, as it was well known that his memory had failed very much for years before the date of the firft will ; and though the fecond will was much too partial to Timothy Greenwood, yet, upon the whole, it did more juftice to *all* the parties concerned than the firft will, with the annexed codicil, did. I afked Timothy Greenwood how the old man's property was difpofed off in the fecond will ? and he faid it was as follows : " The Lower Brook-houfes, free from *all* incumbrances, to Timothy Greenwood and his heirs for ever, befides 100*l*. in cafh out of the perfonal eftate. The Upper Brook-houfes (or Mortimer's Farm) to my eldeft fon Tommy and his heirs for ever, free from all incumbrances alfo. To young W. Birkby and his heirs for ever, the 15*l*. a year eftate at Heckmondwike, which Timothy Greenwood had left in the firft will, free alfo, in lieu of the Lower Brook-houfes. The other 15*l*. a year eftate at the fame place, free from incumbrances alfo, to Jofeph Greenwood and his heirs for ever, and 100*l*. in cafh, befides, out of the perfonal eftate, in addition to what he had received before. The field above Heaton, and the cottages at Heatongate, to John Birkby ; and the remainder of the money equally amongſt William Birkby's daughters." I was not pleaſed with this diſpoſal, becauſe, in the firſt place, it did not correſpond with the old man's foregoing declaration, namely, that he wiſhed to leave the Lower Brook-houſes to my ſon Tommy; and, in the ſecond place, becauſe, by being ſo partial to Timothy Greenwood, it afforded too plauſible a pretext for other people to ſurmiſe that he uſed unfair influence upon the old man, and would look worſe in a court of juſtice. Had the Lower Brook-houſes been left to my ſon Tommy, chargeable with the legacy of 200*l.* to John Birkby, and the field and cottages in Heaton to John Birkby alſo; the Upper Brook-houſes to William Birkby junior, chargeable with the 150*l.* legacy to his youngeſt ſiſter; the two eſtates at Heckmondwike to my daughters Betty and Sally, free from all ties and incumbrances, and the money they had already received; and the ready caſh in the perſonal eſtate amongſt William Birkby's daughters, it would have been a pretty fair and equal diviſion. However, as William Birkby had received (as the old man conſtantly and repeatedly aſſerted) near 1000*l.* from Brook-houſes—which was much more than all my family had received put together—though the laſt will was partial to Sally with reſpect to my other children, yet, everything fairly conſidered, William Birkby's family got their full and fair ſhare even by this will; and though it was not as I could have wifhed it to be, yet, as it did more juftice by far to *all* the parties concerned than the firft will did, for this reafon I wifhed it to ftand much rather than the other.

Jofeph Greenwood and his party now applied to the Chancellor to appoint a guardian for William Birkhead, and in confequence of their application, a jury of eighteen perfons were fummoned to examine the old man, and judge of his intellects. Thefe met at the farther Black Bull, near Birftall church, where they gave in a verdict of *lunacy* againft him. That William Birkhead's *memory* had become very deficient, which it had been for fome years back, fo that he could not recollect any of his former acquaintance, except thofe who were conftantly converfant about him, was a matter of fact; however, he had a good *general* knowledge of his property, and, as far as his memory would ferve him, his underftanding appeared to be very good. He was no more lunatic, in the proper fenfe of the word, than thofe who brought the verdict againft him, nor, I think, could any fenfible perfon who had candidly obferved him, have the leaft doubt but that with a little *honeft* affiftance to his memory from any unprejudiced perfon who was willing that equal juftice fhould be done to *all* the parties concerned, the old man was very competent to have made a juft and equitable difpofal of his property.

It was now expected that a guardian would

be appointed for the old man immediately, by the Court of Chancery; but this was delayed, and the old man died before any such event took place. William Birkhead died on the 3rd day of March, 1797, being about one hundred years old. Upon this occasion the two parties made haste to deliver in the respective wills to the spiritual court at York, in order to their approval. However, the affair hung in suspense in this court till Joseph Greenwood and his party prosecuted the matter at common law, and brought on a trial at the autumn assizes for York, 1797. It appeared that, from some oversight of Joseph Greenwood's attorney, they were likely to be nonsuited; an accommodation was therefore proposed, and the parties agreed to refer it to the sole decision of Samuel Buck, Esq., the recorder of Leeds. This gentleman afterwards made a very unfair decision (in my judgment), establishing the first will, with the unjust codicil, in its full extent. By this decision my son lost nearly the whole of what ought to have been his property. He afterwards sold his trifling annuity of 13*l.* 10*s.* for one hundred and eight guineas. The attorney, D——n, and Joseph Greenwood had assured my son when they persuaded him to sign his name to send up to the chancellor, that it *would not* constitute him a *party*, or make him liable as such, to pay any part of the expense that might be incurred in the affair. I had told him the contrary, and repeatedly and earnestly defired him not to join or give his countenance or affiftance to a fet of fellows whofe chief and apparent defign was to deprive *himfelf* of his fortune, and leave him a beggar; as well to avoid the odium of fuch abfurd conduct, as the further pecuniary inconvenience it would probably fubject him to in the event. However, fuch was the afcendancy they had gained over his mind, that they appeared to be able to perfuade him to do anything, however contrary to his own intereft or difgraceful to his intellects. He accordingly conftantly followed their advice, and neglected mine. However, the attorney carefully watched the moment when he had received the purchafe-money of his annuity, and immediately fent him a charge of 33*l.* as his fhare, or part of his fhare, of the law expenfes, as a *party* concerned in a conteft that had been commenced and carried on (by the party to whom *he himfelf* lent all the affiftance in his power), from the *fole* motive of obtaining and fecuring that very eftate for another man's children, which in all equity and juftice ought to have been his own property, which property he had the *moft urgent occafion for* at the prefent time, and the want of which property was likely to reduce him to the moft pinching diftrefs, and fubject all the future fcenes of his life to difficulties and inconveniences. The attorneys conduct on this occafion gave the lie to his former declaration, namely, that my boy's figning his name to addrefs the chancellor would not conftitute him a party, and that he would never be afked for any part of the law-expenfes ; but fuch conduct as this is not, in general, to be wondered at in men of this profeffion. One hardly knows which to wonder at moft, the ungenerous, unfair, and difingenuous conduct of this party towards an irrefolute, yielding, eafy-tempered, inexperienced youth, or the great imbecility of mind manifefted by my boy on this occafion. However, he was fo much chagrined at the unexpected charge, that he declared he would lie in a jail before he would pay a penny of the money ; or otherwife, abandon his country to avoid that inconvenience ; and he had actually made confiderable preparations for, and was on the point of putting this laft refolve into execution, when he was perfuaded by me and fome others of his friendly acquaintance to fettle himfelf, and follow his bufinefs as ufual, at all hazards ; and it appeared afterwards that the attorney had been perfuaded by fomebody not to urge his claim, at leaft for the prefent. Here the affair refts, and if it happen that the attorney can get paid elfewhere, it is likely he may never renew his claim upon my fon ; if not, it is probable, it may ftill fubject him to future trouble and inconvenience.

Jofeph Greenwood had repeatedly declared in my hearing, that if the difpofition of William Birkhead's will—with which he *was*, or *pretended to be*, unacquainted at the time—had left to his children the eftate which ought to have been left to my fon, as it was reported it had done, that, in that cafe, he would make my fon all the *amends* in his power. What he might have confidered as proper *amends*, or what *kind* or *degree* of amends he might have conferred, if the power of compenfation had remained in his hands, I am not able to fay. I had always thought him in a profperous way of bufinefs; he had taken in a partner the laft year, and about this time they became bankrupt. Jofeph Greenwood attributed very much blame to his partner on this occafion, and faid it was the *unfairnefs* of his conduct that fubjected him to very much lofs, and brought on the bankruptcy. However, this affair entirely difabled him (at leaft, for the prefent) from making any recompenfe to my boy for the deprivation of his expected property, in favour of his children, as aforefaid. Jofeph Greenwood made a demand upon William Birkhead's truftees for money out of the Brookhoufes eftate, to pay the law-expenfes incurred in the late conteft. With this demand I underftand they were not very ready to comply; and it is faid that the affignees of the bankruptcy declare they will fue the truftees if they ftill refufe to advance the money; in which cafe, it is faid, the truftees have declared they will give up their truft into the hands of the chancellor; and in this cafe, it is faid a noted counfel in the law has declared, that the whole eftate would be expended. Here the affair hangs for the prefent, and if the affignees fhould put their threat in execution, I fuppofe they could recover no more, at moft, than what might be deemed Jofeph Greenwood's equal fhare of the expenfes as *one* of the party; and if my fon was confidered as another of the party, he might ftill be liable to pay his full fhare of the expenfe incurred in this deteftable affair, or otherwife take the trouble and expenfe upon himfelf—if this may be feafible —of forcing payment from the Brook-houfes eftate.

Such injurious and unpleafing confequences attend the want of proper attention to paternal admonition. I therefore wifh all my family to take notice of the circumftance, that they may profit thereby if ever it fhould fo happen that any of them hereafter fhould be brought into any fimilar circumftances.

I have now brought the hiftorical fketch of myfelf and my family down to the prefent time. It remains only to take notice, that my daughter Betty, during this interval, bore her fourth living child, a daughter, at Leeds. Mary Ann Greenwood was born in Lower-head-row, Leeds, on Monday, the 12th day of June, 1797.

I will now endeavour to give a fhort account of the important family at Brook-houfes, I mean of the rank and characters of the families they were fprung from.

William Birkhead, grandfather of my firft

wife, dwelt, it feems, at Street-fide, near Dudley-hill,* and followed the trade of making coarfe white cloth.   It does not appear that he was poffeffed of any real eftate, but ranked as one of the lower order of tradefmen in the middle ranks of people. As to his religion, he was a Diffenter of the Prefbyterian perfuafion, and attended divine worfhip at the old Diffenting Chapel,† Bradford.

---

* Street-fide is an old name in the neighbourhood of Birkenfhaw. The high-road from Wakefield to Bradford, after paffing Birkenfhaw, leads over one of the higheft hills in the neighbourhood of Bradford, called Weft-gate hill. A little farther on towards Bradford, a clufter of houfes are named Street-fide, from time immemorial. At the diftance of about a mile, a thickly inhabited diftrict in the borough of Bradford is called Dudley Hill. Within the memory of many now living, the road from Birkenfhaw to Bradford had only a few farm-houfes on each fide, where now may be feen a population confifting of thoufands of the labouring claffes.

† This Diffenting Chapel, Bradford, was the old building ftill ftanding in Chapel-lane. This Prefbyterian place of worfhip was built about the year 1717, but it is probable that there was a diffenting place of worfhip in Chapel-lane before that date. The congregation, about the year 1770, adopted the Unitarian creed of opinions, and have fo continued to the prefent day. It was endowed by Jeremy Dixon, of Heaton-royds, near Manningham, Bradford, yeoman, who by will, dated 22nd Feb. 1724, gave a farm in Denholme, called Birchin Lee, being then of the yearly rent of ten pounds, unto the truftees of this chapel, to the ufe, for ever, of the minifter, being a Proteftant Diffenter from the Eftablifhed Church. Three of the minifters of this place have been learned men, viz., Mr. Heineker, Mr. Ryland, and the prefent minifter, Mr. Freckelton. The interior oak fittings were brought from Howley Hall, on its demolition. The ftone gateway to the chapel was alfo brought from the fame place.

This was the cafe at firſt with his eldeſt ſon William, but the Miniſters of the Calviniſtic ſect called Independents afterwards obtaining poſſeſſion of many of the old Preſbyterian chapels and livings, and this being the cafe in particular at Cleckheaton and Heckmondwike, he and his family became inſenſibly connected with this party, and entered violently into all their ſpirit, principles, and prejudices. He had only one brother younger than himſelf, named Thomas, and three ſiſters. One of theſe married a Joſeph Wooller, a ſhoemaker at Bradford, and left iſſue only one daughter, who married a Mr. Samuel Webſter, a maltſter at Morley, a man of property and a reſpectable family and character. She died without iſſue. Another ſiſter married John Hinchcliffe, near Dudley-hill. They were poor all their life; but their ſon John becoming a dealer in cattle, acquired conſiderable property, took a large farm in the neighbourhood, and provided comfortably for the old people while they lived. John died, leaving a ſon, Joſeph Hinchcliffe (his only child), who reſides at preſent at Newel-hall,* in the road to Wibſey, and occupies

---

* Newel-hall. "On the confines of the townſhip of Bowling, towards North Bierley, lies Newall, or New-hall, anciently one of the ſeats of the Richardſons of Bierley. From an inſcription over the door, within a ſcrolled tablet, it appears to have been built in 1672, by Richard Richardſon, during the life of his ſecond wife, Elizabeth. Though now occupied by cottagers, there are many traces indicatory of its formerly having been a fine manſion. It is built of

the farm belonging to it. He has at prefent a numerous family of feven or eight children, is a man of good character, much bufinefs, and con-fiderable property. The other branches of the family are but in low circumftances. A third fifter married a Julius Whitehead, of Tong, a mafon by trade, an inoffenfive, orderly man, who ranked among that clafs of his neighbours who obtain their bread by their labour.

I return to William and his brother Thomas. Thefe refided at a houfe and fmall farm they had taken at Street-fide, between Dudley-hill and Weftgate-hill, where they joined their ftocks, made coarfe white cloth, and were, it feems, pretty fuccefsful, efpecially during what was called the Ruffia Middle Trade, in which favour-able opportunity, it is generally fuppofed, they obtained the greateft part of their property. They lived together in a ftate of bachelorfhip, till William was approaching towards fifty years of age; he then married a Mary Brooke, a daughter of a John Brooke, a white cloth maker of Cleckheaton. With her he received a *part* of the Brook-houfes eftate as a portion, and

---

large blocks of ftone, and confifts of two wings and a centre. The porch or entrance, according to the ftyle of that day, projects unfymmetrically from one of the wings. The timber and wainfcotting are of black oak, and the maffy door, ftudded with broad-headed nails, ftrongly con-trafts with the light and elegant doors of modern man-fions."—Mr. JOHN JAMES, in his " Hiftory of Bradford." 1848.

paying her father the remaining value, he thus became poffeffed of the whole eftate, partly by gift and partly by purchafe. He immediately erected the prefent houfe, outhoufes, &c., and as foon as it was ready, removed with his family from Street-fide thither, his brother Tommy continuing to refide with the family. Here the family continued till they all died fucceffively, William himfelf, though much the oldeft of the family, being the laft furviving branch of it. His brother Tommy died a bachelor, in the year 1766, leaving his whole fhare of the property to his brother William, except fome trifling legacies of five pounds a-piece to each of his fifters, or their defcendants; thefe, being fome of them in very ftraitened circumftances, exclaimed heavily againft the unfairnefs and difproportion of their brother's donation; but all to no purpofe, it being in general the way of the world to pour into the full cup on thefe occafions. I note here that their two eldeft children, Lydia (my wife) and her fifter Betty, were born at Street-fide, and Willy and Mary were born at Brook-houfes. The old people being careful and faving money out of their income every year, had, during their refidence at this place, firft received in mortgage, and afterwards bought out, the two fmall eftates at Heckmondwike, and purchafed the field in Cleckheaton Upper-lane, and the cottages at Heaton-gate; befides, he had lent upon bond, to Obadiah Brooke, 300*l.*, which he has had in his hands perhaps forty years, and as the old man repeatedly afferted, paid little or no intereft for it. He had alfo lent upon note 10*l.* to Gomerfal Workhoufe (which William Birkby afterwards received), and 10*l.* to Thomas Exley. This was the whole of the property he appeared to be poffeffed of at his death. He had, during his lifetime, paid to my wife (as I mentioned before) 100*l.*, and about 300*l.* amongft my children, which made in the whole 400*l.* on my family-fide; and he often and earneftly declared that William Birkby had received near 1000*l.* out of his houfe, which, with the *partial* difpofals of the will in his family's favour, made a very great, a very unjuft, and a very difproportionate divifion of the fhares which William Birkby and his family, on one fide, and I and my family on the other fide, received out of William Birkhead's property.

There were alfo feveral perfons who were intimately acquainted with the family and its concerns, who thought they had great reafon to believe that fome of their *flatterers*, in the later part of the old man's life, had obtained confiderable fums of money from him—perhaps 400*l.*, 500*l.*, or 600*l.*, more or lefs, which were never accounted for, and for which there appeared no fecurity, and which, if it was fact, were of courfe unjuftly alienated from, and totally loft to, his *own* lawful offspring.

John Brooke, the father of Mrs. Birkhead,

appears to have been a man of a fair general character, and confiderable landed property, and a branch of a numerous, and, at that time, pretty fubftantial family in the neighbourhood; and ranked among the better fort of the middling rank of people. He was by religion a rigid Prefbyterian. He married *three* wives, by the firft of whom he had one child, a fon, named Richard. He turned out wild, enlifted for a foldier, caught a confumption, and died. His fecond wife was from a family at Rooms, near Morley, of the furname of Webfter. With her he had four children, namely, Mary (the late Mrs. Birkhead), of whom we have fpoken before; Samuel, his eldeft fon, who, having offended his father by his marriage, was by him, in effect, difinherited, forfaken by the family, and treated ever afterwards as an alien to their blood; a ftriking inftance, even towards one of their own offspring and the eldeft hope of the family, of the mean pride and unremitting malice inherent in the family, and of which I myfelf experienced from his daughter fo bitter a tafte afterwards. His father gave him two or three fmall crofts, with a cottage and workfhop erected upon them, at a place called Woodfide, between Heaton and Hightown. Having a numerous family of eleven children, he was obliged to mortgage his little pittance for as much money as it would fetch, and ftruggled with diftreffing circumftances all his days. His furviving children, fince his death, have all or moft of them been able to obtain a comfortable fubfiftence by their own exertions. Obadiah, his fecond fon, had the family refidence at Heaton-Green-fide fettled upon him, which ought to have been given to his elder brother. He remained a bachelor to a pretty advanced age, when he had the good fortune to marry a Betty Wood, a daughter of a John Wood, a hardwareman of Bradford. To her management and commercial talents he is entirely indebted, under providence, for the prefent favourable ftate of his family, although, I underftand, his eftate is very deeply mortgaged. He has buried all his children but two fons, John and Obadiah. John has married a quaker, it is faid, with a large fortune, and keeps a hardware fhop, &c. at Cleck-heaton. Obadiah is a bachelor, and fettled at Leeds, where he follows the profeffion of a furgeon and apothecary. Nathaniel, John Brooke's youngeft fon, had a fmall farm called Walftone-houfes, left him near Little Gomerfal, and a few cottages at Heaton-gate; but having a large family alfo of eleven children, was obliged to difpofe of his little eftate in his lifetime, and died in very ftraitened circumftances. His fon Obadiah died before him. Ten of his children furvived him, namely, John, his eldeft fon, who went to the Weft Indies to avoid the perfecution of his father's creditors, and died in Jamaica; Thomas and Jofhua, who obtain their fubfiftence by their labour; Nathaniel and Benoni, who enlifted for foldiers, and are, I fuppofe, ftill in the fervice; Edmund, who had fits, was thrown upon the town, and died; Hannah, who went as a fervant to London, married there, and died; Mary, who married a blackfmith in Lancafhire; Lydia, his youngeft girl, who turned out bad, and followed the foldiers; and Betty, the eldeft girl, who has done much the beft of any of the family, having lately married a Benjamin Fearnley, only fon and child of a John Fearnley, a man of confiderable property in Cleckheaton, who is lately dead, and has left property to his fon, it is faid, of upwards of 2400*l*.

Thus, I have given as fair and impartial an account of this family on both fides, as I am able; their predeceffors, themfelves, their defcendants, and the collateral branches of the families on each fide; from whence it will appear, that they were not fprung from princes; that a few of them were in eafy circumftances, but far the greater part in a low fituation; that they themfelves, (notwithftanding their accidental good fortune in accumulating a little wealth on fome favourable occafions, which made them, in this refpect, a *little* better than *fome* of their neighbours,) were of mean education and low attainments in knowledge. They bore, indeed, a pretty fair character for honefty in their dealings in common with many of their neighbours, and paid a ftrict attention to the formalities of their religion; but had no juft ground, I conceive, for that mighty felf-importance which they feemed defirous of affuming over their neighbours ; and I think I may be allowed, without vanity, to fay, that either with regard to my family, fortune, education, mental abilities, or moral character, I myfelf was, at leaft, as refpectable as they or any that belonged to them ; and that therefore the arrogance, abufe, and contempt with which they continued to treat me to the day of their death, evinced their weaknefs, pride, and vanity, and the badnefs of their hearts ; was infufferable, wicked, deteftable, and blameable in a very high degree.

I come next to their religion, of which I fhall endeavour to give as clear and concife an account as I can.   I fhall next give an exact relation of their behaviour towards me and my children during my connection with them.   I fhall then contraft that behaviour with their religious pro- feffion, and fee how they agree together.   Among thefe obfervations I fhall have occafion to make fome ftrictures on the conduct of feveral other perfons, particularly fome of their religious fra- ternity, who appear to me to have been acceffors, prompters, or affiftants to one or both the old people in their very blameable behaviour towards me and my eldeft fon in particular, and whofe conduct appears, on this occafion, to have been very inconfiftent with their duty as profeffing Chriftians.

The religious fyftem of the old people was

Calvinifm, and they entered into all the bitter prejudices common to the party, againſt thoſe ſectaries who differ from them in opinion, eſpe-cially the *Arminians*, ſo called. They were church-members (as they term themſelves) of the ſect called Independents, meeting together for divine worſhip at Heckmondwike Old Chapel. They paid a conſtant attendance twice every Sunday to hear their preachings, were conſtant partakers every month of *the ordinance* (the cant term of the party for the Lord's Supper), attended the extra lectures and preachments of the party at the neighbouring chapels, had prayers in their family morning and evening every day, and taught their children, &c. the aſſembly's catechiſm, had a kind of religious meetings among the brother-hood at each of their houſes by turns; till they came round, where they ſung and prayed among themſelves, and concluded each viſit with good cheer and common converſation; they refuſed to call the firſt day of the week *Sunday*, but in-ſtead thereof, the *Sabbath*, or the *Sabbath-day*. They had a like objection to ſay *Chriſtmas*, but inſtead thereof ſaid the *Winter-holidays* or Play-days. In ſhort, they came nearer the nice, ſcru-pulous *formality* of the ancient Phariſees than any other party which I have been acquainted with; and I have too much reaſon to believe that this was *eminently* the caſe with reſpect to their *ſpirit* and *diſpoſition* likewiſe.

From all this oſtentatious parade of religious

formality, I thought I had fome reafon to expect that, though I had married their daughter without their confent, and thereby given them *fome* occafion for difpleafure, yet, after their firft refentments were over, their good fenfe and Chriftianity (if they *really* had any) would induce them to behave with fome reafonable degree of refpect towards me, if it was but for the fake of the peace and comfort of their own child, efpecially if, as I intended, I endeavoured to conciliate their affection by behaving as refpectfully towards them and their daughter as lay in my power; but in this expectation I was terribly difappointed. They had before our marriage fpoke of me with the highest contempt and difapprobation imaginable; and, indeed, in fuch very depreciating terms, that if I had heard of *all* they had faid before our marriage, I believe it would have ftaggered my refolution for the match.   On occafion of our marriage their fury arofe well-nigh to madnefs, and their refentment gave vent to itfelf in the moft bitter, degrading, and indecent language; language fo mighty felf-important, abufive, and indecent, as—confidering the little or no difparity between us in my disfavour in any refpect, and their high pretenfions to religion—was matter of aftonifhment to moft of our furrounding neighbours and acquaintance.   The old man wifhed his knife in my heart, faid he would never forgive me, nor ever give me a penny with his daughter, with much more to the fame purpofe.   The old

woman's malice, if poffible, exceeded his, and,
indeed, I always believed fhe had much the worfe
heart of the two, and that the old man's anger
and prejudice would have remitted, if it had not
been artfully increafed and kept up by her evil
influence and mifreprefentations, by which fhe
induced him to look upon me as one of the worft
of characters, and rivetted his prejudice againft
me to the day of his death. In fhort, their whole
conduct on this occafion could not have been
worfe if I had been the vileft mifcreant in the
Britifh dominions. However, I bore all with
ftoical patience, and endeavoured to conciliate
their refpect by the moft gentle and fubmiffive
behaviour, though, the reader will eafily perceive,
their repeated infults were peculiarly difagreeable
and difgufting. Some fhort intervals of apparent
peace and reconciliation fucceeded, but thefe were
always of fhort duration, as they foon found fomething, or nothing, as an occafion to affume their
black looks and difrefpectful behaviour; fo that
I was finally obliged to drop all intercourfe with
the family. My wife, however, *would* continue
her vifits, and being a weak girl, by conftant abufive and degrading language, they foon alienated
her affection from me, and completely infpired
her with their own fpirit and prejudices, which
foon difcovered itfelf in a want of proper efteem
and regard for me, and a total careleffnefs of my
welfare, which entirely overturned all the peace
and comfort of our family; and, as I always

gave her all my cafh to keep, and received it from her again as our occafions required, without taking any account of it, relying entirely on her faithfulnefs, without the leaft fufpicion, I have fince found much reafon to believe that her parents induced her to defraud me of feveral fums of money fecretly, under the fpecious pretences of getting back again what they had lent us, for fear I fhould fhut it,* and faving it for her and the children ; a circumftance which tended much to haften my embarraffments.   Nay, fhe was fo weak and imprudent (as I have been informed fince), as to rail on me behind my back, to the vulgar fellows we had working in the fields, though they laughed her to fcorn for her pains ; and in this fpirit they kept her as long as fhe lived.

When they had thus deprived me of the affections of my wife and the peace of my family, they did all that lay in their power to injure my moral character ; and in order to gain credit for their own conduct, and throw all the odium upon me, they fpoke of me with the utmoft contempt, and flandered me in the moft unjuft manner, to all their party and acquaintance ; and, in the opinion of thofe who did not know me, and thought well of them and their profeffion, they doubtlefs did me much injury ; but in the opinion of all who knew me better, it was out of their

---

* *Shut it*, i. e. fpend it.   A common Yorkfhire word.

power, I believe, to hurt my moral character. Not content with this, they said and did all that lay in their power to deprive me of my children's affections, and endeavoured with all their might, from their infancy to maturer age, to inftil into their minds a diflike and averfion to their own father! Confidering the anxious attention I always paid to my children, the paternal tendernefs with which I had always treated them, and the great affection I always had for them, this part of their conduct hurt me worfe than all the reft, and quite overpowered my patience; and on occafion of the old woman's refufing to let my daughter come and fpeak with me, when I one day fent for her, I differed with her feverely (as I have before related), took both my children home with me, and never came at the houfe again till her death; and I appeal to the heart of every feeling parent, if they can think me greatly blameable, at leaft, on this account, under fuch a trying provocation.

During my widowhood they never came at me, only to get what they could from me. Her youngeft fifter came and wheedled me out of all my wife's clothes, and her mother came and rifled my houfe in my abfence of all my mother's clothes, part of which they fuffered to be ftolen or deftroyed, or wore themfelves, and encouraged my children to convey things fecretly from my houfe, under their ufual pretences, as I have before related. After my fecond marriage, they endeavoured with all their might to perfuade my children to behave with infolence and impropriety towards me and my wife, and thus once again deſtroy the peace of my family; though, by appealing to the good fenfe and affection of my elder children, with fome correction, I was enabled in a good meafure, though not altogether, to prevent the bad confequences of their evil influence. In fhort, for anything that appeared to the contrary, they carried their evil propenfity againſt me to the grave.

After their death a new fcene of malice and undermining villany difplayed itfelf, in the manner in which the old woman and her accomplices had difpofed of the old man's property. As I have given a hiftory of this bufinefs in the preceding pages, I fhall only now add fome additional circumſtances, and give fome account of the mean, ungenerous, and unjuſt practices made ufe of by the perfons who concerned themfelves in this affair, in order to induce Mrs. Birkhead to deprive my fon of his property in favour of thofe who had not fo great a right to it as he had, as the old man himfelf juftly obferved; and attempt to inveſtigate the motives by which they appear to have been each of them actuated.

I have before given a very particular account of the unfortunate affair of my fon with Mifs Rother.* This circumſtance was eagerly laid

---

* This account has been carefully taken out of the manufcript, and this allufion to it is all that remains.

hold of by thofe who were not well-wifhers either to me or my fon, and reprefented to the old people in the moft exaggerated manner, particularly the circumftance of his having promifed the girl marriage. I believe this affair might have been fettled with a trifle, fuppofing the girl had ever advanced any claim, which, perhaps, fhe never would have done; but granting the worft in this cafe, why fhould the eldeft male branch of the family, who, fince his misfortune had given manifeft proofs of his rectitude of conduct, be dealt with much worfe than the youngeft female branch of it, and in a manner difinherited : contrary to the old woman's folemn promife to me in her lifetime; contrary to his uncle Willy's dying requeft, and the old people's folemn promife to him in his dying moments; contrary to the old man's *mind* (as it evidently appeared from his own words afterwards), and contrary to all natural juftice and equity. Or, if any claims from Mifs Rother were feared, why fhould not a *better* annuity than the paltry one of 13*l.* 10*s.* have been fettled upon him for life, and the reverfion of the eftate to his family, as had been done to his younger fifter; or, in default of a family, equally between his fifters or their iffue, at his death; as equity and natural juftice required? This would have fecured it from any poffible claims of Mifs Rother, and have been ufing him with fome juftice and mercy; but to deal with him as they did, and leave his family (if he had

one, and as he was likely to have) without a
shilling to support them with in cafe of his death,
was fo exceflively inconfiderate and cruel, that I
cannot forbear fufpecting (as I have hinted before)
that the old woman herfelf—bad as fhe was—was
impofed upon by the will-maker and her other
aflociates in this affair, who appear to have been
actuated on this occafion by a more infernal
malice, if poffible, againft me and my fon, than
the old woman herfelf.

Another circumftance which the watchful
enemies of my boy laid hold of to prejudice the
old people againft him, and deprive him of his
expectations from them, was as follows.   The
old people were rigid Calvinifts in their religious
fentiments (as I have before obferved).   I myfelf
was of a directly contrary opinion, and efpoufed
the doctrine of Free-agency and Univerfal Re-
demption.   I fcorned to diffemble my fentiments,
to flatter their vanity, but defended them freely
and boldly to the beft of my abilities, though
with decency and good manners—as I had a right
to do—whenever I was attacked by them or any
of their party.   This rendered me obnoxious to
the whole party, and drew upon me their diflike
and difapprobation, and they fpoke of me with
great contempt, and meanly and unjuftly caft
invidious reflections upon my moral character
behind my back upon many occafions, efpecially
the Calviniftic bigots at Brook-houfes.

My fon, during his apprenticefhip with Mr.

Nicholfons (while yet a child, indeed, and before his judgment was matured to form juft conclufions of religious difficulties), had unhappily imbibed from the younger Nicholfon fome biafs to *Deifm;* and, after he came to Leeds, was *incautious* enough to fpeak flightingly of the Bible, and utter his crude conceptions too freely in the hearing of Jofeph Greenwood and others. This was playing a fecond time into his enemies' hands, and was once again the very thing they wanted; for, though no perfon worth his ears would have carried the unwary expreffions of an unfufpicious, unexperienced, unreflecting youth to the perfons with whom it was likely to do him the greateft injury; yet, by fome perfons, inftigated probably by *malice* againft him, or me, or both of us, and by fome other perfons inftigated probably by *felf-intereft*, the wicked tenets and affertions of my fon, with all their aggravations, were prefently whifpered in Mrs. Birkhead's ears; and one flandering, character-murdering, back-ftabbing fcoundrel (old O. B. of Cleckheaton), had the impudence to tell his fifter in the hearing and prefence of my own child (Sally), that my fon was—what? not a *Deift*, as one might have expected, but an *Atheift;* and that I myfelf had taught him Atheism, and that it was a fad thing for a father to teach his child fuch bad principles. A fad thing, indeed! had the charge not happened to be utterly unfounded. Did he not deferve his tongue nailing to the door of the houfe, for uttering fuch a falfe and injurious flander? This injurious report was bandied amongft them for fome time before it reached my fon. At length fome acquaintance told him, that it was reported in the country that he was an *Atheift*. He treated this intelligence at firft with the fmile of contempt, as not fuppofing that anybody would believe it; but at laft the old woman herfelf fent for him, to queftion him upon the fubject. He then began to perceive that it was likely to do him a confiderable injury, and that it had been raifed and propagated by defigning perfons, for this very purpofe. He then fet about finding out the original author, and traced back the report to the late Rev. Mr. James Dawfon, the Independent minifter at Cleckheaton, to whom he immediately wrote the following letter :—

" To the Rev. Mr. James Dawson, Cleckheaton.

" Rev. Sir,   " Leeds, May 12th, 1795.

" Some time fince I was informed by feveral perfons, that it was reported that I was an Atheift. This information, being as new as it was falfe and abfurd, was received by me with the fmile of contempt. I did not think that any evil effects could proceed from fuch a report, for I did not believe it would be credited. Having, however, found that it has operated much to my own difadvantage, and caufed uneafinefs to my friends, I have, therefore, made careful inquiry to find

out the original author of this calumny; and
after tracing it from one perfon to another, have
at laft found, that the fuppofed circumftance was
mentioned by you to a certain gentleman of
Cleckheaton, who, mentioning it to others, has
fpread the invidious report. I have therefore
taken the liberty of requefting that you will inform me *who* was the perfon that told you I was
an Atheift. This requeft I think you ought to
comply with, as well for my fatisfaction as for
the fake of your own character; and I am not
without hopes that you will, by fo doing, fupply
me with a clue by which I fhall have it in my
power to difcover at laft, in the original author
of this flanderous report, either the fecret machinations of the moft abominable villain, or the
agency of fome filly, intermeddling blockhead.

   " I am, with all due refpect,

     " Your humble fervant,

      " THOMAS WRIGHT."

Above a week having elapfed without his
having received any anfwer, he wrote a fecond
letter as follows :—

  " To the Rev. Mr. JAMES DAWSON, Cleckheaton.

" REV. SIR,   " Leeds, May 21ft, 1795.

 " When I lately wrote to defire a fmall favour
from you, I had no doubt but that you would
readily comply with a requeft fo reafonable, and

respecting a matter so *important* to *me*, and of so *little* moment to *yourself*; but I have been totally disappointed in your silence. What can be the cause of this, I am ignorant. Perhaps you think that the affair is not of sufficient importance to deserve your notice; but surely common civility required a civil answer. And besides, you had reported the calumny in question to a person of your acquaintance; a calumny for which it is impossible you should have any just foundation. This circumstance made it requisite that you should either give up the author, or apologize for the ungenerous conduct of having propagated so vile a slander, without knowing from whom you had heard it. If you have never propagated any such report (and I shall certainly take your word for it, if you deny it), then I have detected a very respectable gentleman of Cleckheaton in a wilful falsehood. If I have addressed you somewhat in the language of invective, I hope your candour will make an allowance, and confider that the insulted pride of an honest mind may be expected to defend itself with some warmth, against the dark designs of the hidden assassins of its reputation, without respect of persons. Can anyone tamely bear so sensible an injury without resentment against its authors? This calumny, Sir, which has been invented against me, is calculated to produce the most serious effects; to strip me of character, to deprive me of the sympathy and good-will of my neighbours, and even to wreſt from me the means of procuring an honeſt livelihood. After all, if you ſhould not chooſe to give the information deſired, and if it be not in my power to find the author of this calumnious report, what can I do leſs than contradict ſo groſs a falſehood, by making a public diſavowal of having ever embraced the atheiſtical ſyſtem; and point out to the world thoſe ungenerous perſons who have been, on this occaſion, the viſible agents of the moſt malicious and injurious ſlander and calumny.

"I am, Sir, with all due reſpect,

"Your humble ſervant,

"Thomas Wright."

However, before he put this letter in the poſt, he received from Mr. Dawſon the following anſwer to his former letter :—

"To Mr. Thomas Wright, Leeds.

"Sir,　　　　　"Cleckheaton, 22nd May, 1795.

"Yours, dated 12th inſtant, came to hand. I ſhall not trouble you with any remarks upon it, but ſhall comply with your requeſt. You aſk me, '*Who* was the perſon that told me that you was an Atheiſt?' I have heard Mrs. Birkhead more than either once or twice, ſay that ſhe was informed that you was an Atheiſt; and if ſhe will, ſhe can tell you *who* gave her this information.

"I am, with all due reſpect, yours,

"J. Dawson."

It is evident from this letter of Mr. Dawfon's, that this injurious flander had been paffing among them for fome time ; and every candid mind will allow, that whoever was the author of fuch a wicked flander, they muft be blameable in a very high degree. My boy was fo extremely timid and bafhful, that I could never perfuade him to fpeak to the old people in his own behalf, and this timidity was fo much increafed by the confcious fhame he felt upon his mind on account of his unhappy affair with the aforefaid girl, that in fpite of all I could fay—and I made repeated trials—and the abfolute neceffity of it for his own welfare, I could never engage him to furmount it. This timid bafhfulnefs and want of fpirit was injurioufly imprudent in his then circumftances, and operated much to his difadvantage, though it afforded a ftrong proof of a tender and ingenuous mind. His brother-in-law and fifter Greenwood encouraged him in this conduct, and diffuaded him from vifiting the old people, contrary to my advice ; for what reafon is beft known to themfelves, though, in my opinion (from circumftances that have fince turned up), their conduct on this occafion does not bear a favourable afpect. He accordingly kept himfelf at a fhy diftance from the old people, and fcarce ever paid them a vifit for feveral years. This weak and impolitic conduct gave his enemies their full fcope to raife and fix the old people's prejudices againft him, without oppofition or difturbance, and afforded thofe perfons who had defigns upon his expected property, the beft opportunity they could wifh to eftablifh their undermining plans, and put their bafe defigns in execution; and of this opportunity—as he found to his coft afterwards—they did not fail to avail themfelves to the full.

Another occafion which his enemies laid hold of to ruin him in the favour and good opinion of the old people, was his premature attempt to begin bufinefs, and its unfavourable confequences. I had no hand in this affair, and had rather (and it had been better, much better for him) that he had gone out as a journeyman for fome time, till he had been more perfect in his bufinefs, and waited the event of the old people's death, which was not likely to be far diftant. My boy and Mrs. Birkhead were perfuaded into this tranfaction, and both completely impofed upon in it, by the artful manœuvres of the younger Nicholfon, who, wanting money, took this method to fupply his pockets, at the expenfe of this unwary couple, by exchanging his old fhop-goods, which were comparatively of little value, for Mrs. Birkhead's ready cafh. I believe my boy afterwards never fold them for one half of the money which was paid for them; but this was not the worft. His connexion with this perfon led him into his fatal connection with Mifs Rother, which, plunging his mind in confufion, and adding greatly to his expenfe, both goods and money were foon diffipated. This laid the foundation for all his future misfortunes, and fupplied his enemies with a plaufible reafon for perfuading the old woman that he would be like his father, and would never be good for anything in trade (though his future fobriety and diligence has fince fully confuted this uncandid furmife); that if they left him anything, it would certainly be fpent, and that they had better cut him off with a trifling annuity for life. This unrighteous advice Mrs. Birkhead thought fit to follow, and engaged her difhonourable will-writer to frame a codicil which cut him off from the eftate which the old man had left him in the will itfelf, in lieu of the Lower Brook-houfes, which fhe had quirked him out of *before*, in favour of William Birkby's family ; and by this codicil fhe tricked him out of this eftate alfo, and quit him with a trifling annuity for life (without regard to any family he might have), which was worth little or nothing in comparifon of what fhe had left the other branches of the family. This roguifh codicil, fhe and her affociates perfuaded the poor old doting man to fign, when I believe at the fame time they might as eafily have perfuaded him to have figned his own death-warrant. He afterwards called Tommy into the garden feveral times, told him repeatedly that he *had* left him the Upper Brook-houfes, faid it would be a pretty thing for him, and wifhed him to take care that nobody cheated him out of it, and never manifested the most distant idea of the codicil; and I firmly believe, that as far as his recollection would serve him, the old man died in the full persuasion that he *had* left Tommy John Mortimer's farm. However, the die is now cast, they have put their wicked and spiteful designs in execution, and he is now labouring, and is still likely to labour, under the difficulties and inconveniences brought upon him by the malicious or interested efforts of his and my enemies, in the deprivation of his justly expected property.

It does not appear that my son ever questioned Mrs. Birkhead after the writing of the aforesaid letters, as to *who* had informed her that he and his father were Atheists, otherwise he might possibly have been able to have ascertained with greater precision *who* was the *real* author of this execrable slander. However, the persons who appeared to concern themselves most in this nefarious business were, Joseph Greenwood, of Leeds, who appears to have been actuated (perhaps altogether) by motives of *self-interest;* Thomas Exley, of Spen, and Obadiah Brook, of Cleckheaton, who appear to have been actuated chiefly by what I beg leave to call *religious malice;* for to the best of my knowledge, I never gave either of them any *just* occasion for ill-will towards me, nor ever any *other* occasion than that of happening to differ from them in my religious principles, and taking the liberty of defending those principles from scripture and reason, to the best of my abilities, whenever I was attacked by any of their party. But this is enough to make a man pafs with many, perhaps with moft Calvinifts, for a fool, a knave, a Deift, an Atheift, and every-thing that is weak, wicked, and contemptible; and I believe thefe two perfons were the more willing to do my fon a ferious injury, becaufe they could thereby gratify their fpleen and malice againft his father. I do not know that either my fon or me ever gave the leaft fhadow of occafion to any perfon under the fun, to believe or fuppofe that we were Atheifts, or ever manifefted the leaft tendency towards the atheiftical fyftem. I can fay the fame for myfelf with refpect to Deifm, which I never believed as a fyftem, or inclined to believe, though I have feen and read fome of their capital authors and arguments; but ever fince I was able to form a rational judgment, have uniformly believed and received the Chriftian doctrines, according to the beft of my apprehen-fions; and I have taken no fmall pains to obtain a juft knowledge of the Chriftian fyftem, and afcertain what was truth, and what was error, among the different fyftems of profeffing Chrift-ians. This, I conceive, it was my duty to do, and this, I conceive, it is the duty of every other perfon to do, according to their talents and oppor-tunities. And though I believe that I have a right to fay, if I think fo, that I believe another perfon's fentiments to be *erroneous*—giving my *reafons* for fuch my judgment—yet I do not believe that either I or anybody elfe have a right to mifreprefent, contemn, flander, vilify, and perfecute any other perfon becaufe his religious fentiments happen to be different from, or contrary to ours, any more than becaufe our countenances happen to be different. I therefore think that fuch a conduct is highly blameable, and a certain mark, fo far, of a bad fpirit.

I recite the following circumftances, containing the *reafons* for the *motives* I have afcribed to the *conduct* of the perfons above referred to.

William Birkhead frequently altered his wills, or rather, made new ones, in confequence chiefly of the changes made in his family by death. Towards the clofe of his life, and for fome confiderable time *before* what was called, during the late law conteft, his *firft will* was made, it was well known he was become exceeding defective in his memory, and was fallen, in a degree, into what is commonly called dotage. Under this circumftance the whole direction and management of family concerns fell into Mrs. Birkhead's hands, and fhe could influence the old man to fay, or do, or fign anything fhe pleafed, with the fame eafe fhe could influence a child. Taking advantage of this ftate of his mind—contrary to natural juftice, and, I believe, his own *uninfluenced* mind—fhe and her youngeft daughter, while fhe lived, over-perfuaded the old man to leave William Birkby's youngeft fon, the *youngeft* male branch of the family, the Lower

Brook-houfes, inftead of leaving it to my fon, the *eldeft* male branch of the family, as natural juftice required.   But to make him fome compenfation for this unfair partiality, he, at the fame time, left him the upper part of the eftate, or John Mortimer's Farm.   However, after fome time, when the old man's mind was ftill more debilitated by increafing age, urged by her malignity againft me, and the advice and influence of her malicious or interefted affociates, fhe and they framed that deteftable codicil, and perfuaded the old man to fign it, when, I believe, he did not know what he was doing; which cut my fon off from this eftate alfo, and quit him with the paltry annuity aforefaid.

I was well aware that Jofeph Greenwood had taken no little pains to infinuate himfelf into Mrs. Birkhead's good opinion, and had been equally folicitous to obtain the good graces of her chief counfeller and fcribe, Thomas Exley; and by an artful application to their particular foibles, and the *apparent* profperous circumftances of his trade at that time—which induced Mrs. Birkhead to believe him to be a *great manager*— he fucceeded in a great meafure in his defign, and they entered pretty eagerly into his views. As I myfelf was out of favour with the old folks, and had never come at them for ten or twelve years, and as my children had no fpirit or refolution to fpeak to the old people for themfelves, or make the leaft attempt to counterwork the *undue* influence of the other family, I thought this circumstance not amiss at the time, as it might serve to balance accounts with the sinister endeavours of the contrary party, never once imagining that his design was to undermine the interest of my own child—my eldest and only surviving son by this connection, and deprive him of that property he had a right to expect, and procure it to be transferred to his own children. This, however, appeared from following circumstances to be the real fact, for though Joseph Greenwood pretended to be unacquainted with the particulars of the first will, yet his uncommon eagerness to establish the validity of this will, was an undeniable proof that he *knew* it was made very much in his, or his family's favour; and that he *knew* this was done out of what ought to have been given to my son, appears, I think, first, from his advising my son—so contrary to good policy and his apparent interest— not to visit the old people after his misfortune, to apologize for his fault, endeavour to regain their favour, and prevent his enemies from taking the advantage of his misfortune and his absence. It is true his *sister* joined in this advice, but whether she judged so *ill* as to believe the advice to be proper for his interest, or had any sinister view in the case, is a matter that admits of some doubt to me, and causes many a painful reflection in my mind, whenever I think upon it. In the next place, although Joseph Greenwood and his party made *Doctor Greenwood's designs to cheat the rest of the family*, the great bugbear of their proceedings, yet the futility of this pretence was evinced beyond a doubt in the sequel; for when the contents of the *last will* came to be known, it appeared that Joseph Greenwood had a *better* fortune left by this will than by the first will, excepting that the rascally codicil alienated Tommy's portion, which the old man had left him in the will itself, in favour of William Birkby's girl and Joseph Greenwood's children. Therefore, if Joseph Greenwood had been a fair, and equitable, and a generous man, when he knew this, he would have dropped the contest immediately, and scorned to have advanced another step, or spent another farthing in such a shameful cause; but as he did not, but persevered in the prosecution of it till he had attained his unrighteous design, it is an incontestible proof that to obtain Tommy's portion for his own children and Birkby's girl (by which he left Tommy in a state next to beggary), was the sole motive of his conduct throughout this whole affair. A further proof of this is, that Thomas Exley was overheard to tell him, that he must support the first will, at all events, as it was made very much in his favour. I have also a violent suspicion that the wicked and execrable slander of *Atheism*, and other injurious reports, *originated* at Leeds; though they might be *improved* and further propagated by his assistants at

Spen, Cleckheaton, and probably others of the
party we know not of. I fufpect this, firft becaufe
Tommy was wont to exprefs his fentiments the
moft freely and incautioufly at Jofeph Greenwood's houfe—not about *Atheifm*, to which I
never knew him in the leaft inclined—but about
the validity of the Bible, of which he feemed to
have fome doubt, and to manifeft a difpofition to
Deifm; and fome *wife* people are hardly able to
make a diftinction between the fyftems, though
they are as different as light and darknefs, and a
difpofition to *Deifm* is eafily improved by fuch
reporters into a *firm belief* of it, and a firm belief
of it into Atheifm. Again, I have heard Jofeph
Greenwood make remarks on this fubject, and
fpeak on feveral occafions with the greateft contempt of Tommy's fchemes, talents for trade,
&c. Again, I have heard both Jofeph Greenwood and Betty fay, that if the old people left
Tommy anything, they had beft leave him an
annuity. To this I fhould have had no *great*
objection, had they left him a genteel annuity,
adequate to what they left the other branches of
the family, and the reverfion of the eftate to his
family, if he fhould leave one, at his death ; but
to leave him fuch a paltry annuity as they did,
and that for life only, deferved dafhing back
again in their teeth. In the laft place and above
all, I fufpect this, becaufe fuch a flanderous afper-
fion on Tommy and his father, was fo capitally
calculated to promote their bafe purpofes, and

accomplish their interested or malicious defigns.
I was yet more vexed, if poffible, that Jofeph
Greenwood fhould induce my fon to view the
affair in fo falfe a light, and in confequence of this
to perfuade him to act with fuch exceffive abfurdity
as difgraced his intellects, by affifting a fet of
perfons with all his might in a caufe whofe chief,
if not fole, object, was to accomplish his own
ruin, by depriving him of that property which
the old man would fain have left him, and which
was his *only* and *laft* expectation of pecuniary
affiftance in this world. Great is the injury
which Jofeph Greenwood has done to my fon
as well as to himfelf and my younger daughter,
by his ill-timed, ill-omened, and ill-judged conduct on this occafion. In the firft place, I am
perfuaded it has injured himfelf by breaking his
time, neglecting his bufinefs, and expending his
money ; and by breaking into his ftock, has moft
probably haftened his bankruptcy, which has
given occafion for what was fairly and honourable left him at Brook-houfes to be immediately
alienated from him, and he and his family thrown
upon the mercy of his friends and the world.
In the next place, it has deprived Tommy of the
Lower Brook-houfes, which the old man would
certainly have left him but for his interference.
In the next place, it has deprived him of the
Upper Brook-houfes, which the old man *had*
left him in lieu of it—the vile codicil cutting
him off from this alfo, and leaving him, in com-

parifon of the others, next to nothing. In the next place, it has occafioned my younger daughter's hufband perhaps as much trouble, inconvenience, and expenfe as all he has got is worth ; and it has thrown perhaps more than two-thirds of the property into the hands of the *other family* at the *expenfe of mine,* without *their* being obliged to be at any trouble or expenfe on the occafion ; and all this appears to have been done merely to fecure the *reverfion* of the Upper Brook-houfes at Tommy's death (loaded with a legacy of 150*l.* and intereft out of it to the other family) to Jofeph Greenwood's children. It has occafioned another very great evil. It has fown the feeds of diffenfion and malice between perfons and families who ought to have been the moft kindly-affectioned to one another, and which is not likely to be foon or eafily extinguifhed, and which exifts at the imminent hazard of the *future* happinefs of every perfon who indulges it.

Such is the injurious and unpleafing confequences attending this ill-judged conteft. It will be faid, perhaps, that Tommy was under great obligations to Jofeph Greenwood ; that he had been at the trouble and expenfe of following him to Sheffield to difengage him from Mifs Rother ; that he afterwards afforded him the fhelter and convenience of his houfe in his diftrefs, and affifted him with fmall fums of money to begin his bufinefs with again, &c. This is true, and both Tommy and his father wifhed to be grateful, and to make him every reafonable return, if ever it might be in the power of either of them to fhow him as great, or a greater favour. But this did not entitle him to what ought to have been Tommy's property, or juftify or excufe him in unfair and ungenerous attempts to obtain it. Could Tommy have had what he had a right to expect, he both *could* and *would* have made him every return that could reafonably have been expected from an honeft, grateful, and generous heart ; but being deprived of this, it renders him unable to manifeft his gratitude to the extent he could have wifhed, and he muft remain *apparently* under an unreturned obligation ftill ; though Jofeph Greenwood has got Tommy's expected property for his own children, and thereby deprived him in a great meafure of the means of making a comfortable provifion for his own fubfiftence.

I remark next on the conduct of Thomas Exley. This man had made a long and high profeffion of religion ; and was confidered as one of the chief pillars of the religious fociety with which he was connected : one would therefore have expected from a perfon of fuch a profeffion and character, that he would have fpoke and acted with refpect to *every man* he might have any concern about, with the equity, candour, love, and kindnefs of a *chriftian* ; but this did not appear to have been the cafe to me. There are divers perfons who fuppofe that Thomas

Exley ſtood ſo high in the good opinion and eſtimation of the old people, and that his influence over them was ſo great, that if he had thought fit, he could eaſily have perſuaded them to have made a more equitable will. However, be this as it may, I blame him for writing ſo ſcandalouſly unfair a paper, as the codicil eſpecially, at all, ſo I told him. He ſaid, if he had not wrote it, ſomebody elſe would. Be it ſo; then ſomebody elſe ſhould; I would have ſcorned to have had a hand in ſo dirty a buſineſs; and I think I know even ſome attorneys who, from a principle of honour, would have refuſed to have wrote, even for pay, ſuch an unjuſt paper as the codicil. I blame him, in the next place, for *prevarication*, if not for uttering a *wilful falſehood*. I met with him at the public-houſe where the jury met to decide upon the old man's intellects. I there told him what I had heard reported of the diſpoſals in the old man's will, and complained with ſome warmth of their great *injuſtice* to my boy, if the report was true. He adviſed me to be patient till the will was made public, and *aſſured* me that things *were not*, or *were not ſo bad*, as I ſeemed to fear, or as had been reported; hence I was induced to hope that matters might turn out more favourable for my ſon, than I had been led to imagine. However, when the will came to be known, it turned out to be *much worſe* than had either ever been reported, or than I had ever imagined it to be. Now, it was evident that Thomas Exley

defigned, by what he faid, to quiet my apprehen-
fions, and make me believe that matters were
left better for my fon than they really were ; and
as he was the will-writer, he muft be perfectly
acquainted with its contents : I afk, therefore,
was fuch double dealing as this confiftent with
the Chriftian character ? I blame him, in the
next place, for indulging a very unchriftian fpirit
towards me. He was converfing one day with
a friendly acquaintance of mine on the fubject of
the old man's will, fome time previous to its
being made public ; he told him that my fon
was difinherited, and quit with a trifling annuity,
and faid, with a farcaftic fmile, " How Tommy
Wright of Birkenfhaw would ftorm if he knew
this ! " and feemed to enjoy, by anticipation, a
malignant pleafure in the chagrin which he fuppofed the knowledge of this circumftance would
excite in my breaft. He afterwards, indeed,
when I charged him with it, denied that he had
made the obfervation ; but as I have no reafon
to doubt the veracity of my friend, who could
not poffibly have known the circumftances he
related to me, if Thomas Exley had not informed
him of them ; and as Thomas Exley attempted
to deny what I heard him fay with my own ears
at Birftall, by fkulking behind a flimfy falvo, I
have reafon to believe his motives and conduct
much the fame on this occafion. But fuch a
fpirit and fuch a *conduct* but ill comports with
Chriftianity.

I next remark on the conduct of Obadiah Brook, of Cleckheaton. This perfon is another religious brother of the fame community, and had repeatedly manifefted a malevolent difpofition towards me; and there is reafon to believe that the old man would have rectified his will, and done juftice to my fon, as well as to the reft of the family, if it had not been for his impertinent and malicious interpofition, as I have obferved before. Thefe circumftances, together with that of his falfe and injurious flander to his fifter, that my fon was an atheift, and that I had taught him atheifm, difcover fuch a degree of the moft rancorous and infernal malignity towards me and my family, as I think, the moft candid perfon would find no fmall difficulty to reconcile with the genuine fpirit of Chriftianity. I proceed to compare the conduct of thefe people with their religious profeffion.

When I determined to marry William Birkhead's daughter, notwithftanding the unfavourable difpofition of her parents towards me at the time, I entertained a pretty confident hope that, when the firft paroxifm of their fury was over, and they had given every circumftance a fair confideration, their refentment would fubfide, and we fhould foon become reconciled to one another. I founded this expectation, in the firft place, upon the circumftance of there being *little* or *no real* occafion between us for their violent difapprobation of the match; and, in the next place, upon their religious character ; concluding, that if *indeed* they poffeffed in any tolerable degree the genuine *fpirit* of the religion they had made fo long and fo high a profeffion of, they both *muft* and *would* act accordingly, and that mutual goodwill, peace, and quietnefs between the families would be the happy and neceffary refult.   In order to obtain this defirable end, I had refolved to behave towards the old people with all the *reafonable* refpect and fubmiffion that I could.   I accordingly condefcended to acknowledge the impropriety of my conduct in marrying their daughter *without* their confent, and to afk their pardon in the humbleft manner, as I have noticed before.   I told them I fhould be glad to live on friendly terms with them, and to do all that lay in my power to oblige them, and make their daughter happy ; but all would not do, for, except fome very fhort intervals of *apparent* fociablenefs, during which they were ill able to conceal and fupprefs their prejudices, their general behaviour towards me to the day of their death, was marked with the keeneft averfion and contempt, and the moft inveterate malice.   When I could no longer fee them with any fatisfaction, I refrained the houfe as much as poffible.   However, I indulged my wife in this refpect, as fhe *would* vifit them frequently ; and I often fent the maid (when we had one), or went with her myfelf, to carry the child, till we were near the houfe, and then returned, and met her again when she came back. This was a disagreeable circumstance, and a woman of any spirit, or who had had any regard for the honour of her husband, if *he* could not have seen them in peace, and with good acceptance, would have scorned to have come near them herself. But I soon found the bad effects of this intercourse. It has appeared since, that her parents—especially her mother—during these visits were perpetually vilifying and abusing me to my wife in the most malignant manner, and endeavouring with all their might to instil into her mind a mean and contemptible opinion of her husband, and to deprive me of her regard and affection. This vile purpose they finally effected, and rendered her not only *indifferent*, but even *inimical* to both me and my interests, and, of course, entirely overturned the peace and comfort of our family; and in this unpleasing state of mind, with respect to her husband, through the evil influence of her parents, she appeared to remain to her last moment. Death itself did not seem to soften their enmity, or appear in the least to meliorate their minds; even on this awful occasion they continued to manifest their utter contempt and disregard of me in the most striking manner, by refusing to send either me or the children the least notice of my wife's death, though it so nearly concerned us, and I had earnestly desired it of them the night before; nor did we hear anything of the event, till the neighbours, who came occafionally to our houfe, brought us word in the morning. They behaved precifely in the fame difrefpectful and ill-natured manner towards me fome years afterwards on occafion of the death of my youngeft fon. During my widow-hood they took Sally, and brought her up from that time, for the moft part; but would never fend her to any place of genteel education (except a few weeks at Leeds when fhe was up-grown), and the petty learning fhe had I paid the fchool wage chiefly myfelf; but fhe never learned one liberal fentiment from them during their lives, and it had been much better for her if fhe had been brought up elfewhere. They took my youngeft fon (Willy), with my confent, from the nurfe, and took great care of him while he lived. They feemed to have a great affection for this child, efpecially the old man, who appeared to forrow more feverely for this child's death, than even for that of his own fon. This was a proof of a feeling heart, and mended my opinion a good deal of the old man's difpofition, though he appeared to retain his antipathy againft me to the laft. But the poor old man, I believe, was very much impofed upon, and his diflike and ill-opinion of me artfully fomented and kept up by his wife and her affociates for malicious or interefted purpofes, and is therefore entitled to greater allowance in this refpect. I believe, had my fon Willy furvived, he would have ftood a fair chance for a good fhare of the old people's property. However, they continued to exert all their influence to deprive me of my children's affection, and infpire them with a fupreme contempt for their father; and as my fon Tommy had always manifefted a warm attachment to, and affection for, his father, I have much reafon to believe that their unjuft and fcandalous behaviour towards him at laft, arofe in a large meafure from their hatred to me, for fear (fhould I afterwards ftand in need of his help) he fhould have it in his power to afford me any affiftance. Now, even admitting that I had been a perfon of a bad moral character and conduct, would it not have been their duty as Chriftians, and fhould not common prudence and natural affection to their own child, have induced them to do their beft to promote peace, harmony, and happinefs between us? It certainly ought to have been the cafe, but as they could raife no juft objection to my moral character, and I did my beft to be on good terms with them, were they not, therefore, doubly blameable, and uncommonly perverfe, conftantly to abufe me to my wife, to alienate her affection from me, and to give fome colour to fuch an ungenerous proceeding, to endeavour to blacken my moral character; to withhold her fortune from her, to the embarraffment and final ruin of my temporal circumftances; to endeavour to deprive me of my childrens' efteem and affection from their infancy to maturer age, by fpeaking of me to them in the moft contemptuous and degrading manner, and thus, as far as they could, to ruin the peace of my family; and finally, to deal unjuſtly with my children in the difpoſal of their property, by nearly diſinheriting my eldeſt ſon, and turning him and his family out to beggary; and diſpoſing of far the beſt and greater part of their property to the youngeſt daughter's offspring, contrary to the ſolemn promiſe the old woman had made to me while ſhe lived, contrary to the ſolemn promiſe they had both made to their own expiring ſon, and contrary to every rule of natural juſtice and equity? Could ſuch a conduct as this be confiſtent with a ſingle grain of *real* Chriſtianity, I leave it with the reader to determine; but ſurely, as the poet juſtly and ſtrikingly ſays,—

> " Accurſed is the wretch,
> To ſocial life the moſt inhuman foe,
> Who, in the nice, the tender ſcenes of life,
> Dares raſhly meddle and ſow,"

or promote, diviſion and diſagreement betwixt a man and the wife of his boſom, betwixt a father —a tender and affectionate father—and the off-ſpring of his own bowels. Yet this have they done to me at Brook-houſes; this did they con-tinue to do as long as they lived; and in the old man's will (ſo called) matters were ſo unfairly ordered in the difpoſal of their property, as to foment and continue the ſame infernal ſpirit of ſtrife and contention, animoſity and malice, amongſt the different branches of the family (amongſt whom I have the misfortune to number three of my own ſurviving children by this con-nection), which has cauſed ſome hundreds of it to be ſquandered amongſt the lawyers, has ruined my eldeſt ſon, and done very conſiderable injury to my other two children, and is not unlikely to tranſmit the ſame bad ſpirit of enmity and ill-will to future generations.

APPENDIX.

ELEGIAC STANZAS ON THE DEATH OF AN INFANT

(MARY WRIGHT, MY SECOND DAUGHTER AND SECOND CHILD).

Wherein some observations are occasionally introduced on that opinion entertained by some religious professors, that all the children of those who are not Christian believers, who die in their infancy, are damned.

> " Happy the babe, who privileged by fate,
> To shorter labour and a lighter weight,
> Received but yesterday the gift of breath,
> Ordered to-morrow to return to death."—PRIOR'S *Sol.*

" And they brought young childen to him that he should touch them ; and his disciples rebuked those that brought them. But when Jesus saw it, he was *much displeased*, and said unto them, Suffer the little children to come unto me, and forbid them not, for of such is the kingdom of God. Verily, I say unto you, whosoever shall not receive the kingdom of God as a little child, he shall not enter therein. And he took them up in his arms, put his hands upon them, and blessed them."—*Mark* x. 13—16.

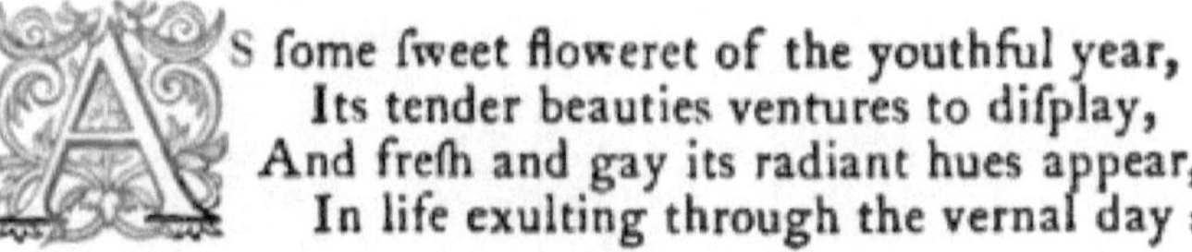

S some sweet floweret of the youthful year,
   Its tender beauties ventures to display,
   And fresh and gay its radiant hues appear,
   In life exulting through the vernal day :

At night shrunk up by some unkindly blast,
   Its unabiding, shadowy beauties fly,
Its blooming honours to oblivion haste,
   And droop, and sicken, fade away, and die.

So thou, fweet babe, juft op'd thy infant eyes,
    This fin-diforder'd fcene of things to view,
But blafted by the noxious damps that rife,
    Thy tender foul to happier climes withdrew.

Farewell, my lovely innocent, farewell!
    By thy cherubic guards attended, rife
High in thy heavenly Father's houfe to dwell,
    In blifsful manfions of the eternal fkies.*

Well haft thou fcaped the thoufand ills that fwarm
    In baneful troops o'er earth's infected fhore;
Safe art thou lodged beyond the reach of harm,
    Where pain and grief can never touch thee more.

Whate'er of fin from thy firft fire † derived
    Subjected thee to pain and death below,
Thy Saviour's blood has of its fting deprived,—
    The little children He receives, we know.‡

Shall any hard, unfeeling bofom dare
    Suppofe that innocence like thine may go
To fuffer dire, infernal torments there
    Where raging fiends inhabit endlefs woe?

Accurfed thought! abhorrent muft it be,
    Greatly abhorrent to the tender heart;
Dire, horrid, fhocking to humanity;
    Enough to make the vileft tyrant ftart!

Vile thought, moft gracious God! vile thought of thee;
    Difgraceful to thy goodnefs muft it prove;
Difhonourable to the laft degree
    To thee, whofe nature and whofe name is Love.

Ye infant-damners, lend a candid ear,
    While I attempt the tender babes' defence;
The little children's advocate appear,
    And plead the caufe of infant innocence.

---

* See Matt. xviii. 10. "For I fay unto you, that in heaven their angels do always behold the face of my Father which is in heaven."

† Adam.

‡ See the motto, and the correfpondent places in the other Evangelifts, "Suffer the little children to come unto me, and forbid them not."

" Of infant-innocence," methinks I hear
    Some gloomy, ftern, auftere profeffor cry,
" They all deferve the wrath of Heaven to bear,
    They all deferve for Adam's fin to die.

" To die eternally, their lot to have,
    In foul-tormenting, everlafting fire ;
To howl, and fcream, and fhriek, and writhe, and rave,
    In vengeful flames that never fhall expire."

Oh, horrid, horrid tale ! enough to make
    The moft unpitying bofom thrill with pain ;
To caufe a heart of adamant to ache,
    And freeze the life-blood up in every vein.

Can this be any *parent's* voice, that deals
    Damnation round in fuch a lavifh ftrain
Amongft the helplefs infant tribes, nor feels
    One pang of forrow, grief, remorfe, or pain ?

Can any *father* act fo dire a part ?
    Or tender *mother* fuch opinions bear ?
Where are the yearnings of a *father's* heart ?
    The founding of a *mother's* bowels, where ?

Oh, what fond parent's heart could unopprest
    Behold their offspring ficken and expire,
Torn from the nurfing mother's tender breaft,
    And plunged in oceans of devouring fire ?

But oh, my foul, the dreadful thought forbear,—
    A thought too dreadful far for me, I own :
In this refpect, whatever others are,
    My heart is made of flefh, and not of ftone.

But you fome falvo have in this refpect,
    Whereby more favour will to yours be fhown ;
You a believer are, you are elect,
    And think by this that you fecure your own.

Your narrow foul, it feems, without regret,
    Can half a world of other infants fee
(Be yours but fafe) thrown headlong to the pit,
    To feed the flames to all eternity.

For loving Chriſtians a ſad ſpirit this,
  And as ſtrange Chriſtian doctrine this indeed ;
This genuine ſupererogation is,
  If *your* believing ſave your infant ſeed.

But when did God the ſolemn oath annul,
  Which in His ſacred Word we find him make ? *
Does he at length invert his ancient rule,
  And ſave or damn them for the parent's ſake ?

See that poor heathen ; in her cloſe embrace
  While kindly ſhe her tender babe ſecures,
It ſweetly ſmiles in its fond parent's face,
  As free from blame, as innocent, as yours.

Will God, their common maker, think you, deal
  So differently with theſe, as yours to ſave,
And ſend the heathen infant's ſoul to hell,
  Whene'er he ſends its body to the grave ?

'Cauſe you have heard the ſound, and have receiv'd,
  Believed, and truſted in a Saviour's name,
In which the unhappy heathen ne'er believ'd,
  Becauſe, alas ! ſhe never heard the ſame.

Unequal, cruel conduct this indeed,
  With which you charge a gracious God, my friend ;
Strange goſpel ! which I'm ſure I never read,
  And which, I think, you never can defend.

'Tis true, God does permit the little ones
  (Though they in *perſon* ne'er could ſin, we know,)
To cry, complain, and weep ; to utter groans,
  And ſuffer a variety of woe.

For their exiſtence, by their father's † fault,
  So circumſtanced was, that they, 'tis plain,
Could into perſonal being not be brought
  Without being ſubjected to ſuffer pain.

---

* See Ezek. xviii. 3 and 20. " As I live, ſaith the Lord God, the ſon ſhall
not bear the iniquity of the father, neither ſhall the father bear the iniquity of the
ſon."   † Adam's.

Howe'er, the light afflictions they endure,
    Which are but for a moment ere they ceafe,
Are greatly countervail'd, as they enfure
    A weight of glory, and eternal blefs.*

So God ordains.   When our firft father fell,
    And in his loins his whole included feed,
God juftly might have fent us all to hell,
    As making *one* with our corrupted head.

This *muft* have been the cafe, if juftice had
    Eternally to punifh us devifed,
So far true equity had been difplay'd,
    The fin and punifhment had harmoniz'd.

For as *unconfcious* of our father's crime,
    We finn'd *in him* without our own confent,
We then fhould have been punifhed *in him*,
    Without a *confciousnefs* of punifhment.

But Mercy interpofed, and Goodnefs cried,
    (Infinite Goodnefs!) let the finner live ;
I have a ranfom found, my Son has died,†
    (Died in effect) I can his fin forgive.

Through this Redeemer, all his future race,
    Together with their fire, may be forgiven,
May all obtain, through His redeeming grace,
    Repentance, pardon, holinefs, and heaven.

And as for thofe the monfter Death fhall feize,
    And in their infancy of life diveft,
'Twill infinitely better be for thefe
    Than if their perfonal being were fuppreft.

For as through the *offence* of Adam, *all*
    (He and his unborn feed) were doomed to die,
Even *fo* the *righteoufnefs* of Jefus fhall
    Retrieve them *all*, and freely juftify.‡

---

* See 1 Cor. iv. 17. " For our light afflictions which are but for a moment,
worketh for us a far more exceeding and eternal weight of glory."
    † Job xxxiii. 24. " Deliver him from going down into the pit, I have found
a ranfom."
    ‡ See Rom. v. 18. " Therefore, as by the offence of one (Adam) Judgment
came upon *all men* to condemnation, even *fo* (in the fame *manner and extent*) by

And by my great and glorious name, I fwear,*
  No fon fhall fuffer for his father's crime ;
Eternal mifery, I mean, howe'er
  They undergo grief, pain, and death in time.

Hence, gentle innocents, ye all are fafe,
  Ye ne'er fhall occupy the infernal den ;
God is your friend, you may fecurely laugh
  At the vain notions of erroneous men.

What ftrange, unworthy notions muft they have,
  Of that † all-loving, good, and gracious mind,
Who think they honoured him whene'er they gave
  Him fovereign right to damn the infant kind.

What a ftrange Chriftian muft that mortal be,
  Who can the cruel fentiment maintain,
Or could with any fatisfaction fee
  Poor, harmlefs infants doomed to endlefs pain !

The Saviour feems of quite a different mind,
  " Forbid ye not the little ones," ‡ fays he,
Welcome to Jefus are the infant kind,
  " Suffer the little babes to come to me."

" Yes, truly, this fhall be your certain doom,
  Ye in no wife fhall ever be forgiven,
Except like little children you become ;
  Of fuch is the fociety of heaven."

---

the righteoufnefs of one (Chrift) the free gift came upon (the fame) *all men,* to juftification of life." This paffage (I think) fully proves the point, as to the juftification of all infants (at leaft), exhibits Jefus Chrift as great a Saviour as Adam was a deftroyer, and makes the plaifter as wide as the fore ; and I am apt to think, that no perfon of good fenfe and penetration, who candidly confiders the paffage, without party-prejudice or views to pre-conceived fyftems, can poffibly think otherwife.

  * See Ezek. xviii. 3 and 20. " As I live, faith the Lord God, the fon fhall not die for the iniquity of his father." This muft, I conceive, refer to *uncommon* judgments and *future* fufferings, for by the law of our prefent degraded ftate, we fuffer many diftreffes and inconveniences of a *temperal* nature, from the wickednefs, folly, or imprudence of our parents ; nay, the body is fubject to pain, diffolution, and death, becaufe of fin of young and old, good and bad together.

  † See Pfalm cxlv. 9. " The Lord is good to all, and his tender mercies are over all his works." See alfo 1 Tim. ii. 3 and 4. " God our Saviour will have all men to be faved, and to come unto the knowledge of the truth."

  ‡ Mark x. 4. " Suffer ye little children to come unto me."

Jefus was *much difpleafed* with thofe (I read)*
  Who thought fo meanly of his love and grace—
Whofe yet contracted breaft would have forbid
  The little children from his fond embrace.

Who can but be difpleafed, as Jefus was,
  Yea, *much*, yea, very much difpleafed with thofe
Who would exclude poor infants from his grace,
  And doom the little ones to endlefs woes.

But, hail, ye little lovely creatures, hail!
  Tho' fome ftrange mortals would no pity fhew
Towards your helplefs innocence, 'tis well
  Your Saviour has a kinder heart for you.

Whate'er *morofe* would you of heaven deny,
  I am well pleafed to hear the Saviour blefs; †
Whoever are difpleafed to hear it, I
  Rejoice fincerely in your happinefs.

Not in the happinefs of *mine* alone;
  That were unworthy of a generous breaft
(Tho' two of my dear babes are thither gone); ‡
  No, I rejoice to think you *all* are bleft.

If e'er thro' boundlefs mercy I obtain
  An humble place upon that happy fhore,
Where error and miftake, where grief and pain,
  Difeafe and death, and parting are no more;

Methinks, conducted by fome heav'nly guide,
  I then fhall gladly hafte to feaft my fight
With the fweet heav'n where infant-faints refide,
  And view their happy train with vaft delight.

Methinks, on ftrong imagination's wing
  Tranfported, I already view the place;
Already hear their happy manfions ring
  With thankful fongs for their Redeemer's grace.

---

* Mark x. 4. " Jefus was much difpleafed."
† Mark x. 16. " Jefus took them up in His arms and bleffed them."
‡ Before the finifhing of thefe ftanzas, a fecond child of the author's died.

See ! what a blaze of lucid brightnefs decks
    And beams delightful o'er the blifsful plain ;
What *equal** ray of ftreaming glory breaks
    From ev'ry faint thro' all the countlefs train !

Hail, virgin fouls! ye little cherubs, hail !
    Firft objects of your Lord's redeeming care ;
Thro' Him poffefs'd of joys that ne'er fhall fail,
    And all the blifs you poffibly can fhare.

'Tis true your infant-fouls cannot contain
    So large a fhare of happinefs as they
Who fought and conquer'd on the hoftile plain,
    And bore the heat and burden of the day.

Howe'er, you fhare pre-eminence in this ;
    For furely you had leaft to be forgiven,
Tho' not poffefs'd of fuch a height of blifs,
    Tho' not exalted to fo high an heaven.

But where (methinks I afk the angel fair,
    And eager queftion thus my glorious guide)—
Where is the place, the heav'nly manfion where,
    The happy fpot where my fweet babes refide ?

Where yonder grove of heavenly palm † afpires,
    And forms beneath its fhade fweet fhining bowers,
There tuning their celeftial harps ‡ and lyres,
    Abide the happy fouls you claim as yours :

Or frequent follow with their fellow train
    The Lamb of God,§ combined in grateful ftrife,

---

* For as none of them were capable of abufing or improving their inferior talent, they are admitted with it to an *equal* as to *themfelves*, though to that of adult faints an *inferior* degree of glory.

† Rev. vii. 9. "And they had palms in their hands."

‡ Rev. v. 8, and xiv. 2. "And having every one harps. And I heard the voice of harpers harping with their harps."

§ Rev. xiv. 4. "Which follow the Lamb wherefoever he goeth." *Query.* Whether the 144,000 (a certain number, it feems, put for an uncertain) fpoken of in this paffage, as not defiled with women, as virgins, as following the Lamb, as redeemed from among men, as firft fruits unto God and the Lamb, as without guile, and without *fault* before God,—be not fpoken of thofe who die in their infancy, and therefore could never commit a *perfonal* fault ? I know commentators explain it otherwife, but their interpretation admits, I think, at leaft of a doubt.

Whene'er He leads them o'er the happy plain,
  By living ſtreams among the trees of life.*

Lo, there they ſtand, ſurrounded by a throng
  Of fellow-ſaints, who equal raptures prove,
About, it ſeems, to ſing ſome heav'nly ſong,
  And celebrate their Saviour's matchleſs love.

Know ye your earthly parent, gentle lambs?
  (Suſpend awhile your ſacred ſong and ſhew)
Know ye, my lovely babes, the man who claims
  A loving, tender father's part in you?

Yes! they reply, while heav'nly ſweetneſs flows
  In bliſsful ſmiles from either charming face,
And each its arms around me kindly throws,
  And claſps its father in a fond embrace.

Yes, we diſcern and love our father dear;
  Yes, we our kind, our tender parent know;
For *love* and *knowledge* are extended here †
  Beyond the reach of thought in worlds below.

But higher motives here our paſſions move,
  More god-like views our pure affections join,
And every earthly motive here above
  Is loſt in love, ſuperior and divine.

Our ſire is welcome to theſe ſeats of bliſs,
  Welcome with us celeſtial joys to prove,
Thrice welcome to our heav'nly paradiſe;
  Come, join with us to praiſe the Saviour's love,

They ſaid, and ſtriking their celeſtial lyres
  To correſpondent notes from ev'ry tongue;
In lofty praiſe the pleaſing ſtrain aſpires,
  And heav'n reſounded with their ſacred ſong.

---

* Rev. vii. 17, and xxii. 1, 2. "And he ſhall lead them to living fountains of waters. And he ſhewed me a pure river of water of life, clear as cryſtal. And in the midſt of the ſtreet of it, and on either ſide of the river, was there the tree of life."

† See 1 Cor. xiii. 12. "For *now* we ſee through a glaſs darkly, but *then* face to face; *now* I know in part, but *then* ſhall I know, even as alſo I am known."

Such melting ſtrains, ſo raviſhing an air,
  So ſweet, ſo heav'nly, ſo divine the lay,
'T might cheer a ſoul even in the laſt deſpair,
  And charm the agonies of death away.

Their Maker's and their Saviour's praiſe they ſung;
  This the bleſt ſubjeƈt of their happy theme—
The Saviour's praiſes flowed from ev'ry tongue,
  And ſacred many a grateful ſtrain to him.

Say, Muſe, their ſong, for thou remembereſt well
  The ſacred ſubjeƈt of their grateful lay :
Repeat the heav'nly ſtrain ; for thou canſt tell,
  Thou heard'ſt, and canſt each circumſtance diſplay.

Glory to God (they ſung), and endleſs praiſe ;
  Glory to God who reigns enthron'd above,
The God of ſaving univerſal grace,
  The God of boundleſs everlaſting love !

Glory to Thee, Almighty Father, Thee !
  Great Fountain of Exiſtence, ſource of bliſs ;
Thou awful Father of Eternity !
  God of all grace, and peace, and happineſs.

'Twas love amazing ! love beyond degree !
  Goodneſs Divine ! which prompted Thee to form
Each creature, from the higheſt dignity
  In heaven, down to the meaneſt mortal worm.

Thy god-like principle of aƈtion this,
  To ev'ry creature to communicate
As large a ſhare of happineſs and bliſs
  As each was able to participate.

Thanks to Thy Name for Thy creating love ;
  All glory, bleſſing, honour, power, and praiſe,
Be rendered Thee by all the hoſts above,
  And all below, in earth, or air, or ſeas.

Glory to Thee, incarnate Son of God,
  Gracious Redeemer of our fallen race !

Glory to Thee, thro' Whofe atoning blood
　　We now exift,* are bleft, and fing Thy praife.

Great was the grace, ftupendous was the love
　　Which made Thee not difdain the Virgin's womb,
But gladly leave Thy Father's throne above,
　　And there like us a little child become.

Great is the myftery of Thy love divine,
　　Aftonifhing the firft-born fons of light,
Which even archangels never can define,
　　But earneftly defire to view the fight.†

To Jefus thanks for His redeeming love;
　　Bleffing and honour to His faving Name;
Glory to Him who fills the throne above
　　Be ever given, falvation to the Lamb!

Glory to Thee, eternal Spirit Divine;
　　Glory to Thee, benign celeftial Dove;
Eternal glory, power, and thanks be Thine,
　　And praife unwearied as Thy patient love!

Thanks to Thy Name for Thy *renewing* grace,
　　Thy fanctifying influence on the foul,
Whereby Thou doft the works of fin efface,
　　And all the raging powers of hell control.

Glory to Father, Son, and Holy Ghoft,
　　The myftic Three that bear record in heaven‡
(Which yet are One), by all the heav'nly hoft,
　　And fons of earth, eternal praife be given!

---

* That is exift *perfonally*, for had it not been for the Redeemer, juftice and mercy in conjunction *muft* have required the *perfonal* punifhment of Adam and his confort *alone*, as they *alone* finned *perfonally*, when they had power afforded them by their gracious Maker to do otherwife, in which cafe not one of Adam's feed had ever enjoyed a *perfonal* exiftence, but had fuffered *as* they had finned, without the leaft *confcioufnefs* of the matter, in a ftate of *feminal* exiftence in the loins of Adam.

† 1 Peter i. 12. "Which things the angels defire to look into."

‡ 1 John v. 7. "For there are three that bear record in heaven, the Father, the Word, and the Holy Ghoft, and thefe three are one."

What thanks from us to Love Divine is due
  For our Almighty Father's tender care,
Who from yon dangerous fcene our fouls withdrew,
  And placed them in a ftate of fafety here!

What praifes to a gracious God we owe,
  Whofe kind affection fnatch'd us from the womb;
Who feafonably call'd us from below,
  And timely took us from the ills to come!

Perhaps our gracious heav'nly Father faw
  Some dire temptation forming to betray
Our minds to vice; fome dangerous fnare to draw
  Our fimple, unexperienc'd fouls aftray.

He therefore hous'd His pleafant plants in time
  T' avoid the withering blaft and fcorching flame;
Remov'd our fpirits to a happier clime,
  Before the dread, the fierce temptation came.

What grief and pain, what mifery and woe,
  What direful fcenes in yonder world abound;
What foul-diftreffing cares are known below,
  What bitter groans from all its coafts refound!

There many wallow in the laft excefs,
  As if in hafte with raging fiends to dwell;
And moft, regardlefs of their future peace,
  By folly antedate the pains of hell.

There ev'n the good man ftruggling thro' the throng,
  And agonizing in the arduous fray,
Conflicting with temptations, many and ftrong,
  Is almoft ready to refign the day.

What bitter floods of fierce contempt arife—
  What raging billows of temptation roar,
To intercept his paffage to the fkies,
  To bar his progrefs to the heav'nly fhore!

But by wife order of our heav'nly Sire,
  Beneath the load of *actual* fin to groan,
And be expofed to fierce temptation's fire,
  Is what our favour'd fouls have never known.

Be everlasting glory to our King;
   Unceasing thanks be to our Jesus given;
Honour and blessing to His Name we'll sing,
   And praise eternal as the days of heaven.

O, could our praises equal our desires,
   Or bear the least proportion to our theme,
To honour Jesus as His love requires,
   In blessing, praising, and adoring Him.

But vain th' attempt; our efforts here must cease;
   Our loftiest strains the arduous task resign:
Lost! lost! lost! in th' uncircumscrib'd abyss,
   Th' unfathomable depths of Love Divine.

Here ceas'd their grateful song. Enraptur'd I
   Exclaim, O happy, happy, happy train!
Worthy is Jesus, fervently reply,
   And to their praises add my loud Amen.

Amen; thanksgiving, honour, glory, praise,
   Wisdom and strength, be to our Jesus given;
His praise be sung in everlasting lays,
   By all the sons of earth and hosts of heaven.

But from this pleasing visionary scene
   To yonder clod I must descend again.
Alas! what sin and sorrow lies between,
   E'er I your happy peaceful state attain.

Enjoy, ye favour'd souls, your heav'n enjoy;
   Be ever blest, and still your bliss improve;
Happy, thrice happy in your sweet employ,
   To praise in thankful strains the God you love.

Farewell, my babes, my happy babes farewell,
   Till at the final summons Death dismiss
My soul by grace renew'd with yours to dwell,
   "High in salvation, and the climes of bliss." *

---

* A line from MILTON's *Paradise Lost*, B. 11, l. 708.

ON THE DEATH OF JOHN WRIGHT,

THE AUTHOR'S THIRD SON AND SIXTH CHILD, WHO DIED
SUDDENLY, IN HIS AFFLICTED FATHER'S ARMS, ON SATUR-
DAY, JULY THE 19TH, 1797, AGED EIGHT YEARS AND
SIX MONTHS.

S my beloved gone?
　　And is my darling fled?
　　In one revolving day cut down,
　　　And numbered with the dead!

Yes, Death in *one* short day
　　Has seiz'd the blooming prize,
And snatch'd my much-lov'd child away
　　From my desiring eyes.

Commission'd from above,
　　The frowning tyrant see!
The gloomy king, my dearest love,
　　Severely frown'd on thee.

His deathful bow he drew,
　　And wing'd the deadly dart;
The fatal shaft unpitying flew,
　　And pierc'd thy tender heart.

Now drooping, pale, and wan,
　　My infant lies distrest,
Convuls'd with agonizing pain,
　　With mortal anguish prest.

While tossing to and fro
　　Upon his dying bed,
He struggles with his latest foe,
　　And hastens to the dead.

Alas! for thee, my lamb,
  My poor afflicted one,
What anguish tore thy tender frame,
  My lovelieft, deareft fon!

Oft did I wifh for thee
  (But the fond wifh was vain),
To bear thy mortal agony—
  To fuffer all thy pain.

O, could thy father bear
  (How oft did I exclaim)
Thofe dire convulfive throes, my dear,
  That fhake thy inmoft frame!

While o'er his face I hung,
  And mark'd his painful fmart,
How ev'ry pang he fuffer'd wrung
  His father's aching heart!

He rais'd a languid look,
  His weeping fire to view;
And tho' delirious with the ftroke,
  His weeping fire he knew.

Struck with his father's grief,
  His little arms he fpread;
T' afford my forrowing mind relief,
  He rais'd his drooping head;

And with the tendereft love
  And pity in his eyes,
With eager reach my neck he ftrove
  To clafp, while thus he cries:

"Come, daddy! come my joy!
  Whom beft on earth I love;"*
As if inviting me to go—
  To fly with him above.

---

* His words were, "Come daddy, come joy, come joy, come joy!" exprefled with a look and accent of the tendereft love and pity for his father, when he faw me weeping over him, at the fame time ftretching out his little arms and embracing, kiffing, and bleffing me, with the greateft ardour of filial affection, a few moments before he expired.

Then in a laft embrace,
  With filial ardour preft
His much-afflicted father clofe
  To his beloved breaft.

His laft fweet words I heard,
  To give me comfort ftrove,
And in his laft fond looks appear'd
  Unutterable love.

With dying lips on mine,
  A parting kifs he preft,
And with his laft expiring breath,
  His forrowing father bleft.

O Death! relentlefs king!
  In all his blooming charms,
How could'ft thou kill my child, within
  His weeping father's arms?

But foon th' unequal ftrife—
  The conteft foon was o'er;
My darling child refign'd his life,
  And funk to rife no more.

No more on earth to rife,
  Till that great awful Day
Th' Archangel's trumpet from the fkies
  Shall wake his fleeping clay.

Then with new life endued,
  His lovely form fhall fhine
In beauty, ftrength, and youth renew'd,
  Immortal and divine!

This glorious hope we owe
  To Jefus' dying love;
O may we fhare his grace below,
  And fing his power above.

Till that great Day come on
  (A period none can tell),
My loving, my beloved fon,
  My darling child, farewell!

Or rather, John, farewell
   Till I ſhall be ſet free,
And Death diſmiſs my ſoul to dwell
   In Paradiſe with thee.

Then, if Almighty Grace,
   Deſcending from above,
Shall fit me for that heav'nly place,
   And perfeĉt me in love.

Then free from grief and pain,
   Of perfect bliſs poſſeſt,
I then ſhall meet my child again,
   And claſp him to my breaſt:

There hand in hand again,
   Recount our former loves,
While ranging o'er the happy plain,
   Or through the blifsful groves:

In praiſe to Jeſus join,
   His love and goodneſs tell,
And bleſs the gracious hand Divine
   That order'd all things well.

For ſure Thy filial love
   (A ſpark from Love Divine),
Can ne'er in heav'n deficient prove,
   Or ſuffer a decline?

And mine to thee, my dear,
   Can ne'er impaired be;
Can ne'er become indiff'rent there,
   Or e'er grow cold to thee.

Our love ſo deep, ſo kind,
   Was ne'er to periſh given;
Improv'd, exalted, and refin'd,
   But not annull'd in heaven.

But O, my deareſt love,
   Thy mortal conflicts o'er;
Thou by a ſudden quick remove
   Haſt gain'd the peaceful ſhore.

Thy painful throes below
  A final period have,
And ev'ry mortal grief and woe
  Is buried in thy grave.

While left behind to mourn,
  Thy father wanders here,
With heart-corroding anguiſh torn,
  A prey to grief and care.

By ſin and ſorrow preſt,
  I long to follow thee;
O may the God of Love cut ſhort
  His gracious work in me.

And when from ſin ſet free,
  Of perfect love poſſeſt,
Call up my ſoul to dwell with thee,
  In everlaſting reſt.

Till then, in lonely walk,
  I mourn thy timeleſs fall,
And to thy fancied ſhadow talk,
  As though thou heard'ſt my call.

Thy dear, dear name repeat,
  My love to thee declare,
And fondly call thee kind and ſweet,
  As thou, my John, waſt there.

Tell me (I cry), O tell,
  Thou ſoul of him I love,
In what new region doſt thou dwell,
  With happy ſouls above?

Tell me, my deareſt love,
  Ah! whither art thou fled?
To what delightful world above,
  Among the happy dead?

Doſt thou e'er hover near
  My walk, my charming ſaint?
Or does my lov'd one ever hear
  His father's fond complaint?

Doſt thou e'er mark my moans,
  Or know my griefs and fears?
Doſt thou e'er hear my ſighs and groans,
  Or ſee my ſtreaming tears?

Or if detain'd above,
  Where living pleaſures flow,
Thy happy ſoul no longer ſees
  What paſſes here below.

Amongſt the ſpirits divine,
  Who human actions ſee,
Has no informing angel told
  Thy father's griefs to thee?

How, while I wander wild,
  Dejected and forlorn,
I weep for my beloved child,
  And for his abſence mourn?

Each field or path I find
  Where he was wont to run,
Recalls my darling to my mind,
  What he hath ſaid or done.

He here around me play'd,
  On that ſame ſpot of ground;
This little obſervation made,
  That little wonder found.

In that ſame flowery vale,
  Beneath that ſhady tree,
He told his little childiſh tale,
  And prattled on my knee.

I there have ſeen him ſtand;
  To climb that tree he tried;
There hung upon his daddy's hand,
  Ran tripping by my ſide;

While his dear loving chat
  Would all my cares beguile,
And ev'n while preſt with anxious thought,
  Would make me fondly ſmile.

" Blefs you, my daddy, doy," *
  Oft has my lov'd one faid ;
" From heaven ten thoufand bleffings flow
  Upon my daddy's head !

" I love you, daddy, well—
  You may your child believe—
How well I love, no tongue can tell,
  No human heart conceive.

" You dearer are to me
  Than all the world would prove ;
I better than ten thoufand worlds
  My deareft daddy love.

" O if unpitying Death
  Should my lov'd father flay,
Your poor forfaken, forrowing child
  Would weep his life away.

" Nor would I choofe to die,
  For this, becaufe I find
I could not love to leave you here
  In this bad world behind.

" O, I fhould greatly mourn,
  And weep from you to part ;
'Twould much diftrefs me to be torn
  From your indulgent heart.

" Your neighbours all confpire,
  Your tendernefs t' approve,
And all your babes will witnefs bear
  To your paternal love !"

From my lov'd infant's lips,
  Such tender prattle flowed,
And fuch the warm affection which
  In his lov'd bofom glowed.

---

* The firft feven verfes in this page, are the words my departed child has often
expreffed to me, as near as the verfe would admit, which I have put in the fame
child-like language he was wont to make ufe of when fondly prattling to his
father.

Whene'er we chanc'd to part,
  Some little tale he'd tell,
Then turn about, his father kifs,
  And bid a kind farewell.

And oft—to fee his fire
  My child took fuch delight—
He oft would afk me there to ftand,
  While he remain'd in fight.

And when he reach'd the place
  Of utmoft view, would ftand,
Look at me there, with eager gaze,
  And wave his little hand.

How pleas'd, how fond was I
  To mark his guiltlefs play,
While full of life he round me ran,
  All active, brifk, and gay.

Pleas'd when his father feem'd
  His little acts t' approve;
Affection breath'd in ev'ry word,
  And every look was love.

My child! and muft it be?
  And muft we, muft we part?
My deareft John, the lofs of thee
  Will never from my heart!

Thy death to my fad foul
  Such lafting anguifh gave,
As finks thy mourning father down
  With forrow to the grave.

O who can e'er exprefs
  The pungent grief and fmart,
The bitter woe, the fore diftrefs,
  That tore my aching heart,

When on that fatal day,
  In all his youthful charms,
My dear departing infant lay
  Expiring in my arms!

Ah! thofe fond looks, my dear,
　Thofe laft fond looks from thee,
In fancy's eye ftill feem to fhed
　Their pitying rays on me.

Thy tender accents ftill
　I fondly think I hear,
And thy beloved voice yet founds
　In lift'ning fancy's ear.

No time can blot the trace,
　Or bid thy form depart;
Succeffive years can ne'er efface
　Thy image from my heart.

In my diftracted mind *
　While mem'ry holds a feat,
My dying infant, fweet and kind,
　I never can forget.

While life remains, I ftill
　Shall thy remembrance find;
The dear idea for ever will
　Be prefent to my mind.

In the laft mortal pain,
　When death fhall let me free,
If confcious memory then remain,
　I ftill fhall think on thee.

In that dread moment when
　I clofe my eyes in death,
O will thy loving fpirit then
　Attend my parting breath?

And while my lifelefs clay
　Remains with thine to reft,
Point out thy father's fpirit the way
　To manfions of the bleft?

Hear I, or think I hear
　My happy infant fay,

---

* " While memory holds a feat
In this diftracted globe."—SHAKESPEARE.

" Yes, daddy, I'll attend you there ;
   Will point you out the way.

" Yes, if the Will Divine
   With my defire comply,
Your child your angel-guard will join,
   To waft your foul on high,

" To that divine abode,
   Thofe manfions of the bleft ;
Thofe peaceful feats prepar'd by God,
   Where fep'rate fpirits reft.

" Meantime, by Jefus taught,
   Refign your darling up,
And forrow not as thofe without
   The Gofpel's bleffed hope.

" In mercy, truth, and love,
   Th' afflictive ftroke was giv'n,
To fix your thoughts on things above,
   And draw your foul to heav'n.

" 'Twas Love and Mercy mild
   Took me from ills to come ;
'Twas Mercy fent your darling child
   To fill an early tomb.

" Now placed beyond the reach
   Of fin and Satan's power,
No further mifery e'er can vex
   Or ever touch me more.

" In forrowing fancy's eye,*
 . If ftill your child you fee,
Still hear your lov'd one's dying cry,
   ' Come, daddy ! follow me !'

" O may the thought infpire
   Your foul with holy zeal,
To mount on wings of heav'nly fire
   To yon celeftial hill !

----

* See firft two verfes in page 307.

" There free from grief and pain,
  On that eternal fhore,
There you and J fhall meet again,
  Shall meet to part no more."

ON THE ANNIVERSARY RETURN OF THE
DAY ON WHICH JOHN WRIGHT
DIED, JULY 19TH, 1783.

" Unhappy day ! be facred ftill to grief,
A grief too obftinate for all relief ;
On thee my face fhall never wear a smile,
No joy on thee fhall e'er my heart beguile.
Why does thy light again my eyes moleft ?
Why am I not with thee, dear youth, at reft ?
For thee all thoughts of pleafure I forego ;
For thee my tears fhall never ceafe to flow ;
My bofom all thy image fhall retain—
The full impreffion there fhall ftill remain,
Till I with thee, upon my dufty bed,
Fo.get the toils of life, and mingle with the dead."
                                        MRS. ROWE

PART I.

TH' unwearied flight of Time, once more
    Returns the fatal day
  Which from my heaving bofom tore
    My darling child away.

Deep was the wound, my deareft John,
    And lafting was the fmart
Inflicted by that ftroke, upon
    Thy father's aching heart.

Still, ftill I feel the piercing pain,
    The bitter grief renew,
While fond remembrance calls again
    Thy image to my view.

Yes, bufy thought prefents again `
    The fad diftrefsful day,
When rack'd with agonizing pain
    My ftruggling infant lay.

Ah! ftill I fee thee gafping there,
    Still hear thy plaintive moan,
And pour afrefh the ftreaming tear,
    And heave the mournful groan.

Beneath the heavy hand of Death
    (Nor could thy father fave)
I faw thee yield thy infant breath,
    And fink into the grave.

Since then, as fad I frequent ftray'd,
    Withdrawn from mortal fight,
Beneath the awful folemn fhade
    Of all-concealing night;

What floods of tears my eyes have fhed,
    While with deep anguifh preft;
For thee what heart-felt groans have fled
    From my afflicted breaft!

Oft have I, funk in penfive thought,
    Beneath the midnight fky,
Bedew'd with tears the facred fpot
    Where thy dear relics lie.

And oft along the lonely walk,
    I mourn my infant gone;
To thy imagin'd fhadow talk,
    And cry, My John! my John!

Thou too waft wont, my deareft love,
    (Thus to myfelf I fay),
With me along thefe fields to rove,
    And round my footfteps play;

With little active limbs addreft
    Would climb th' afpiring tree;
Would rifle there the lofty neft,
    And bring the fpoils to me.

Then thro' the hazel copfe would'ft beat,
  And oft difcover there
The little fongfter's clofe retreat,
  Then fhow thy father where :

Would pluck each flower of fweeteft fcent,
  And moft variety,
Then form the nofegay, and prefent
  The flow'ry wreath to me ;

And fondly fmiling, bid me fee
  If I thy choice approv'd ;
Then fit and prattle on my knee,
  And tell how much thou lov'd.

" By me "—thus would my prattler fay,
  While round my neck he clung,
And fweetly kifs'd my cares away,
  And blefs'd me with his tongue,—

" By me whate'er beneath the fkies
  The circling fun can view,
Ten thoufand worlds are not fo priz'd,
  So dearly lov'd as you.

" Much, much may be th' affeſtion which
  In other children fhine,
Yet O their love can never reach—
  Can never equal mine.

" May heav'n to you all goodnefs fhew,
  Its choiceft influence fhed ;
And may ten thoufand bleffings flow
  Upon my daddy's head !"

Such was thy foft engaging talk,
  Such thy fweet chat to me,
When in the folemn evening walk
  I trod thefe fhades with thee.

Ah ! oft to fee thee play about,
  And mark thy infant wiles,
Would foften my feverer thought,
  And melt me into fmiles.

And oft to my remembrance brought
  My infant days, when, free
From thorny care and anxious thought,
  I pafs'd the time like thee.

But now with lonely ftep I glide
  Along the gloomy vale,
No little prattler by my fide,
  To tell his pleafing tale.

Thofe fmiling eyes that wont to fhine,
  Now wither and decay;
Thofe little active limbs of thine
  Lie mouldering in the clay.

Cut off amidft thy fprightlieft bloom,
  And clos'd thy eyes fo bright;
Remov'd into the filent tomb,
  Out of my longing fight.

But never from my heart remov'd,
  While circling feafons roll,
My deareft, fweeteft, beft belov'd,
  Thou darling of my foul!

I fooner could myfelf forget,
  And all the fun can fee,
Than thee forget, my deareft John,
  Than ceafe to think on thee.

Yes, thy dear mem'ry fhall furvive,
  In fpite of time and death,
While in this mortal world I live,
  And draw my vital breath.

Where'er thy little feet have trod,
  Or climb'd th' afpiring tree,
Some fond memorial there I'll make,
  My deareft love, of thee.

Within the bark I'll carve thy name,
  In ev'ry fhady grove;
Memorial of thy little fame,
  And my paternal love.

O name to me for ever fad,
    To me for ever dear;
Still breath'd in many a heart-felt figh,
    Still utter'd with a tear.

Long muft thy father's aching heart
    With deep-felt anguifh moan;
And long my forrowing foul deplore
    The lofs of thee, my John!

PART II.

UT may not this affliction giv'n,
        Divine monition be?
    What is the voice of gracious Heav'n
        In this event to me?

For yet that fage remark is juft,
    And ftill a truth is found;
Affliction fprings not from the duft,
    Nor trouble from the ground.

Waft thou withdrawn, my deareft love,
    To urge thy father's rife;
To draw my heart to things above,
    And call me to the fkies.

When tofling on thy dying bed,
    Did I not hear thee fay,
" From earthly cares, and earthly loves,
    Come, daddy, come away?

" The mortal pleafures we purfue
    In this dark dreary vale,
Are tranfient as the morning dew,
    And fleeting as the gale.

" Sin has involv'd thefe earthly fcenes
    In mifery and woe;
In vain the fons of Adam feek
    For happinefs below.

" 'Tis fin that with a fatal ftroke
   Now points the deadly dart,
And tears, with unrelenting hand,
   Your darling from your heart.

" Then, daddy, if your bowels yearn
   For your beloved John,
If overwhelm'd with grief, you mourn
   O'er your expiring fon ;

" As e'er you ardently defire
   To meet me in the fkies,
When my dear Saviour fhall require
   My fleeping duft to rife ;

" As e'er you wifh to join me there,
   On that eternal fhore,
Where pining grief and anxious care,
   And parting are no more ;

" From fin, that fatal mifchief, ceafe,
   And you fhall be forgiv'n ;
And in the paths of holinefs,
   Come after me to heav'n.

" O think, and may the affecting thought
   Your nobleft paffions move,
Till all your willing mind be brought
   To feek the things above.

" O think of each endearing fcene,
   Each action paft review,
The tender love that pafs'd between
   Your darling child and you.

" When wont around you to rejoice,
   Along the field or grove,
And blefs you with the genuine voice
   Of undiffembled love.

" Think of the laft fad parting fcene,
   When, 'midft my youthful charms,
Unpitying Death his victim feiz'd,
   And tore me from your arms.

" Think of the laſt fond words I ſpoke
  Upon my dying bed,
Wherein you heard me Heav'n invoke
  For bleſſings on your head.

" Remember my laſt dying call,
  The laſt fond kiſs I gave ;
That laſt embrace e'er yet I ſunk
  Into the ſilent grave.

" And when your mortal life ſhall ceaſe,
  Then (all your ſins forgiv'n),
Then may you cloſe your eyes in peace,
  And follow me to heav'n."

Yes, my dear prattler, may I be
  Renew'd by grace divine ;
Made by my gracious Saviour free,
  And in His image ſhine !

Then I ſhall up to heav'n aſcend,
  From mortal anguiſh free,
In unimagin'd bliſs to ſpend
  An endleſs year with thee !

ON JOHN WRIGHT FOUR YEARS AFTER

HIS DEATH.

FOUR times round the central ſun,
    Journeying through the azure ſkies,
  Earth its annual courſe has run,
    Since my darling clos'd his eyes :
  Cropp'd amidſt his vernal bloom,
  Sent to fill an early tomb !

Sacred be the ſpot my dear,
  Where thy lovely limbs repoſe ;
Reſt thy precious reliĉts there,
  Till the laſt dread trumpet blows ;
Till thy loving Saviour ſay,
" Riſe ! my love, and come away !"

Oft thy father paſſing near,
　　Wrapt beneath the midnight ſhade,
Oft has pour'd the ſtreaming tear,
　　Where thy dear remains are laid ;
Oft expreſs'd the heaving ſigh,
Where thy ſleeping aſhes lie.

There, while ſunk in penſive thought,
　　Muſing over thee, my John,
To my mind fond mem'ry brought
　　Many an action thou hadſt done ;
Buſy fancy call'd anew
Thy lov'd image to my view.

Sportive o'er the flow'ry mead,
　　Lively, active, briſk, and gay,
Thou with me was wont to tread,
　　Round me run in youthful play,
Or beneath the ſhady tree
Sit and prattle on my knee.

Ah ! my lovely fondling boy !
　　Rudely from my boſom torn,
Late thy father's deareſt joy,
　　Now condemn'd for thee to mourn ;
From my fond embraces fled,
Mingled with the ſilent dead.

Through the well-known flow'ry vale
　　Now forlorn and ſad I ſtray ;
Hear no more thy prattling tale,
　　See no more thy active play ;
Death the fatal ſummons gave,
Sunk thee to the gloomy grave.

Raviſh'd from my longing eyes,
　　Shall I never ſee thee more ?
Art thou fall'n no more to riſe,
　　Held by Death's eternal power ?
Will not He, the Prince of Day,
Re-awake thy ſleeping clay ?

Yes! the lip of Truth hath said ; *
   Why should sorrow then complain ?
Tho' thy much-lov'd child be dead,
   He shall surely live again ;
Rescued from the greedy grave,
He shall prove My power to save !

Haste the happy glorious morn
   When my child again shall rise !
When from dust and ashes borne,
   I shall meet him in the skies;
Join him there our God t' adore,
Join him there to part no more.

ON JOHN WRIGHT'S DEATH, 1788.

FLED, alas! my child is fled
   From my fond embraces,
To the regions of the dead,
   Those undiscover'd places !
Whither is my darling flown ?
   To what blissful regions ?
From his father's bosom gone,
   To join the angelic legions.

Shall I never see thee more ?
   Shall grim Death dissever
Those who lov'd so dear before
   For ever and for ever ?
Nay, I hear the Saviour say ; †
   " Cease thy grief and mourning ;
He shall rise again that day—
   The day of my returning !

---

* John xi. 23, 24, 25. "Jesus saith, Thy brother shall rise again. Martha saith, I know that he shall rise again in the resurrection at the last day. Jesus said, I am the resurrection and the life." &c.

† See John xi. 23, 24, 25.

He shall prove my pow'r to save,
  Over death victorious;
Rescu'd from the greedy grave,
  All perfect, bright, and glorious.
Then with me to heav'n ascend,
  Thro' the bright expansion,
To the joys that never end,
  In yon celestial mansion!"

Glorious Saviour! strong to save;
  Jesus, we adore Thee!
Thou hast triumph'd o'er the grave,
  Death, hell, fall down before Thee.
Everlasting praise be Thine,
  Great, Almighty Saviour,
For a blessing so divine,
  For such a god-like favour.

Yet indulge, immortal King,
  A father's fond complaining,
While in pensive strains I sing
  My dear departed darling.
Dearest, sweetest, loveliest youth!
  Still for ever thought on;
Thy dear filial love and truth
  Shall never be forgotten.

Mournful mem'ry marks the day,
  In yon meadow straying,
Fresh in life, in beauty gay,
  I saw my lov'd one playing;
Down in that same flow'ry vale,
  Near yon tree so shady,
Oft I heard the tender tale
  Of my dear prattling baby.

There my boy would fondly tell,
  While we stray'd together,
In kind praise, how much, how well
  He lov'd his dearest father:
Better, would my darling say,
  While my life remaineth—
Better than the world itself,
  And all that it containeth.

Deareſt prattler! fare-thee-well,
　Till the trumpet ſounding,
Call thee from thy ſilent cell,
　To heav'nly joys abounding;
Endleſs life thence to retain,
　Thro' the great Retriever,
Then we both ſhall meet again,
　To part no more for ever!

ON JOHN WRIGHT.

(The four firſt Stanzas a little altered from Mr. Thomſon.)

ELL me, thou ſoul of him I love,
　Ah! tell me, whither art thou fled?
To what delightful world above,
　Appointed for the happy dead?

Or doſt thou free at pleaſure roam,
　And ſometimes ſhare thy father's woe,
Where, void of thee, his cheerleſs home
　Can now, alas! ſmall comfort know?

Oh! if thou hov'reſt round my walk,
　While, under ev'ry well-known tree,
I to thy fancied ſhadow talk,
　And ev'ry tear is full of thee.

Should then the weary eye of grief,
　Beſide ſome ſympathetic ſtream,
In ſlumber find a ſhort relief,
　O viſit thou my ſoothing dream.

When thro' the ſilent ſhady grove,
　With lonely ſteps I muſing ſtray
Thro' tracts where thou was wont to rove,
　In purſuit of thy childiſh play.

Then mem'ry fond recalls the time,
   And marks the path where thou haſt ſtray'd,
The tree which I have known thee climb,
   The moſſy bank where thou haſt play'd.

Struck with the ſadly-pleaſing thought,
   Swells my ſad heart with heaving ſighs,
While down my cheeks in ſtreamlets flow
   The briny ſorrow from my eyes.

Dear, lovely youth! caught from my hopes,
   How greatly dear to me thou art;
Far dearer than the vital drops
   That viſit my ſad drooping heart!

But peace, my weary troubled mind,
   Let peeviſh grief no more complain;
I ſhall not long remain behind;
   I ſoon ſhall meet my child again!

Meet him where ſin no more can blight,
   Or pain oppreſs, or ſorrow fade;
Where fever's rage no more can ſmite,
   Or cauſe to hang the drooping head:

Meet him where Death diſarm'd of power,
   For ever drops his fatal dart,
And where the tyrant can no more
   With anguiſh pierce the feeling heart.

Meet him in yonder bliſsful ſkies,
   Baſking in life's meridian ray,
And with my much-lov'd darling riſe,
   To triumph in eternal day!

A HEROIC POEM IN PRAISE OF RICHARD HILL, ESQ.

BEING A COUNTERPART TO MR. HILL'S HEROIC POEM IN PRAISE OF MR. WESLEY.

> " All fools have still an itching to deride,
> And fain would be upon the laughing side."—POPE.

TO RICHARD HILL, ESQ., AT HAWKESTONE, NEAR WHITCHURCH, IN SHROPSHIRE.*

SIR,

HAVING seen "A Heroic Poem in praise of Mr. John Wesley," in a pamphlet of yours lately published, entitled, " Logica Wesleiensis, or The Farrago Double Distilled," I have taken the liberty to send you the following, which please to accept as a counterpart to yours.

THE AUTHOR.

ITHER, ye *chosen tribes*, repair,
  " I've welcome news to tell;"
Whate'er your *iniquities* are,
  " My dose can suit you well."

For let your sins be great or small,†
  Of low or high degree,
Resisted or indulged, 'tis all
  The very same to me.

---

* The following poem was sent by the author to Mr. Hill, in a letter by the
†.
  See Mr. Hill's " Five Letters to the Vindicator of Mr. Wesley's Minutes,"
  27, 32.

The great *Herculean* tafk, a man
  Shall find in this refpect,
Is firm believing (if he can)
  Himfelf to be elect.

Such who my *noftrum's* virtue tries,
  Shall find his bufinefs done;
Sin flies my pill, as darknefs flies
  Before the rifing fun.

Sin in the chofen ones, I mean,
  The fins of the elect,
In *fuch* my famous pill is feen
  To work a rare effect.

But hence, ye reprobated brood!
  " Who hearken not to me,"
But dread to father upon God
  John Calvin's *black decree :*

Who teach the world the Father gave
  His Son to die for *all*,
And ranfom each unhappy flave
  That fell in Adam's fall.

But oh! my brother, babe, or friend,
  Thefe doctrines don't believe;
For *Calvin's Gofpel* ftill contend,
  And cordially receive.

Perhaps you know not who I am,
  What battles I have won?
What! have you never heard my fame?
  What wonders I have done?

I'm Dick the giant-killer, I *
  That leading *hero* who
Goliah flew, and forc'd to fly
  The proud *Oxonian* foe!

---

* Should any perfon imagine that this line is too vulgar to be applied to a gentleman of Mr. Hill's quality, &c., he muft confider that it is altogether as genteel and juft, if not more fo, as "brave Jack of all trades," applied by Mr. Hill to Mr. Wefley. Mr. Hill wrote a pamphlet upon occafion of the expulfion of the fix ftudents from Edmund Hall, which he ironically entitled "Goliah Slain;" and another on the fame occafion, entitled, "Pietas Oxonienfis," that is, Oxonian piety, or the piety of Oxford.

Poor Wesley, friends, 'tis true derides,
   And calls me THE CATSPAW,*
But what! I've bang'd him back and sides,
   For his presumption though.

And if his crabb'd *associates* would
   But have restrain'd their ire,
The poor old heretic I could
   Have trod into the mire.

But oh! that sturdy *Swifs*,† he makes
   My bosom beat with fears,
And with *Helvetic* bluntness shakes
   My system by the ears.

Swifs honesty! Truth's candle! too, ‡
   I like them not, not I;
They all my labour'd sophisms show,
   And ev'ry corner spy.

From this rough mountaineer, my friends,
   I've suffer'd many a pang;
And many a dang'rous shaft he sends,
   And gives me many a bang.

For solid *argument* I long
   Have answer'd him with fun;
And for his *reasons* clear and strong,
   Return'd a cutting *pun*.

And oft my brave auxiliar troops
   Of *scandal* lend supplies,§
Which in his face I dash, in hopes
   To put out both his eyes.

---

* See Mr. Hill's "Heroic Poem," eleventh stanza; and Mr. Wesley's "Remarks on Mr. Hill's Review," p. 40.

† The Rev. Mr. John Fletcher, Vicar of Madeley, in Shropshire, who is a native of Switzerland.

‡ See "The Farrago Double Distilled," p. 7. In another publication Mr. Hill and his brother express their dislike of Mr. Fletcher's "Illustrations," which he (Mr. Fletcher) calls the candle of the Lord, or the candle of truth.

§ Alluding to the slanderous stories Mr. Hill and his associates pick up and publish, in order to bring Mr. Wesley into ridicule and contempt.

Though all is ineffectual, yet
    Who knows what may betide? *
He by and bye may take the pet,
    Perhaps may change his side.

But cheer, my friends, I'll never yield,
    Though I should suffer pain;
I'll brandish *Calvin's* sword and shield,
    Till ev'ry *giant's* slain;

I'll make them, with sarcastic jokes,
    Like madmen skip and leap;
Reviews, Farragos, Finish'd Strokes,†
    Shall drive them on a heap.

I'll raise John Calvin's ghost to fight,
    All grizly, stern, and pale;
And if his *horrid front* ‡ wont fright,
    I'll turn his *filthy tail!* §

What! shall the precious babies lack
    The soul-reviving dose,
'Cause 'tis abused by a pack
    Of corrupt-minded foes? ‖

No; I'll the privilege declare
    So pleasing to old Adam—
That thing call'd flesh, I mean—whate'er
    It be to Him who made 'em.

---

* While Mr. Hill attacks Mr. Wesley with all the virulence and animosity of an irreconcileable enmity, not discovering the most distant desire of an accommodation with *him*, he at the same time manifests a willingness to be friends with Mr. Fletcher, whom, though lately honoured with the title of " *Young-Ignorance*," he now kindly condescends to call his " *able antagonist*," but intimates that he must purchase his friendship, if not by turning Calvinist, at least by remaining neuter in the present controversy, and so deserting his friend and what he himself esteems to be the cause of truth together. A mighty generous intimation indeed! See his " Farrago Double Distilled," towards the conclusion.

† The titles of several of Mr. Hill's pamphlets in the present controversy.

‡ The doctrine of Absolute Reprobation.

§ The impure Nicolaitan doctrines of the Antinomians, which maintain that a man may be a pleasant child of God while he is defiling his neighbour's bed, and embruing his hands in his brother's blood; and which, we think, may be justly considered as the spawn of Calvinism.

‖ " Five Letters," p. 33, 34, 27, first edition.

Mark then this *scroll,* obferve it well,
  'Twill ferve a time of need,
And many a charming tale 'twill tell
  To *Calvin's chofen feed.*

To *Calvin's faints* a pleafing fight,
  And comfort to *all thofe*;
But caufe of horrible affright
  And terror to our *foes.*

It fays the faints of Calvin's God
  May lie, or fwear, or whore;
Slander their neighbour, fhed his blood,
  Opprefs or rob the poor.

But though they into whoredom fall,
  Their neighbour rob or kill,
Yet in thefe very acts, they all
  Are *pleafant children* ftill.*

Their fouls though *really black* with fin,
  In Chrift are *really fair*; †
And though *polluted* all within,
  In Him they're *clean,* O rare! ‡

Nay, with the help of *Crifp* I trow
  " I've learn'd to conjure too,"
And prove the work is *finifh'd now,*§
  Which yet *remains to do.*

Your fins fhall fly, I'll not leave one—
  " *Prefto, hey pafs!*" I' th' name
O' Doctor Crifp at once they're gone;
  They're gone before they came!

With fneer and banter long I tried
  To lay old Goodwin's ghoft;
Abufe and flander next applied,
  But all is labour loft;

---

* See Mr. Hill's " Five Letters," and his " Review," where he publicly maintains that David was a pleafant child of God, while wallowing in adultery and murder.

† " Five Letters," p. 27, 28.

‡ O rare! an exclamation Mr. Hill frequently makes ufe of in his " Farrago Double Diftilled."

§ The abfurd doctrine of Finifhed Salvation.

For ftill each vile *Arminian fnake* *
  My fyftem will oppofe,
Will counterwork my plots, and take
  My doctrines by the nofe.

There's *Cobler Tom* † and Mountain Jack,‡
  With that fierce fiend *Sellon*, §
Befides *th' arch heretic* ; ‖ good lack !
  I fear we's be out-done.

Help, Toplady, thou foul-mouth'd thing,
  With thy auxiliar aids ;
Thy Billingfgate artill'ry bring,
  To drub thefe tefty blades ;

Like any *Hector* tread the ftage,
  Put on thy terrors, man ;
Threat, bully, blufter, vaunt, and rage,
  And fright them if thou can.

Say that I fill an *efquire's* room,
  And tell them for their good,
That many of our friends are come
  Of *honourable* blood.

With us the *rich* and noble are,
  And *doctors* of degree ;
How fhould *plain Swifs* and *Cobblers* fhare
  As much good fenfe as we ?

A noble *magazine* ¶ of arms
  We have, 'tis furely known,
With cutting fcandal ftuff'd, and charms
  Peculiarly our own.

----

* Mr. Hill calls Mr. Fletcher a fnake that bites the Calvinifm minifters.—
"Review," p. 70.
  † Mr. Thomas Olivers, a lay preacher under Mr. Wefley.
  ‡ The Rev. Mr. John Fletcher.
  § The Rev. Mr. Walter Sellon.
  ‖ The Rev. Mr. John Wefley.
  ¶ "The Gofpel Magazine," as it is falfely called, fays Mr. Sellon ; "that
monthly medley of *truth* and *error*, *found words*, and *blafphemy*, trumped up as a
vehicle to convey Calvinifm and flander round the nation." M——n and could'ft
thou Gofpel add ; O name, O facred name of Gofpel thus profaned !

Have at thee,* thou *Arminian knave!*
  Thou *Bell-wether! thou Pope!*
Thou merits *sending for* a *slave,*
  Or *hanging in a rope.*

Thou *Proteus! conjurer!* thou *quack!*
  Thou *whore of Babylon!*
Thou *lying sophister!* thou *Jack*
  Of all trades! good at none.

Religious gambler! coward! both,
  In *forgery* employ'd;
Thou *Jesuit,* of *justice, truth,*
  And *common honour* void!

Blind leader of a blinded clan,
  Thou teacher of *free-will!*
Apostate, heretic, carman,
  Old plagiary, windmill!

Thou *lurking, sly assassin,* thou
  Beneath the level gone
Of *chimney-sweep* or *oyster-frow,*
  Thou false, thou *perjur'd* one!

Thou plays a mean, dishonest part,
  As any man may see;
A *nuisance* and a *pest* thou art
  To all society!

Come then, my worthy friends, nor lag
  Behind, nor shun the fight;
Afford your help, and soon we'll drag
  This monster out to light.

My *principal,†* with loud alarms,
  Denounc'd the sound of war;
Summon'd three nations up to arms,
  The glorious toil to share!

---

* See Mr. Toplady's " Letter to Mr. Wesley," and Mr. Hill's publications in the present controversy, where the abusive names and *scurrilous* language which compose the six following stanzas may be found, either directly or indirectly, in a positive or comparative sense, applied to Mr. Wesley, besides a great variety of Billingsgate language liberally bestowed upon him from time to time by a great number of Calvinistic writers upon other occasions.

† The Rev. Mr. Shir—y. See his " Circular Letter."

Our friends in order to excite
  To help without delay,
Proclaim'd aloud with all his might,
  Free quarters, if no pay.

Down with the *heretics!* cried he,
  Defend the *good old caufe* ;
We join'd the cry, and *herefy*
  Our word of battle was.

The found aroufed my martial flame ;
  I flew to his relief,
Refolved to fignalize my name,
  Beneath this mighty chief.

But fcarce had he perform'd a feat,
  But flyly flunk away,*
And left his friend to bear the heat
  And burden of the day.

But, O thou brazen-fronted friend,
  Exert thy founding lungs ;
Thy voice to all our brethren fend,
  Of *parties, people, tongues.*

Should all ftill prove too weak when come
  To ftand *th' Arminian* fire ;
Why, then, we'll fend exprefs to Rome,
  To fetch the *Popifh Friar.*†

But if the field, through hoftile ire,
  Should e'er become unfafe,
To *fort contempt* we'll then retire,
  And from the ramparts laugh.‡

Nor fear t' incur the coward's doom,
  'Tis courage in difguife ;
For if we can't our foes *o'ercome,*
  We can our foes *defpife.*

---

* Mr. S——y, after publifhing his " Narrative," wifely flipped his neck out of
the collar and gave up the cudgels to the prefent Calviniftic champion, Mr. Hill.
  † See the " Dialogue with the Benedictine Monk at Paris."
  ‡ See Mr. Toplady's " Letter to Mr. Wefley," p. 12.

"Thus, Sir," I have returned your favour, by "giving you a few hobbling rhymes in the exact language of" your own publications, and those of your allies, "from whence I have borrowed" every *shocking* doctrine, all the *Billingsgate* language, and "every *abusive* appellation" which my verses contain; and this I have done with a sincere desire that it may prove a means of shewing you "the great impropriety as well of *your own* and of *your*" *allies'* "manner of writing," as of the great shame and disgrace attending your manner of conduct towards two eminent ministers of Christ, which is such as utterly unbecomes you, either as a man, a gentleman, or a Christian, and more especially the last; for as you are one of those who esteem themselves the chosen ones of God, one might justly have expected to have found you more ready to have put in practice the Apostle's advice, where he exhorts the elect of God, as such, to put on bowels of mercy, kindness, humbleness of mind, meekness, long-suffering; forbearing one another, and forgiving one another, if any man had a quarrel against another, even as Christ forgave them. And you ought certainly to remember, on such occasions as these, that good advice of his in another place, that the servant of the Lord must not strive, but be gentle unto all men, apt to teach, patient, in meekness instructing those that oppose themselves, if God peradventure may give them repentance to the acknowledging of (Calvinism, if Calvinism be) the truth.

Now, sir, should you be offended at the freedom of my conduct upon this occasion, I shall only apologize for the liberty I have taken in the words of a celebrated poet—

> " Example strikes
> All human hearts, a *bad* example more."—YOUNG.

I am, Sir, your humble servant,

THOMAS WRIGHT.

Lower Blacup, near Hightown, near Halifax in Yorkshire,
August, 1775.

POSTSCRIPT.

HOULD any perſon objeƈt againſt this performance (as one of no mean name has already done)
that it is "railing for railing," I think ſuch
objeƈtors ought to conſider that there are circumſtances
wherein it may not only be allowable, but even neceſſary
to take the wiſe man's advice, and to anſwer a fool
according to his folly, leſt he ſhould be wiſe in his own
conceit. I allow this ought *ſo* to be done as not to render the reſpondent like the fool he anſwers; and this, I
conceive, is a very nice and difficult point to hit upon.
Mr. Hill profeſſes that the ſole motive which induced him
to write the ſarcaſtic piece upon Mr. Weſley, was *only* to
convince him of his error, and to bring him to a deteſtation
of (what it ſeems he thinks) his opprobrious way of writing. Were this faƈt, I think it might be a ſufficient ex-
cuſe for Mr. Hill's performance, but I think the contrary
appears very evident from the circumſtances and manner of
its execution. It is allowed by all good judges, that *vice*
and *folly* are the *only* proper objeƈts of ſatire; but if a divine
of good natural parts and great learning ſhould think fit
to write not only upon divinity, but natural philoſophy,
phyſic, politics, &c.; or ſhould he venture to give his advice
with reſpeƈt to the drinking of tea, or a perſon entering
into the marriage ſtate; muſt the doing of any or all of
theſe *neceſſarily* imply that the perſon who has done them
muſt either be a vicious man or a fool? Yet all theſe are
circumſtances which Mr. Hill, in his poem, attempts to
turn into ridicule. He likewiſe ſeleƈts ſome other circumſtances which he repreſents in a very unfair and unjuſt
manner, whereas ſatire ought always to be founded in the
ſtriƈteſt truth and juſtice. From all this, it appears to me
that Mr. Hill's motive in writing his poem was not (what
it ſeems he would fain have the world believe it to be) a
kind, good-natured intention of leading Mr. Weſley out of
his error, &c., but rather an ill-natured deſign to reproach
him, and by repreſenting him in as abſurd and ridiculous a
view as poſſible, to bring him into the greateſt diſeſteem
and contempt. However, I think what Mr. Hill only
pretended to be his motive in writing was *really* mine. I
thought thus retorting upon Mr. Hill might poſſibly prove
an occaſion of ſhewing him the great abſurdity, weakneſs,

and folly of his own conduct and of that of his allies, as well as that of his religious fyftem, by exhibiting a proof if both thefe lay much more open to juft farcafm and ridicule than either the conduct or religious fyftem of thofe himfelf had been fo earneftly labouring to bring into contempt. I hope I have not been guilty of the fame faults myfelf which I have been cenfuring in Mr. Hill. I think I have given a fair reprefentation of the circumftances I mention, and that they juftly deferve to be held forth in the ridiculous view in which they appear in my verfes; however, I leave this to the judgment of the candid reader.

OBSERVATIONS ON A PAMPHLET LATELY PUBLISHED,

ENTITLED "POLYPHEMUS, OR A CYCLOPS COMBATTING TRUTH."

> "All fools have ftill an itching to deride,
> And fain would be upon the laughing fide."—POPE.

> "On any point if you difpute,
> Depend upon it he'll confute;
> Change fides, you but increafe your pain,
> For he'll confute you back again."—PRIOR.

TO THE READER.

KIND READER,

HAVE no hard names or allufions to heathen fables to explain to thee, like the Calvinift, nor fhall I make any apology for what my pamphlet contains; but what follows may ferve to explain the Introduction. Some Calvinifts returning in a poft-chaife from one of their lectures,[*] where the author of "Polyphemus" had been firft vending his ware, and in their way paffing by a Methodift preaching-houfe,[†] the vehicle ftopped; out leaps a Calvinift, runs to

---

[*] Heckmondwike.

[†] The Height preaching-houfe above Hightown. [The Height Chapel ftood on an eminence which is now in the centre of Hightown, over againft the Lower Blacup farm. It was pulled down partly fome years ago, and altered into cottages, but the gable ends are ftill to be feen. The old chapel would be lefs than half a mile from the poet's home.]

the preaching-houfe, and attempts to force one of the giant-titled pamphlets under the door—mightily tickled, no doubt, at thinking how the poor Methodifts, at their next vifit, would be frighted to find fo horrid a monfter ftalking about the place!   However, as the found truth of the Methodift doctrines repell all the vain arguments and malicious attempts the Calvinifts make ufe of in order to overturn or injure them, fo the firmnefs and clofenefs of the preaching-houfe doors repelled the vain attempt of this Calvinift to force " Polyphemus " into the place ; he therefore runs next to the ftable-door, the bottom of which not being quite fo clofe, he thrufts " Polyphemus " half way through into the horfe-ftand (a place too good for him); but the poor giant, alas! fticking faft by the middle, his friend was obliged to leave him in that condition, with his pofteriors expofed to a brifk fhower of rain, which happened to fall at that time.   This had fuch an effect in foftening the giant's hinder parts, that when an obferver came afterwards to difengage him, he feparated in two pieces!   The Calvinift returned to his carriage again and drove away, laughing in his fleeve at the arch trick he had played the Methodifts.

INTRODUCTION.

Being an account of an adventure of one of the pamphlets in queftion.

TH' other day as I happen'd to pafs on the road,
I obferved a great number of people abroad,
And afking the meaning, was made underftand
The Calvinifts had a great lecture in hand.*
A lecture, faid I ; what's the meaning of that ?
Why, a meeting of people to hear and debate,
To pray, preach, and fing, and to eat, drink, and chat.
I thankfully nodded, but queftion'd no more,
And journey'd along, as I had done before.

* At Heckmondwike. [Formerly, "on the firft Wednefday after the fecond Sunday in June, an annual religious feftival was held here, called the ' Lecture,' which was attended by a great number of Calviniftic minifters and people of that perfuafion, from the furrounding country, the objects of which were the arrangement of certain matters relating to the miniftry, and the promotion of vital religion."—BAINES' *Directory of Yorkfhire*.]

It happen'd, I having fulfill'd my intent,
At night I returned the way that I went;
When sudden a rumble, saluting my ear,
Inform'd me some kind of a carriage was near.
A chaise soon appear'd, not far from the place,
And whirling along it approach'd me apace.
Now, reader, you here may observe if you will
A Methodist preaching-house stood on the hill.
The chaise bounc'd along in its wonted career,
But what there was in it did not yet appear;
However, when just 'gainst the chapel it stopp'd,
The door it flew open, and out of it popp'd
A Predestinarian, I think, by his mien,
Or something as like one as ever was seen.
He stepp'd to the house, cast a proud, scornful eye on't,
Then turn'd from his pocket a fierce new-born giant.
As it happ'd to be rainy, the tender young thing
Would gladly have enter'd, but could not get in;
It struggled for entrance at bottom o' th' door,
And got in its head, but could get in no more;
Not one hair's breadth further a way could it find,
Though its friend puff'd and thrusted hard at it behind.
In this painful posture, and struggling amain,
Its posteriors exposed to the wind and the rain,
He said something of God, and the house, and its father,
Some prayer, or some sneer on the Methodists rather,
Then strode back the way he had measur'd before,
Leap'd into the carriage, and fasten'd the door;
Where being composed and adjusted aright,
The steeds quickly whirl'd him out of my sight.
I stepp'd o'er the road to see if I could find
What the poor thing was doing he'd just left behind;
When, strange to relate—but, betwixt me and you,
I assure you, kind reader, 'tis certainly true—
'Twas transformed to a pamphlet! a pamphlet, indeed,
With an outlandish tail, and a monstrous head.
But the rain having much, sir, bedabbled its tail,
Had rendered it weakly, and tender, and frail;
And when to have taken it up I design'd,
The tail, sir, came off, but the head stuck behind;
Howe'er, when I join'd the two pieces anew,
It's terrific title flash'd full in my view.

OBSERVATIONS ON THE TITLE PAGE.[*]

"POLYPHEMUS! *a Cyclops!*"[†] Lord blefs me, thought I,
The monfter I fear will be rude by and by.
"*Combatting,*" O fie, thought I, that is not well,
That thofe fhould write Latin who Englifh can't fpell.
"*Truth!*" aye, fir, but this is a general term,
And yours I fufpect is not fterling and firm.
The practice is common in thefe days, you fee,
For profeffors of every name and degree,
Howe'er contradictory their fyftems you know,
To lay kindred claim to the goddefs below.
See Proteftants, Papifts, Turks, Pagans, and Jews,
How diff'rent foe'er their opinions and views,
Although twice five hundred ways they divide,
All, all, fir, alike find fair Truth on their fide,
Are as pofitive in turn as yourfelf, 'tis well known,
And their *ipfe dixit's* as good as your own.
"*A Poem!*" that's fomething, I fancy, like mine,
In rhyme and in meafure, neat, pretty, and fine.
    We next have the mottos infcrib'd on its fore-face,
From Virgil, the author, St. Paul, and old Horace,
And fomebody elfe too, but who I don't wift,
"*Veritas non eget defenforibus ift—*"
Your readers will here, fir, be loft in a mift;[‡]
Not one in five hundred, rare fcholar I ween,
Ev'n of your own party, can tell what you mean!
"*Tantæne animis cæleftibus iræ?*"
For this fome kind ignorant friend may admire ye;
Cry out, what a wonderful fcholar is this!
He's a man of rare parts, to be fure that he is:
You fee he writes Latin, he is fo far learned,
Though by moft of his readers 'twill not be difcerned,
But doubtlefs it gives the *Arminians* a fmack;
I darefay it trims that fame blackfmith his back;

---

[*] The quotations will be all along enclofed in double commas.
[†] "Polyphemus! a Cyclops!" a fcornful allufion to Mr. Taylor's original occupation—a blackfmith. How difingenuous this in Mr. Knight, who was him-felf originally a collier!
[‡] I difapprove of the practice of making ufe of Latin and Greek terms and quotations, in publications where very few of thofe who are likely to read them underftand a word of the language. I think it is unmeaning and abfurd, and only ferves to fhew the vanity of the author.

He too talk'd of hammering Latin you know,
But the Collier * has given him his bellyful now.
If such the fruits of PERFECT LOVE,
'Tis not descended from above.
But then, kind fir, you ought to prove
Cyclops profefles *perfect love;*
Or otherwife, you know, my lad,
Suppofe his book or good or bad,
It can't be th' fruit of that, you know,
Which he makes no pretenfions to.
Th' advice you give from Paul, 'tis true,
Is good for him, and good for *you;*
For *you* particularly, fir,
Whofe arrogant affuming air
Declares you (if I err not wide)
Far gone in prejudice and pride,
Right willing, were it in your pow'r,
To bite, afperfe, traduce, devour;
But thanks to favouring Heaven for't,
Th' unlucky heifer's horns are fhort.
And fince the caufe of *genuine* Truth,
Embrac'd by the Cyclopean youth,
Among your quondam friends is fafe,
Permit us, fir, a friendly laugh,
While you will falfify and rail,
With Horace at your title's tail.

THE ADVERTISEMENT.

WHAT next, fir, our attention claims?
A comment on his heathen names.
We likewife find this author tries,
With fome concern, t' apologize
For that acute and dreadful fmart,
He feems to think his poignant dart,

---

* I difapprove of the great difingenuity of this author's fpirit, in endeavouring
to caft contempt upon *Philalethes*, by a fcornful allufion to his original occupation
(that of a blackfmith) in his title page, as the Cyclops, it is well known, were
fabled by the ancient poets to be gigantic journeymen blackfmiths to Vulcan in
forging arms for his heroes, &c. Now, a poor man may be born with a good
natural genius, which if he improves and makes ufe of for the good of fociety, he
is a worthy man, and deferves refpect, notwithstanding the lownefs of his birth or
occupation.

Unerring, acrimonious, dire,
Will caufe the object of his ire.
Dear *Collier*, be advifed by me,
And let not your good nature be
Too much alarmed on this occafion;
The *Blackfmith*, fir, is on good fafhion;
So far from having pierc'd within,
Your weapon never raz'd his fkin;
He did, when firft your book he faw,
Feel fomething tickle like a ftraw,
But then his limbs and life were fafe—
It only made the *Blackfmith* laugh!

REMARKS ON THE POEM CALLED "POLYPHEMUS." *

Now hark ye, kind reader, a word in your ear;
I only fhall notice a place here and there,
Where this writer I find wand'ring widely, poor man!
And fet him as gently to rights as I can.
" *He greatly admir'd her:*" † he tells you not fo,
But that he much doubted her genuine or no, ‡
And that afterwards, when he ventured to try,
He found her a *baftard*, not fprung from the fky;
No *goddefs*, the offspring of heav'nly plains,
But the fpurious produce of Calvinian brains.
" *He writes, juft efcaped:*" he does not, indeed;
I wonder you'll truft to your blundering head.
'Tis " *lately efcaped*," fure, if you will look;
But 'tis common with you, fir, to talk without book.
To " lately efcaped," he tells the blind youth,
He ought to have added, " from the arms of Truth."
But rather it fhould be, I think, honeft friend,
From the dang'rous errors Calvinians defend.
" *Said Hephaiftos*," fo here your poor readers may feek
Long enough for the meaning of this heathen Greek;
What need for it, pray, but to fhow on th' occafion
Your own learned vanity and affectation?

---

* The name of a huge cruel Sicilian giant mentioned by Homer in his
" Odyffey," with only one large eye in the middle of his forehead.
　† Viz., Calvinifm, which this author, with a great deal of dogmatical affurance,
dignifies with the name of *Truth*.
　‡ See the third page of his own pamphlet, in his addrefs to Mr. Wefley.

Omniscience to God we deny not, *you know,*
His *decrees,* right defined, we likewife allow ;
And if "*Turks, Pagans, Jews, have in every age*
Afferted your doctrine, both pious and fage,
And Chriftians in this and in every nation
Have drunk in the tenet of predeftination,"
You ftill muft allow the *Cyclopean* youth,
That the *age* of a tenet's no *proof* of its *truth ;*
Nor does it authenticate error, I ween,
How *num'rous* foe'er its abettors have been.
" But clofe not in argument "—Calvinift, fie ;
Your proud intimation joins clofe on a lie ;
Your puffs are unmeaning, your boafting is vain ;
We fear not the *Calvinift* nor his *whole* train.
That *Fletcher* you hint at has given you your fill,
Has drubb'd your bold champions, Toplady and Hill,
Has come to clofe quarters, much *clofer* I trow
Than fome of you like, that we very well know ;
If this writer thinks not, let him try if he can
(He yet is unanfwer'd) to anfwer the man—
To bring down this high-foaring Swifs to the ground,
His books are in print, and may eafily be found.
" *We eftablifh old chance ;*" fir, we do not indeed,
'Tis but a miftake of your own muddy head.
" *And may ye fucceed, but 'tis more than I hope :*"
Here too, fir, we think you are wide of your fcope.
In general it feems, if we truft to old fame,
The *Calvinians* are playing a faft loofing game.
" *Untaught to examine, forbid to debate* "—
Such falfities how can this writer relate ?
Of your pens or your parts, fir, we ftand in no dread ;
We fear not your ableft productions to read,
To give them a fair and a candid review,
And canvafs your ableft arguments through.
However, good fir, that of crowds of your own
The line is defcriptive, is very well known.*
" *And crafty Ulyffes ;*" dear fir, have a care,
And be not fool-hardy, but cautious, beware !
Touch lightly on *Fletcher,* your teeth he will fpoil ;
You remember the tale of the viper and file ? †

---

* The Calvinifts, to our knowledge, in many places ftrictly charging their people
not to read Mr. Fletcher.
† See the twenty-third fable of Æfop.

Z

The *Calvinift*, fir, may be certain of this,
He nor is, nor e'er will be, a match for the *Swifs*.
" *Quite darken'd the eye in poor Polypheme's front* "—
Now don't write abfurdly, good poet, pray don't.
" *When truth he beheld;*" how! what, man, do you fay?
Could the *Cyclops* fee *truth* without eyes, fir, I pray,
When his *eye* was quite darken'd (you feign he'd but one),
And poor *Polyphemus* was " *blind as a ftone?* "
Our poet poffeffes rare talents indeed,
An invention-furprifing, and accurate head!
          " *But the goddefs,* * *indeed,*
" *Had Veritas* † *legibly wrote on her head.*"
Don't you think you miftake now? I think, fir, you do;
The medium is falfe which you look at her through;
Or fomething's the matter, whatever it be,
For *Truth* on *her* forehead you never did fee.
You'll fay I am pofitive; excufe me, fir, do,
Example is catching, dear poet, you know.
It is not long fince this Calvinian *elf*
I met on my way, fir, and faw her myfelf;
Examin'd her clofely, and truly can tell
I remember her perfon and look very well.
Since then, I have feen, fir, you muft underftand,
Her portraiture drawn by a mafterly hand; ‡
And for your advantage and profit, dear man,
I'll try to defcribe her as near as I can.

A FIGURATIVE SKETCH OF CALVINISM.

HER perfon's genteel, fair-proportion'd, and tall,
Her countenance comely, but haughty withal;
Her *genuine* name (for I faw't in her face
Infcrib'd on her forehead) is *Wanton-free-grace.*§
Howe'er, th' appellations are diff'rent fhe claims,
And fhe paffes herfelf under various names;
Sometimes *Orthodoxy,* and fometimes *Free-grace,*
Curtail'd of the addition infcrib'd on her face; ‖
Sometimes the *Pure Gofpel* herfelf fhe'll affirm;
And fometimes *The Doctrines of Grace* are her term;

---

* Calvinifm.   † Viz., Truth.
‡ Mr. Fletcher.   See his " Hiftorical Effay," p. 21, preceding the firft part of his " Equal Check."
§ Viz., Abfolute Election.   ‖ Viz., Wanton.

Then *The Truth* or *The Gospel,* to thefe fhe'll lay claim,
As if none but herfelf e'er deferved the name.
An ugly black boy* you'll be certain to find,
That bears up the train of her mantle behind;
Her conftant attendant, ne'er feen from her fide,
And by the fraternal relation allied,
But as confcious, it feems, of his own frightful look,
Very artfully hides himfelf under her cloak.†
　　When firft I difcerned him, I ftepp'd to the place,
And took up the train that o'erfhadow'd his face;
But (fave me kind Heaven, and merciful be!)
So horrid an afpect I never did fee!
Remorfelefs ill-nature appear'd in his air,
And perch'd on his head fat the *Fury* Defpair;
His breath fent around a fulphureous fmell,
From his broad glaring eyes flafh'd the lightning of hell;
For fingers dire fharp crooked talons appear'd;
His roar the moft dreadful that ever was heard;
His fplay cloven feet might be feen as he went,
And plainly betray'd his infernal defcent;
His name is FREE WRATH, fir, which vifibly ftood
Infcribed on his forehead in letters of blood;
In one fingle line his character to tell,
He was fierce as ten furies, and horrid as hell!‡
His dire afpect—which ftill frighted fancy retains—
E'en caus'd the warm blood to run chill in my veins.
I ftarted with horror, turn'd back from the view,
Implor'd Heaven's protection, and hafty withdrew;
Retir'd to a diftance, beneath a frefh fhade,
And fat down to notice the progrefs they made.
She walks through the world (her attendant behind);
And as fhe proceeds through the crowds of mankind,
She picks up fome fav'rites, a few here and there,
And fawns over thefe with peculiar care;
She hugs them and foothes them, and fmiles in their face,
And tells them they're all the dear offspring of grace;
That fhe loves them all dearly, and will do for aye,
Let them do what they will, or behave as they may;
Should they murder with David, or curfe, fwear, and lie
With Peter, or like him their Saviour deny;

---

* Abfolute Reprobation.
† Alluding to the general backwardnefs of the Calvinifts to fpeak on the fubject of Reprobation
‡ " Fierce as ten furies, terrible as hell," is a line of Milton, B. 2, L. 671.

Or commit what fome people adultery call,
She affures them they never fhall finally fall;
But fooner or later, howe'er they've behaved,
Shall be *made* to repent, and believe, and be faved.
But fhe looks on all elfe, fir, that ever were born,
With contempt, indignation, and infinite fcorn,
And tells them exprefly fhe always view'd them
With wrath everlafting, and hatred fupreme.
She calls them and makes them mock offers of grace;
If they come, fir, fhe taunts them and fleers in their face,
Reproaches them as a vile reprobate brood,
Appointed for Tophet, and hated of God.
When they dared to complain, fir, I heard her declare,
With a haughty, imperious, and infolent air,
She was fure her proceedings were not to be blam'd,
That their fuff'rings were juft, and they ought to be
    damn'd;
And queftion'd them fternly how fuch a vile brood
Durft prefume to complain or reply againft God?
For that fix thoufand years ago, or thereupon,
The crime that deferved thefe pains they had done
In the garden of Eden, when, at Satan's fuit,
Our old grandfather Adam eat forbidden fruit.
When they further prefum'd, fir, to reafon the cafe,
And told her they never remember'd the place,
And faid (like the lamb in the fable * forlorn)
That the time fhe had named was before they were born,
That they could not conceive how God juftly could fend
Them to torments infernal and pains without end,
As they themfelves never were able to choofe,
Nor e'er had a power to accept or refufe;
'Twas as hard with a crime to be chargeable made,
Of which, fir, they never were *confcious* they faid—
For a crime to be hated, rejeƈted, forlorn,
Another committed before they were born;
And earneftly begg'd fhe'd confider their cafe,
And try them at leaft with one grain of true grace,
That they might (though but fmall) have fome chance for
    falvation,
Before they were fent to eternal damnation.
Here the lady put on, in a furious fit,
A frown, fir, as black as the bottomlefs pit;
She huff'd and look'd fcornful, and proudly declar'd

---

* See the fecond fable of Æfop.

Such dull coxcombs as they were beneath her regard;
She call'd them perverse, and of reprobate mind,
And free willing heretics, stupid, and blind;
Blaspheming Arminians, that truth they betrayed—
'Twas horrid and shocking to hear them, she said;
That 'twas true they'd no pow'r to accept or deny,
And declar'd that Free-agency all was a lie;
That how strange a matter soe'er it may seem
To such shallow short-sighted creatures as them,
With such things as these, she would have them to know,
Common sense, sir, and reason had nothing to do: *
She wonder'd, much wonder'd, such wretches as them,
To censure their Maker's decrees should presume;
Though they fell on themselves with a terrible weight,
They should hold their peace, go to hell, and be quiet;
And as heaven's great Sovereign it seems had thought fit
To doom them to burn in the bottomless pit,
They ought not to murmur, but humbly submit,
To yield to the sovereign disposal he claims,
Nor complain for his pleasure to fry in the flames.

Here she frown'd and look'd wrathful, averted her face,
And declar'd they should ne'er have a grain of *true* grace;
Contemptuous she turn'd, disregarded their cry,
And finally passed the poor reprobates by.

No sooner she turned, but the monster behind,
Perceiving they now for the flames were design'd,
First view'd them with infernal pleasure a while,
And grinn'd o'er them horrid a grim ghastly smile,†
Then stalk'd through the crowd with his cloven splay feet,
And tost them by shoals to the bottomless pit!
But what shock'd beyond measure and harrow'd my mind,
Was to see the grim fiend seize the poor infant kind!
For myriads of infants the *Wanton* pass'd by,‡
Not regarding their moan or their heart-piercing cry.
I watch'd the fierce *Fury*, and saw him, sir, stand
With a tender young infant gripp'd fast in each hand;
His talons pierced thro' them, and down from each wound
The warm blood in streamlets distill'd on the ground.
To have heard their sad shrieks and their pitiful moan,

* This the author heard a Calvinist assert in express terms not long ago.
† "Grinn'd horrible a ghastly smile."—Milton, B. 2, L. 846.
‡ If the Calvinists deny this, I present them with the following note taken from Mr. Fletcher's "Scripture Scales," part second, pp. 281, 282, second edit.:—"When Calvin speaks of the absolute destruction of *so many nations*, which ('una cum

Would have pierced a heart even harder than ftone;
They writhed in an agony, tortur'd with pain,
And fpread out their poor little arms, fir, in vain!
I wept o'er the babies, I could not forbear
(I, fir, am a *father*, excufe the fond tear);
My bowels yearn'd o'er the poor innocent lambs;
And when the foul fiend caft them into the flames,
I ftepp'd to the fide of the pit and look'd in;
But O, my dear Calvinift, what a fad fcene!
Whole myriads of infants of different degrees,
Some but a fpan long, fome yet fmaller than thefe,
In furious burnings lay weltering there,
Though they knew not for why they fo miferable were;
Convulfed and rack'd with unfpeakable pain,
They feebly fcream'd out, but their fcreams were in vain!
O horrid and cruel, I cried out, difmayed;
It feems the dire couple o'erheard what I faid,
For no fooner the words from my lips, fir, were flown,
But they both caft upon me an indignant frown.
I was frighted, as well you'll fuppofe I might be,
For fear thofe dire talons fhould faften on me.
I turned about, in a hurry withdrew,
And bade them a long and a willing adieu!

END OF THE SKETCH.

> " *I fay 'tis chance alone bears rule,*
> *And who denies this is a fool;*
> *The Almighty Ruler of the fkies,*
> *I dare affirm, is not all-wife.*
> *I fay 'tis falfe that when man fell,*
> *His cov'nant feed deferved hell.*

---

liberis eorum infantibus') *together with their little children, are involved,* WITHOUT REMEDY, *in eternal death by the fall,* he fays that ' *God foreknew their end before he made man.*' And he accounts for this *foreknowledge* thus: ' *He foreknew it becaufe he had ordained it by His decree* '—a decree this which three lines above he calls ' *horribly awful.*' ' Et ideo præfcivit quia decreto fuo fic ordinarat.' ' Decretum quidem *horribile* fateor.' And in the next chapter he obferves, that ' *Forafmuch as the reprobates do not obey the Word of God, we may well charge their difobedience upon the* WICKEDNESS *of their hearts, provided we add at the fame time that they were devoted to this* WICKEDNESS; *becaufe by the juft and unfearchable judgment of God, they were raifed up to illuftrate his glory by their* DAMNATION.' ' Modo fimul adjiciatur, ideo in hanc pravitatem addictos, quia jufto et infcrutabili Dei judicio fufcitati funt, ad gloriam ejus fua damnatione illuftrandam.'" This Calvinifm unmafked may be feen in " Calvin's Inftitutions," third book, chap. 23, fect. 7; and chap. 24, fect. 14.

'Twould be unjuſt ſhould God not love
With like affeċtion all our race,
And give to all men EQUAL *grace!*
We diſapprove the Word that ſays
'Tis God diſpoſes all men's ways;
Nor can we own him for a Methodiſt,
Who ſays he can do nothing without Chriſt.
We Calviniſm WHOLLY *diſapprove,*
And HATE *to them conſiſts with* PERFECT *love.*
The tranſvers'd ſhilling fix'd my faith, *
Which I'm reſolv'd to hold till death."
I'll tell thee what, Calviniſt, 'twixt thee and I,
'Tis mean, and unmanly, and wicked to lie.
Of all theſe aſſertions thy pen has let fall,
There is not one grain of ſound truth in them all.
That our open belief of theſe points we declare,
Your conſcience, I think, will not let you aver;
That with juſtice and truth they can fairly be drawn
From our principles, is what I never have known;
And 'tis well enough known to this candid good man,
That our fixed belief is that they never can,
And therefore to miſrepreſent as you do,
Is unfair, and ungen'rous, and cowardly too.
  "*That men by works are* juſtified
We preach."   So does Saint James beſides.†
"*We . . . . make it plain*
That God muſt FIRST *be lov'd by man.*"
Write greater untruth they who can.
"*We prove that God may love to-day,*
To-morrow take his love away."
The ſame will honeſt *Hoſea* ſay;‡
The ſame *Ezekiel* ſaid before,§
And *John,*‖ and *Paul,*¶ and twenty more.
Calvinians "*ſay God's*" ſtill "*the ſame.*"
Who, think you, can this author name
That thinks the ſentiment amiſs,
Or ſays the contrary to this?
"*And whom He loves and makes His friend,*
He loves and ſaves them to the end."
The very ſame the *Blackſmith* ſaith,
If they continue in the Faith,

---

* Viz., Mr. Weſley's.
† See James ii. 24.
‡ Hoſea ix. 15.

§ Ezek. xviii. 24, 26; and xxxiii. 13, 18
‖ John xv. 6.
¶ Rom. xi. 22.

Grounded and fettled, nor give up
The genuine Gofpel's ftable hope.
  " Some truths there are, we can't deny,
Yet dare by no means preach them." Fie!
Now is not this, dear fir, a lie?
" Somethings we DISBELIEVE, *yet they* *
Will have them preach'd, and we obey.
. . . . *"* We hope
Though we do give our confcience up
(Small harm, if good may come from thence),
God with our weaknefs will difpenfe."
O fie for fhame, Calvinift, fie, fie for fhame!
Did not confcience here whifper thou'rt highly to blame?
Where one of thofe Methodift preachers, I trow,
(Come name them and fhame them) where one doft thou
        know,
That fuch a bafe, vile, wicked maxim receives,
Or preaches contrary to what he believes?
But if thou canft not, then repent as 'tis o'er,
And write fuch bafe, vile, wicked flanders no more.
" Profane and ungodly and Methodifts join'd,
United in purpofe, in heart, and in mind."
I cannot help thinking, dear fir, in this place,
This remark comes from you with a very ill grace.
Thought I, 'twould do well this Calvinian elf
Would take Paul's advice † and confider himfelf,
Keep his vile intimations upon his own ground,
Where *profane* and *ungodly* enough may be found.
" In fpite of them all, I the fceptre yet hold."
But where, fir, reigns Calvinifm fo uncontroll'd?
That erroneous fcheme you fo ftoutly aver,
And difhonour the truth by comparing't with her.
" Forbear then, O Cyclops, for triumph I muft,
When thou and thy forces are laid in the duft."
A mean, empty, low, and poor paltry vain boaft.

---

* Viz., the Wefleys.   † See Gal. vi. 1.

CHISWICK PRESS:—PRINTED BY WHITTINGHAM AND WILKINS,
TOOKS COURT, CHANCERY LANE.

www.ingramcontent.com/pod-product-compliance
Lightning Source LLC
Chambersburg PA
CBHW021713110726